PŪKOKO:

A HAWAIIAN IN THE AMERICAN CIVIL WAR

BLOOD RED:

HE KANAKA MAOLI I KE KĀUA KŪLOKO `AMELIKA

PŪKOKO:

A HAWAIIAN IN THE AMERICAN CIVIL WAR

BLOOD RED:

HE KANAKA MAOLI I KE KĀUA KŪLOKO `AMELIKA

WAYNE MONIZ

Pūnāwai Press
1812 Nani Street
Wailuku, Maui
Hawai`i 96793

Copyright 2014 by Wayne Moniz
Cover Art Copyright 2014 by Joseph Aspell
Format and Editing by Cheryl J. Kauha`a-Po
Book Cover Production by Amy Sirota
Author Photo by Nagamine Studio, Inc.
Printed in the United States

Distributed in America and Worldwide by
Pūnāwai Press and Amazon Books.
For more about the book and author, search online for the title
and/or for Wayne Moniz.

Moniz, Wayne
Pūkoko: A Hawaiian in the American Civil War = Blood Red: *He Kanaka Maoli I Ke Kāua Kūloko `Amelika* / Wayne Moniz. — Wailuku, Maui, Hawai`i: Pūnāwai Press, ©2014.

ISBN-13: 978-0-9791507-4-6
ISBN-10: 0-9791507-4-4

Includes glossary of Hawaiian and Spanish words as well as Hawaiian and International Locations.

1. Hawai`i — Fiction. 2. Maui (Hawai`i) — Fiction. 3. American Civil War — Fiction. 4. War Story — Fiction. 5. Romance. I. Title: Pūkoko: A Hawaiian in the American Civil War. II. Title: Blood Red: *He Kanaka Maoli I Ke Kāua Kūloko `Amelika.*

This is a work of fiction. Names, characters, businesses, places, events, and incidents are either the product of the author's imagination or used in a fictitious manner. Any resemblance to actual persons, living or dead, or actual events is purely coincidental.

CONTENTS

MAHALO AND DEDICATION Page vii

PREFACE Page xi

PRONUNCIATION OF HAWAIIAN WORDS & ABOUT KAONA Page xiii

CHAPTER CONTENTS

Prologue – *The Makali`i and The Mosquito Fleet* Page 3
Chapter One – *Waters of Destruction* Page 5
Chapter Two – *In the Garden of the Gods* Page 9
Chapter Three – *The Evasive `Elepaio* Page 17
Chapter Four – *The Cloud Kapa of Hina* Page 25
Chapter Five – *The Red Fish* Page 31
Chapter Six – *On the Edge of the Fishhook* Page 35
Chapter Seven – *The Browns are Banned from Bowling* Page 41
Chapter Eight – *In the Wake of the Kino`ole* Page 47
Chapter Nine – *The Red Lotus* Page 51
Chapter Ten – *The Winds of Kaua`ula* Page 59
Chapter Eleven – *The White Mantle of Lilinoe* Page 65
Chapter Twelve – *The Tempest and the Tea Pot* Page 79
Chapter Thirteen – *Chrysopylae* Page 97
Chapter Fourteen – *Along the Barbary Coast* Page 109
Chapter Fifteen – *Mauve Crosses and Fool's Gold* Page 117
Chapter Sixteen – *Upon This Bank and Shoal of Time* Page 131
Chapter Seventeen – *All God's Chillun Got Wings* Page 143
Chapter Eighteen – *Ke Alahao: The Iron Road* Page 153
Chapter Nineteen – *Escape from Rat Hell* Page 161
Chapter Twenty – *Follow the Drinking Gourd* Page 171
Chapter Twenty One – *West through the Williwaw Winds* Page 185
Chapter Twenty Two – *Ho`i Hou I Ka Iwi Kuamo`o* Page 197

KAONA CONTENTS

Lehua Mau Loa Page 207
The Everlasting Lehua
Dedicated to Kino`ole and Larry Spieler
In Memory of Henry Ho`olilo Pitman

E Inu o Ka Pūnāwai Mau Loa Page 208
Drink from the Everlasting Spring
Dedicated to Edna Ellis
In Memory of James Bush

Ka Lauhihi Page 209
The Plumbago
Dedicated in Memory of Joquina Martins Texeira

Ka Ua Ho`opala `Ōhi`a Page 210
The Rain Ripened Mountain Apple
Dedicated to the Memory of Ida Rodrigues Moniz

Ka Pa`a Male Paina Page 211
The Ironwood Couple
Dedicated in Memory of Chuck and Marlene Powell

Ka Lei o No`e Page 212
The Mist Lei
Dedicated in Memory of Charlotte Hanako Onna

NOTES ON THOSE WHO SERVED Page 213
GLOSSARY OF HAWAIIAN & SPANISH WORDS Page 217
HAWAI`I AND INTERNATIONAL SITES Page 226
SOME BOOKS ON THE SUBJECT Page 230
MAPS OF HAWAI`I AND MAUI Page 232
BY THE SAME AUTHOR Page 234
ABOUT THE ARTIST Page 237
ABOUT PŪNĀWAI PRESS Page 238

MAHALO

My gratitude goes out to the men of Hawai`i who served in the American Civil War, their descendants, and the believers who inspired the novel including: James Bush, Ordinary Seaman, U.S. Navy (served on U.S.S. *Vandalia* and U.S.S. *Beauregard*)—Edna Ellis (descendant); Henry Ho`olulu Pitman, Private, Twenty Second Regiment Massachusetts Volunteers, U.S. Army, (Battles of South Mountain, Antietam, and Sharpsburg)—Kino`ole and Larry Speiler (descendants); the two dozen from O`ahu College (now Punahou School) who served; Hawaiian whaling ship crew members who were impressed into the Confederate Navy; and those who enlisted or volunteered in the Army or Navy.

Many thanks to those who made *Pūkoko: A Hawaiian in the American Civil War* a reality: Cheryl J. Kauha`a-Po, Format and Editing; Joseph Aspell, Art Design; Charlotte Boteilho, Assisting Editor; Amy Sirota, Book Cover Production; Laurel (Seeti) Douglass and Guy Gaumont, Hawaiian History and Audio Book Consultants; and Professor Austin Dias, Spanish Language and Mexican Culture Consultant. Thanks to Producer Tom Moffatt, Slack Key Artist Patrick Landeza, Actor/Singer Eric Gilliom, Singer/Composer/Actress Amy Hanaiali`i Gilliom, and *San Francisco Examiner* Reporter Rhys Alvarado for their kind words.

My appreciation for the inspiration and support of Dr. Justin Vance, Professor of Military History, Hawai`i Pacific University, and Todd Ocvirk, Film Director and Writer of the documentary film *Hawai`i Sons of the Civil War*.

Mahalo to those who assisted in my book tour of *Beyond the Reef: Stories of Maui in the World*: Pat Rickard, Principal, St. Anthony High School (Maui, Hawai`i); *Maui Time Weekly*, Editor, Anthony Pignataro; Barnes and Noble (Lāhainā, Maui); James Presbitero; *Kumu Hula* Holoamoku Ralar and *Nā Keiki o Nā Pua o Kapiolani*; Patrick Landeza; Sandy Miranda Robinett, KALW (San Francisco, CA); Vern Chang, KKUP (San Jose, CA); Michael Keene, KVMR (Grass Valley, CA); Barnes and Noble Hillsdale Shopping Center (San Mateo, CA); Craig Bridges; *Kumu Hula* Kau`i Isa-Kahaku and Hālau Nā Wai Ola; Robert Markham and Tom Stevens, The Works (Pacific Grove, CA); Lani Oliveira Bandhauer, KZSC (Santa Cruz, CA); Rick Riccotelli, Books Inc., Opera House Plaza (San Francisco,

CA); *Kumu Hula* Kawika Alfiche and Hālau `o Keiki Ali`i; Keolani DeSa, Aloha Fest, San Mateo County Fairgrounds; Arnold Kotler, Koa Books; Kīhei Sunrise Rotary; Kīhei-Mākena Rotary; Kahului Rotary; the Soroptimist Club of Maui; Elyse Ditzel, Whole Foods Maui; Hawaiian Chamber of Commerce; The Bailey House and Museum; Sheldon Brown, Kevin Brown, and Joe Bommarito (Waiehu Sons); Audrey Rocha Reed, KNUI (Maui); Alaka`i Paleka, KPOA (Maui); Shane Kahalehau, KPOA (Maui); Chris Vandercook, HPR (Hawaii Public Radio); Cindy Paulos, KAOI (Maui); Trisha Eagar and Karlen Peterson and the Kula Book Club; the Wailea Women's Literary Society; the Aloha Writers' Conference; Ritz Carlton (Kapalua, Maui); Tom Peek; and Rosemary Patterson.

A shout out to my constant supporters: Val and Dan Bridges, Miriam and Rob Chipp, Tom and Laurie Dankwardt, John Holland, M. Denise C., Theresa Keith, Deb Peyton, Chris Keith, Paulette and Joe Medeiros, Virginia and David Sandell, David Peyton, John Duarte, Joe and Julie Cecchi, Tom and Michele Allen, Rodger and Georgia Bridgen, Uncle John and Aunty Marlene Moniz, Raiatea Helm, Austin Dias, Natalie Lee Kwai, Karl Kahui, Aunty Ruthie Deponte, Larry Singson, Beverly Salomon, Mike Kretzmer, Aunty Evelyn Hew, and Aunty Margaret Duarte.

DEDICATION

This novel is dedicated to those who advocate peace.

"Blessed are the peacemakers for they shall be called the children of God."
Matthew 5:9

"Peace will come soon to stay
and so come as to be worth keeping in all future time."
Abraham Lincoln

"Peace comes from within. Do not seek it without."
Gautama Buddha

"Peace is always beautiful."
Walt Whitman

PREFACE

I was on tour with my first book of short stories in California when Arnie Kotler of Koa Books, editor of my book, *Under Maui Skies and Other Stories*, sent me a clipping from the *Honolulu Advertiser* that reported a special ceremony at Punchbowl Cemetery. There had been a gathering of descendants and interested parties to honor Hawaiians who had served voluntarily or involuntarily in the American Civil War.

I was surprised. What? Hawaiians fought in the American Civil War? Many others have been equally astonished, never associating the two. Why? How? The answers to these questions were the inspiration of the topic I was seeking in regards to my first novel.

I did some initial digging. Kamehameha V had maintained the neutrality of the Kingdom of Hawai`i first declared by Kamehameha IV in 1861, five months after the start of the War Between the States. So the question still remained: how did Hawaiians get involved in the battle between the Yankees and Confederates?

Eventually, I discovered that the graves and memorials of prominent white men from Hawai`i who served in the Union Army were contained in a special area called The Army of the Grand Republic in O`ahu Cemetery. However, there were no obvious stone memorials to Hawaiians who served.

I contacted Edna Ellis and Kino`ole Speiler, descendants of Hawai`i veterans, whose names I had garnered from the *Honolulu Advertiser* article. They invited me to the second annual ceremony of the new section memorial at the Cemetery of the Pacific at Punchbowl dedicated to *Kanaka Maoli* who volunteered, were drafted, or were impressed into service during the conflict. These *kūpuna* were joined by Professor Justin Vance, a Hawaii Pacific University military history instructor, and members of the Civil War Roundtable of Hawai`i, a group that meets regularly to learn about and discuss American Civil War history. Some of these American Civil War buffs actually showed up in civil war uniforms for the observance. They were helpful in sharing their information. I continued to gather details.

In the meantime, Todd Ocvirk, a Hawaiian film writer and director, contacted me. He was planning a documentary on the very subject. We agreed to share and exchange research material on the topic.

After I finished the tour of my second book of short stories, *Beyond the Reef: Stories of Maui in the World*, I dove full time into the civil war research at libraries and archives. I read a number of books on the war. What had I waded into? I had waded into a very complicated armed conflict but I had the essentials for a novel: war, romance, travel, Hawaiiana, and a period piece set between 1843–1865. It would be my *Nalowale i ka Makani.*

I have attempted to be true to history. The time line is compatible to the events of Hawai`i, the United States, and the World. Mo`ikeha is not based on one particular person but is a composite of the hundred plus men who served.

In my homage to Stephen Crane and his classic, *The Red Badge of Courage*, the characters are titled generically, (e.g. The Boy, The Father, The Captain of the *Kino`ole*, The Two Homely Sisters etc.). Major characters from history are mentioned initially and then referred to generically. (e.g. Admiral Farragut—The Admiral, Abraham Lincoln—The President.) The names of fleeting coincidental fictitious or real characters are mentioned briefly but only Mo`ikeha and Ho`oipo's names are referred to throughout. The main character's namesake was one of the great travelers from Polynesian oral history who crossed the Pacific to Tahiti and back several times just as this Mo`ikeha travels to the American continent and back.

The journey that unfolded before me as I wrote was equally as fascinating at Mo`ikeha's odyssey. I hope you enjoy his journey as well.

PRONOUNCING HAWAIIAN WORDS

The Hawaiian alphabet consists of twelve letters—five vowels and seven consonants. The vowels are pronounced similarly to Latin, Spanish, Italian, and Japanese, except the letter "e," which is pronounced like the "e" in get. Hawaiian consonants are similar to those in English, but have less aspiration. Under certain circumstances, (after i and e, and optionally after a or as the initial letter), the letter is pronounced as a soft v.

Generally, the accent of words is on the second-to-last syllable. The *`okina*, or glottal stop—it looks like a "left apostrophe" between certain vowels—is a quick stopping of the flow of air, causing each of the vowels to be enunciated separately. The *kahakō*, or macron—a line placed over a vowel—indicates that the syllable should be held for approximately two beats, rather than one. When pronouncing certain diphthongs (ei, eu, oi, ou, ai, ae, ao, au), emphasize the first vowel, and then roll into the second.

KAONA

Following *Pukoko: A Hawaiian in the American Civil War,* there are six *kaona*. A *kaona* is a re-directed metaphor that describes a person's particular traits by means of, for example, a flower, a waterfall, a tree, a bay, or another natural phenomenon. Nothing human is mentioned. Traditionally, it would be recited directly in Hawaiian to the person or next of kin for whom the *mele* was dedicated. These particular poems are in memory of two Hawaiians who fought in the American Civil War, my grandmothers, and dearly departed friends.

Pūkoko

He Kanaka Maoli i Ke Kāua Kūloko `Amelika

A Hawaiian in the American Civil War

by

Wayne Moniz

PROLOGUE
The Makali`i and The Mosquito Fleet

Even though he was on a sloop and better able to navigate through shallows, Mo`ikeha had been warned to keep a lookout for jagged shoals or shifting sandbars infamous along the Mississippi. He posted two men port and starboard on the bow to keep an eye out for natural or man-made obstacles. Poles were at their sides in case the river had to be probed. The sloop had been painted black and its sails were of dark canvas. The crew and captain kept their fingers crossed, hoping that they would not encounter a rebel ship patrolling the outer banks. They knew that they were near their destination when they observed with their spyglasses some lanterns hanging from the forts in the distance. No sentinels were spotted. The crew of the *Makali`i* was nervously elated that no one had discovered them, thus far. The murmur of crickets marked the night. Suddenly, Mo`ikeha heard a sound that he had never heard before. It was an irritating reverberation coming from a low clump of pines. He grabbed one of the local crew members. "What the hell is that?" he asked, concerned that a rebel was hiding in the grove and sending signals.

The sailor laughed softly and whispered, "Oh, that's a cicada, Captain." Mo`ikeha gave him a further look of confusion. "An insect, Captain, not a rebel, although as ugly as one. Sometimes they are in chorus but this guy's a loner, probably a refugee from New Orleans."

The ship sailed on in the stygian dark. He felt like Charon, the ferryman, from Dante's *Inferno* in *The Divine Comedy,* the epic poem he had endured at Lahainaluna School. Fortunately, their final destination was not Hades but New Orleans.

They approached the new boom stretched out across the river, the blockade made up of eleven hulks of Confederate schooners chained together. Only the right end chain opposite Fort Jackson had to be dislodged. Once dismantled, the remainder of the discarded ships would flow down the Mississippi and hug its left bank like a wounded river snake. The river would then be wide open for the Union Navy's advance. Mo`ikeha grabbed a spyglass and looked past the boom into Plaquemine's Bend. There it was! The Mosquito Fleet! He counted ten wooden ships beyond the barrier and, to his dismay, two Confederate ironclads, the *Louisiana* and the *Manassas*. He had seen enough and commanded his crew to head back downriver before they were detected.

Death could be stalking the Maui captain and his fellow Union crew around any bend. It could come from a sniper in the shadows. They could be killed before they reached the safety of the fleet.

When he got back to the U.S.S. *Hartford*, he would report what he had seen to The Admiral. Mo`ikeha and his crew would then return on another day and dislodge the obstacles. As soon as the blockage was eliminated, The Admiral's flotilla would be free to move north to the Crescent City.

Mo`ikeha would soon be facing the likelihood of battle. Doubts swirled around in his head like eddies along the banks of the Big Muddy. He was sure that any normal sailor had last minute apprehensions before facing the enemy. Yet, he had made a commitment to Admiral Farragut and Commodore Montgomery. He had also embarked on journey out of wanderlust to experience other places than Hawai`i and had learned quickly that danger was more probable when he left the security of `Īao Valley and stepped out into the world.

He recalled, as they cut through the inky night, his first encounter with danger. He was only twelve years old. By the end of that experience he was looking for something beyond the limits of Maui.

CHAPTER ONE
Waters of Destruction

The riverbed resounded. The Boy could feel it vibrate under his feet. The others weren't as sensitive as he was to the river's personality. They merely enjoyed the valley as their playground but The Boy was the one who was its caretaker. They had playfully wandered a long way up the narrowing valley before the sun had reached its zenith, unaware, as the day moved on, of the impending danger. Suddenly, a soft rumbling roar began. It grew louder like the building growl of a watchdog at a stranger.

"Pele is angry!" yelled back one of the boys, thinking it was an earthquake and wrongly blaming the goddess of fire. "The *`āina* is moving!" The quivering words were overlapped by the commencement of crunching, gnawing, pounding sounds. The Boy had heard that echoing rumble before—but from high ground. He had never experienced the coming onslaught of a flash flood while he was actually in the riverbed, nor at a dangerous distance from easily accessible high ground.

"Run!" he yelled, "Up and away from the destruction! Big water is coming!" They feared for their lives as they began to leap from boulder to boulder down the stream, the walls in the immediate area too steep for climbing and without ample footing to escape the wild onrush of water.

"Kāne, protect us!" yelled another to the god of *wai*, hoping the deity of water was listening. As he looked back toward the bend of the now-rising stream, The Boy's Friend could see the tops of the *kukui* shaking like the very legs that ran to safety. The trees finally succumbed and were toppled by the torrent.

The sound got louder and more destructive. The wrathful waters slapped, surrounded, and submerged the giant boulders. The Boy couldn't believe how the most serene stream in all of the islands of Kamehameha had suddenly turned into a raging *mo`o*. The unleashed lizard wound its way down the meandering course, crushing all impediments, and taking the living with him.

"*Ka hema*!" yelled the `Īao caretaker. He commanded the boys to move to the sharp incline at the left that was forested by a grove of towering *kī*. But before they passed through the *ti* leaf thicket, one of the boys slipped on a slimy rock, a mossy hazard even when the stream slid along casually on uneventful days. He toppled over into the muddy stew of debris in the swollen stream that was now rising above his waist. The Boy leaned over and yanked his *hoaloha* out of the baptism of destruction.

They clawed their way up the dirt incline like their ancestors, the sons and daughters of Kahekili, the former king of Maui. The warriors of Kamehameha in their conquest of the island had cornered Kahekili's defenders near these very cliffs. The voracious watery serpent gnawed at the soles of their contemporaries, chomping the *kī*, dragging it, and swallowing the leaves into its liquid bowels.

The water licked at their feet, splintered spears aimed for their legs. The boys clambered their way up about ten men high, grasping onto the hillside's face like insects. There they hung precariously, panting, and waiting for the wall of water to pass. After some time, the stream would still be high but the boys would not be subjected to a gauntlet of *pōhaku* to be stoned or shards of *kukui* to be pierced.

As they clung there like *`ōpe`ape`a*, The Boy knew that just above within reach of him and his fellow human bats, if they had the strength to crawl up any farther, was one of the caves of his ancestors. Many generations before, Kāka`e, an ancient *mō`ī*, had designated the valley as the burial place of all the great *ali`i* of Maui and leaders of the other islands as well. Those ruling chiefs had been stripped of flesh, their *iwi* secluded in high cliff caves. He was constantly amazed how skilled the cliff-climbing hiders were to expertly scale the towering walls. Along with the hidden bones, the caves contained treasured belongings that could be of some assistance in the after-life, perhaps a feather war helmet or a *koa* spear.

As he embraced the basalt precipice, The Boy, Mo`ikeha, reminded himself again that this monster water was the exception to the rule. The meandering stream was normally peaceful and as clear as the blown glass that white men drank from. The streambed was littered with gems, actually multi-colored rocks bejeweled by the sunlight filtering through the *kukui*, its leaves spinning like children's pinwheels in the trade winds.

He would some day be the valley's protector. His father, a direct descendent of Kahekili, the feared chief of Maui, had been chosen by Governor Kānehoa to continue to care for `Īao Valley. Mo`ikeha was therefore raised to respect his island's last mō`ī, Kahekili, the king who had defeated Kamehameha the Great in the Big Island's first attempt to conquer Maui. Kahekili's warriors, men and women, had lain in wait, hidden beneath the sands of Wailuku, with hollow reeds in their mouths to breath the above-surface air. Once the warriors of Kalaniōpu`u, the Chief of the Big Island of Hawai`i, and his then assistant, Kamehameha, stepped into the snare, the Maui homeland defenders rose from the sediment and, with sand cascading from their bodies, plunged their sharpened *koa* wood daggers into the chests of their enemy. The Big Island Chiefs were sworn to vengeance. Kamehameha returned with *Lopaka*, the cannon with a human name. The mounted gun was no match for wooden spears and shark toothed weapons and Maui was conquered.

However, seventy-five years had passed. Times had changed. Old grudges had dissipated. The third Kamehameha, Kauikeaouli, was their current monarch. The Boy was sure that there would be no change to his eventual stewardship of the valley. Kamehameha III was a fair and just man as well as Paul Nahaolelua, the newly appointed Governor of Maui. The respect that the king and governor had for The Boy's family would synch their continued *kuleana* of the valley, where Maui the demigod once lived.

Suddenly, a piercing cry from one of the boys rattled the already tense situation. "*Kanapī*!" The cry of centipede came from near Mo`ikeha. The Friend's face matched his stiffened body. Luckily, Mo`ikeha found some ample footing and managed to claw his way across the face of the cliff until he was alongside his panicked companion. There, on his friend's arm, crept the fat red predator, ready to sting at any movement.

"Be still!" whispered his savior. "I'm going to flick him off your arm." The forehead of his friend was oozing beads of sweat. With one hand holding him to the hazardous face, dangling from the precipice, The Boy yanked a *laua`e* protruding horizontally from the cliff face near him. He paused to aim, then, with precision, swatted the venomous intruder with the fern. The invertebrate and its stingers toppled to the boulders below into the now slowly subsiding stream. The aromatic scent of the *laua`e* and the now eliminated creeper brought a relieved smile to the victim's face. It was followed by a faint, but grateful, "*Mahalo.*"

The water had now cleared the tops of the boulders in the stream. "*E iho*!" The Boy called with authority. The other boys followed his order and slowly made their way down the escarpment onto the *pōhaku pa`a*. They would leap from one large rock to another until they reached the now muddied trail that came out under Kūka`emoku, a thousand foot phallic rock created by the collapse of the ancient caldera wall, part of the greater range of Mount Kahālāwai.

What would Father think of his son and his friends wandering off from their *lo`i*, the taro patches that needed tending? If his *makuakāne* had been downstream near the *hale* on the bluff he would have certainly seen the rampaging waters rushing down to the sea. And the elder had seen it. Racing from a distance toward the soggy muddy youth was The Boy's frantic father. Mo`ikeha anticipated a barrage of "See, see, see!" and perhaps some kind of punishment for his negligence.

"Mo`ikeha, boys? *Pehea `oukou*? Are you all right?"

"We are fine, Father," The Boy answered, the rest of his companions nodding their heads in agreement. He hugged his son with *aloha*, and then grabbed at the shoulders of The Boy's friends.

"I'm sorry, Father."

"No need to explain, Son. Your *makuahine* has been worried, though. She raced to the *lo`i*, now cluttered with debris, and found you missing. She thought the worst. We must get to Mother as soon as possible to relieve her fears that you were not swept away."

He turned to the boys and urged them to return to their equally concerned *`ohana*. "*Aloha!*," they shouted as they dashed toward Wailuku.

With the human lei, his father's arm, around his neck, The Boy walked up to their compound with a new sense of seriousness as a result of his adventure and his brush with near death. It had also resurrected, in his mind, a secret. He thought that his father would have an adverse response to the longing in his heart.

CHAPTER TWO
In the Garden of the Gods

The Boy's secret had something to do with where he was headed. He was bouncing along the *pali* trail that transitioned from `Īao, his green and vibrant protectorate in Wailuku, to the bleached landscape named after the cruel searing sun—Lāhainā. His father, wagon reigns in hand, was goading old Pōhūhū to move and not glance down the steep precipice. The horse wasn't allowed to peek down the plummet, but The Boy never tired of peering off of the high winding coastline.

He mused as he looked down off the high cliffs to the *uli* ocean below. It was similar in color to the darkest unwrinkled blue of an *`uki `uki* stained *kapa* fabric. He spied for *koholā* on the stiff azure cloth-like sea but saw no whales. He was occupied with the thought that perhaps if he had never left the confines of the central valley, he would have remained ignorant of the bigger, more alluring world that Lāhainā offered.

He was told and warned that the missionaries looked upon the former capital as Sodom or Gomorrah or both. Even Princess Nāhi`ena`ena had been exiled from Lāhainā to Wailuku by the godly men with the white collars. They wanted to prevent her from the temptations aroused by rum and tobacco provided for the heathen whalers.

Mo`ikeha would be dropped off in Lāhainā to stay for weeks at a time to be of some assistance to his aging grandmother, a descendent of Governor Hoapili. She lived on his property back of the sacred Moku`ula or Island of Red Mists. The residence of former *ali`i* was now old and neglected. The capital had been moved from Lāhainā to Honolulu, leaving Moku`ula's remaining structures, pools, and docks to slowly crumble into disrepair.

It was here in the whaling port that his grandmother, inspired by the conversions of the Hawaiian Queens, Ka`ahumanu and Keōpuōlani, trained him in the Christian religion. He was escorted every Sunday to the service at Waine`e Church. But, he, like his ancestors, was torn when he surveyed the beauteous terrain of his island home. Ancient rhythms called no matter where he went. The gods of old were there when he witnessed the red rain of Lāhainā, the splashing stream of `Īao, the cascading waterfalls preceding Hānā, or the lei of clouds that circled imposing Haleakalā. He was awestruck at the same time with the power of Jesus who had claimed the hearts of the island's most beloved royalty.

He wanted to tell his father his secret as the elder prepared the wagon to return to `Īao. The wagon was now some distance down the road, when he yelled out, "Father…!"

"Yes?" he called back.

He instantly retracted his revelation. "Ah…*Aloha*, Father. See you at the end of the month." What he wanted to express was something stronger than religion and equally stronger than his *kuleana*, his responsibility for taking care of the valley of `Īao.

The catalyst had actually occurred two previous summers when he was ten years old:

"Watch out for those drunken sailors!" Grandmother yelled at Mo`ikeha as he and his shadow burst out the veranda door. They raced down the sandy pathway that ran from Moku`ula to Waine`e Beach.

Mo`ikeha and his cousin, also ten, made it their daily ritual to meander along the coconut tree-lined beach toward Lāhainā Roads, the anchorage with Lāna`i and Moloka`i as background. On excruciatingly hot days, they lounged fetal-like in the bend of coconut trees extended over the shallows. Sometimes they played *nīele*, curious to see what a fisherman had snagged in his cast net, sometimes they watched surfers catching combers beyond the reef, and sometimes fished and surfed themselves. On eventless days, they proceeded on to the harbor to watch the crazy white men that had been ferried to shore from the pack of international whaling ships that bobbed out in Lāhainā Bay. They were bound to witness a scuffle or even an all-out fight if they managed to capture a ringside seat outside a beer or grog shop.

But today would be different. A surprise! There, washed upon the shoreline, was an overturned dinghy, looking like the carcass of a beached whale. Judging from the barnacles that covered its bottom and deteriorating paint, Mo`ikeha figured that the small boat had busted loose from its mooring and had drifted apart from one of the more than fifty ships and whalers anchored off shore at any time. It had probably been missing for weeks, months.

"Cousin, we are the proud owners of a new...well, old, boat!" declared an excited Mo`ikeha.

"Cannot, Cousin. It doesn't belong to us," negated his companion.

"Look. It's in disrepair. It most likely came from...who knows where... Moloka`i, Lāna`i, The Big Island...maybe `Amelika!. If you show me the owner's name, we'll return it. If not, we find, we keep."

"It's all busted up," remarked The Cousin, looking for anything to indicate ownership, noting that the boat's name was indecipherable because of inflicted scrapes and wave-worn peelings.

"We can fix it. *Tutukāne*'s tools are still in his shed, as well as a couple of paddles." He stood there for a minute to remember his grandfather's passing and the skills of canoe building that went with him. "We'll hide our find in the abandoned boat house at Moku`ula and work on it everyday until we can christen it like the Lāhainā shipbuilders. Here, lift it." The boys became headless as they bore the dinghy along the beach path to The Island of Red Mists, their weaving walk akin to a drunken turtle.

Within a week, sometimes sneaking out at night to the boathouse, the youngsters had completed the major repairs: the barnacles scraped loose, some *puka* filled, the seats fixed, splinters eliminated. Now all they needed was to re-place the peeled hull with a fresh coat of white paint.

Several days later, the paint dried. The boys were now ready to give her a name. "How about *Palaoa Pae*?" suggested Mo`ikeha.

"`*Ae*," approved his partner. "It did look like a giant whale washed ashore when we found it at the beach." As Mo`ikeha dipped the brush into the black paint in the container to begin the lettering, he deliberated, unbeknownst to his partner, about the next risky chapter in the adventures of the *Palaoa Pae*.

A double mango summer was nearing when Mo`ikeha returned for an extended stay to care for *Tutuwahine* and her bout with an influenza virus. Scurrilous tittle-tattle had spread that she had succumbed to the smallpox virus now plaguing Lāhainā. Mr. Baldwin put the rumor to rest. He had inoculated her earlier and went on to play doctor to bring relief to the bulk of the residents of Lāhainā and beyond. *Tutuwahine*'s house was just outside the downtown quarantined area, so the summer life of boys would resume as usual.

The mango trees planted along Waine`e Road were now overloaded in August. The ripe fruit dropped like ambrosial bombs, exploding on contact with the ground. The Boy and The Cousin gathered as many as they could; Grandmother made the sweetest mango seed on the West Side.

"Are you ready for our grand adventure?" Mo`ikeha asked The Cousin, as he tossed rocks upward to dislodge the hanging ripe beauties.

"Of course," he replied, unaware of the other's meaning.

"We may have to tell some little white lies to accomplish it."

"What do you mean? What lies?"

"You will tell your mother and father that you'll be staying at my grandmother's house and I'll tell Grandmother that I'll be staying at your house for the same period of time until Sunday service at Waine`e Church."

"Well, where will we be?" The Cousin queried.

"On Lāna`i."

"On Lāna`i? What…?"

"Well, we couldn't row or sail to the Big Island…"

"…Sail? Big Island?"

"…That's too far. Kaho`olawe is out of the question—only goats or a prisoner or two left behind. To get to Moloka`i, we'd have to lug the *Palaoa Pae* all the way down to Nāpili.

"Sail?"

"Don't worry. I've got it all worked out." He threw a couple of more mangos in the sack.

As they sauntered back to *Tutuwahine*'s *hale*, The Cousin had as many questions as hesitations. Danger was the first thing that came to his mind. "Not to worry, cousin. You know how *māli`e*, how calm the `Au`au Channel between Maui and Lāna`i is. It's rightly named—water to bathe in. Of course, we'll choose a day when the ocean is as flat as a fish pond, no choppy, windy days, for sure."

"If it's flat that means that we'd have to row all the way. I don't know if these skinny arms could endure that," objected the ten-year old.

"It's only eight miles across. We've walked much farther than that in our explorations together. Besides, I've dragged out some of

Tutukāne's old maps. One current will take us; another will bring us back. And…" he said if his cousin continued to argue, "I've made a small sail from some canvas I found under the house, in case we can't depend on your skinny arms." He shifted the mango bag to the other shoulder.

His cousin had the look of a *pua`a* about to be sacrificed. "Your piggy eyes still show doubt. I promise if there's any problem, we will immediately turn around and come back. *Hiki nō*?" The Boy expected his cousin/friend to say no, so he was prepared to use his last weapon in his emotional arsenal—the defense of his cousin's manhood. But before he'd accuse him of cowardice as a last resort, his cohort avoided that taunting by issuing a still dubious confirmation, "`*Ae*."

"Okay," Mo`ikeha said, grabbing a branch of *hale koa* from alongside the road. "Kneel!" he commanded. "Come on." The Cousin looked at him quizzically as he slowly genuflected. He tapped his assistant's shoulders then head with the switch declaring, "I, Captain Mo`ikeha, appoint you my first mate. Declare your little white lie to your parents. If there be fair weather, we sail before sunrise on Saturday for Lāna`i! Now, let us quickly remove our booty to grandmother for mango seed." The two ran down the road laughing, excited with the adventure that lay before them.

The two boys couldn't sleep for several nights with the anxiety of possible outcomes: Would they break up on the two-mile reef that ran along Lāhainā Roads? Would sharks attack them? Would they end up like Jonah in the belly of a humpback? Would they drift off course? Would a Kona squall blowing from the south sink the *Palaoa Pae*?

In the early morning darkness, The Boy joined The Cousin in the grove of *kukui* back of the dilapidated boathouse. Both carried their belongings in rice bags: an extra set of clothes, some crackers, a jug of water, flint, smoked meat, and *Tutuwahine*'s mango seed. From the boathouse, they waddled toward the shoreline trying to balance the dinghy, the sail pole and canvas, and the sack with their belongings. Several times, at the insistence of The Cousin, they plopped the boat down for a rest, but, after some endurance, they finally made it to the deserted beach.

The sun's rays were just about to peek over Haleakalā as Mo`ikeha prepared the *Palaoa Pae*. The silence of the early dawn was deafening, except for an occasional morning bird soaring over the calm sea.

Mo`ikeha shoved off, his first mate occupying the bow seat. There was a light breeze but The Boy was sure that once they got out past the reef, the agreeable current would carry them to their destination. He handed the first mate his *Tutukāne*'s old spyglass.

All the anxiety caused by the unnecessary bad dreams of several nights seemed to dissipate with the slowly rising sun. Bravado filled their souls with the encouragingly flat channel; `Au`au would live up to its name on this day. Their only fear was that a passing schooner would tattle to authorities that they had spotted a couple of vagrant children adrift between Lāna`i and Maui.

Several hours passed. The current glided the *Palaoa Pae* toward the increasingly larger island. Now they had hoped for something more adventuresome but their only encounter was a shower of *mālolo*. Hundreds of *keiki* flying fish leaped across the bow and stern nearly striking the two A.W.O.L. sailors, but the young winged creatures faded into the distance, ricocheting down across the tranquil channel surface like skipping stones.

The sun began to drop behind Lāna`i. The first mate was now concerned that they would have to land in the dark. The captain reassured the reluctant crew that they were merely a mile out and that landfall was expected within the hour.

The sky blushed in several phases from orange to pink to *pūkoko*. "Beach, ho!" yelled The Cousin, lowering the spyglass from his eye. Excitement stirred within the two. They had done it. "What beach is it, Captain?"

"There are several possibilities." He read from *Tutukāne*'s map. "Keōmuku, Lōpā, Naha…" He looked up from the paper suddenly, more concerned of running the dinghy onto rocks. His companion was encouraging, citing a rock-less sandy strand ahead.

"Then get ready to put those skinny arms to the test. We'll have to row now and maneuver a clear passage to the beach."

Watching the boys maneuver their way onto Lōpā Beach were two fishermen. They observed the boys falling to the ground, kissing it like British colonists, and hugging each other at their accomplishment. The two boys looked up and noticed that they had a welcoming committee.

The Tall Fisherman said to the other, "I don't recognize these boys. You?"

The other responded by shouting out to the two novice sailors, "Where you boys from?"

"Maui!" shouted out the first mate. The captain elbowed him into silence, and whispered, "*Lōlō,* why did you tell them?"

The two fishermen laughed at the Maui answer. "No. Come on. Where are you two from? Visiting with relatives on the north side?"

A moment of pride suddenly filled the captain. "No. We are from Maui. We're going back." He yanked the first mate and bee-lined back to the boat.

The two fishermen were stunned at the thought that these two little urchins had sailed the eight miles on their own. The Taller Fisherman insisted, "No. You boys can't go back. The sea is choppy with white caps and the sun is about to set. You can't cross in the dark."

"We'll sleep at the beach and cast off at daybreak," said Mo`ikeha. The Cousin nodded his head in agreement.

"Look. No cloud cover. Lāna`i can get cold at night. You have no blankets. I insist that you come with us. We were just about to return home, nothing biting today. You must have scared them off."

The Tall Fisherman added, "You can return tomorrow morning after some *`ai* and a good night's *moe moe.* Mama's prepared some *akule* we caught off Keōmuku the other day, some *poi*, and sweet potatoes from our own patch."

The boys gave the look to each other that there weren't many other choices. They proposed that their bounty be part of the dinner meal. "We've got some smoked meat and *Tutuwahine*'s mango seed."

"Now, you're talking," said The Short Fisherman. "Let's go." They loaded the fishing equipment and The Boy's rice bags with their belongings onto a small makeshift wagon. The men clicked their cheeks to revive their old mare. The *makule* horse headed around the south point and up the bluff to Kaunolū Village.

Oil lamps warmly greeted the fishermen and the tourists. *Aloha* filled the air for the rest of the night with *`ono* food, the singing of the *mele* of old, and *mo`olelo* of Lāna`i. Ignorant of an island so close to Maui, the boys listened attentively to the storytellers, descendents of the island's savior. They dramatically told the tale of Kaulula`au, the mischievousness son of a Maui king who drove away the *akua `ino*, the goblins and ghosts of Lāna`i. The marathon of storytelling continued until the boys fell asleep.

"*Aloha Kakahiaka*, sailors," came from the dark. The Boy opened his eyes to see the morning stars still with their silver glow shining through the *puka*. "It's time to get ready. Come eat some *`ulu*, oh, and, besides the breadfruit, the chickens were kind to lay some eggs for you.

Then we'll head down the road, and get you back to your `*ohana* while the `Au`au is flat."

The hearty morning meal was served, the fishermen's wives and children bid their fond *aloha* and safe traveling, and the old horse pulled the hosts' two man canoe down to Lōpā Beach where the *Palaoa Pae* rested in the cool morning sand.

"We'll follow you out, until you`re safe at Lāhainā Roads. We don't want your claim to fame to be a one-way trip. After that, you two navigators are on your own," said the Tall Fisherman.

Good time was made. Now with the sun in its full glory, the canoe pulled up alongside the dinghy. "*Pōmaika`i, `elua kelamoku. Ā hui hou aku.*" The two fishermen wished the two novice sailors good fortune until they'd meet again. The canoe of the Lāna`i elders turned around and slowly faded.

The boys turned to see the whitewashed school buildings of Lahainaluna in the distance high above the port. They were welcoming signs for the two young adventurers who had sailed on their own to another island, an achievement they would share with their own ten-year-olds some day.

CHAPTER THREE
The Evasive `Elepaio

The Boy's Father never found out, likewise the parents of The Cousin. A compact was made never to tell the elders of their great adventure. The experience compelled The Boy to become even more desirous of a life on the sea.

"We must work in the *lo`i* today, Son," said The Father, "now that there will be no more visits to Lāhainā until next summer. We shall celebrate your twelfth this evening with *kālua* pork and *poi*, but now we must go down to the *taro* patch with your brother. The *`auwai* has plugged up with sediment and debris from last week's rain. Once the ditches are cleared, you may enjoy the day with your friends."

His birthday wish had been lingering in his mind ever since his voyage to Lāna`i. Although he was up to his knees in mud unplugging the blockage and allowing the stream to flow freely again, he felt, now with his father by his side, that the time was appropriate.

"Father? Would you say that today I am a man?"

His father replied loud enough to preach the sermon only once to each of his two boys. "Manhood is not about years, Mo`ikeha. One Hawaiian word for it is *o`o*. Like fruit, maturity is different for different males. I know many that call themselves men but act like children. They do no good. One way to check if one has obtained manhood is to observe if he's following *The Law of the Splintered Paddle.* These rules were uttered by our former king, Kamehameha the Great, who gained maturity the hard way. One day as he was passing by a beach in his canoe, he decided to take by force the hard-earned catch from a couple of poor gray-haired fishermen. Not knowing who he was, they ran away from the *ali`i* but he chased them. During his pursuit, the chief who conquered and united the islands got his foot caught in a lava fissure. One of the fishermen returned to where Kamehameha was snared. He raised his oar and knocked The Lonely One on his head. The *ali`i nui* learned his lesson. The splintered paddle represented his insensitive arrogance and the reminder to share *aloha* and to *malama* the elderly, the sick, the needy, the children, and your family. Of course, Son, manhood is also achieved from bravery in battle, from the *pūkoko* wound inflicted, and from the ultimate sacrifice—giving up your life to protect your homeland or another human. I believe you become a man when you react with maturity when these situations present themselves."

The Boy appreciated his father's response, but he was hoping that the answer to the proposed question would be yes. He had a plea that he did not want dismissed. "Father, I have a request."

"What is it?" asked The Father, yanking at some weeds that had sprung up in the *lo`i* over the last week.

"Father, I'd like to have my own canoe." He waited to hear a no, but it didn't come.

"If you do it the traditional way, you may have one."

Luckily, Mo`ikeha was in tandem with his father. He wanted a *wa`a* the traditional way as well. His father added some of the specifications of the protocol of canoe building. "This includes finding the appropriate *koa* and having the *kahuna* perform all the ceremonies. We can't afford to buy one like the white man, but if you build your own canoe, you will treasure it and not disrespect it like a childhood toy. Sleep on it. It will come to you in a dream. Now yank the debris and muddy buildup at the bottom of the next patch so that the rest can get fresh water." Upon loosening that mucky barrier, The Boy felt akin to the freed water that would nourish the lower *lo`i* and that would continue on to the sea at Waiehu.

The dream came that night as he heard the *pueo* hoot outside his window. He saw himself walking through a dale. Eventually he recognized it as Olowalu Valley—an Eden-like canyon on the west side of Mauna Kahālāwai, lush with fern, *kukui*, a sweet bubbly stream, fresh splashing elfin waterfalls that sprinkled the trail, a mirror of his own `Īao. The vale was located just past the *pali* several hours by wagon to Lāhainā. Olowalu and `Īao valleys were connected, though separated by a sheer cliff and scalable only with the help or hindrance of slimy moss covered ropes. It was this cliff at the top of Mount Kahālāwai that was clawed and climbed by the retreating Kalanikūpule, the son of Kahekili, and his entourage who escaped the cannonballs and spears of

Kamehameha the Great in the Battle of `Īao Valley, the final campaign that united Maui to all of Hawai`i.

But there was something else in this positive dream besides the huge *koa* he imagined that grew far up in Olowalu Valley. He had no idea what it was, but he felt that more good was coming his way when he would sleep beneath the tree that would be transformed into his canoe.

Luckily, The Neighbor had to take his wagon and trade his vegetables, fruits, and breads for some bags of cooking flour over in Lāhaina. His wife, a resourceful maiden he had married from Madeira, was a master of the big outdoor oven and produced the most delicious *pão douce*, a skill for baking sweet bread that she had acquired along with stomping the grapes of the world-renowned wine and crocheting doilies. The Neighbor would stay overnight not too far from Olowalu so he gladly dropped off Mo`ikeha with his blanket and a few necessities to spend the night in the valley. The Boy also had with him red fish, black fish, and some pork that he would eat, a portion of which was required to be offered in supplication to the gods.

The Boy jumped from the wagon as it pulled up in front of Olowalu Village. Mo`ikeha waved a goodbye and *mahalo* to The Neighbor. The village, a *pu`u honua* or place of refuge, was once an active hamlet, housing hundreds of people, until Metcalfe appeared on the scene. The hot-blooded Captain of *The Eleanora* was one of the first ships to explore Hawai`i after Captain Cook's demise. The British commander decided on bloody retaliation when one of his dinghies was stolen and his watchman killed off of Mākena. He sailed to Olowalu to avenge the loss of the ship's property and the dead crew member. The boat had been looted for its nails, valuable to a non-industrial Hawai`i. The Captain of *The Eleanora* under the guise of trading sent a message to Chiefess Kalola, the *mō`ī wahine* of the valley. "The natives are welcome aboard for bartering." A multitude of canoes headed out while hundreds of inhabitants lined the beach to see the ships that they called floating islands. When the Hawaiian canoes were halfway out, The Captain of *The Eleanora* fired his cannons, including nails of reprisal. The shrapnel and cannonballs inflicted injury and death to over two hundred villagers. The slaughter was called *Kālolopahū*—the spilled brains.

The horrible day in Hawaiian history and the stripping of the sandalwood from the valley did not deter Mo`ikeha from his destiny.

`Īao Valley, after all, despite its spiritual and natural beauty, had also been at one time, a valley of carnage where the river ran blood red. He was sure that the irony held true for many battlefields across the world—the most beautiful peaceful places were also sites of gory destruction.

The Boy made his way past the remaining homes up to the mouth of the valley, but a pounding sound distracted him. It wasn't the sound of shovels or metal hammers. It came from one of the compounds. His ear-filled curiosity led him to a backyard. At once he recognized the unfathomable feeling from his dream.

The Girl stopped the pounding of the *kapa*, aware that someone else was staring at her. Mo`ikeha fell into a stupor. Her piercing eyes of invitation were as brown as the wood rose. Her smooth youthful skin was like burnt umber and her hair cascaded down her back like Honokōhau Falls. Her body was slim and graceful despite the rigorous striking of the bark from which *kapa* cloth would be made.

He also observed a band of boys under a *kamani* tree ogling every stroke she made with the *kapa* beater.

"Can I help you?" she asked.

The Boy tried to speak but only phrases and half sentences spilled out. He finally offered a complete thought. "*`A`ole*. I just heard the tapping and was *nīele*. I…I was on my way to find my canoe."

"You left your canoe in the valley?"

He laughed. "No, I am in search of one. I will sleep there tonight to discover if it is the one."

"You will find it," she added. Mo`ikeha wondered if it was merely a polite answer or if she had some insight into his search. "Have a good night's sleep." She continued on with the beating and making of Hawaiian cloth.

The Boy proceeded up the valley, embarrassed by his incoherent responses and stares, wishing that this would not be the last visit in spite of the brood of other boys fluttering their feathers in the nearby shade. Why, he had not even asked her name. "*Hūpō*!" he said out loud, marking himself as stupid.

The trailhead distracted him for the time. He passed the right side wall entrance filled with pictures from pre-contact time. The hieroglyphs included humans, animals, and the things of common life. The trail continued on. Parallel to it was the stream that went from quiet to bustling. It was bordered by fern, an occasional `*ōhia* tree, and *ti* leaf plants. The same birds and dragonflies that flitted in `Īao also darted and danced their aerial hula across the stream leading The Boy toward his destination.

A gushing waterfall some ten feet above the left side of the towering canyon wall was a welcome shower to rid the sweat accumulated after an hour of hiking up a gradual incline. The *wai* splashed on his head—a welcome relief to the searing sun that broke through the canopy along the way.

Another hour farther upstream, he began to believe that The Girl's prediction was merely out of kindness. Perhaps the *koa* he was looking for had been stripped along with the Sandalwood trees and sent to China to bolster the kingdom's coffers.

The sun started to set out on the Lāhainā Sea and the valley darkened. But thanks to the gods, as he turned a craggy corner, there it was! It was not the grandest of *koa*—but still perfect for a one-man canoe. It was a handsome tree, a rich brown similar to the striking complexion of The Girl in the garden. He stared at the wooded behemoth for sometime looking for certain signs, but the *`elepaio* was not spotted anywhere around the *koa*. He would be disappointed if the bird was tapping at its trunk, for it was an omen that the bark was worm-filled—the insects a sign of a deficient canoe.

He dipped his small carrying water gourd into the sweet *wai* of the stream, rolled his blanket out, cradled himself in the roots of the *koa*, un-wrapped the fish, took little bites, and then placed the bulk of the remainder on a rock as an offering to the gods. Then he enjoyed his own sparse but desirous meal of sweet potato and *kulolo*. He stared upward into the tree and envisioned his canoe, a gift of the immortals.

The repetitive ripple of the stream drowsed Mo`ikeha, but not before he heard the rustle of an *`auku`u*, a Hawaiian fisher, making his twilight journey downstream, the zigzag flutter of *`ōpe`ape`a*, and the call of a *pueo*. The bird, bat, owl, and The Boy all became one; it was time to sleep and to *moe`uhane.*

He would not remember the dream until the forest woke him the next morning. The Girl came in the night vision. He felt embarrassed at first for she was without clothes. He dared not look up at her, lest he would show her by his embarrassment that he was still a child. But she calmed him, "'*A`ole pilikia.*" She embraced him. He was no longer shy. He felt strong. However, he wondered for a time if The Girl pounding *kapa* was also a dream. Was he imagining her because she represented all that he wanted in a *wahine*? But her embrace was real. She stirred a feeling in him that he longed for but never felt before. Oh, he knew that his parents and *`ohana* loved him; it was their *kuleana*, their responsibility. But, now, here was someone who loved him merely for who he was. Warmth came over his body in spite of the evening sea breeze that had cooled the valley down. A sudden loud rush of the stream awakened him for a second. He turned his body, pulled up the blanket, and finished his sleep, without dreams.

The still drowsy boy brushed his face. A pesky fly seemed to return to his cheeks despite every wipe of his countenance. He finally opened his eyes but it was no bothersome insect. It was The Girl, brushing a stem of *laua`e* across his nose. She giggled. He was shocked as to how close she was to his body.

"How was your dream? Is this your canoe?" she said looking up at the towering *koa*.

The awkwardness he had experienced when he first saw her seemed to rush back. "Ah… fine. I…I need to wake up. *E kala mai ia`u*. Let me splash some water on my face so I can join the real world."

He wiggled on his cut pants beneath the blanket and, shirtless, bent over to scoop handfuls of stream water onto his head. The Girl stared at The Boy's body that was turning to that of a man as her body was turning to that of a woman. Desires stirred in her as she watched water trickle down his splashed face onto his silky dark chest and back.

"So, was the omen good or bad? Did you see the people?"

"How do you know about canoe dreams?" he asked, almost blushing, forever mum that she was the positive nude omen in the nocturnal vision. "It's not the *kuleana* of a *wahine*."

"It wasn't the concern of a woman a hundred years ago. But, I couldn't avoid learning about it with five brothers in the family."

"The omen was good. This is the tree, at least up to this point. Now the *kahuna* must be brought here to confirm my feelings about the *koa*. Oh, I almost forgot!" He suddenly remembered that he had to meet The Neighbor out on Pi`ilani Road, returning to Wailuku. He quickly gathered up his things. "My neighbor is coming from Lāhainā. I need to wait for my ride at the road."

"I'll wait with you," she said, following The Boy downstream. "Oh, by the way, *O wai kou inoa*?"

"My name? Mo`ikeha, as in Mo`ikeha the Restless. He was one of the first sailors who traveled back and forth from Hawai`i to Kahiki.

"`*A `oe?*"

"Ho`oipo."

The rushing stream that rambled down Mauna Kahālāwai to the sea smothered her name. "Sorry, I couldn't hear it. `*Ōlelo hou.*"

"Ho`oipo!" She repeated it, loudly and clearly. The name bounced off the canyon walls, echoing in joy, as if the valley and all its inhabitants were confirming this happy day when The Boy met The Girl of, and in, his dreams.

CHAPTER FOUR
The Cloud Kapa of Hina

The sun was setting over Mauna Kahālāwai as The Neighbor's wagon leaned down the hill into `Īao Valley. A *mele* came to The Boy's mind; the song went: "*Hanohano i ka maka, ke `ike aku, Mauna Kahālāwai o Maui*". The missionaries had translated it into English as "Great wonders to the eyes to behold the mountain of the meeting of waters." Most newcomers to the Hawaiian language, rather than getting their tongue twisted, soullessly called Mauna Kahālāwai—the West Maui Mountains.

It made The Boy proud that he, his parents, his younger brother by four years, and his eight year old twin sisters had been privileged to have `Īao Valley as their *kuleana*. `Īao Stream was part of *Nā Wai `Ehā*, the four streams of Central Maui, and one source of *Ka Wai Ola*—The Life Giving Water of Kāne. He thanked the Hawaiian god of creation as well as Jesus' Father for their beautifully scenic gift.

However, despite the *makana* of Kāne, despite the gift of Jesus, and the love he felt for `Īao and Maui, he felt restless, just as The Girl had described him.

Mo`ikeha jumped off the wagon, thanked The Neighbor, and rushed to his father and mother. "*Makuakāne, Makuahine*, I have a canoe! I have a canoe!"

His parents, brother, and twin sisters raced to their excited sojourner. "It was in Olowalu Valley, just as I dreamed it."

"We are so proud of you, Son," proclaimed The Father. "We must, as soon as possible, call on a *kahuna* to ask him if he would perform the ceremonies for felling the tree, preparing it, removing it with protocol from the forest, and supervising the building of it before you take it for its dry run."

"That can wait, Husband. Come eat, Son; you must be famished," said an equally excited mother. "Come and tell us all about it while we `*ai*. Father traded some of his *poi* for some *mūhe`e* from the cousins in Waihe`e. We had a sample of the tender squid the other night. You'll love it; it's `*ono*."

He confirmed the delightful taste at the dinner table by taking a second helping. The dinner buzzed with all the details of The Boy's experience, save one episode. He held it in secret, less he be scoffed as a silly child falling in love.

The next forenoon, work in the valley continued as usual. This time the family spent the morning moving rocks to allow the stream to flow smoothly. Rough rushing water over the last couple of days had moved the smaller boulders. They blocked a steady continuous movement of the *wai* into the patches and the surrounding fruit trees. The weeding was ongoing.

"Father!" called out The Boy from across the river, loud enough to overpower the splashes and gushes of the stream. "You mentioned a *kahuna*. But who is this man?"

"There are several that still perform the ancient ceremonies. I'm thinking of one that lives just outside of Olowalu Valley, considering his proximity to the future canoe."

The Boy's ears perked up. "Could it be? No, merely coincidence," he confided to himself.

"The *Kahuna* is an expert. He not only performed the ceremonies for five sons but performed protocol for many paddlers up and down the coast. Perhaps you even passed his *hale* when you went up Olowalu in search of your canoe."

The Boy feigned ignorance. A smile appeared upon his face—The Boy's Father aware of the grin but confused of its nature.

"Perhaps we can visit him together. It is almost *Nana*, according to the Hawaiian moon calendar—a time perfect for canoe building."

As days passed, The Boy wished that the gap between `Īao and Olowalu Valleys was easy to cross. He couldn't believe that he was missing someone. The rift not only separated the two areas of the islands but the couple with the blossoming love as well. He looked forward to the day when he would meet The *Kahuna* but even more excited to re-visit The *Kahuna*'s Daughter, the beauty who appeared in The Boy's dreams.

Nana arrived, the moon already showing a silver slither in the western skies. The excitement of seeing The Girl again had been building for days. Father announced that they would visit The *Kahuna* on horseback the next day.

They were up, saddled, and off to Lāhainā by the time the sun peeked over its hiding place, Haleakalā. Before noon, The Father and his son were trotting down the *pali* and onto Pi`ilani's shoreline trail. After lagging a little behind, The Boy caught up with the elder. "Father, I forgot to ask you how you knew this *Kahuna*."

"Your grandfather from Lāhainā knew him and introduced me to him when we attended the wedding of your Uncle Kāpū. He married this *Kahuna*'s sister."

"Is he spooky, Father? From what I read about *kahuna*..."

The Father laughed, interrupting what he expected a child's notion of *kahuna* to be. "Of course not. You'll be surprised at both his youth and his kindness. He's no crusty old greybeard and lives *aloha*. He'll make us feel like we're family."

The Father noticed another odd smile form on The Boy's face at the word family.

The Boy's heart pounded like the beating of *kapa* as the horses turned off the road. He could hear her in the distance creating new cloth from fresh mulberry bark. The pounding came to a halt at the snorting of the visiting horses.

"Father, our visitors from Wailuku are here," called out The Girl as she moved to the front of the compound. Her jaw dropped when she looked at The Boy on the horse. A throng of people spilled out of the house: father, mother, sisters, brothers, *tutukāne* and *tutuwahine*. "Aloha, our dear friends. Welcome to Olowalu."

"*Kala mai*, boys, time to go home. We have visitors." The *Kahuna's* Wife urged the throng of admiring teens sitting under the *kamani* tree to leave.

"Let them stay," uttered The Boy's Father.

"Oh, no. They're only intrigued by our dear daughter's *kapa*-pounding skills." The girls in the family giggled at their mother's comment, coaxing a smattering of jealousy in The Boy. The wooers left.

"Come, come sit in the backyard, and have some fresh mango," urged The Girl's Mother. "The tree in the garden is doing well and it looks like it will bear fruit twice this year. They're so delicious; I won't be surprised if this fruit will be growing all over Lāhainā before you know it."

The hour was spent discussing the protocol of canoe building and the steps to be taken, all within several moons. The *Kahuna* would replicate what The Boy himself had done. If the same thing happened it would be confirmed. With the serious discussion aside, the adults broke into *wala`au*, conversation about who was sick, who had died, the ones they caught and the ones that got away, the growth of Lāhainā, and the invasion of decadent sailors.

Pretending they were unnoticed, The Boy broke away with The Girl. He led her across the road and down onto the coral-strewn beach. There was silence for a while, until they both spoke the same sentence at once, "Your Father... is nice." The coincidence made them both laugh and erase away the awkwardness.

"I was surprised to see you again. I didn't expect my Father would be *kahuna* to your canoe. I thought that your family would have chosen an experienced elder on the Kahului side," said The Girl.

"Well, I was equally surprised when I heard that my father's choice was a *kahuna* from Olowalu." He calmed his nervousness by tossing fist-sized coral into the placid sea.

"On second thought, I'm not surprised. Maui is small," replied The Girl. "The gods have looked down on us. They created opportunities for us to see each other for several months. I'll look forward to your visits." They sat as the sun turned *pūkoko*, Hina's kapa clouds tinted red like Ho`oipo's fabric creations, nature's hint that visiting time was over.

All eyes were on them when the two returned. "We've solved your problem, my dear daughter."

"What conspiracy have you formed while we were gone?" mused The Girl. "What are you talking about, Father?"

"Those hangers-on have been stuck like sandalwood paste under that *kamani* tree for months on end. It is time to cut them loose."

"I cannot be so rude, Father. I don't want to hurt their feelings."

"It's also cruel to lead all of them on. You need to choose one." The Girl looked at the Boy awkwardly. Before she could object, her father slipped in a proposal. "But, I do have a solution. How about a competition—for your hand—like they did *i wā kahiko*, in days of old?"

"You mean, like a race?"

"With canoes. If all goes well, Mo`ikeha, here, will have his canoe cured in two months; it should be constructed and completed by the end of the summer break at school. It'll give everybody time to practice."

Under his breath The Boy whispered, "Are any of those competitors especially good?"

She whispered back in *sotto voce*, "From what I've seen, you have a definite chance to take it. They're definitely landlubbers."

On their way back up the *pali* and on to Wailuku, the Father shared the *Kahuna*'s specifics of the race with his son. The *Kahuna* decided that a race from One Loa, the magnificent beach at Mākena, to Molokini Island would be an ideal challenge. The prize was a *lei niho palaoa*, an award to the victorious in the ancient times. It was comprised of human hair and a fish-hook carved from bone. He would place a replica of a *lei niho palaoa* on the island, one for each competitor. The first one back with their reward would be the winner of the race.

At the top of the *pali*, the father and son looked down from the steep cliffs onto the placid bay below. Molokini, the little island in the shadow of Kaho`olawe, appeared as a mere dot in the distance. As he looked at his goal, The Boy questioned his father again. "Father, don't you think it's quite silly to do an old fashioned challenge like that? We just learned in school about that Greek story, *The Odyssey*. Penelope fought off the suitors, unraveling her weaving until Ulysses returned, and challenged all of them to a feat with his bow and arrows. But that was then. This is modern times. A *wahine* is won by charm and attention nowadays."

"Well, luckily, son, you don't have a hundred suitors—only five. The *Kahuna* is merely narrowing the field in a fun way. The losers will get the hint and move on to other female fish in the ocean."

"But what if I lose, Father? I will lose..." The Boy stopped, already revealing too much about the feelings in her heart.

"Then we have to make sure you don't lose. We'll construct the best canoe and prepare you day and night. Are you up to it?"

He could not lose Ho`oipo. His heart spoke out loud. "We will win, Father. We will win."

CHAPTER FIVE
The Red Fish

Reverend Alexander who was now preaching at Wailuku was approached by The Boy's Father about the possibility of getting him into Lahainaluna School not merely to allow proximity to the canoe he was building but to provide his son with a quality Christian education. The school located up on the slopes above the whaling town was starting to gain a reputation for producing competent businessmen and bureaucrats. The Boy would eventually be guaranteed a good job, in addition to his care of `Īao Valley after his father passed on.

During the transition from Hawaiian religion to Christianity, The Boy's Father had, under the inspiration of Queen Ka`ahumanu, been converted to the new religion. It was not an absolute conversion for him or his family. They still took pride in their traditions. Their Jesus God was seen initially as a God above all other deities. They still clung on to those gods under the One *Akua* who were responsible for all the things that affected their daily lives—the winds, the sea, the mountains, and the rain, among others. Surely, those local spirits were more evident every day than the one that walked the shores of Galilee. No matter what their beliefs, the lure of the guarantee of eternal life was the bottom line.

Reverend Alexander, who had been a former administrator at Lahainaluna and who had admired The Boy's family for their Christian qualities, couldn't resist submitting a letter of recommendation in support of The Boy. Mo`ikeha received good news several weeks later. He would enter Lahainaluna School at age 14. He would not board like most of the students but stay with his grandmother near Moku`ula. He would trudge up the hill from her house in the wee hours of the morning and perform the chores required by all students for free attendance at the school. He fed the pigs, cattle, and chickens before sunrise, the glow of the lanterns of Lahainaluna and the lighthouse at harbor-side the only guiding beacons in the late-night town.

As soon as school got out and the boarders punched in at the old clock at the entrance to the farm, The Boy headed down the hill to *Tutuwahine*'s *hale* where the *koa* tree had been transported with protocol by hand in the old way, then on a wagon by The *Kahuna*. The original *hālau wa`a* that had been constructed by his late grandfather many years prior would be used to house and protect the canoe as well as shade the carvers from the cruel sun.

Soon, by the beginning of The Boy's summer break, the imagined canoe began to take shape. So far, only good omens presented themselves. The time had arrived to paint the outrigger's name with the *pā`ele* or black paint made from a combination of shrubs and trees. The canoe was christened *Laniakea*, the Hawaiian version of *Ra`iatea*, the Tahitian island visited by his namesake. Launch day was quickly approaching.

There was excitement throughout the compound on the day of the trial run. A number of aunties and friends were busy preparing the meal, the men cooking a pig in the *imu*, all part of the ritual. The food would be consumed if all went well. What the missionaries called *butterflies* were a-flutter in The Boy's stomach.

The ceremony for the trial run—the original launch—was called *Lolo kai wa`a ka hala*, translated "the imparting of brains to the canoe". The canoe would not only depend upon The Boy but The Boy would depend upon the canoe.

The last step before launch was finally here. A live pig was brought forward. If the pig positioned at the stern would run to the bow and leap out of the canoe, it was the sign of success. The *Kahuna* stepped forward with the *pua`a*, wiggling and squealing. The slippery little porker had one thing in mind when he was plopped down in the stern—to get away from the boisterous crowd and back to the security of his pen. He sped up to the bow and leaped out, his owner in pursuit. The gathered crowd laughed and The Boy let out a sigh of relief.

A conch shell was blown to announce the procession from the canoe *hālau* to the beach. All those who had helped construct the vessel walked beside it. The *Kahuna Kālai Wa`a*, The Girl's Father, followed at the back, the many invisible gods behind him. The sight of the canoe attracted more onlookers along the way. The whole throng finally arrived at the beach, the same one where The Boy and The Cousin had launched the grounded dinghy on their daring trip to Lāna`i. The Boy's Cousin stood among the well-wishers, beaming at the accomplishment of his old captain.

The Boy proudly held the paddle of his grandfather that had been handed down through the centuries during the final *oli*. During that last chant, he lovingly gazed at his parents, at his family, and at The Girl. As the chanting progressed, he surveyed the crowd further, worried if bad omens would arise. He had even tied a line to the stern in hopes of catching a red fish—the final traditional insurance of a faithful canoe.

Now, it was time. He shoved off. Salutations of *pōmaika`i*, good luck, filled the air. He dug deep and hard, slicing at an ocean of blue glass. The faces and bodies on the beach slowly became indistinguishable. Before long, now away from pressure and anxiety, did Mo`ikeha finally realize the beauty of the day. The sky, the sun, the sea, the canoe, and The Boy all came together as one. He praised Jesus and all the gods around him about how fortunate he was here in Lāhainā, on Maui, in his very own canoe. He had never traveled around the world but knew in his mind that Hawai`i, his homeland, the land of perpetual summer, was special. He could feel the breath of his grandfather on his back with every stroke of the paddle. He paused for a moment to bait the line for the red fish then continued on. To his right was the port, the whaling ships sitting like bobbing ducks at the Lāhainā Crossroads. He restrained the urge to paddle around them and shout out his excitement. That was for another day.

And, as he thought about the red fish omen, the line went taut. He grabbed it, bringing the something up, hand over hand, to the surface. Would the blue sea bring forth the color he was hoping for? There, wriggling its way to the surface was the *pūkoko* he was looking for. He headed back to land holding his trophy high so all those on the beach could see it.

The *Kahuna* called out as he got closer, "Is everything well? Is the canoe good?" The Boy jubilantly shouted back, "It is!" His mind was already advancing to the day when he would prove himself to The Girl.

The feasting lasted into the late afternoon with plans made to sail the canoe from Lāhainā to Kahului. At the seaside village below Wailuku near the mouth of the `Īao Stream, a *hālau* to house the new canoe had been built. During the *pā`ina*, the family decided that the canoe would stay at *Tutuwahine*'s place and set sail the next day.

At dawn, as the sky transformed from purple to gold, The Boy embarked on the canoe, paddling close to shore around the *pali* cliffs. The family, from their wagon high above on the summit road, followed along, keeping watch on their precious son, brother, and now sailor on the verge of manhood. They would meet him at Mā`alaea and from there transport the gift of the forest by wagon to Kahului. The Son, like his father, realized that he was not ready for the lengthy trek either around Nāpili and Kahakuloa to the north, Kaupō and Hānā to the east, or Mākena to the south.

Now home for his break from school, his day was divided by working the land in the morning in the valley where the demigod Maui once lived and practicing for the big race in Kahului Bay every summer afternoon. He had not lost his love of the valley. When the wind swept down the cliff, he could still hear `Īao, Maui's daughter, calling for her lover, Pu`uokamoa, now frozen as a rock formation. That lava peak looked like a sailor's bodkin for sewing canvas so the white folks had nicknamed it The Needle. He could hear the whispers of the *ali`i* whose bones or *`iwi* had been secreted in the high cliffs of the valley by Chief Kāka`e years before.

Everyday, as soon as the sun hit its zenith, the Boy walked the path that paralleled the stream from the valley down to the canoe *hālau* on his uncle's land at the edge of the ocean. With two months of practice, his skin darkened, arm muscles formed, and control of the canoe was mastered. His canoe runs were getting longer day-by-day. He had made it to Kahakuloa as well as Māliko Bay in the opposite direction. Oh, he had swamped his canoe on a number of occasions but with time he got better at getting it upright faster. He knew, that in a crisis, the quick maneuver could mean life or death.

CHAPTER SIX
On the Edge of The Fishhook

The fishhook lay where it had been created 230,000 years ago. To the ancients, Molokini was the woman who had a spat with Pele, the goddess of fire, over the same man. Pele's anger had hardened Molokini into lava rock—her body stretched out, her head now Pu`u Ōla`i, the red cinder cone at One Loa, the big sandy beach at Mākena.

It was on Molokini that The *Kahuna*, The Girl's Father, landed his canoe, crawled up the exposed narrow path of the partially sunken crater, and placed five small *lei niho palaoa* about half way up the crescent-shaped formation. These lei were imitations made of animal hair instead of human, copies of necklaces that adorned the *ali`i* of old. But the whale's teeth that were carved into hooks and hung at the end of the braids were indeed the same as the ones ancient kings wore. The *Kahuna* had extracted them from a dead beached whale off of Launiupoko Beach several years back.

The sun was about to subtly reveal itself over the peak of Haleakalā and radiate a corona atop its ridgelines. The *Kahuna*'s two and a half mile paddle from One Loa Beach in Mākena across a most typical placid morning sea was meditative, spiritual. The Girl's Father was here to set up the five *makana* for competition long before the arrival of most of the young paddlers who would try to capture the heart of his beautiful daughter. Before he headed back to the wide white beach, he surveyed the entire scope: Haleakalā and the green patches of `Ulupalakua were to his left and Kaho`olawe Island another five miles to his right.

Down in the sunken caldera of Molokini, he could see a rainbow of fish. He and the other men would return after the race to catch from the bounty that lay within the fishhook-shaped crater. Several larger splashes within the natural fishbowl caught The *Kahuna*'s eye.

He hoped it was a *nai`a*, a spinner dolphin, many of which frequented the area. Maybe it was a large turtle, a monk seal? Because he did not see the origin of the splash, thoughts crossed his mind that it might also be a predator, perhaps a white tipped reef shark searching for its morning meal. He presumed, however, that all the noise of the oncoming boisterous gaggle of young men heading to the islet in their canoes would probably chase off any fish, even bigger dangerous ones.

As he headed back to the Mākena shore, he spotted many more bodies. His family had arrived and camped the night before, as well as some of the boys who had no wagons to haul their canoes. They had paddled to the spot all the way from Lāhainā the previous afternoon to assure a good night's sleep in preparation for the big day.

The *Kahuna* could see Mo`ikeha's wagon slowly winding its way to the water's edge. The buckboard with the new canoe was followed by another one spilling over with the `Īao family who had come along to encourage their Wailuku son. All the rivals arrived within the hour and shared a communal breakfast.

"*E ho`ākoakoa*!" The *Kahuna* called everyone together after the dishes of the morning meal were washed and stored. The *pā`ina* would continue as a celebration meal after the competition.

Five contenders had shown up to give Mo`ikeha the challenge. The Boy identified each one by their traits or qualities. There was Tall Boy whose arms were meant for paddling. Laughing Boy found everything funny even the weather. `*Ehu* Boy got his title from sported shades of `*ehu* or red in his bushy top. Squinting Boy looked at everything Mo`ikeha said with gravity as if he was being investigated. Judging from his quizzical look, Squinting Boy would most likely end up as a constable. Finally, there was Pretty Boy, Mo`ikeha's obvious rival. Besides his devastatingly good looks, Pretty Boy obviously had the most experience with a canoe. The Boy noted his rigorous practice sprint as the competitors warmed up for the race. The *Kahuna* announced that at the sound of the sandalwood whistle, which he had proudly carved for the very occasion, the race was on. The challengers would paddle to the island, scale the islet's narrow path, grab one of the *lei niho palaloa*, scurry back down to the canoe, circle the fishhook, and return to One Loa.

The Girl, who Mo`ikeha now teased as Helen of Olowalu after the Trojan woman who launched a thousand ships, went over to each of the boys, wishing them the best. The Boy's heart pounded as The Girl leaned over and pecked him with a kiss of *aloha*, the sweet moment interrupted by the ready signal.

"*Mākaukau*?" asked The Girl's Father. The competitors were indeed ready, their canoes aligned at the edge of the ocean. "`*Ekahi, `elua, `ekolu*!" On the count of three, the whistle broke the silence of the quiet morning. The Five Boys shoved off, Laughing Boy having the most difficulty but giggling it off like a little child. Of course, Pretty Boy took the lead, but Mo`ikeha spoke to *Laniakea*, his canoe, and prayed to his invisible grandfather to help him catch up. He petitioned his namesake, "Oh, Mo`ikeha, who I am named after and who settled in Hawai`i after crossing the vast Pacific, help me with these mere two miles." His ancestors seemed to respond. The *ihu wa`a* closed in on Pretty Boy's *muli*. Mo`ikeha's bow was only a couple of feet from Pretty Boy's stern.

Squinting Boy moved in on the starboard side, giving Mo`ikeha a curious look as if the boy from `Īao had committed murder. Tall Boy was on his port side; his gangly arms were merely an illusion of power. Farther back, `*Ehu* Boy's red hair served as a beacon for Laughing Boy who brought up the rear.

The shouts of encouragement diminished as the canoes reached open sea. The gods and Jesus couldn't have created an easier crossing. An early morning flurry of flying fish flitted across the ocean like a silver rain shower. Mo`ikeha started to move past Pretty Boy, with Squinting and `*Ehu* Boys still staying parallel to him. Tall Boy and Laughing Boy had now made up for lost time and were now a stone's throw behind the other three mariners.

Suddenly, Laughing Boy was no longer laughing, but shouting. It was inaudible to the rest but clear to Tall Boy. "I saw a shark!" Tall Boy had not seen anything.

"Paddle! Stop complaining! If it is, he'll have to eat a whole canoe before he gets to you," argued Tall Boy.

"I tell you. I saw his fin. He went under my canoe!"

"*Nai`a* have fins too."

The four competitors had formed a phalanx in their assault of Molokini, each separated by only a few feet. Squinting Boy cast aspersions at Mo`ikeha and Pretty Boy. He accused the former as a newcomer who hadn't earned his dues by spending enough time under Ho`oipo's *kamani* tree and the latter as someone with good looks that alone didn't win challenges.

The islet loomed larger as they closed in on it. The voice of Mo`ikeha's grandfather was now heard again. "*Ho`oikaika*! Effort! Effort! Ask Mo`ikeha, your namesake, to cut the water with strength." With that whisper, the canoe began to skim through the water like one of those toy *ti* leaf boats Mo`ikeha used to plop down in `Īao Stream as a child. Now The Boy's Father's voice added to the chorus of encouragement. Mo`ikeha recalled his words, "You can do it."

He was now ahead by a mere canoe. He would be first at the bottom of the fishhook and the first to get the Hawaiian booty.

He slid the canoe onto the little lava rock finger and raced up the narrow pathway. Pretty Boy began his race up the crater's lip just as Mo`ikeha snatched one of the *lei niho palaoa*. Mo`ikeha paused briefly and turned toward One Loa Beach with both hands raised like a conqueror. He was hoping his father would see him through the spyglass he had brought along. The Father saw his son's pose of success and relayed the triumph to the gathered throng, much to the joy of his family and the contained delight of The Girl. The brief act of victory was ended abruptly as Pretty Boy almost knocked him off the edge on his way up to the spoils of love.

Mo`ikeha raced down the gravel path back to the canoe. He hopped into *Laniakea*, courteously allowing space for Squinting Boy and `*Ehu* Boy to beach their boats. Pretty Boy rolled down the rim like a barrel hoop, leaped like a frenzied *mo`o* over the two as they disembarked, and cut at the water with his paddle in pursuit of the leader.

The sea at the back of the islet was a totally different game. The spine of Molokini faced the open sea so the course was no longer placid. Large heaving waves now made paddling a real challenge. But it would not be for long, once they looped around the crater.

Mo`ikeha was temporarily distracted to note that Laughing Boy had finally reached the crest of the islet. He was yelling "*Manō*! *Manō*!" to the leaders and pointing toward the sea. The developing morning wind re-interpreted shark as *manu* or bird, the other boys confused as to why Laughing Boy wanted them to look at birds. From his viewpoint, high above, he could see the definite outline of the predator. Laughing Boy was frozen on the spot.

Tall Boy called to Laughing Boy from his canoe. He was about to shove off from the collapsed caldera. "Come on. What are you waiting for?"

"The shark! I see it from here!" Tall Boy disregarded the warning as part of Laughing Boy's vivid imagination and hopped into his canoe.

From his perch high above, Laughing Boy watched as the shadow of the *manō*, a white tipped reef shark the length of their boats, glided under Squinting Boy's bow. When the shark surfaced in front of Squinting Boy, both he and `*Ehu* Boy now realized that it was not *manu* that Laughing Boy had been shouting.

Both Mo`ikeha and Pretty Boy turned at the same time to hear the screams of the paddling congregation of new believers and the developing accident. `*Ehu* Boy panicked when he saw the hungry predator head directly for his canoe. Fearful, he turned it suddenly to avoid the impact and rammed his boat into Squinting Boy's, puncturing it with a sizable hole. `*Ehu* Boy's canoe flipped on the impact, the outrigger crashing down on his head.

Mo`ikeha was now in the lead, but matters of life and death had raised its unfortunate head in the form of a shark. To the puzzlement of Pretty Boy who continued on to the finish line at One Loa, Mo`ikeha turned his canoe around and headed back out to the center of chaos. Squinting Boy was trying to keep his canoe above water to no avail; he finally gave in to the thought that he could not save it. He let it go; his boat spiraled down into the deep blue ocean. `*Ehu* Boy, dazed from the blow from the *ama*, clung tentatively on the hull of the flipped craft. The *manō* circled the semi-conscious boy, preparing to attack. Squinting Boy moved toward the injured boy and tried to accomplish three impossible things at the same time—overturn `*Ehu* Boy's canoe, save the panicked youth, and keep the shark from taking a bite out of his own legs, dangling below the surface.

Luckily, Mo`ikeha closed in, occasionally pounding the side of the canoe, hoping the racket would repel those hungry jaws. Mo`ikeha pulled `*Ehu* Boy onto his own canoe, giving Squinting Boy the energy to return his overturned canoe to its upright position. From the periphery of his eyes, Mo`ikeha saw the *manō* approach. He raised grandfather's paddle high, waiting for the shark to circle back. As soon as it got close, The Boy, with as much energy that he could muster, speared the cold deadly eye with his paddle like a seasoned harpooner. The plunderer got the message from the mighty blow to his face and skidded off to open sea.

Now clear of the menace, Laughing Boy started laughing again. He moved down the lip of the caldera and headed back to shore the same way he had come. As the exhausted competitors limped back to land, they could see that Pretty Boy was already on the beach shaking hands, the crowd casting their accolades on the winner, unaware because of distance of the near tragedy in the shadow of the islet.

As the remaining paddlers beached their canoes, the crowd of family and friends raced down to the water's edge, their attention turned from the apparent winner to the excited talk about a shark, Mo`ikeha's diversion from the race, and his concern for brothers in trouble.

Still gasping for breath, Squinting Boy squeezed out, "If it wasn't for Mo`ikeha, we would have ended up in the belly of that *manō*." The crowd started to re-evaluate the true winner.

As he beached his canoe, Mo`ikeha diffused the notion of heroism by convincing the throng that Squinting Boy was trying his best to save both paddler and canoe at the same time.

The nervous giggles of Laughing Boy could be heard even before he landed on the beach. His family ran toward him and hugged him as he re-told the whole story from his vantage point high above the action.

The elders announced that the victory meal would soon be ready. While the fishes were flipped for its final scalding on the fire and the celebratory food was laid out, The Girl grabbed Mo`ikeha and whisked him away from the crowd. A naturally fallen tree served as a bench for the couple in the clearing of a burgeoning *kiawe* forest.

The golden sprouts of sweet *`ilima* adorned the site. "I have to be honest with you, Mo`ikeha. It wouldn't have mattered who won. After all, it was only a game. You would have still been my choice. But I'm glad that we held the contest. It was by following the *Law of the Splintered Paddle*—like that of our great *ali`i*, Kamehameha I—that you revealed your chivalry. You cared for those in need." She leaned over to kiss him, the affection interrupted by a clanging pan—the signal to *pule* then *`ai.*

During the prayer before the meal, the parents of Mo`ikeha and Ho`oipo noticed the loving hand grasp of their son and daughter and concluded each in their own minds that the real winner of the race was not Pretty Boy but Mo`ikeha. Even Pretty Boy caught the hint and turned his affections elsewhere in the days that followed.

Now only one boy would sit in the shade of the *kamani* tree and observe The Girl as she pounded *kapa*.

CHAPTER SEVEN
The Browns are Banned from Bowling

The Boy matured mentally that summer but he also grew physically, now on the verge of passing his five-foot-eleven father by a half inch. The summers were spent in the cool of verdant `Īao. His canoe trips were longer, eventually encompassing all the shorelines of Maui.

Those who embraced the Christian way found it scandalous when he took The Girl out along with him for a trip north to Kahakuloa or south to La Perouse. Lahainaluna did not admit girls and with little access to a horse, Mo`ikeha had to rely on his canoe, *Laniakea*, to sail to Olowalu for occasional visits with his *kapa*-making *ku`uipo*. These meetings with his sweetheart were limited because of his newly required farm duties at the campus. He felt the same angst of Romeo when the English language teacher shared the story of the star-crossed lovers to the class one spring day. Like all the elderly characters in the Shakespeare play, the adults in The Hawaiian Boy's life were quite vocal about him not rushing into any kind of serious relationship.

His time with The Girl would be further limited when he was urged to get an extra job for needed cash. There were still remnants of trading and bartering going on, but the times were changing and they seemed to benefit the foreign settlers, newcomers, and especially those with the American dollar. His wise father hoped that The Boy's accounting class and related studies at the missionary school would put him in equal footing with future aggressive competitive white businessmen.

And the perfect opportunity arose during the summer of Mo`ikeha's fifteenth year with the help of The Girl's Father. The *Kahuna* had done some work for the owner of G.D. Gilman and Company, the primary ship chandlery in Lāhainā. The chandler was looking for a reliable strong stock boy. The re were ten wholesale/retail stores in the whaling port that sold some ship supplies, but Gilman's was the exclusive provider for the more than forty whaling and merchant ships that anchored at the Lāhainā Roads.

The Boy's job would be simple: to keep the shelves stocked by retrieving the items from Gilman's extensive inventory in several small warehouses at the back of the store. He hauled rosin, turpentine, linseed oil, whale oil, tallow, lard, varnish, twine, ropes and cordage including hemp and oakum, tools along with nails, spikes, and hooks, hand pumps, cleaning supplies, leather goods, and paper. The excess contents sat under canvas beneath a spreading monkeypod tree at the back of the premises. It was a simple task done with earnestness much to the appreciation of the owner. The Boy likewise was pleased with his fifty cents an hour job. With three hours of work in the late afternoon and more on Saturday, The Boy would save enough money for marriage.

When school resumed he would be approaching his third year, quite an accomplishment since a number of boys had forsaken their schoolbooks for a job in town or on farms as soon as they had acquired basic knowledge.

The Girl's Father had convinced Mo`ikeha's Father that the job would provide a perfect opportunity for The Boy to make contact with shipowners, captains, and recruiters to satisfy his growing desire to work on-board a sailing vessel. The opportunity would unveil itself in a crisis.

It was now the summer of 1859. It was one of those hot, humid summers—a reason why the town had changed its original name, *Lele*, for the more relative *Lāhainā,* the Hawaiian word for *the cruel sun.*

At 5:00 he locked the shop. The Chandler was off in Honolulu to purchase more products. The sun would be dipping into the Lāhainā Sea within two hours, hopefully bringing the sea breeze to Puamana.

Sweat clung uncomfortably to Mo`ikeha's work shirt as he trudged over to *Tutuwahine*'s cottage near Moku`ula. Grandmother was asleep on her rocker on the veranda. He quietly opened and closed the squeaky screen door, tossed his soaked clothes in the hamper, slipped on swim trunks, and headed out to the beach for a swim to beat the heat. Luckily, the weekend would soon be here. He could hide out and cool down in the shade of `Īao Valley's *kukui* groves and in the inviting water of its stream.

He lounged in the sea like he always did—face up to the sky, holding in his breath, and bobbing in the water like a human float. The pain of every irritable customer and heavy box of the day seemed to slide off his body. He had known for a long time the soothing healing of the *malino* sea. He had covered the American adventurers in his history class, recalling Portola's term for this God-given sea when he first discovered it—*Pacifico*. The Boy and The Explorer's impressions were the same: what a calm, beautiful ocean.

He waited for the green flash, the natural emerald light that flared on the horizon at sunset. It was his signal to head home to *Tutuwahine*'s when suddenly the town fire bell started ringing excitedly. He instinctively raced along the *Alanui Ali`i* toward town, shirtless, his bathing trunks still wet. As he sprinted along the King's Highway, he hoped the black smoke he saw blocks away was not The Chandler's; he imagined the accusatory scenario as he ran, his boss lambasting him for his inattention at closing, and his eventual unemployment. "Please," he pleaded to himself, "let it not be Gilman's."

He beat the volunteer firemen to the site. It was the Ten Pins Alley—two buildings away from the Ship Chandlery! The Owner of the Goods from China Shop was running around frantically and shouting, "No good. Idle boys. No school. Smoke in back of bowling alley. I chase. *Kanaka* boys. No recognize." He seemed more concerned about the culprits than the crisis at hand.

"Grab buckets, Mr. Ahpun. We'll let the constable take care of that! Get buckets. We'll form a line to the canal as soon as others get here." The Owner of the Goods from China Shop ran off to get pails. The Boy's main concern was the chandlery. He grabbed an old mop bucket on the sidewall of the bowling alley, raced to the pump, and filled the container up the brim with water. He lunged forward with the container flinging the contents onto the wall of the chandlery in an attempt to wet it down in case the fire jumped. Luckily, no winds were blowing now. The orange flames reached up like quivering hands toward the indigo evening skies.

Eugene Bal, the manager of the Hotel de France across the street, burst out the swinging doors of the only licensed inn in town, buckets in hand, and joined The Boy at firefighting.

Within a short time, the volunteer fire brigade arrived with their personal buckets, pre-announced by the Owner of the Goods from China Shop wailing Cantonese exclamations while running and juggling multiple containers. It was not the brigade's first fire, nor would it be their last. The wooden structures of old Lāhainā were worn by sun, rain, wind, and termites, easy prey to a carelessly thrown match, a knocked over lantern, an unattended stove or, in this case, as the Owner of the Goods from China Shop called it—"Arsons done by good for nothing *kolohe*."

The brigade tried to save the tin roof of the alley but it was to no avail. It caved in. The fiery debris from the spectacular crash sent sparks and cinders sailing across the canal and onto the roof of the almost-completed Market Building. The debris and unused timber from construction made the edifice flammable. The volunteer commander shouted, "Johnny, take B Boys across and try to save that building." He realized that the small crew would be fighting a losing battle but he was committed to giving his best effort.

Mo`ikeha tried to engage the local boys standing around to join in. One yelled above the din, "Help the white man? Does he help us? Brown boys are not allowed to bowl. Let it burn down!" Without the added help, he turned to Jesus and all the Hawaiian gods pleading that the winds stop or at least blow in from the ocean. Then, suddenly, whether a miracle or not, the latter happened. The sea breeze stirred up. Gusts forced the remaining flames engulfing the bowling alley into the opposite direction, sending the airborne embers onto neighboring fallow potato fields. Eventually, only lingering smoke filled the air.

Secure that a few volunteer firemen would keep vigil for the night in case there were some undetected smoldering hot spots, The Boy dragged his sooty self toward Moku`ula. There in the light of a street gas lamp, he saw *Tutuwahine* headed his way. There was a worried look on her face, a blanket in one hand, and a jug of water in the other. "Grandson, are you okay?" He nodded, exhausted even to speak. She placed the blanket on his shoulders, hugging him simultaneously. His answer was garbled as he poured water from the container over his head, wiping the ash from his face.

"Mr. Kahui, says you were quite brave, and right in the middle of all the action. He ran to town to help but couldn't stay long because he was watching the babies; his wife's at a funeral in Hānā." The Boy took a hearty swig of water. "He works for the inter-island shipping company. He said to stop by when you can. He said he could use a responsible fast thinking employee."

Most of what grandmother had said would have to be repeated the next morning because The Boy was too tired to think, his mind blurred, his nose stuffed by the smell and dusting of cinders. A hearty bath and a full night's sleep were the only prescriptions for an exhausted junior firefighter.

CHAPTER EIGHT
In the Wake of the Kino`ole

"You've done a terrific job, son," proclaimed The Chandler on his return from O`ahu. "Mr. Bal said that you took charge and showed those adults how to deal with a crisis. The head of the volunteer fire brigade said that they'd like you to join the group. I'm happy to have such an employee. Perhaps you'll take over as manager some day."

Mixed feelings stirred within The Boy. What The Chandler didn't know was that The Boy had met with Mr. Kahui of the Pacific Navigation Company. He was not the owner but the Captain of the *Kino`ole* that plied trade between the islands, the ship named after the beloved *wahine mō`ī* of the Hilo and Pana`ewa areas, an *ahupua`a* that ran from the mountains to the sea. He favored giving responsible native boys an opportunity.

When he approached his father about the possibility, the elder reminded Mo`ikeha about finishing his schooling at Lahainaluna. "I just want to make sure that you understand that your education will travel with you and keep you afloat for a lifetime. Schooners come and go—sometimes to the bottom of the sea. And, within the year, those sailing ships out at the Lāhainā Crossroads are going to be replaced by new steam ones. Oh, I'm not stopping you from working on the *Kino`ole*, Son, but only if they allow you to work on weekends. If they do, I'd say go ahead and give it a try."

The Boy thanked The Chandler and bid his boss a good day. He kept the meeting with The Captain of the *Kino`ole* hush-hush, leaving the proper time of resignation for another day.

That day came. Upon hearing that The Boy wanted to work on the *Kino`ole*, The Chandler made what he thought was a generous offer. After the proposal of a five-cent raise was turned down, The Chandler resigned himself to the reality that wanderlust was part of The Boy's character. He said he was saddened that he'd be losing a great employee and gave him his blessings, cordially reminding him that he'd return to the ship store occasionally for supplies for the *Kino`ole*.

Mo`ikeha was the jack-of-all-trades on the inter-island ship: ticket collector, docker, a steward to serve the privileged on-board, bouncer for those too inebriated to travel, and occasionally even a helmsman. The *Kino` ole*'s weekend route was simple—Lāhainā to Honolulu, with an occasionally supply stop at Moloka`i. He would race down the hill from Lahainaluna every Friday at 2:00 p.m., grab his gear from *Tutuwahine*'s house, and get to the Lāhainā Wharf by 3:00 when he'd start collecting ticket fees.

The rich, pampered with coffee, tea, a meal with napkins, and wet face towels, unknowingly caused their own seasickness by nestling down in the hold where every rise and fall of a wave was felt in the gut. The rare but occasional *akamai* native traveler settled on the top deck breathing fresh air, chewing ginger to fight sea-sickness, and consuming the delicacies of home cooking.

After the passengers spilled off onto the Honolulu docks, the job was half done. Now the merchandise was hauled out of the cargo hold and piled on wagons headed to the wholesaler's warehouse. The primary goods that the *Kino`ole* carried were Irish and sweet potatoes. The Boy heard rumors that the King was considering experimenting with sugar cane as his major crop but for now the vast fields of Kama`ole and Lāhainā made potato king.

Between a busy school week and an even busier maritime weekend, little time was available to spend with the love of his life. Luckily, a broken rudder on a Thursday forced the *Kino`ole* into dry dock for the weekend, the intended cargo transferred to another ship and crew. The opportunity allowed Mo`ikeha to attend the wedding *pā`ina* of The Girl's older brother on Saturday night in the coconut grove adjacent to the Waine`e Church grounds.

The wedding celebration gave the couple the opportunity to slip away across the church graveyard past the tombs of many beloved *ali`i* that included Keōpūolani, the highest-ranking wife of Kamehameha the Great. They found a comfortable spot at the edge of the property in a smaller grove of coconut trees.

The moon hung in the sky like an oversized silver dollar, its luster polishing the Lāhainā Sea. The couple predicted that, with the growing changes to the island, they would reminisce years later that the moon, the gentle trades, the colorfully clad wedding well-wishers from that little community, the flickering torches, and the preciously prepared *`ono* food would be what locals would call Old Hawai`i. There was another word for it—romantic, the perfect seasoning for young lovers.

The Girl initiated the conversation after the couple stared at each other, almost hypnotized by the luminescent *mahina*. "I'm so glad that old rudder broke or it would be days before I'd see you again."

"I know," apologized her lover, "but I hope you realize that all of this is to make sure that your future husband can provide his future wife with a happy and comfortable future life."

"What good is a marriage if we rarely see each other?"

"But we will soon. Time is flying. I'll graduate from Lahainaluna within a year. I'll be shifting to a day job, finally with lots of time on weekends and nights to spend with you...and our children."

"A little too early to speak about children..."

"For the white man. Our Hawaiian predecessors were ready for childbearing at around sixteen." The fronds of the swaying palms cast alternating primitive shadows and light on the passionate duo.

"Before we start talking about offspring, let me first finish my reading, writing, and arithmetic at Olowalu/Ukumehame School. Besides, I have a more serious concern about you. I overheard The Chandler tell a customer that his former employee, you, had an extreme case of wanderlust. I was worried and thought it was a disease. When I got home I ran to the English dictionary and found out the meaning of the word—the desire to travel. If this is true, it contradicts your desire to be with me more often."

The Boy was without words. The silence allowed the couple to hear the crash of combers in the near distance from the beach where his compulsion for wanderlust originated.

The Girl continued. "I'd hate to be a wife like Pīhoihoi Kahele—a woman without a man months at a time, her husband gone again, crossing dangerous seas. She always seems sullen each time he departs on those filthy whaling ships. She then begins her routine of worry, unsure that he'll ever return."

The Boy tried to explain a desire as strong as his love and concern for Ho`oipo. "Well, for one thing, I'd never set sail on a ship to kill *koholā*. It puzzles me why foreigners don't have the same love for our gentle giants. I'm concerned that with forty plus whaling ships annually anchored out at the crossroad, the whales will soon be extinct like the Black Mamo."

"I hope your love for whales and birds is less than your love for me…" She interrupted herself on hearing her own words. "…I'm sorry; that sounded selfish, making you pick and choose, as if you couldn't love us all…as well as the drive in your heart to travel."

The Boy tried to explain his impulse to sail but remained silent about his interest in sailing as far as America. "Maybe I just need to get it out of my system. Once my stomach has had its fill of topsy-turvy seas and bad food, I'll be ready to settle down with you in the peace of `Īao Valley."

Ho`oipo tried to stay positive. "Father has talked to Mr. Whitney about getting me a job at the new post office as soon as it's completed and when I graduate from school. So if you intend to go globe trotting at least I'll be there to receive your letters as soon as they arrive."

"Perfect," said The Boy, "I promise that no matter where I sail, whether across the channel or across the Pacific, I will send letters of my love to you. Even better yet, I'll make a supreme promise that my seafaring days will end in five years at twenty-two. If I have not proposed to you by then, you will be free to marry another."

Ho`oipo leaned on Mo`ikeha as the couple watched the lanterns being lit along the *Alanui Ali`i*. The responsible sailors had returned to their ships or taken lodging at private homes. The Constable was out and about looking for ship crew stragglers and drunks who had not obeyed their sunset curfew.

Under the canopy of moon and stars, as she stared into his yet untested face, she wanted to tell Mo`ikeha that she would never love anyone else. But she was also aware that many things could happen in five years.

CHAPTER NINE
The Red Lotus

The Boy had been so caught up in his multi-tasks that he was unaware of the changes to the sky and the sea. The slapping of the halyards drew his attention followed by a shout from The Young Chinese Sailor. "*Mō`ī* —pot side!" As he tightened the ropes, The Boy laughed at the Young Chinese Sailor's attempt to say port and tickled at his abbreviated name for The Boy—Mō`ī or Hawaiian for king.

So far the voyage out of Lāhainā Harbor to Honolulu had been smooth sailing. The *Kino`ole* was loaded up with Irish potatoes and passengers. The prized tubers, harvested from the slopes of Kama`ole and Lāhainā, were purchased for five to ten dollars a barrel. A small portion would be sold to Honolulu markets, the bulk of it headed for San Francisco and the gold fields at thirty dollars a barrel.

As they crossed the watery separation between Maui and Moloka`i, a squall hiding behind Lāna`i decided to extend its playground to include the Kalohi Channel. The Young Chinese Sailor continued. "The captain say for tell those on deck fo go below and then batten the hashis."

The Boy ushered the deck passengers below and attempted to secure the hatch. The downward flow was interrupted by a customer making her way in the opposite direction. Mo`ikeha had avoided her ever since she had boarded and had pulled his cap down prior to taking her ticket. He called her The Lips, not only for the body part with which she had seduced many a sailor in Lāhainā, but also for the gossip she spread about her triumphs whether real or imagined. He couldn't avoid her anymore.

"*Kala mai*, miss, but a squall is making its way toward us. You'll have to stay down below until she passes over."

Above the increasing howl of the wind she bellowed, "Eh, I know you. The Lahainaluna schoolboy! You the one with the skinny girlfriend from Olowalu, yeah? You work on this boat?"

The two rocked back and forth during the interrogation as the first showers of the passing gale began to pelt them. "It's the captain's orders for all passengers to go below. Even a brief blow like this can cause havoc."

"Do you have a stay-over in Honolulu?" she asked, rolling her eyes flirtatiously.

As The Boy answered with a curt no, The Young Chinese Sailor emerged from the hold. "You go down, Missy. Wind blow hard." The Lips descended the stairs staring back with the eyes of Jezebel at the two young men.

The Boy was happy that the Young Chinese Sailor had put a stop to the grilling of the licentious gossip. The Boy was no match for The Young Chinese Sailor, either about women or the open sea. Although he was only three years older than Mo`ikeha, The Young Chinese Sailor had crossed the Pacific a number of times from Canton, initially fleeing the poverty of his village. Like The Boy, he was filled with the same yearning to travel. Suddenly, however, his maritime experience was put on hold. A rouge gust tore across the bow, flinging the fore boom into the direction of The Young Chinese Sailor's head. The crack slammed him onto the deck. He was out cold.

Mo`ikeha swatted him lightly on the face. "*Pung Yaou*," he called, having learned the Cantonese word for friend from the now immobile mariner. No answer. He raced over to the scuttle bucket on deck and hurled a ladle-full of water onto his face, but to no avail.

With few remaining options, he raced to the captain's cabin and roused him to the deck. When they reappeared, The Young Chinese Sailor was groaning, showing signs of consciousness, his arms and legs gyrating like a wounded praying mantis.

"Take him down to his bunk and get up here quickly and fasten the boom. When we get into port, I want you to take him to the Sailor's Home on Bethel; sometimes there's a doctor there. Stay the night and get rid of that mean headache. I'll get the other crew members to do the unloading. We'll leave at eight o'clock tomorrow morning. Be there."

As The Boy did so, the sneaky squall slithered southward. After the boom was secured, the passengers erupted forth from the bowels of the ship and up onto the deck to take in the scenery of Moloka`i as they sailed onward to O`ahu and the capital.

It had been only ten years since Kamehameha III had moved the seat of the monarchy from Lāhainā to Honolulu. Māmala Bay was already crowded with over one hundred whaling and commercial ships. As they neared the island, the passengers could see, through a forest of masts, the town of Kou and its more general surroundings now known as Honolulu. The nautical scene was highlighted by the setting sun.

The Captain of the *Kino`ole* paid the driver of one of the waiting buggies to transport The Boy and the woozy Young Chinese Sailor. "No need!" insisted the injured.

"Just check and have a good night's sleep," maintained The Captain of the *Kino`ole*, as he tossed their ditty bags to them. "You're my best men. Get ready to load up tomorrow morning."

As the buggy headed toward Bethel Street, The Young Chinese Sailor protested a night at the Sailor's Home. "Why?" asked The Boy.

"Who want `*uku* and smelly seamen?" The description of fleas and foul smelling sailors did not appeal to Mo`ikeha either.

"But you need some care."

"My sister can play doctor," proposed The Young Chinese Sailor.

"I didn't know you had a sister here in Honolulu."

"She live Hotel Street. You will like her; she pretty."

"You know I have a future wife," claimed The Boy.

"You also know what Yankees say, 'When cat away, mouses go crazee.' But before we go there, we go visit Joe Booth. Driver, go Joe Booth's." The Boy scratched his head, unaware of his fellow passenger's friend.

The buggy made a left and within minutes The Boy naively discovered the identification of Joe Booth. It was emblazoned on a large blood red sign followed by the word saloon.

"But you need rest. You had a hard blow," insisted The Boy.

"*Mahalo*, driver." The man with the reins gave a few clicks from the side of his mouth and headed back to the newly constructed harbor esplanade. "Whiskey heal all wounds. We rest later." The two paused briefly before the swinging doors hoping to catch the green flash as an amber sun dropped into the cerulean sea.

A din of gab and someone attempting to master the banjo

previewed their entrance. The Boy was amazed at the crowded bar. The Young Chinese Sailor read the novice's mind. "Look like you've never been in saloon before. Patrons having libason before *kaukau*."

"Oh, I've peeked inside some in Lāhainā before, but if Father ever…"

"Not to worry. No one know you here."

"Eh, *Pākē* sailor from Maui," bellowed The Saloonkeeper, "where the sweet potatoes you promised me?" The sailor pulled a sack from his sea bag and tossed them to The Saloonkeeper. "*Mahalo, pung yaou*. The usual for you and your friend?"

"I don't drink!" The Boy objected as The Saloonkeeper poured two whiskeys. Besides his father's stern warnings, the site of drooling disheveled sailors collapsed on the boarded walks outside many of the fifty Lāhainā grog shops had kept him away from the devil's elixir.

"I think you mean you never drink before. Try for first time. See if you like or no like," coerced The Young Chinese Sailor.

The Saloonkeeper chuckled heartily enlisting the men crouched over their drinks along the counter to encourage the tenderfoot. "Hey, fellas. We got here a virgin."

Now Mo`ikeha's manhood was at stake. His companion educated him. "Swallow in one gulp best way." The line at the bar stared him down, waiting for the commencement of his alcoholic baptism. He couldn't back down now. Surely, one wouldn't hurt. He tilted his head back, closed his eyes, and swigged the jigger of Kentucky bourbon.

The Boy didn't gag like most neophytes but sat silent, seemingly unaffected, although The Young Chinese Sailor was convinced that he saw smoke coming from The Boy's ears. The mute moment was finally followed by a loud, "Whew!" A cheer went up from the patrons followed by back pats to celebrate the greenhorn's accomplishment.

"How do you feel?" inquired The Young Chinese Sailor.

"A little warm, that's all," smiled the fledgling, his watery eyes larger than when he had parted the tavern's swinging doors.

"See! You never *make', die, dead*. We have one more then *pau*," promised his fellow crew member.

The saloon seemed to have now come to life. "One more and that's it."

The Young Chinese Sailor put a fifty-cent piece on the counter. "A final drink for me and friend, saloonkeeper. I have to pay visit to sister." All the men at the bar snickered.

The sailing duo from Maui downed the amber contents, grabbed their ditty bags, and bid *aloha* to the patrons. The Boy wiped his mouth with his sleeve as the two burst out of Joe Booth's Saloon. "How you feel?" asked the Cantonese sea dog.

"Fine," said The Boy, a fixed grin on his face from ear to ear. He seemed more conscious of the offshore breeze that bathed his face and his wicked partner's countenance aglow from the flicker of the recently lit street lamps. "This is certainly not Lāhainā," Mo`ikeha said loudly, his voice intensified by the whiskey. "Look at all the people still walking about."

The Boy's tempter informed him in his broken English, "In *Holy Bible*, Sodamn and Gomorrah never have clocks. More strict Lāhainā. Everybody go *moe moe* early."

"Speaking of sleep, we better head to your sister's. Maybe she has to work early; we don't want to disturb her."

"Oh, no. The Red Lotus work hard all night. Here, this way, up Hotel Street."

"You call her The Red Lotus?"

"Sisters in family named after all color of lotus. She the red one."

After a wobbly short hike, the two stood before Akiulau's Laundry, The Boy now wondering if his companion needed his clothes cleaned. "No washy. Room upstairs in back."

They disappeared into the shadows of the back alley, frightening and being frightened by a few black cats feasting on the spill of overloaded trashcans. A dilapidated wooden span connected the upstairs of the laundry to the adjoining building. They climbed up the rickety stairs toward a small lamp and little bell outside the uppermost door.

The Young Chinese Sailor rang the bell. A little red curtain was swept aside from behind the small *puka* in the door, the hole big enough to fit a half-face. He talked to The Eyes in rapid Chinese until the door was unlocked.

"Same usual?" asked The Eyes, almost a shadow in the dim entrance. With very little light, The Boy could not see what the two stuffed into each other's hands.

"Same." The Eyes led the young men down a drab hall past curtained doors, their feet forcing the floor to eek out eerie creaks, the Boy unsure of the particular pungency that permeated the building.

The Eyes parted a door drape emblazoned with a dragon. The room was dim. When his eyes had adjusted, The Boy noticed that bedding and an assortment of mismatched pillows pretty much covered the floor, the walls adorned with childlike drawings of plum, peony, camellia, and lotus.

"What is this place?" pleaded Mo`ikeha.

"Someplace to rest tired sea bones," his fellow crew member said as he slid a tray of items and long pipe out of a chest against the wall. He lit a small lantern with a cowboy match. "Lie back and relax."

The Boy shook his head, finally realizing his naivety. "It's an opium place!"

"Your attention to detail make you one good constable some day," taunted the tempter.

"That's exactly what I'm worried about. The constable will bust in here at any moment and haul us off to the stockade."

"No need worry, little brother. This licensed *Punti* den."

"Why should I believe you now? You tricked me to go to Joe Booth's, and now to this den."

The Young Chinese Sailor heated the pipe bowl with the special lamp. "Go. Go out in hallway. Look at certify that hang on wall." The Boy left and returned as quickly as he left, though now less paranoid.

"See. I told you all legal. Get Kingdom of Hawai`i Seal, yeah? You like puff?" he said as he released a stream of smoke. He predicted what the answer would be, though aware that the fumes that filled the room would eventually find its way into The Boy's mind. "Relax. When I finish, we go to sleep at The Red Lotus, you know, sister's place."

Mo`ikeha uneasily lay down and watched The Young Chinese Sailor relight, inhale, and release more shafts of opium smoke. The Boy started to loosen up, his eyes transfixed on the details of the flowers that adorned the wall. The clouds from the pipe eased his resistance and stimulated his curiosity. "Well, only one time."

"Just inhale. I help vaporize with lamp." The Boy sucked in a huge volume that sent him into a coughing fit that finally subsided.

"Whew. I think I see angels," proclaimed The Boy, as he surrendered to the pillows under him.

Although his body was now like putty, he listened to The Young Chinese Sailor mumble on a number of topics. "I like this room. Look. We high enough fo see waves breaking in harbor. And when poppy extra strong, mind make me see *Mō`ī Wahine* Mālama still surfing her spot."

The blanket of opium mist settled on Mo`ikeha. He continued to dream of angels.

Time passed unknowingly to him. "Go with her, *pung yaou*," whispered a voice. The Boy barely opened his eyes. Through the clouds he saw an Asian angel in a red kimono.

"Follow me," she said softly. She lifted him tenderly. He walked on clouds out of the room with the flowers, floated across the span into the adjoining building, and landed in a room lit subtly only by a small red lamp.

She lay him down and pulled off his shoes and clothes. The last image that he remembered was the beautiful girl with long silky black hair cradling his torso. She stroked his chest tenderly, repeatedly, until he fell into a deeper sleep.

Morning came obnoxiously. Pounding was followed by, "Friend! Crewmate! We must go, now. Only half hour before we go back to Maui." It was the Young Chinese Sailor standing in the doorframe of the room of The Red Lotus with their ditty bags in his hands.

"Oh, my God!" Mo`ikeha leaped up from the bed, wiped the *makapiapia* from his eyes, slid on his trousers, and tied his shoes. "Where's your sister? I need to thank her for..."

"Not to worry," urged the veteran seaman. "The Red Lotus used to sleepy sailors racing to ships. We say *mahalo* next time."

The shirtless Boy followed his companion down the rickety stairs. Halfway down he turned and noticed the snitch emerging from the same building that housed The Red Lotus. The Lips combed her tousled hair and shouted, "E Lahainaluna boy, mum's the word!" Her heinous laugh echoed down the seedy alley.

Mo`ikeha slipped his shirt on and the men bolted toward the harbor as the morning sun highlighted the Ko`olau Mountains.

CHAPTER TEN
The Winds of Kaua`ula

The Boy had hacked at the *hale koa* for an hour despite the blustery breeze and hand delivered the weeds to the cows that had been making a racket until the green offerings had been placed in their sacred trough. Now, finished with his required duties at the school, Mo`ikeha raced down the hill toward the compelling event. He was equally excited that Christmas break was only several weeks away. He would be able to spend more time in the peace of `Īao Valley, hopefully with the love of his life.

It was a Tuesday so he wasn't there to perform his maritime work. Oh, he'd stop by the customhouse to garner his pay of the previous weekend, but there was something exciting happening at the harbor this day.

But he didn't feel right. He always felt that way when the Kona Winds were blowing or when, like today, The Winds of Kaua`ula came whipping down the valley adjacent to Lahainaluna School. Its fierce gale had in a previous decade leveled the old Waine`e Church to the ground; its bell found later near the seashore. Those often-destructive breezes had been living up to their reputation. They had been blowing strong and steady even from the lighting of the first lamps by the kitchen staff preparing breakfast for the dormitory boys when they returned from their required pre-school chores.

The Kīlauea was coming to Lāhainā! He was as excited as a kid waiting for his five cents worth of sweets and sours from one of the large jars on the shelf at Mr. Lau's crack seed store. Oh, other steamships had poked their heads into the Lāhainā's Crossroads mainly to show off the eventual replacement of sailing ships. But *The Kīlauea* was different. The 399-ton screw steamer from the Regular Dispatch Line was going to replace the sunken *Akamai* with regular runs between Lāhainā and Honolulu.

As he approached the port town, he thought he heard a band playing above the howling wind and indeed it was a mish-mash of anyone in town who owned an instrument. A ragamuffin raced up to Mo`ikeha. "Did you hear the news? Abraham Lincoln is president!" Mo`ikeha had almost forgotten about the November election, though not surprised that the news had taken several weeks to get across the continent from Washington, D.C. and almost three weeks to arrive from California. The deliverer of the news raced away to a throng of people celebrating the victory. The Winds of Kaua`ula seemed to add its own confetti to the festivity; blowing leaves and paper swirled around the jubilant crowd. Their signs read: *Abolition Now*, *Stop Slavery*, and *God Bless Abraham Lincoln*. The Boy was not unfamiliar with their efforts. Ever since he had first visited Lāhainā he had occasionally witnessed small groups marching along the oceanfront businesses informing the public about their abolitionist cause. His missionary teachers at Lahainaluna had also made him aware of the struggle to stop slavery. After all, most of them had come from Boston or the East Coast where black men were free to come and go with less harassment, unlike the South.

The Boy had even managed to obtain a copy of *Uncle Tom's Cabin* left behind by a passenger on the *Kino`ole*. He was moved to tears reading about the sufferings and humiliation of Eliza and Uncle Tom and hoped that he would never see the likes of a Simon Legree. Mo`ikeha could not understand how white people believed that the color of one's skin made him or her inferior. Perhaps, if he were on the North American Continent, he would end up in bondage. An unfamiliar white woman emerged from the throng, shoved a placard reading *All Men are Created Equal* into his palms, said "Thank you, brother," and rejoined the crowd.

"Hey, Lahainaluna schoolboy!" A familiar ominous voice halted him in his tracks. He wasn't wrong. It was The Lips calling from the upstairs balcony of The Hotel de France, her kimono open in anticipation of the arrival of the *Kīlauea*'s crew. "You going fight for the ablushions?" Her third grade literacy forced him to utter a *tsa!* of disregard and to keep walking.

When he reached the pier, he strained his eyes down the channel. In the distance he saw ceremonial columns of smoke being puffed skyward. It was the *Kīlauea*! As it got closer, a flock of boys on boards and canoes paddled strenuously toward it. The group of Lincoln revelers halted their activities temporarily and congregated dockside to witness and wave their hankies to greet the modern marvel.

Mo`ikeha was filled with awe as he stared toward the spanking new vessel. Within the hour the ship's crew dropped anchor. The inaugural passengers were herded onto the shore boat and sent toward the harbor.

The travelers were riddled with questions about the journey as they set foot on ground. Within the hubbub, a crew member stuck a flyer in Mo`ikeha's hand. He scrutinized it with extreme interest. It read: "Experienced crew needed for the *Southern Cross*—California bound. Contact customhouse for details."

His peaked interest was interrupted. "Mo`ikeha!" He turned to see Ho`oipo advancing toward him.

"What a surprise! What are you doing here?"

The Girl had to raise her voice above the din. "The same thing you're doing. Actually, Father drove me into Lāhainā with those *kapa* cloths I've been working on for so long. Mō`ī Liholiho has purchased the whole lot."

"Kamehameha the Fourth, himself?"

"Yes. It'll go to Honolulu when the *Kīlauea* embarks tomorrow."

The Boy sensed sullenness even in her short response. "And where is your father?"

"He met up with some old friends. They'll *wala`au* about fishing and old times. We planned to meet later. Could we talk somewhere that's less noisy?" she yelled over the howling wind and the babble of politics and passengers.

The Boy mused as to the topic of the conversation. "And cool. How about the little garden on the ocean side of Hale Piula?"

"Under the *kou* tree? Perfect."

The Boy grabbed The Girl's hand and took a short cut through the voluminous indigo shrubs and across the Hale Piula lawn. They sat on the natural bench contrived from the fallen branches of the shady *kou*.

Mo`ikeha sensed Ho`oipo's anxiety. "What's the matter? Is there something wrong?"

She backed into the talk. "How was your trip to Honolulu?"

He recoiled but answered, "Fine. The Young Chinese Sailor got a mean bang on his head. The Captain told me to take him to The Sailor's Home for a checkup."

"And did you?"

The interrogation was suspicious. "No-o. He seemed to shake off the blow so we slept at his sister's house. No `*uku* there."

"You sure she was his sister?"

"Well, we went to a saloon first…"

"A saloon?" She scrunched up her face in disapproval, but then suddenly surrendered. "Oh well, what did I expect from you hanging around sailors and their vices."

The Boy finally blurted it out. "It was The Lips, wasn't it?"

"The Lips?"

"Yeah, that floozy that welcomes every sailor to port."

Ho`oipo laughed. "You call her The Lips? My friends call her The Scarlet Lips."

Mo`ikeha laughed. "Well, we're pretty close. Where did you see her?"

"She yelled down to me from the hotel balcony and asked me if I approved of you sleeping with a lady of the evening."

"She's the town bitty. You don't expect to believe anything that comes out of her mouth, do you?"

"All I want you to do is to tell the truth. If you're going to be my husband, then the least I can expect is honesty." There was a moment of awkward silence. It was followed by, "Well?"

"I don't know."

"What do you mean? You don't know if you can be honest?"

"I am. I just don't know most of what happened that night. I was drowsy. I don't remember much."

"How many drinks did you have?"

"Two glasses of whiskey. That's all."

The Girl stood. "I think my father's calling. You're either a lousy liar or an easily intoxicated drunk!" She stormed off as a blast of The Winds of Kaua`ula shook the *kou* tree, its leaves showering The Boy.

"Ho`oipo! Wait!" He leaped over the indigo bushes and chased after her.

"Daughter!" The Girl's Father, The *Kahuna*, called, simultaneously waving goodbye to his friends. The Boy advanced. "Son, longtime no see. Busy student/busy sailor, yeah? *Pehea `oe*?" He pressed his nose against him. "You two off making sweet talk?"

The Girl shrugged her shoulders and avoided eye contact. The Boy took advantage of the intervention to press what he had planned to tell her before she ran off. "I was just about to ask Ho`oipo to come and stay at `Īao for Christmas at my parents' invite."

"That's a good idea. I think she needs a break from school and *kapa*. Did she tell you?"

"That The King bought it? Yeah, he'll love her work."

"I don't know..." replied the girl.

"Please, Ho`oipo. You've been working night and day on the *kapa* quilts. Go enjoy yourself," suggested her father.

On second thought The Girl finally agreed, figuring that the relationship needed to come to a better understanding, aware that in spite of her aggressive inquiry, she loved Mo`ikeha dearly.

"Gotta get to the custom house before it closes. *Aloha*, *Kahuna*. *Aloha*, Ho`oipo." The Boy ran toward the building and his future, swept along by the Winds of Kaua`ula.

CHAPTER ELEVEN
The White Mantle of Lilinoe

Christmas was unknown to the Hawaiians until the missionaries arrived but even The Boy couldn't resist the story of the little child born in poverty who eventually saved his people. When Mo`ikeha first heard the story he could not help but make the connection to Hawaii's greatest leader, Kamehameha The First. Like Jesus, a bright star was seen on the winter night of his birth. His mere nativity threatened leaders who called for the death of newborns. He fled with his caretakers far away where he prepared himself for the world.

Friday, December 25, finally arrived. Horses, buggies, and wagons lined up along the road to Lahainaluna to carry the liberated away. The clanging of the school bell previewed the sudden rush of the hooting and hollering freed inhabitants. The day students shouted "Merry Christmas!" to their classmates and to the world in general and raced down the hill toward the ocean—the saltwater sanctuary that most would retreat to every day during the twelve days of vacation.

The boarders leaving for their villages tossed their lockers and laundry onto their parents' vehicles or fastened them on the backs of horses. The Boy was saddened that some had to stay because they were from other islands, lacked money, or were bereft of loving parents. How he wished he could take them home to the warmth of his family.

"Mo`ikeha!" It was The Neighbor from `Īao. "Ready?" He pulled the rein of the horse and jumped out, helping The Boy with his trunk. "Your father said we are to pick up Ho`oipo at Olowalu."

"`*Ae*. She should be waiting for us along the road."

Although it was end of the year in Hawai`i, a newcomer would not be aware of the subtle changes between winter and summer. The breezes along the shoreline were cooler. The waves past Puamana broke larger, their glassy days on vacation until summer. The Girl stood waiting along the road under the shade of a clump of coconut trees, her mother and some bags at her side. "Whoa, Leo," The Neighbor commanded.

"*Aloha*, my friend," Ho`oipo's Mother said to the driver. "Here are a few coins for some of that tasty sweetbread made by your wife. Just bring it back the next time you're out this way." She turned to Mo`ikeha. "*Aloha*, son. *Pehea `oe*?" The Boy had been culturally raised to answer in the affirmative even when he wasn't fine. He jabbered on hospitably about how he wouldn't face the stress of books, and tests, and reports for two weeks. The Girl said nothing, her mind still clouded with unanswered questions. "What's the matter, Ho`oipo? Did a *mo`o* steal your tongue? Give my *aloha* to all."

The Girl managed to squeeze out a faint goodbye. "I think that last night's *poi* was too sour for my *`ōpū*," she feigned. The Neighbor reached into one of his sacks of produce gathered at Lāhainā. "Ah, here. Good for upset stomach." He broke off a piece of ginger and handed it to The Girl. She pretended to nibble.

"Thank you, neighbor and *a hui hou*, daughter. Have a nice Christmas. Oh, Mo`ikeha, you and your family must come here for a *pā`ina* to celebrate New Year's. Please invite them." She addressed The Neighbor. "And you and your wife as well."

"Will do. *Mahalo* and *aloha*." The wagon moved off, heading up towards the narrow winding road of the *pali* that led toward Wailuku then `Īao.

The Neighbor, thankfully, did all the talking. His commentary on places and people along the way prevented any awkward moments between the couple. Within several hours they had passed Waikapū. They made a left turn at Ka`ahumanu Church, named for the most noted wife of Kamehameha the Great who had broken a number of *kapū* before she embraced Christianity. In minutes, they reached the crest of the hill where Kamehameha I had placed *Lopaka*, the cannon that routed the forces of Kahekili and conquered Maui.

The Boy would avoid the eventual discussion and let The Girl to herself. She needed a restful sleep after the arduous ride anyway. In the morning he would take her to the uppermost end of `Īao to the connecting spot where their two valleys joined. There, they would hopefully come to a meeting of minds.

The Boy was first to spot his father banging away at a wagon that Mo`ikeha had never seen before. "Mother!" The Twins yelled out in harmony, "They're here!" The cry of Mo`ikeha and Ho`oipo's arrival was heard by all and everyone raced to bunch themselves in front of the *ti* leaf hedge. The Girl forgot about her bone of contention for the time being as she was hugged and squeezed by all the members with affections of *aloha*. The twin girls instantly adopted her as their big sister, each one clutching either hand.

The *lū`au* stew and rice was a most satisfying dinner, everyone noting the droopy eyelids of their tired guest. "*Makuakāne*," The Boy noted, "whose wagon are you working on?"

"It's ours. I got it from Uncle Kilolani from Waihe`e," replied The Father.

"Poor thing," *Makuahine* added, "his eyes all foggy, almost blind."

"It even has a name, *Ke Ka`a Hokū* , painted on the back," added The Boy's Father, "a perfect name for all the stars that it will carry that are seated at this table."

"When will it be ready, Father?" asked The Younger Son.

"As soon as I scrape off some rust. Our neighbor's legs are failing. He cannot work the *lo`i* any more. He has given us Leo's offspring in exchange for a weekly keg of *poi*. Leolani is now old enough to haul all our big *`ōkole* around the island."

The Twins giggled at the mention of large fannies. *Makuahine* waved her finger at her husband with a slight smile on her face. "Girls, go get Ho`oipo's bed ready. The poor, tired girl, *maka hiamoe*. She almost dipped her nose in the *lū`au* stew."

"Oh, *kala mai*," said the exhausted Ho`oipo. "I'll help you clean up."

"No need be sorry. *Mahalo*," said The Mother. "And same to the rest of you. As the *haole* man say, 'Scram!'"

"If you don't mind, I'll wash up and go *moe moe*," said The Girl. "I'm sure I'll feel better tomorrow. *Mahalo* for the *`ono `ai*. *Aloha*." The Twins trailed their new sister like chambermaids in training.

The Boy sauntered out to the porch to catch a glimpse of the evening stars through the leaves of the *kukui*. His father followed him out and lit his pipe. "What's the matter, Son? Ho`oipo seems more than tired. Any *pilikia*?"

"No trouble that can't be fixed in the morning. I'm taking her up to the headlands and up to the gap. All should be better when we return."

"She's a good girl, Mo`ikeha. Be kind and loving."

The two stood silently on the porch, staring at Hōkūle`a, the star that guided his ancestors to this fair land. "`*Ae*, Father. I will." The elder exhaled in satisfaction, the smoke disappearing into the dusk.

The morning came; a light breakfast was served. "Here, Son. I've made a small meal for the both of you for midday," said The Mother. "Here's an *ipu*. Fill the gourd in the stream before you head up. Put these in your shoulder bag."

"*Mahalo, Makuahine*. Have you seen Ho`oipo?"

"She's waiting for you at the edge of the *lo`i*, ready to go."

"Well, we're off. See you by supper."

Mo`ikeha bounded down the stairs and called across the yard, "Ho`oipo, you ready?" She nodded. They walked quietly for a while taking in the serenity and beauty of the valley. "Have you ever been here before?" he asked her.

"I've visited with Father. We ate a meal at the *kepaniwai*. Father told me of the *iwi* of the great *ali`i* hidden away up on those cliffs that made this valley sacred."

"How the hiders got the bones of the chiefs up those steep cliffs is still a wonder to me," said Mo`ikeha. "When he was a boy, Father said he went climbing up one of those high ridges and accidentally discovered a cave. When he peeked inside, he saw not only the *iwi* that he expected, but a whole canoe, as well."

"There's the *kepaniwai*," announced The Girl as they approached the man-made earthen dam at the end of the road. "I've never been beyond here. I've been longing to see Pu`uokamoa."

"Reverend Andrews calls it the spear that pokes the heavens."

The Girl commented, "The white man likes to give simple definitions of words. Father told me that Pu`uokamoa suggests the whole story of the merman's forbidden love of Maui's daughter, `Īao. Her father cruelly cast him into stone, the needle that `Īao could always gaze at. It's sad to think that two people who loved each other dearly had to keep their affections secret from their families."

"Like Romeo and Juliet?" he said.

"I don't think I know them. Do they live in Wailuku?"

The Boy smiled. "No, they're from this play we read at school."

"Well, I'm so happy that unlike them we have loving and encouraging parents. Anyway, I've been thinking over how I acted in Lāhainā and wanted to apologize for being *lili*, filled with jealousy brought about by the town gossip."

"I should apologize for drinking and..." insisted The Boy.

His lover cut him off. "Actually, I was fascinated that you weren't a boy anymore, but a man. I, in turn, acted like a silly girl and not like a sensible woman. I just want you to be honest and to share with me both good and bad."

"Even if it hurts?"

She echoed, "Even if it hurts."

They continued up the trail. She stopped to admire the valley across the stream with her seven waterfalls, each one below the other. "It must be gorgeous when those falls are gushing."

"I've recently christened them *Makali`i*, The Little Eyes of The Pleiades—*Ka Maka* of The Seven Sisters."

They finally reached the area where the `Īao Stream split. Ho`oipo stared up in awe at mighty Pu`uokamoa that seemed to slice the clouds that gathered at its peak. The stone sentinel would watch them as they climbed up the island between the forked *kahawai*.

"This way," The Boy indicated as he dipped the drinking gourd into the stream. "It's a challenge but, once we get to the top of the bluff, it will be an easy gradual climb to our destination." They crossed the river, hopping from one boulder to another. The Girl counted the natural rock steps in her head as they ascended, announcing the number seventy-seven out loud when they reached the top. Her shortness of breath was replaced by the stunning view of the valley below, the divided stream to her left and right, the latter winding like the tail of a giant *mo`o*, a large lizard, down to Wailuku, Kahului, and the ocean in the distance. He hugged her from her back around her waist. "You can see how torn I am to leave this *kuleana*."

They trudged onward and upward along the root-laden path. The timing couldn't have been more perfect. With the sun at its zenith, they reached the meadow—a wonderful grassy opening that ran from one ledge to the other. A *milo* tree was the only shade in the middle of the sunny field, a perfect place for a lovers' lunch.

After The Mother's fried `*ulu* and shredded pork were consumed, the couple lay down under the shelter of the *milo*. They sipped the cool stream water from the gourd. They gazed at the whisking clouds playing tag overhead.

Mo`ikeha broke the news. "I picked up information about being a crew member on a ship bound for the West Coast of America. They said the chances were pretty good."

"That's something I wished I'd never hear. You can't go now. You still have school."

"Oh, this won't happen until after graduation this coming summer. It will be carrying sugar that will be refined in California."

"It will be difficult without you here."

"You told me to be honest and, as I mentioned before, I must follow this impulse. I wish I could take you with me but it won't be for long. I'll come back more experienced. We could then settle down and take care of this valley—this precious prize of *Akua*."

"It won't be easy, but I'll wait and work on a special *kapa* that will shelter us, like this lovely tree, on the day we become husband and wife." Ho`oipo turned over and kissed Mo`ikeha. She rested her head on his chest and listened to his heartbeat. The moment drowsed them into a short slumber.

The chirping of a honeycreeper in the *milo* tree woke them from their fleeting but refreshing nap. "Ho`oipo, I'd like to stay here all day but we still have a way to go."

The lovers dusted away their drowsiness and clothing and exited the meadow and continued back onto the trail to the upper rain forest. *Ti* leaf and fern bordered the little trail that switched back and forth, the couple occasionally stopping to sample *`ūlei* and *`ōhelu* berries.

Time passed. *`Ama`u* and *hāpu`u* ferns created tunnels forcing The Boy and The Girl to stoop-walk their way up the path. Mo`ikeha was impressed by his lover's identification of various plants like the purple *`uki`uki* berry that she had to learn because of the dyes used to tint her various *kapa*.

The winds had gotten much cooler when they broke out of the wet forest into the open space and red dirt of the summit. Now only occasional *`ōhia lehua* and *nī`oi* trees jutted up in the barren upland.

The sun was starting its journey down behind Pu`u Kukui, the range's highest peak. "We've reached it," announced The Boy pointing to a twenty-foot precipice.

"All I see is a cliff."

"On the other side of it is your valley, Olowalu, the same route Kalanikūpule, the son of King Kahekili who defended Maui, took to escape Kamehameha's advancing warriors. Travelers traversing this barrier used sedge ropes to pull themselves over the top. All the rest is downhill. See, you and I are separated only by a small ridge." The couple hugged each other at their accomplishment.

"I hate to be a spoiler, Ho`oipo, but we'd better be getting back. It will be dark by the time we get down. Mother might get worried."

They began their descent noting how colder it became the more they descended.

The Boy, sensitive to the environs of the valley, commented on how the approaching dark had a green tinge to it. "There seems to be a lot of *mana* in the air. With all this power, perhaps a tempest is headed this way. I remember a storm over Haleakalā when I was twelve; the dome of the volcano was bathed in emerald, bolts of violet lightning attacking its summit. Sailors said it was St. Elmo's Fire."

Their last remaining steps across the stream were taken with care to avoid a tumble in the dark. Finally, they were on solid footing and on the large path that wound around the cliffs, the stream to their right, forty feet below.

The Boy was suddenly alerted by his partner. "Look, Mo`ikeha! There's a light down in the stream."

The Boy squinted at the orange-red light that unexpectedly moved from the riverbed up towards the couple. "*Akua lele*!" he yelled. "Run!" The twosome sprinted in terror, the stories of the demonic fireball racing in their heads. *Kahuna* said that if it flew over one's dwelling, someone's death was imminent. The missionary teachers differed with Hawaiian priests and explained it away as pockets of methane gas seeping upward from decomposing humans or animals ignited by spontaneous combustion. The scientific theory was plausible. `Īao Valley had been littered with the bodies of Kahekili's *Nā Koa*, his warriors buried in graves along the river's edge when Kamehameha The Great came to conquer.

Somehow a science lesson seemed inappropriate at a harrowing time. The duo zigzagged, hoping the fireball would bypass them, but it shifted with their every movement. The ultimate thought bothered The Boy. Was it headed to his family's house or to an unsuspecting home in Wailuku? No matter where it was headed, Mo`ikeha was compelled to stop it. He halted in the middle of the path.

"Mo`ikeha!" The Girl screamed. "What are you doing? Keep running!" The Boy turned abruptly and unloaded every expletive in Hawaiian and every foul English word that he had heard from drunken sailors. He spat a ball of saliva at the fiery fiend from the underworld. The devil-ball exploded, ejecting showery sparks skyward like the exploding fireworks of the *Pākē* man.

Ho`oipo, startled by the vulgar utterances coming from The Boy's mouth, stopped to watch the explosion and demise of the *akua lele*.

She collapsed on the bank of the path. Mo`ikeha raced over to her and dripped the remaining water from the gourd in his bag onto her face. "Ho`oipo! Ho`oipo! All *pau*. It's gone," panted The Boy, his heart still racing from the near-encounter from Hell.

Realizing he was still there and unharmed, she hugged him and whispered, "I'm *maika`i*, just exhausted from running." He helped her to her feet. She added, "Let's go home. Enough adventure for one night."

A light drizzle started as they headed back. "Oh, no," The Girl moaned. "Maybe we spoke too soon." They halted. Their eyes widened, bewildered for a moment at another glow coming from where they were headed. But before they decided to dash back from where they came, they heard a familiar voice behind the illumination. It was Father, lantern in hand, running toward them with The Younger Son. The Father called out, "Mo`ikeha! Ho`oipo!"

"Father!" The Boy called back. "We're all right." He hugged them tight. "We were chased by *akua lele*."

"*Akua lele*?" said The Younger Son. "I heard stories and always wanted to see one."

"You're talking stupid, Son," reprimanded The Father. "I've heard stories too, lived here all my life, have never seen one, and never care to see one."

"You wouldn't want to, believe me," added The Girl, "but Mo`ikeha was brave and stopped it." The Boy refused to admit that during the threatening experience the proclaimed hero had made *mimi* in his pants. He hoped that no one noticed.

"Did you do what is customary under the situation?" asked The Father.

"I apologize to Jesus for my foul mouth."

"I think Jesus would love someone stopping evil, Son."

"I thought Mo`ikeha had lost his mind, stopping and cursing like that," added The Girl.

"Oh, he lost it a long time ago," taunted The Younger Son.

"You, son of a *mo`o*!" Mo`ikeha grabbed his brother around the neck. The Younger Son slipped out of the hold and raced homeward yelling, "Come on, *akua lele*. Catch me if you can." He raced toward their *hale* laughing, his older brother close behind in pursuit. The Father and The Girl likewise picked up their pace as the rain fell harder and colder.

And rain it did all day on the 23rd of December. The temperature hit the fifties in otherwise benign `Īao Valley. Shorts were shed for long pants and parlor games replaced working in the *lo`i*. The Younger Son ventured to the top of the hill during a short break from the downpour late in the afternoon to check on the rest of the island. What he saw caused him to turn around and race back home.

"Father, Mother, guess what I saw?" he shouted, bounding up the steps, bursting into the living area.

"Son, wipe your feet off outside. It's full of mud."

"Snow, Mother! Snow, Father," he gushed as he scraped his feet on the mat. "Haleakalā is covered with *hau*. I saw it through a *puka* in the clouds. Can we go?"

The Twins squealed at the thought. Mo`ikeha joined the chorus. "Let's test out the new wagon. Let's take the stars to the stars."

"What do you think, *ku`uipo*?" The Father asked his sweetheart.

"Only if the rain stops and if the snow doesn't melt."

"We'll prepare to leave at about two or three a.m. No rain, we go. Boys, go pull the big canvas out and attach it to the poles on the wagon. I'll go ask The Neighbor if Leo can join his offspring to pull us up the hill. The poor man is unable to go anywhere for a spell. He's in bed with the gout, his feet all bandaged."

"Supper's almost ready. And if we're going up the mountain, then it's to bed early," announced The Mother. The house buzzed with the excitement of seeing snow. Bedtime prayers asked *Akua* for the sun to stay away and for it to remain cold for at least a day or two.

Two a.m. seemed like it would never come, everyone too excited to sleep. At the announced hour, The Twins ran out to the porch, barefoot and eager to announce the good news and indeed there was. They exclaimed how cold the floor was after they proclaimed, "No rain! Let's go!"

"Make sure everyone's got an extra change of clothes. Mo`ikeha grab all those blankets Mr. Alexander gave us that we never use. Now's the time to initiate them." The Mother then instructed The Younger Son to move the food out to the wagon.

Within the hour, the jubilant clan was out of Wailuku and headed to Kahului. The sun attempted with no success to pry through the heavy cover of grey threatening clouds; a bitter wind whipped down the slopes of the ten thousand foot volcano, much to the delight of the snow-goers.

After a water and relief break in Kahului, the wagon pushed on to Pukalani, the next stop. It reached the two thousand foot level at late afternoon where the horses were watered and the gang prepared for their last leg before nightfall. "I'm hoping that we can stay at The *Paniolo*'s place for the night despite our sudden impulse and little notice. However, our cousin, the cowboy, always encouraged me to come up whenever I want and to bring the family."

The little shack of The *Paniolo* at the junction between the upper and lower Kula trails was finally reached just as darkness was about to fall. On hearing the noise from the approaching wagon, the numerous inhabitants burst out of the *hale* into the chilling night air. The Father presumed that there would be no beds for the visitors.

"My Cousin!" called out The *Paniolo*. "Let me guess. You are up here to see the snow and, of course, visit me."

"It looks like we've come at a bad time. I wish we could have given you fair warning but we came *mana`o ulu wale*, you know, on a whim given this rare occasion. Can you suggest a place where we can stay farther up the road?"

"My son from Pāi`a obviously had the same intentions. But not to worry, the barn is yours. It's cozy at the back. There are even a couple of cots near the rear wall and a small wood stove to keep you warm. Can get nippy up here, you know. It's kinda like a bunkhouse. The cowboys stay there during roundup."

"*Mahalo*, Cousin."

"Come have some *`ai* when you're settled. We have lots of leftovers."

"No need, *Paniolo*. Mother prepared some food. Oh, Son, before I forget, give Uncle and Auntie the coffee, the pickled onions, and chile peppers we brought for them."

"*Mahalo `ia `oukou.* `Īao Valley coffee!" Accepting the gifts, he turned to his wife. "Honey, here. Can you please make it like only you can? Cousins, come on over after you *pau* eat and get the children settled for bed. We'll have some cups of your famous `Īao Valley brew and *wala`au* about your intrepid sailor, his bride to be, and catch up with the rest of the handsome family." He patted The Twins on their heads. "Ho, they getting big. Our *aloha* to all of you. Enjoy your evening. I'll wake all of you up early before I head out to the cattle pens." He retreated back to the house followed by his entourage then stopped and turned. "Oh, please stay tomorrow night on your way down." To The Twins he added, "You going have good fun making a snowman."

The meal, including chicken and sweet potatoes brought out by the hosts' sons, was devoured by the `Īao Valley clan. The Twins and The Younger Brother formed some comfortable beds in the fresh hay and fell asleep without trying. The adults talked story in the cousins' kitchen, its lamp seemingly the only light on the mountain. In its glow, The Father related that The Captain of the *Southern Cross*, the steamship that his son would be working on, decided that, because of Mo`ikeha's experience on the *Kino`ole*, a steward's position would best fit. "He'll begin at the bottom of the ladder as a green boy. Of course, all crew members can be called on at any time to assist others outside their specific talent."

Outdoors, Mo`ikeha and Ho`oipo, wrapped like Indians in Mr. Alexander's blankets, strolled hand in hand and gazed at stars, now even brighter at the higher altitude. Suddenly, flakes began to fall, a preview of the blessings of snow that would manifest itself the next day at the top of the world in the House of the Sun.

The clanging of an old wagon wheel woke the snow pilgrims. "Next stop—Haleakalā!" It was morning, *Paniolo* announcing that it was time to head out. "My son will follow you up with his family. Have a *māli`e* day. I see you tonight."

The sky had remained overcast, the morning air biting as the wagon was loaded up with the basic necessities and the horses watered and hitched. Leo and Leolani clopped their way up the meandering dirt road to the summit with no intention of pushing themselves needlessly. An occasional snow flurry brushed the family, the girls squealing at the thought of the ultimate snowball fight.

As they got higher and patches of snow decorated the ground, the children laughed at their smoky breaths and, at every turn, demanded that the wagon stop. "Not yet. Farther," responded their father. "We'll stop when we get to lots of snow. There's not enough at this level to make a good snowman."

They started to ascend above the clouds, the murky skies now a royal blue. The sun made a majestic appearance. The snow was thicker, so thick that when they got to the nine thousand foot marker, it became a road barrier to the final thousand feet. "This is it!" yelled The Father.

Everyone rubbed their `*ōkole* from the bumpy ride, then charged the landscape. A snowball fight ensued, at first resisted by the ladies until they had had it and proceeded with icy sweet revenge. They pursued the aggressive males with packed powder in hand. The high altitude made them dizzy with delight, their cheeks taking on the color of the Maui rose.

With enough snow down their collars, the girls finally turned to a more benign activity and urged their mother to help them make a snowman that looked like their father.

After an hour of serious snow silliness, The Father suggested to the family that they should all walk up the remaining thousand feet to Pu`u `Ula `Ula. There they would take in the grand panorama of the crater. The offspring heartily agreed to gaze at a wonder only their parents had seen. On the way they were baptized with handfuls of flakes from The Twins like The Snow Maidens of Lake Waiau. The travelers slogged their way up to the highest point. Looking back, they spotted The *Paniolo*'s Son finally pulling his wagon adjacent to theirs.

The sun was now beyond its zenith, as bright and unblocked, as to be admired by and to satisfy the demigod, Maui. Kū and Jesus kept them warm as they climbed the final yards to the crater's edge. Oohs and aahs spilled out of their mouths as they peered down at all the shades of oranges and reds that Pele had painted the House of the Sun. The cinder cones were sprinkled with snow like sugared pastry. They stood there silent like the last family on earth in meditation of *Akua* and Pele's generous gift. While Father described the different areas within the crater and unfurled stories of the volcano to the children, only Ho`oipo noticed another visitor dressed all in white standing on a bluff about a good stone's throw from the family. She must have arrived earlier and wandered off from her company. Ho`oipo swore that her long flowing attire was *kapa*, the pure white gown flowing feely, the woman almost melding as one with the snow.

Father made the dreaded advisory. "Sorry, family. Let's all head back down to the wagon, have some food, and head down to Kula as soon as possible. Riding in the dark on this narrow road can be dangerous." A volley of snowballs pelted the announcer of bad news.

As they reluctantly descended the mountain, *puka* formed in the clouds below. They could see Wailuku and Kahului in the distance, a sign that the snow would soon be melting, but not the memories.

Christmas Eve was spent in The *Paniolo*'s barn, the family hopeful that they would make it to Wailuku to Ka`ahumanu Church for the

Christmas Evening *pa`ina*. They would miss the day service but The Father was happy that the family was together for this special holyday before Mo`ikeha sailed away. As they lay in their place of sleep, both father and son thanked *Akua* and Jesus for the love that bound their family. The final snowflakes of 1860 fell. It was a silent and peaceful night.

CHAPTER TWELVE
The Tempest and The Teapot

"Ladies and Gentlemen, hold your applause until all the graduates are on the stage."

The entry march was played as well as a fledgling band could play it. The parents of the musicians couldn't have cared less about the off-key ensemble. Like the primary school drama skits their offspring appeared in, moms and dads, with a loving prejudice, believed that their son or daughter was the best non-speaking flower or tree.

The play this time was graduation for the young men from Lahainaluna, Class of 1861. The request to hold the clapping down as each graduate approached the dais was as quickly ignored as it was issued. It was now Mo`ikeha's turn. He strolled down the aisle proudly, noting all his family and friends, their arms bedecked with *lei*.

Much to the delight of the students, graduation and the end of the school year had been moved to May. The Hawaiian Mission Board would be in convocation for several weeks with the school as its site.

The assembly had been blessed. The month of May was when Lāhainā began to live up to its moniker—the cruel sun—but the morning had been most pleasant; cool trades raced down the western slopes of Mauna Kahālāwai. Even for the audience layered in their Sunday best, the climate was most *`olu`olu*.

The Girl chuckled as she watched the love of her life trying to keep step with the offbeat of the little musical group. He had complained earlier that cap and gowns made the senior class look like monkeys. He moaned in agreement with his fellow graduates that the wearing of the stuffy outfits was one of the silliest traditions Westerners had ever initiated.

Ho`oipo had mixed emotions: proud that the boy she loved was going to receive his sheepskin as he called it, but at the same time saddened that he would be sailing off to California the very next day. It seemed not enough time for an adequate *aloha*.

The speeches about accomplishments and futures given by balding men in hoary beards were merely background noises to two hearts bearing the weight of distance between far-away lands. Ho`oipo and Mo`ikeha's souls were filled with the anxiety of adjustment. Questions arose: Would he change? What if he met another woman? What if he got injured? Upon considering that question, she dared not even think the worst. She also had doubts about her own feelings. How much absence could she endure without wanting someone in her arms? From the story he had passed on to her about Ulysses, she imagined herself as Penelope having to un-do her stitches every night to keep other suitors at bay while awaiting the return of her world traveler.

And then there was the threat of war. Up to this point it had been all bluster, but word reached Hawai`i at the end of February that South Carolina had seceded from the Union. Mississippi, Florida, Alabama, Georgia, Louisiana, and Texas followed The Palmetto Confederate State. Would that affect California where Mo`ikeha was headed?

The ceremony ended with the issuing of diplomas followed by *E Ola Ke Ali`i Ke Akua*, Prince Lunalilo's prize-winning composition in a contest held for a new Hawai`i anthem. Keeping in step was again attempted as the entry march was replayed for the exit. At the end of the line, caps were thrown and classmates were hugged. Parents and friends rushed the seniors and stacked them with *lei* of all types, colors, and sizes up to their chins and beyond. Mothers raced to their son's aid to keep them from suffocating from the strung garlands.

During the next several hours at the *pā`ina* of *kālua* pig, *lomi* salmon, *poi*, chicken long rice, *`opihi*, *`ōpae*, purple and orange sweet potatoes, *haupia,* and *kūlolo*, the graduates traded stories of their fellow classmates, the liked and disliked teachers, and the sins committed against their alma mater, especially the more outrageous escapades of the dormitory boys.

Ho`oipo pulled Mo`ikeha away for some private time together as the crowd thinned. They walked to the edge of Hale Pa`i, the printing building, and looked down on Lāhainā town, now basking in the copper of sundown. She pulled a *lei* from a small bag. "I thought our island's flower, the *Lokelani,* would be appropriate. I picked it from the area in Olowalu around the *koa* that you chose for your canoe. I didn't want to give it to you earlier, too fragile." She draped it delicately around his neck, kissing him.

"This is the most special *lei* of all. *Mahalo*, Ho`oipo. I'm so glad that you and your family will be here tomorrow to see me leave. You don't know how much it means."

"You promised me that you would write, so you better. I'll be expecting your letters at the post office. But…" She paused to tell him of her concern about the possibility of war.

Just as she said that, the thinning crowd suddenly grew agitated. "Oh, no," was heard more than once. Fearing a fight had erupted to mar the ceremony, the couple ran toward the chaos.

Ho`oipo's father raced toward the two. The *Kahuna* cried out, "They attacked Fort Sumpter!" The Girl, unfamiliar with the place and the villains, was lost for a minute. "The Confederates captured a Union fort. A civil war has started. Troops are amassing," he added.

"Who told you that, Father?" asked The Girl.

"The farm foreman came up the hill with news from the *Southern Cross*."

Most of the people were mildly curious, the war far away, out of sight, out of mind. But anxiety in The Girl increased. She turned to The Boy. "Perhaps you should stay home," she pled.

He tried to comfort her. "One of our teachers said that most of Northern California is pro-union. It's those radicals in the southern part of the state and a few pockets in the Bay Area that want two Californias. San Francisco is safe. Who'd want to attack sugar or whaling ships?"

"Mo`ikeha!" The Boy's Father called as he headed towards Ho`oipo's family. "We should start heading over to *Tutuwahine*'s. *Kahuna*, you and your family come for some coffee before you spend the night at the cousin's."

At *Tutuwahine*'s *hale*, everyone stripped out of their church/graduation clothes down to the essentials, their bare toes wiggling in relief, their shoes now decorating the porch. They had shed the formalities of the day and were now at ease. As he sipped coffee, The Boy listened to the elders' advice of dos and don'ts directed to him, similar to the conflicting counsel of Ophelia's father in *Hamlet*. Ho`oipo noticed the toll on her lover.

"I have an announcement to make," proclaimed The Boy's Father. "Today, my eldest son is no longer a child. In our changing society, it is graduation that makes the man. Mo`ikeha, from this day on, you will never be called The Boy. From this moment you are The Young Man."

"*Mahalo*, Father. And does that mean that Ho`oipo is no longer The Girl?"

The *Kahuna* spoke for his daughter. "`*Ae*. I no longer have my little girl. I now have The Young Woman in my family." Mixed tears of joy and sorrow came to the eyes of the four parents. It was the day they had looked forward to and yet regretted.

With that said, The *Kahuna* gathered up his clan, traded *aloha* to their hosts, and left to get some sleep to be on time for the seven o'clock departure of the *Southern Cross*.

By five thirty the next morning, the wagon had been loaded with The Young Man's locker and ditty bag along with some scones his mother had baked some time during the night, his bulky pea coat tucked under his arm. When they arrived at the pier, Ho`oipo's family was already there. The two clans gathered, The Twins impressed by the big boat. Everyone hugged and kissed The Young Man. Tears were shed by all, their hearts filled with apprehension about their Mo`ikeha leaving little Maui for the big world.

Ho`oipo pulled Mo`ikeha aside. "Here. This is for you. I saw a first mate of a British ship from Birmingham using it. I offered him a *kapa* cloth in exchange for it to make sure you had something that would force you to write. It's called a fountain pen. No more quills. You suck it up from the ink bottle. Just lift this." She then placed it in a little bag that contained several blotters, and writing paper. "No excuse, Young Man," she teased.

"No excuse, Young Woman," he mimicked.

The Young Man upon hearing the firing up of the boilers that echoed across the harbor knew that it was now six o'clock. It was time to get on-board. He made one last round of goodbyes and stepped onto the tender that took him out to Lāhainā Roads where The *Southern Cross* sat anchored. It was an excruciating hour for Ho`oipo and the two families. He would not appear on deck until the ship left.

During the hour, Mo`ikeha's devotees discussed the hundred and forty-nine thousand tons of unprocessed sugar in the hold and its future and gave commentary on the parade of privileged white passengers that filed past them. Finally, The *Kahuna* with spyglass in hand announced where all the crew members were positioning themselves for departure: the Chief Officer on the forward deck, the Captain and Extra Second on the bridge, the Senior and Junior Officer on the aft deck, and the Third and Fourth Officers at the forward and aft gangways.

Winches chattered, windlasses kept a musical beat, the capstans rattled with slacking cables. The docking crew worked the warps and the shout of "Yo. Heave ho!" was finally bellowed out. The anchor was pulled up. A long blast was given and like the curtain call of a play, Mo`ikeha moved out to the deck followed by the passengers to wave one final farewell. He propped up his binoculars, spotted that his supporters were faithfully still there, and thought how diminutive they looked from across the water. He waved widely, their tiny hands responding.

The ship was moving. Maui, his family, and friends were soon out of sight.

No sooner were they out in the `Au`au Channel, when the Chief Officer announced, "All crew on deck!" Like ants at a picnic, the ship workers materialized from all nooks and crannies onto the forward deck. It was *the speech*, the speech delivered by The Captain, the kind of soliloquy given by a leader to his team about various feats to be accomplished like those at *Makahiki* games. Whether the speech dealt with sport events like *Makahiki* or ship work, it was about each person doing their job, helping each other when necessary, and about not stirring up trouble. The Captain pledged that he wouldn't get into anyone's hair if they didn't get into his. A few sailors snickered. He had not much of a mop. During the maritime monologue, The Young Man wrestled with all the terminology that he had to learn. Luckily, as an apprentice to the steward, he would have normal hours, stalling him from immediately memorizing the bell schedule or all the terminology. He would work the entire day and sleep at night and be spared of the horrid middle watch from midnight to four a.m.

After they were dismissed, The Young Man raced to refresh and fill the scuttle buckets on the ship. As he dashed around the back stairs, The Captain proceeded back to the pilothouse. The commander missed his step, tried grasping for the rail, fell backwards, and slid down the stairs. The Young Man raced over. "Captain, are you okay?" He propped his shoulder under his superior. "Here. Try to stand."

"Maybe sit," suggested The Captain. He plopped down on one of the stairs, felt his ankle, and straightened out his jacket and slacks.

"Shall I fetch someone?" The Young Man asked.

"Oh, no," I'm fine. It's going to take more than one fall to put away this old sea salt. Besides," he whispered, "it's embarrassing. Mum's the word to help me save my face."

"I know nothing," smiled The Young Man.

"Say," said The Captain, finally collected, "you're the *kanaka* from Maui, aren't you? Your name is Mokini..."

"Mo`ikeha, Captain. How did you know?"

"I hired you. Remember?"

"Oh, yes," he embarrassingly recalled.

"I love the *Kanaka*. So I'm sure I'll treasure you. Such good sailors, quite adaptable, and carefree. I think it's that *aloha*. So what made you take a job on this ship?"

"I've been sailing for a long time. Perhaps I'll get a chance to steer my own schooner someday. The Captain of the *Kino`ole* let me do it often and, of course, I've built my own canoe."

"Well, you've got work to do and so do I. Perhaps I'll get you up on the bridge sometime soon to feel the ropes. Goodbye for now, son."

The Young Man raced to finish filling the deck buckets when he ran into The Chief Officer. "Green boy, haven't you filled those buckets yet. It's been some time since we left the Lāhainā Roads. What have you been doing?"

"I was speaking to The Captain."

"We don't speak to The Captain. All queries are posed to The Chief Steward and he to me."

"Yes, sir." Mo`ikeha took it all in stride, knowing the hierarchy of a ship.

His general job was to assist The Chief Steward and The Cook in the preparation and serving of meals. Of course, in reality, he was merely an assistant to The Steward's Assistant. In addition to making sure everyone was fed and on time, he was assigned to perform the most menial tasks: scrubbing something almost endlessly, getting rid of trash and garbage, as well as sweeping and swabbing decks, stairways, and passages.

The veteran Chief and Assistant Stewards had become jaded by the pampered class that traveled in the handful of cabins for passengers. Even their flamboyant wealth was questionable. The Chief and Assistant Steward eagerly handed the duty of mollycoddling them to Mo`ikeha who would have to put up with the finicky demands of the rich.

Mo`ikeha tried to memorize the list initially by identifying them by their vocations: The Sugar Man, The Heiress and her Pomeranian, Fifi, The Heiress' Daughter and her Lawyer Husband, The Missionary and His Wife, The Saloon Keeper, The Diplomat and His Wife, and The Retired Whaler. The Chief Steward commented to the neophyte that the question was not where they were traveling to but what they were fleeing from.

The Pomeranian from the get-go was a problem. The Sugar Man, with his recent purchase of Pioneer Mill in Lāhainā, was off to The Golden State to arrange the future of processing and to encourage new markets. Fifi didn't take to ships and barked as soon as her paws hit the deck. The Sugar Man complained so Mo`ikeha was sent in to console the *kō* baron and discuss the issue with The Heiress. Eight bells was quickly approaching. The Young Man tried to balance serving lunch with serving as peacemaker.

Everyone gathered in the small dining room. During dinner, Mo`ikeha noticed that the dog went quiet. Perhaps that was the solution. He whispered to The Heiress while pouring her another glass of Lāhainā grape, "Feed Fifi these snacks as soon as she begins to bark." He inconspicuously slid a bag of beef jerky on the owner's lap hoping the pet would chew in silence.

This road to Hell was paved with good intentions. The beef jerky did not take well to the Pomeranian. Later that evening, while heading to his cabin, the crusty Retired Whaler almost broke his neck. "Shit!" he yelled. And indeed it was, a gift from Fifi. He slipped. His wooden leg went one way, his good one another, creating a human scissors. He lambasted the Chief Steward. "None of the whaling ships that I served on from the Aleutians to the South Pacific ever allowed mutts on-board, especially those with incontinence problems." The Chief Steward called Mo`ikeha to task and The Young Man was sent on poop patrol.

The Diplomat and His Wife cornered him as he lugged the bucket and mop down to remove the *kūkae*. "Excuse me, darkie, but we'd like to report an odor coming from outside our cabin."

The Wife added, "And it smells like...well, it smells. Can you see to it?"

"*`A`ole pilikia*," replied the poop patrolman.

"I beg your pardon," retorted The Diplomat's Wife, never having tried to master what she called the 'gibberish of the Hawaiian language' during her short stay in Honolulu and Lāhainā.

"No problem," Mo`ikeha translated. "It's done." He scurried off with the mop and bucket in hand.

No sooner was the task completed, then he was off and running to prepare for dinner at 6:00. The Cook had it under control so The Young Man finished stocking the pantry with the provisions picked up in Lāhainā, then later dropped off washcloths, hand towels, and bath towels outside each cabin.

A note was attached to the Heiress' door excusing her from dinner. "Not feeling well." Perhaps she had been embarrassed by the antics of her pet.

Mo`ikeha noted through the porthole that the sun had drifted behind a layer of thick clouds. Perhaps, rain was on its way.

The guests ate better than the crew. The dining room table had a spread of prime rib, halibut, tossed greens, baked potatoes, plum pudding and wine. The Diplomat delivered a sermon about the destruction to the U.S. economy with the abolition of slavery. He rambled on with more crazy thoughts like Abraham having slaves. A rumble of thunder silenced the zealot. "The gods must be bowling," teased the green boy. The privileged party remained laugh-less.

The Missionary asked the group about the absent heiress. Mo`ikeha, while filling their water glasses, volunteered the woman's excuse of not feeling well. The Daughter of the Heiress found it odd. "She was fine when we walked her to her cabin after lunch."

"At least we'll have some relief from that mangy cur," blurted The Diplomat's Wife. The Heiress' Daughter responded by giving the Diplomat's wife what Mo`ikeha regarded as *stink eye*.

"I'll check on her after our game of bridge," the progeny announced.

The Chief Officer knocked at the dining room door and entered, a strong gust of wind pushing behind him. "Excuse me, ladies and gentlemen. I hate to disturb your dinner. I hope all is well. It looks like there's a storm up ahead. We'll try to steer around it without adding more time to the voyage. I know you all have appointments in San Francisco. I'd advise staying in your cabin and off decks until I give an all clear. Tonight might be a little rough." The boom of a thunderclap accentuated his exit.

Rain was falling heavily as the privileged patrons scurried to their suites. Mo`ikeha proceeded to clean the dining room, set out the night lunches for those on watch, check the breakfast menu, and finally make the rounds to the cabins with tea pots.

He donned his rain gear and delivered lunches to the men on watch. As The Young Man balanced his way back across the slippery deck, he heard the whining of a dog. It was Fifi! She was soaking wet, hiding under the stairwell. "Fifi, what are you doing out here?" Mo`ikeha found it strange that the dog had strayed from the constant side of The Heiress. Obviously, she had gotten out. He scooped up the dog and grabbed a towel on the way to her owner's cabin.

He knocked on the cabin door while wiping Fifi down. "Miss," he called in a loud voice, "this is the assistant steward." There was no response. He pounded on the door louder, but to no avail. He grew more concerned. Perhaps she was seriously sick. He pulled out the master key.

Fifi scampered to the side of The Heiress who lay crumpled on the floor. "Oh, no!" Mo`ikeha cried out loud. He moved quickly to her side to feel her pulse. There was nothing. He looked at her face; her eyes were dilated, bulging, her body wrung wet with sweat, her dress soiled.

He got up, locked the cabin door, and raced to the Chief Steward who was about to settle down for the night. "What is it, green boy? Looks like you've seen a ghost."

"She's dead," claimed The Young Man.

"Who's dead?"

"The Heiress. She's got no pulse."

"Go get the Captain. We'll meet at her cabin."

The noise of ship personnel rushing to and from the cabin had alerted the rest of the elite including The Heiress' Daughter. The partners of the bridge party followed her. They were jammed outside the dead woman's compartment, The Chief Steward's arms outstretched across the cabin door like a reluctant messiah demanding no entrance or questions until The Captain appeared.

The stately Captain and Mo`ikeha came rushing down the corridor. His command was even. "Everyone, please return to your cabins. I'll meet with you later." They were slow in returning. "Come on, folks. Come on." He directed an exception to The Heiress' Daughter. "Except you and only you."

"It's your negro lackey!" yelled The Diplomat as he headed for his room. The Captain ignored the accusation.

The Captain entered, felt the woman's pulse, and noted the condition of her body. "She was perfectly well when my husband and

I left her here after lunch," said The Heiress' Daughter in a quivering voice.

"How old was your mother?" asked The Chief Steward, suggesting that it might have been her advanced age that resulted in her death.

"Oh, she's…" The Heiress' Daughter began to sob and speak at the same time. "She was seventy but in excellent condition. Mr. Baldwin recently gave her a clean bill of health."

"Chief Steward, take the lady and Fifi back to her cabin. And notify the others that we need to secure this room and that we'll give them information as soon as we've investigated the situation. Oh, and Miss, mum's the word until I contact you again." The Chief Steward offered the lady a handkerchief and ushered the weeping woman and her lawyer husband to their cabin.

The Captain turned to Mo`ikeha. "How did you do in your chemistry class at Lahainaluna, son?"

"I got an A," The Young Man replied.

"Take a look at the bottom of the tea cup. What do you see?"

Mo`ikeha swirled it around. "It's purple, Captain."

"Our tea's not purple. I think the residue is a poison. I believe this woman was murdered. Of the five major poisons, there's only one that's purple."

"The Deadly Nightshade!" concluded The Young Man. "But it's not common in Lāhainā. The only place I've seen it was in Reverend Richards' garden. His neighbor's horse got to it and eventually collapsed, sweating, heaving, his eyes dilated like saucers."

"Exactly the same symptoms as The Heiress. Look." At that moment, a flash of lightning pounded outside the ship, highlighting the effects of the belladonna on the woman's body. "Perfect night for a murder, eh?"

"Who would want to kill this kindly woman?" said The Young Man after he eeked out a small laugh in reaction to The Captain's sardonic jest.

"Most obviously the one who gets to benefit from her death?"

"She has no husband and only one daughter…"

"…who had easy access to her. But let's not jump to conclusions. I'm off to get some men and a bag and move her body to the cold locker. You stay here, my junior detective, and go through all her belongings. Report to me anything you find relevant." The Captain hustled off.

Mo`ikeha started rifling through her belongings. He came across a Tiffany jewelry case opened, its contents missing. Robbery? Maybe. But if that was so, the culprit was either selective or in a hurry. He or she had left behind a diamond ring and pearl bracelet in the victim's purse.

Besides clothes and personal items, the only item of interest to Mo`ikeha was a sizeable box filled with articles from the *Pacific Commercial Advertiser*. Stashed under the clippings was a folder of documents, letters, and under that—the Holy Grail—the woman's diary! He skimmed to the last entry. It read: "I know and I'm going to tell."

"What are you doing, green boy?" demanded The Chief Steward, barging in upon his return.

Startled, The Young Man dropped the news stories on the diary and folder, hoping The Chief Steward had not seen the last two items. "Oh, you scared me. The Captain commanded me to go through all of The Heiress' belongings. I was skimming through this box of newspaper clippings. Looks like a hobby. There are so many in here."

"So she was a hoarder. I'll take over from now on. Time for young boys like you to get to bed."

"Do you mind if I take this box with me?"

"Going to catch up on your reading of past history and sales at Hackfields?" snickered The Chief Steward. "Go, green boy. I'll wait here till The Captain gets back. Scram! Just get out of my hair." The boy lugged the box of news stories out the door.

The perennial midnight oil was burned that night in The Young Man's cabin. The ship bucked like a wild horse, thunder rolled from east to west, lightning flashed like cannons of war, but Mo`ikeha read on. Within several hours, he came to a startling conclusion.

He jotted down a note with the fountain pen that Ho`oipo had given him, tossed on a raincoat, and headed for The Captain's quarters where he attached the missive to his door to meet as early as possible in the morning.

The dawn came soon enough, the atmosphere grey. A thick mist enveloped the ship, a preview of the famous San Francisco fog. The Young Man woke up way before the passengers. The Captain, having read the note on his door, found Mo`ikeha preparing for breakfast. "Chief Steward, Mo`ikeha will be aiding me. I'm sure you and the Assistant Steward can carry on."

"Aye, Captain," said The Chief Steward somewhat reluctantly.

"Let me grab a box from my cabin and I'll meet you at the..." Mo`ikeha gulped at the unbelievable words he was saying "...murder scene."

The Captain was scouring the now body-less cabin with closer scrutiny when the green boy reappeared with the evidence. "Anything missing?" asked The Captain.

"Only a ring...from Tiffany's. But what's strange, Captain, is that the killer thief left behind two valuable pieces of jewelry."

Mo`ikeha spread the articles out on the bed. "Look!" he said excitedly like a kid with a treasure map, "These travelers all had ties to The Heiress... and mostly bad ones. They are all connected to the company that made her wealthy, Colonial Empire. Here, for example: The Sugar Man—Colonial reneged on a deal to buy Central Maui land. He lost thousands of dollars."

The Captain scanned the clips about the Saloon Keeper. The Heiress was President of the Lāhainā Prohibition League. The organization had been formed to close down some of the fifty saloons in the port town. Their blacklist resulted in the shut down of his questionable establishment. They were after his tavern in particular, claiming he was unlawfully mixing his *`ōkolehau* with toxic fillers like *kiawe* beans.

Mo`ikeha next shared the Retired Whaler's story from a Lāhainā newspaper article. "It says here that The Whaler and his crew took to the streets protesting the decommission of several whaling ships from Colonial Empire without advanced notice. The Heiress refused their call for assistance, proclaiming that, with the discovery of ground oil in Pennsylvania, the whaling industry was going to be replaced. She also complained that the Humpback and Grey species were also diminishing because of over whaling. She finally made note that a number of whaling ships carrying precious oil for fuel and munitions had already been sunk by the Confederacy on the East Coast."

"What about that racist diplomat and his equally racist wife?" asked The Captain.

"The Diplomat and His Wife were leaving the Islands. He was brought in from somewhere in the South by Foreign Minister Wyllie because they saw eye to eye on the Confederacy and slavery. But unlike Wyllie, The Diplomat was blatant, outspoken about his dislike for coloreds including Hawaiians. The Heiress put the pressure on the

Foreign Minister to remove the bigot and his wife. His wife buttered it up by claiming that it was a transfer and that she couldn't stand the hellish sun and the lazy brownies, anyway."

"Finally," said Mo`ikeha, "there's The Missionary and His Niece. You might recall it, Captain. This clipping should jog your memory. Here. His wife left to visit a family member back East in New Salem, Massachusetts and never returned. Her niece then arrived to take care of her husband."

"He later claimed that his wife had died back there. But I don't see the connection to The Heiress," commented The Captain.

"This might be closer to the truth," claimed the green boy turned detective. He handed a correspondence found in the folder. "It's a letter of response to The Heiress from a Massachusetts private investigator claiming that there was no such woman or relatives in New Salem, or funerals of her namesake. It seems The Heiress may have had some doubts about the woman's demise."

"And this so called niece?" added The Captain. "Mo`ikeha, go fetch The Chief Steward. Tell him that The Captain requests all passengers to be at the salon for breakfast at 8:00. After they're there, search all passenger cabins. We're looking for a necklace with a Tiffany engraving. I'll go through the diary for any further clues." Mo`ikeha ran off.

At breakfast, the stewards set up a buffet with eggs, toast, fruit, hotcakes, and sausages with hot coffee. The Captain waited until the feast was consumed before he began the grand inquisition.

The Captain entered the room as the patrons supped their Lāhainā brew. "Good Morning, Ladies and Gentlemen," announced The Captain. Mo`ikeha listened while he cleared the buffet table. "I'm sure you're aware that I'm here to fill you in on the passing of The Heiress. But before I do that, I have a question to ask all of you. Who in this room knew her?" A silence pervaded the salon. The Heiress' Daughter raised her hanky-cradled hand. "I mean, other than her daughter and son-in-law." There was again no response. "Ladies and Gentlemen, I suggest you tell the truth. Murder is a serious situation."

"Murder?" The group gasped, uttering the dreaded word. Her daughter wept loudly. "How?"

"Someone here poisoned her tea," proclaimed The Captain.

"Poison?" The group gulped. The Daughter continued gushing tears.

The Captain directed his attention to the Sugar Man. "You, Sir, knew this lady." The group feigned surprise. "The Heiress and her company, Colonial Empire, reneged on a deal to buy Central Maui cane land. How much did you lose, Sir?"

"Thousands," said The Sugar Man. "Do you think I like opening old wounds? Business is business. You win some; you lose some. It's no excuse for murder."

"He had nothing to gain," blurted out The Saloon Keeper.

"Revenge is very powerful," countered The Captain.

"Her daughter will inherit a whole company and, I'm sure, a hefty insurance claim," accused The Whaler. "Interrogate her, not us."

"Did you know her?" The Captain asked The Whaler.

"Okay, okay. Her company sold a number of ships, including the one I worked on, without notice. My crew and I were thrown into the streets penniless. We begged for some compensation while looking for other jobs. We despised what she had done but most homeless and hungry people don't kill the ones that fired them."

"Well, most at least," added The Captain.

The Whaler pointed to The Saloon Keeper. "She ruined his life as well. Tell him. The Captain seems to know all about us."

At that moment, one of the staff members searching the passenger cabins knocked outside the salon. "Excuse me, Captain. Can I see you for a minute?" Mumbles were heard outside the door. The Captain returned with a bag in hand.

"Well, sir," The Captain asked The Saloon Keeper, "what's The Whaler talking about?"

The latter responded. "I didn't want to tell anyone out of fear of embarrassment. And believe me, I've gone straight. It was her banning of saloons that started the whole mess. I paid my time and lost my pub, but I've moved on. I only saw her name on documents. I had never met the woman and didn't even realize that my fellow passenger was the owner of Colonial Empire."

The Diplomat re-confirmed that there was no relationship between him and his wife and The Heiress. "We've only been in Lāhainā for four months. My wife hated the humidity and…"

"…the dark skinned natives?" completed The Captain. Mo`ikeha cringed at the prejudice directed to his people by those who stayed no longer than a sailor could grow a beard. "You, unfortunately, have been spewing your intolerance about our Hawaiian host culture, and, in particular, directing hate language to my interracial crew. According to newspaper articles and her diary, The Heiress persuaded The Foreign Minister to relocate you to an all-white utopia. Oh, by the way, this was found in your room." The Captain pulled out the necklace from the bag. The group sighed somewhat, presuming theft to be the motive. "It's The Heiress' bracelet."

The Diplomat's wife protested. "It could be my jewelry."

"But it's not," argued The Captain, "especially when it's a Tiffany piece, with The Heiress' name engraved on it."

He glanced over to The Missionary and His Niece. "The *Pacific Commercial Advertiser* carried your story. You want to tell us all about it?"

"Well, I didn't know The Heiress that well. She was a friend of my wife until…" He paused to reflect on his wife again. "…until she left Hawai`i to go Back East."

"But she never returned from New Salem," added The Captain.

"I was in despair when I found out that she died on the way there. I couldn't leave my mission and had to mourn from afar. I'm glad her niece came to comfort and assist me."

"It would have been helpful if all of you had been forthcoming." He pointed to Mo`ikeha. "But my junior sleuth here did all the work. And despite the fact that everyone had a motive, only one is responsible. The robbery was to divert suspicion, and as Mo`ikeha noted, if robbery was the motive, why weren't the other expensive jewels taken from the most obvious place—The Heiress' purse? But the murderer had to move in and out of the room quickly. The bracelet was dropped through the cabin porthole of the Diplomat and His Wife and found on the floor right beneath the window by one of the crew—an obvious set up."

"Then who is it, Captain?" asked The Diplomat's Wife, somewhat relieved.

"It's a person who has murdered before. And only one of you has been involved with missing persons that we mentioned previously."

"I wouldn't kill my wife. I am a servant of God. I loved her dearly," protested The Missionary."

"As much as you love your niece?"

"What are you insinuating, Captain?"

"Oh, I'm not insinuating. The Heiress left behind a diary." He pulled out the little book. "She made an entry about your wife, every time she visited her. She complained to The Heiress about your inordinate temper, showing her bruises and burns covered up by the long sleeved, long skirted Mother Hubbards. Then, shortly before she went missing, she revealed to The Heiress your lusty affair with a Honolulu saloon maid. Your niece? Your wife attempted to send a letter to the Mission Board about your fall from grace. You discovered the letter; your wife went missing shortly after that."

"This is ridiculous. She died in New Salem," objected The Missionary.

"Not according to the town coroner. A family with her married or surname never lived or died there. The Heiress had hired a private investigator and he sent her a revealing report concerning her dear friend."

The Heiress' Daughter posed the question about the kind of poison. "The Deadly Nightshade," answered The Captain, "dropped in the tea pot. The only place in Lāhainā my green boy knew where belladonna for medicinal purposes grew was in the missionary garden. Obviously, The Missionary and The Heiress had a discussion about the missing wife at some point after they boarded. She threatened to turn him in once we got to San Francisco. The last entry in her diary was 'I know and I'm going to tell.' It was also her last day on earth. I'm guessing that her body is someplace in that garden. I'm also guessing that the handwriting on the note on the cabin door is not that of The Heiress but yours. As certified by maritime law, being the justice officer of the open sea, I arrest you and your so called niece for the murder of The Heiress."

The Captain called in the two burly sailors waiting outside the door. "Take them to the brig."

The niece or mistress objected strenuously. "I'm innocent. He told me that his wife had died. He lied to me." She was obviously trying to save her own neck.

"Tell it to the judge after they extradite you back to the islands. Take them away, men." He turned to the group. "Make it easier the next time: tell the truth. I hope the rest of your trip is better." He went over to console The Heiress' Daughter.

As Moi`keha began to leave for the kitchen with the piled dishes, The Captain stopped him. "*Mahalo*, my junior sleuth. Come up to bridge on your break tomorrow and we'll let you steer the ship for awhile." The Young Man/part time investigator beamed while balancing the breakfast dishes on his way to the scullery.

The sun came out as if connected to the clearing of the crime. The day proceeded with the normal rigor of meals and cleaning. After the evening dinner, after all was put away, Mo`ikeha made his way up to the deck. The sky was painted red much to the delight of the sailors. Like their predecessors during the glorious days of sailing ships, the crew celebrated their free time telling tales, mending, playing cards, challenging each other to checkers or chess, playing a variety of instruments, or writing letters.

As the music men plunked out nostalgic tunes, Mo`ikeha pulled out his fountain pen and continued his letter to Ho`oipo. He added the skinny of the murder and his part in the drama. With *Greensleeves*, *Barbara Allen*, *The Willow Tree*, *Blow Ye Winds Blow*, and *The Girl I Left Behind* either instrumentally or with song as background, he told her that The Captain had invited him up to steer the ship and that in a few days they would be passing through The Golden Gates of San Francisco.

CHAPTER THIRTEEN
Chrysopylae

Like the crew, Mo`ikeha grew more and more excited as California and San Francisco got closer. The weather had been balmy but word was that San Francisco in summer was cold and definitely foggier than in winter. The distant shoreline had been spotted by spyglass. The Young Man was so busy serving meals, cleaning brass, and taking final inventory that he even failed to hear "Land Ho!"

An hour passed. Mo`ikeha was in the middle of his duties when The Captain summoned the Maui sailor to the bridge. "I promised you when you took the wheel several times that I'd have you back for our final approach to the Golden Gate. Second Officer, let Mo`ikeha steer."

"Aye, Captain," answered The Second Officer. Mo`ikeha beamed proudly as he navigated past the Marin Peninsula to the north and the San Francisco Bay Peninsula to the south. "Steering a steamship is nothing like the good old days of sailing," noted The Captain. "Oh, you still have to be alert but the power of steam keeps her pretty steady. This bay is one of the easiest to navigate. She's got an ideal sheltered port and she's twelve miles wide so there's little chance of running a ship aground."

It was as easy as threading a needle through its *puka* for sure. As he passed through the headlands of Marin and San Francisco, the sun broke out, reflecting gold from the wild yellow daises, indigenous poppies, and profuse dry grasses. "It's a golden gate for sure, Captain," The Young Man declared.

"John C. Fremont gave the area its name, *Chrysopylae* or Golden Gate, after the famous Byzantine harbor. Okay, Mo`ikeha, let's return the wheel back to The Second Officer. You hurry along back down to assist The Chief Steward to prepare for docking."

The *Southern Cross* maneuvered her way and was moored at the

Vallejo Street Wharf. The passengers disembarked and added twelve more bodies to the fifty-six thousand dreamers that already populated the Bay Area of California, the state now only eleven years old. The harbor constable was notified and the murderer and his mistress were hauled off to the pokey. The crew wouldn't touch ground for a few hours until all their duties had been settled. The consulate and harbormaster messengers scampered onto the ship with missives for The Captain.

An hour later, The Captain called for Mo`ikeha. "I have a message from Commodore Montgomery that may interest you. He's looking for recruits. I thought you might be attracted by the pay—fifty dollars a week. I'm sure that it looks substantial compared to the eight dollars a month you made working on this ship."

"Fifty dollars! What's the job?" queried The Young Man, thinking of his future wife and family.

"I'll let The Commodore fill you in. His letter said that interested recruits are asked to report to Mare Island on Friday. There's nothing to lose. If you change your mind, the *Southern Cross* sails on Saturday. I'd hate to lose a good sailor to The Commodore but I think it's a real opportunity for a young man like you. Here are the specifics." He handed him the dispatch from The Commodore.

Mo`ikeha turned to leave. "Oh, *mahalo*, Captain." He prepared to depart again and turned once more. "Oh, Captain, with all the excitement, I forgot two important things. Are there any affordable hotels nearby and how do I get to Mare Island?"

"There are boarding houses and hotels from fifty cents to five dollars a night all within walking distance from here and a ferry leaves for Mare Island every morning at eight from the adjoining pier. Good luck, son."

An hour later, Mo`ikeha dragged his bag down the gangplank. The stevedores were in position to start unloading the precious cane crystals. He learned from The Captain that sugar cane production in the South had been halted with the outbreak of war and that Hawai`i could pick up the slack. He had his earned eight dollars, the fifty dollars that he had saved from crewing on the *Kino`ole* for over a year, and the twenty-five his father had given him. There was no other choice. To be able to eat, catch the ferry, and pay for lodging, he had to stick to a fifty-cent-a-day boarding house.

There were many lodgings along Battery and Clay Streets. With his bags growing heavier by the minute, he stopped on Commercial Street where he spotted a familiar name—Eureka! the expression screamed at Sutter's Mill upon the discovery of gold. It was a better place in contrast to all the flophouses that he passed along the way that were obviously quickly and cheaply constructed at the onset of The Gold Rush.

"How much are the rooms?" he asked the little lady at the front desk.

"Fifty cents a day up front."

"Perfect," responded The Young Man in the new land. He signed in.

"Second floor. Bathtub and shower with cold water and toilet at the end of the hall. Hot water Saturdays only." The proprietor handed him the key. "No rowdiness. And quiet after six o' clock. Make sure your door is locked at all times. Some mug got himself rubbed out across the street a couple of nights ago."

Mo`ikeha was concerned about the last admonition as he lugged his meager belongings up the stairs. A couple of barrels had been placed along the hallway for trash, the smell from rotting food emanating from them. He justified the splintered door, the squeaky bed, the ripped armchair, and the lock that only worked when you slammed it hard by acknowledging that that's what you get for fifty cents.

He also reminded himself that the second rate hotel was just a place to store his bags and sleep. He'd be out and about The City tomorrow to take in the sites. After a cold shower he raced back to his room and threw himself under the covers, staring out the window as the fog crept in like a mute white panther. Before long, the buildings across the street were no longer visible. He tried to sleep, believing the clerk had been pulling his leg about no noise after six o'clock. Doors banged all night, heated discussions in Chinese were heard down the hall, and a drunk sang a merry tune off-key.

Mo`ikeha questioned his decision to see the world when he had the most peaceful, sublime life in `Īao Valley that most could only dream about. It would be times like this when he would feel most lonely and desirous of Maui—his home, his family, and Ho`oipo. He combated the noisy night with paper and fountain pen, writing letters to all his loved ones. He announced that he had finally made it to California. Of course, he left out the part about the pathetic boarding house and that he had an appointment for a lucrative job. The latter omission had to be made, at least for now, less they'd think that he'd never return. He finally fell asleep with Ho`oipo's pen in hand at about four a.m. At last there was peace, for even drunks had to eventually snooze.

No alarm clocks were needed to wake The Young Man. Early shift workers in bulky boots tromped their way down the hall, the cans from a noisy milk wagon rattled against each other, and a fire wagon clanged its way down to the waterfront. He looked out the window. The fog panther had slipped out before morning. It was nippy but the sky was cloudless, a most opportune day for playing tourist. He pasted his hair down with water, slipped into his clothes and light jacket, and headed in search for the perfect cup of coffee.

He skipped down the stairs, turned the corner, and bumped into a human curiosity waiting near the check-in desk. It was a man wearing a beaver hat, a blue uniform, his coat topped with golden epaulets highlighted by a boutonniere. A cavalry sword hung at his side, a walking stick in hand. "Oh, *E kala mai ia`u*," exclaimed Mo`ikeha. "I mean excuse me..." Considering the colorful character's regalia, he couldn't help adding, "...Sir!"

"A *kanaka* from The Sandwich Isles!" proclaimed the uniformed man.

"How did you know?" asked Mo`ikeha.

"There are quite a few of your fellow countrymen living in The City. They work the ships between the Islands and the West Coast. There's even a town in Washington named after Kalama, a sailor from Hawai`i, who married into the Cowlitz tribe and produced a huge brood. Now what specific island do you hail from?"

"I'm from Maui," declared The Young Man.

"Ah, Lāhainā, Haleakalā. Do you have a name?" asked the sword-toting gentleman.

"Mo`ikeha."

"Named after the sailor who crisscrossed Polynesia."

Mo`ikeha was amazed at the man's knowledge. "How do you know all of this?"

"An emperor needs to know as much as he can if he is to serve his people well." The Young Man laughed at the silliness of it. "Would you like to join us? We are about to head out the door for our morning coffee...well, after my often tardy Grand Chamberlain arrives." As if on cue, a middle aged Chinese man barged through the doors.

"Sorry, I'm late, Emperor," apologized The Grand Chamberlain.

"This is Mo`ikeha from Maui. He's here in San Francisco. Oh, I forgot to ask you why you're here. Working on a ship, I presume. Is this your first visit?"

"Yes. I came on the *Southern Cross.* I've only been to Honolulu... and Lāna`i."

"Well, Grand Chamberlain, we have a duty to show our *kanaka* friend our fair city. First stop, the Empire House Hotel to catch up on the news and sip some mocha java. Lead the way, Grand Chamberlain."

As they paraded down the street toward the Empire House Hotel, The Emperor was greeted by passers-by with various regal salutations performed with a slight tilt of the head: "Your Emperor," "Your Highness," "Your Majesty." Mo`ikeha was beginning to believe that perhaps The Emperor was indeed who he said he was. It was further confirmed when he was greeted and escorted by the doorman at the Empire House to a cluster of soft leather chairs in the ornate lobby. A nervous man in a little mustache approached. "The usual, sir?"

"Yes, and a cup of brew for our dear brother Mo`ikeha visiting all the way from The Sandwich Islands."

"Yes, sir." He led them to their table then scampered off to return quickly with the morning editions of *The Daily Alta California* and *The San Francisco Bulletin*. The Emperor handed the Hawaiian one of the newspapers.

"Here, son. It's the time we catch up with the foolishness of the world like that crazy war back East." Big bowls of steaming coffee arrived. "An old friend, A.J. Folger, is making it big on this brew."

The three men sipped, and turned, and folded. The royals were occasionally saluted with passing greetings by the wealthy patrons of the five dollar–a-day hotel. "I was once like these men," the chief potentate whispered, "burdened with fleeting riches all made from the Gold Rush and all lost as quickly as it came."

The Emperor's statement resonated as The Young Man scanned the papers, shocked by the number of suicides. "I believe you according to the number of people in these articles who have taken their lives."

"So sad. When the gold dried up, so did their desire to live. I was near that brink but found out how to let go, that the best in life is free." He took the last sip of the hotel's complimentary coffee, tucked the newspaper under his arm, and urged his entourage to head to Portsmouth Square where, according to The Grand Chamberlain, The Emperor would hold court.

As they entered the Portsmouth Square gate, The Emperor pointed out its origin. "Because your culture treasures the significance of names, you might be interested to know that this square was named after The Commodore's ship."

"Are we talking about the same commodore that I'll be seeing on Friday?"

"If it's the same one who has Montgomery Street named after him."

"He has a street named after him?"

"One of the steepest. May I ask why you're going to see him?"

"Oh, I don't know. The Captain of my ship said that The Commodore would fill me in on it later."

"Mo`ikeha, don't get mixed up in that ugly skirmish. That's why I've declared myself emperor because I'm saner than the idiots who run the country. Brother killing brother. This war will only end up annihilating thousands of young boys. I predict it."

"How do you know?"

"Books. I sometimes wonder if the leaders of the nations even know how to read. Historians have recorded all the horrible wars. No one learns. Power clouds the minds." A group of citizens approached the impoverished sovereign. They were concerned about the lack of horses to pull the new steam fire engines and tired of bucking city hall. They wanted some solutions. He turned back to Mo`ikeha. "See, enough money for cannons but not enough for fire engine horses."

During the discussion, The Grand Chamberlain filled Mo`ikeha in about the The Emperor's compassion for minorities like the Chinese, Negroes, Mexicans, and Hawaiians. He had fought for the Grand Chamberlain's dignity, debated the anti-abolitionists that were peppered throughout the bay, and respected benevolent royalty like Queen Emma whose portrait, he claimed, hung on a ten penny nail in his room.

Petitions were brought before the court until the church bells at St. Mary's struck twelve. "Grand Chamberlain, lead Mo`ikeha and I to Martin and Horton's." He turned to The Young Man. "Lunch. You hungry?"

The title seemed to flow easily. "Yes, your majesty. " The threesome strutted down Clay Street. Like the previous establishment, The Emperor was greeted hospitably and escorted to the elegant dining room. They sat down to decorative china and silk napkins. Mo`ikeha tried to erase the creases from his ship-worn clothing.

"Prince Mo`ikeha from Maui is joining us today."

"Very good, your honor," responded the maitre d'.

"Choose what you will, Mo`ikeha. It's on the house."

How could this ragged man afford the best? The Grand Chamberlain answered the question in The Young Man's head. "Publicity. Simply publicity. The Emperor's exploits are daily fodder for reporters. The restaurants and establishments don't want to look like ogres with bad press."

Steak, baked potatoes, green beans, and toasty buns came and went with glasses of wine. At the end of an hour, the three patted their lips clean, rubbed their tummies, and dangled toothpicks from their lips.

Their final stop of the day was the Bohemian Club. "Know how to play chess, Mo`ikeha?" asked The Emperor.

"No, sir."

"Would you like to learn?"

"Sure."

"Well," he said gesturing to himself, "you have before you one of the best chess instructors."

The afternoon was spent making moves, learning strategies, smoking cigars, and drinking sherry, all on the house, of course. It was time for the late afternoon nap so the triumvirate returned to the Eureka Lodgings. "Tomorrow's the Fourth of July. Perhaps you'd like to join us and get a good laugh from the side show of bragging politicians," urged The Emperor.

"That sounds good," said The Young Man. "See you in the morning. Oh, and *mahalo, Ali`i Nui.*"

"The great chief bids *adieu*," said The Emperor.

"*Adieu*, likewise," echoed The Grand Chamberlain.

The Young Man mounted the stairs one by one to his room, exhausted from a full day of activities with The Emperor and his right-hand man. He dropped onto his bed with the clothes on his back with no need for dinner, having stuffed himself with the savory meal at Martin and Horton's. He fell asleep dreaming of kings and castles.

A low rumble and a mighty shake woke Mo`ikeha up. He lay there in shock watching his room rattle, the ceiling lantern swinging to and fro like a metronome. He shook himself out of his initial rude awakening to realize that it was an earthquake! Luckily, he was still in the previous day's garb. He raced out the door, peeled down the hall, and descended the stairs like a drunk listing back and forth between the staircase railing and the wall. He bolted out the front door of The Eureka into the dark of dawn to join the throng of occupants already gathered outside. The street rippled like big waves at Ho`okipa Bay back home, then stopped.

The Emperor stepped from the crowd to inform and philosophize about earthquakes. "Good Morning, Mo`ikeha. A unique wake-up call, eh? Best not to re-enter the building until the after-shocks have subsided." On cue, the earth trembled once again this time for only a few seconds. "You know, when an earthquake strikes up at Hetch Hetchy, the Yosemite natives run out of their little grass huts and jump up and down. They laugh and cheer at Mother Nature's adjustments. It's us white men that live in fear. We build tall flimsy buildings that collapse and kill. I must say, though, that the Eureka here has some mighty strong termites that hold tight during these tremblers. Some day a mighty one will come. But why am I telling someone who knows Madam Pele well."

"Indeed," said Mo`ikeha. "The goddess of the volcano takes but she gives us more land. Her sister, Hi`iaka, grows the green after the lava cools. Hawaiians are grateful like the Yosemite Indians for Pele's alterations."

Another short shake caught their attention. "That's it. Like the baseball game, we give it three strikes. Are you ready for a cup of coffee? Let's go check our rooms then head out. We can officially survey the neighborhood damage on our way to the Empire Hotel."

The Grand Chamberlain awaited them on their way out, shaken pale from the experience. "Note the damage for me, Honorable Chamberlain." The assistant nodded, took pencil and paper to hand, and started writing. "Brick wall at 203 Clay. Chimney at 147 Montague." The list continued until they reached The Empire. "Survey to continue after coffee." The Chinese assistant tucked the paper and pencil away.

They'd have to wait for a later edition of the news today, the paperboys' routines upset by street closures due to debris and some broken water mains. Instead, they planned a day hosting the Hawaiian tourist. A must visit was a studio on Montgomery that housed the latest invention—photography. The Emperor presumed that Mo`ikeha would love to send a picture back to his princess in the islands. The photographer posed him before a background of faded willow trees. Mo`ikeha's eyes bulged at the unexpected explosion of flash powder so there was a re-take for a more reserved though still serious picture. Next, they took him for a free ride on the sand cars on the Market Street Railway. Later, after lunch, they joined the crowd to witness the Fourth of July marchers and snicker at the orations at City Hall. The Fourth of July fireworks show culminated the night. It was complimented with brandy toasted from a blanket on the grass at Washington Square. The Young Man knew it would be another exhausting day but good times would soon be rare and he was determined to enjoy The Emperor's excursion.

As they watched the aerial bombs burst in the sky like colorful giant jellyfish and umbrellas, The Emperor wished The Young Man luck with his meeting with The Commodore the next morning. "I also wish I could keep you away from the war but I know the importance of making your own decisions. I only hope that you and the nation survive this dismal fist-a-cuff. Your natural instincts should be helpful for, as the Romantics and Mr. Thoreau claimed, you are the noble savage."

As they walked down the hill to their meager lodging, The Emperor implored Mo`ikeha to come by and visit him and The Grand Chamberlain whenever The Young Man returned to The City.

Mo`ikeha packed his belongings that night. If he agreed to The Commodore's request, he would be ready to lodge on Mare Island. If the job was not for the taking, he'd head back to the *Southern Cross* and prepare for his return to Lāhainā. He wrote to Ho`oipo about the possibility of a job, the hospitality of The Emperor, and some details about the earthquake.

The Young Man was restless. He tossed and turned all night, wondering how the meeting with the famous naval hero would go. Dawn came with the usual wake up call from the streets. This day the infamous fog had socked in The City. His bags and body cut through the thick mist like a knife as he headed down to the Vallejo Pier. The ferry departed on time. Mo`ikeha scanned the deck and noted several men whom he intuitively knew were headed to Mare Island for the same purpose. He struck up a conversation with another young fellow who was obviously Irish from his brogue. He proudly claimed he was one of many who had fled their homeland because of famine and had come to California to dig for gold instead of potatoes. When the gold veins dried up, the tall, barrel-chested man had turned to work on ships with the sea-going skills he had mastered back in Letterfrack. He took easily to the *kanaka* from the Sandwich Isles. Mo`ikeha had a new-found friend whom he appropriately dubbed The Irishman.

The two men joined other interested parties in The Commodore's waiting room at the Pacific Squadron headquarters. Mo`ikeha's interview was scheduled for 9:00 a.m. The Irishman's meeting conveniently followed.

Mo`ikeha was finally summoned. He took a deep breath and knocked. "Come in. Come in," urged The Commodore. Much to his surprise, The Commodore was not a stuffy officer. He had a fatherly air about him, often diverting the interview with his adventures in the Mexican-American War. He finally got to the purpose of the meeting. "Young Man, The Captain of the *Southern Cross* has highly recommended you. We are looking for contracted sea captains to aid Admiral Farragut in severing the blockade of New Orleans by the Confederates. I'm quite aware that you are not a citizen of the United States and that King Alexander continues to declare the neutrality of Hawai`i. However, because all hands are needed to stem secession and eliminate slavery, we'd contract you. Oh, by the way, can I presume that your are an abolitionist considering the influence of the Boston missionaries on the converted?"

"Missionaries or not, I believe every one should live the life they want to live. *Aloha* was the foundation of our culture even before we knew about Jesus," declared Mo`ikeha. "Our black brothers are just one shade deeper than this skin," he said pointing to his face. "We all bleed *pūkoko*—blood red."

"Very good, son. You can understand our cause. So, in general, you would man your own schooner, sail or steam. We will train you and willing adventurers like you at fifty dollars a week with room and board right here on the island and ship you out to the Gulf of Mexico by the first of the year. You will be contracted for each mission and can break the agreement anytime after any mission. Admiral Farragut will fill you in on specifics when you rendezvous in the gulf. Do you need some time to think about it?"

Mo`ikeha responded without much reflection. "No. It's now or I'm on a ship back to Lāhainā tomorrow. I'm young and willing to take life like a big wave at Honolua. It's risky, dangerous, but when I catch one, I'm filled with the *hā*, the breath of life. I'll accept, but only with one mission at a time. I have a bride-to-be and family waiting at home for my return."

"You sound like me when I was your age. Very good, then. One of my assistants will see you to the barracks. Is your locker still on the ship? If so, retrieve it. You'll be away for at least a year. Oh, you can catch the afternoon ferry back after you've settled in. Welcome aboard, Mo`ikeha."

The Young Man returned to the *Southern Cross* to pick up his locker and say a final *mahalo* and farewell to The Captain. The First Officer said that he had gone into The City and wouldn't be back until after dinner so Mo`ikeha pulled out his fountain pen and wrote his thanks and regards, noting that he had accepted The Commodore's invitation to help the Union cause. Hesitation arose half way through the message. Was he making the right decision?

CHAPTER FOURTEEN
Along the Barbary Coast

There were days and nights of rigorous training. Mo`ikeha's specialty would be the sailing sloop. The Young Man was proud to find out that he was walking in the footsteps of Admiral Farragut who was Mare Island's first commander.

It was already fall, the fog more occasional now. In sunlight and in darkness, with wind and calm, in hot and cold, Mo`ikeha became familiar with the bay and its fortresses: Fort Point, Camp Sumner at the Presidio, Fort Baker at the Headlands, Fort Alcatraz—the island in the middle of the bay that held incarcerated secessionists, Camp Reynolds at Angel Island, Fort Mason, Point San Jose, and the Benicia Arsenal where Generals Grant and Hooker served.

He carried a crew of twelve with only handguns and rifles. Hopefully, they would never have to use firearms. The mission of the sloop became obvious: to sneak in quietly near or past Confederate ships or barricades, probably at night, judging from the number of trial assignments performed in the dark. Offensive and defensive blockade tactics were employed. The other volunteers were trained on steam schooners with thirteen-inch mortars for the river war in the South.

The West Coast's only threats were pockets of secession. The Young Man found out that General Albert Sidney Johnston who had been headquartered at Benicia and who was sympathetic to the Southern cause had been replaced by General Edwin V. Sumner when Johnston tried to seize the San Francisco forts as well as the arsenal for the Gray. He was shipped out and was heard to have joined the Confederacy. Mo`ikeha also learned that there had been at least three attempts to introduce slavery in California. Finally, there was the ridiculous Pico Act proposed in the state legislature for Southern California to secede from the state. The cavalry from Fort Mojave and Fort Tejon were sent by General Sumner to contain the pockets of rebellion. Sumner also made sure that all of San Francisco's bastions were further strengthened.

The Young Man got to know more about The Pacific Squadron. He discovered from The Irishman that the Pacific naval defense had also been beefed up to prevent Confederate ships from rounding Tierra Del Fuego and seizing merchant ships carrying gold bullion out of Yerba Buena, the native name for San Francisco. Six sloops of war were employed. Most of them were twelve to twenty-four years old, spread thin, and manned only with about one thousand sailors and about a hundred guns. This western navy represented American interests and patrolled a huge area including the West Coast of North and South America, Alaska, Hawai`i, China, Japan, Australia, and The South Seas.

Night after night, eight to ten hours, Mo`ikeha and his fellow new hires trained, sleeping off their nocturnal activities during the day. Finally, feeling that the men had been worked to the bone, The Commodore agreed to free them up on Saturday evenings and early Sundays, snickering that the latter was for church to make up for sins committed on the previous night. "Oh, and don't get shanghaied," he added.

Like most of the trainees, The Irishman suggested that shore leave include a night of cards, some strong booze, and a few sultry women from along the Barbary Coast. Luckily, Mo`ikeha had learned the skills of poker from the boarders at Lahainaluna. As for liquor and the pretty waiter girls, well, he had learned his lesson with The Young Chinese Sailor and The Red Lotus. Even though Ho`oipo was a good two thousand miles away, he somehow believed that she would eventually find out about it. He also figured that if he was sober he might be able make some money to send back to his family and the love of his life.

The blockade-runners had never looked so clean in months. They had soaped their bodies down, greased their hair, and slipped on their frock coats or vests. Mo`ikeha strode alongside The Irishman. Ahead of them was a gang of three who had taken full control of the sidewalk with bravado. As they passed the cow yards and cribs that were obviously heavier into prostitution, they got whistles from the over-powdered girls that stood out in front attempting to lure in lusty men. The sailors were dragged away by their saner companions who convinced them that the best looking girls worked the gambling parlors.

Finally, they approached their destination. Upon entering The Cobweb Palace, one would come to the obvious conclusion as to its moniker. One of the trainees pointed upward at the spider webs that filled the rafters, the arachnid a favorite of the owner. A piano player pounded out a lively tune on the upright in the corner. Through the haze of cigarette, cigar, and pipe smoke, the five men were escorted by a well-endowed greeter with a porcelain face, one of the naval apprentices immediately smitten by something that he had not seen up close for months—the opposite sex. She made them feel at home by flashing her eyelashes and flirting her way to empty chairs at one of the green felt-covered tables. The other two men were escorted to games already in progress. Finally, The Irishman and Mo`ikeha were seated. Their fellow players included a chubby man with a beet-red face sprouting uncultivated white eyebrows, a tall dark man with a goatee who was dressed like a professional gambler, and a red-headed, freckled kid, his legal age for gambling questionable to Mo`ikeha.

"What'll you have, gentlemen?" asked a pretty waiter girl, the two newcomers to the table admiring her long golden curls and pouty scarlet lips.

"Bourbon on the rocks," responded The Irishman.

"And you, sir?" added the server.

"Sarsaparilla," Mo`ikeha said meekly. The men at the table snickered.

"A drink for sissies. Obviously, you're not a sailor like your partner here," commented The Professional Gambler.

"I'm a farmer," Mo`ikeha claimed, aware that his former profession was his salvation.

"What do you grow?" asked The Beet Red Face.

"He grows *poi*." Before the men would question what the hell *poi* was, The Irishman added, "Enough of the interrogation. We came to play poker." The Pretty Waiter Girl left for the drinks and the men ceased the questioning, intimidated by the bulk and the scowl of the Irish sailor.

Mo`ikeha's fortune was riding high from the first deal. He had two aces in the hand and took the four-dollar pot when he finally picked up a third. Mo`ikeha had already made half of one month's pay on the ship. "Beginner's luck," sneered The Freckled Kid, chewing tobacco drooling from his lip.

Five bourbons later, The Irishman was feeling no pain, laughing boisterously, slapping the behind of The Pretty Waiter Girl. Mo`ikeha was still hugging onto his sarsaparilla. The other men at the table had downed an equal number of whiskeys and beers and had obviously become too drunk to count cards much to Mo`ikeha's advantage.

"I think we should leave," Mo`ikeha insisted to The Irishman, concerned that it was getting late and that more drinks might end in the loss of more money. There was also the possibility of a fistfight erupting with another heavily intoxicated card player.

"After you've won fifty dollars?" chided The Professional Gambler. "Give us a chance to win some back."

"One more for the road," demanded The Irishman to The Pretty Waiter Girl. A new hand was dealt. The Irishman downed the bourbon. Within minutes, his head began to nod, his temperament no more jovial, his eyes dazed.

"What's the matter with your sailor friend, *poi* farmer?" The question from The Pretty Waiter Girl lacked the emotion of real concern as if asked a hundred times before.

"Obviously, too many drinks," said Mo`ikeha.

"We'll take him to the back room and sober him out," she said, signaling to the bouncer near the door.

"No," insisted The Young Man with suspicion. "I'll take care of him. We'll leave now."

"A cold shower should do it," insisted The Pretty Waiter Girl. "Go on. Continue your game." She pushed Mo`ikeha down into his chair. The brutish bouncer and another burley male dragged off The Irishman. "We'll take care of it."

Mo`ikeha feigned an okay, his mind now suspicious about the predicament of his buddy. He watched him get carried into a back room. "I have to use the *lua*...er...the toilet," he lied to the other players. "Deal me out of this hand." He headed into the latrine, peered through the crack in the door, and waited for a safe moment when he could duck into the back room unseen. When all the workers were occupied, he slipped through the door marked *Storage*. No one was there. He heard doors slam outside. He exited into an alley that dead-ended at both extremes. The only possible sources of the slams were a pair of cellar doors adjoined to the neighboring building. He quietly pulled them open. Steps led down into the black of Hell. He could hear mumbling trailing away in the distance. He stood there adjusting his eyes to the dark. It was a tunnel. He heard voices again, took off his shoes so as not to alert those ahead of him, and raced stealthily toward the echoing babble.

Now he could make out the two figures dragging and occasionally stopping to prop up The Irishman. A foghorn moaned in the distance, the slapping of rigging against masts. He was surely near the harbor. The light of outdoor night broke through the crypt's exit. He stopped at its edge and peeked around. The abductors were headed along the pier, having some difficulty with the large Irishman. Mo`ikeha wouldn't be able to stop the strongmen by himself and would need help. He sprinted down to the corner frantically looking for aid at this time of night. Luckily, a constable was walking his beat around the turn.

"Police!" he yelled. "They're kidnapping my friend!" Mo`ikeha raced in the direction of the abductee, the copper finally catching up with him. "There they are!" he yelled, pointing at the villains ahead. The Constable blew his whistle. "Stop, it's the law!" The thugs dropped the drugged sailor without concern and fled, The Constable in pursuit. He returned shortly, winded, and apologetic that the culprits had split up and disappeared into the cow yards and cribs of the Barbary Coast.

"You stopped your friend from being shanghaied. They usually add some drops of laudanum or opium to a sailor's drink that wears off after a number of hours. Your friend'll be fine after a good night's sleep. I'm sure he's going to be mighty grateful that he didn't wake up on a slow boat to China. What ship you boys on?"

"We're training under The Commodore on Mare Island," replied The Young Man.

"For the civil war?" asked The Constable.

"How'd you know?"

"Small town, son. Small town. Now, do you have a place to stay?"

After some thought, he answered with a place familiar to him, "Eureka Lodgings."

"Ah, The Emperor's Palace," commented The Constable. "I'll fetch a buggy for you. They run down Montgomery all night taking drunken sailors to their ships. I'll hail one for you." Within minutes a buggy pulled up. Mo`ikeha and The Constable heaved The Irishman onto the seat. "Good luck, son," the policeman yelled as the carriage headed toward Commercial Street.

Sunday morning came. The clanging bells of St. Mary's on California woke The Irishman from the fog inside his head. He opened his eyes to find a man in full regalia including beaver hat and ostrich plume staring down at him, "Are you okay?" asked the stranger.

"Where am I?" he asked, "And who are you?"

A more familiar face came into his view. It was the countenance of Mo`ikeha. "You're at a hotel and this is His Excellency, The Emperor. Do you remember anything about last night?" asked The Young Man.

He searched his head for answers. "I was playing poker...ah...the rest is mush."

The Emperor filled him in on the heroics. "Some hooligans tried to shanghai you, but thanks to Prince Mo`ikeha you're not on some boat headed to China."

The Irishman turned to his friend. "*Mahalo*, as you say, my brother. You'll have to tell me about the whole thing when I'm less dizzy." Then he turned to Mo`ikeha and added quizzically, "You're a prince?"

"It's a long story. How about a cold shower?" suggested Mo`ikeha.

"And some breakfast. I'm sure you're famished. The treat's on me, correction, on the people of San Francisco," added The Emperor.

After a shower and a hearty breakfast at Martin and Horton's, The Emperor escorted the two trainees down to the Vallejo Wharf for the noon ferry to Mare Island. He waved and yelled at them as they departed, "Watch out for them spiders. They weave a wicked web."

A few days later, the second letter from Ho`oipo arrived. The first mailing was merely a hope that he was safe and sound in California. The second letter read:

Lāhainā, Maui
Kingdom of Hawai`i

Dear Sweetheart,

All is well here in Lāhainā. I saw your family last Sunday at services at Ka`ahumanu Church. We were there for a cousin's christening and the *pā`ina* that followed in Kahului. Your brother is getting tall and The Twins prettier. Your parents look fine and miss you. I'm so proud of you in helping The Captain find out who killed The Heiress, but it must have been awful to find a dead person, something I've never experienced, yet. The Captain sounds like a good man especially going out of his way to recommend you to The Commodore. I can't believe that you'll be paid fifty dollars a week. What kind of a project is it? I'm praying it's nothing dangerous.

It was nice for The Emperor to take you under his wing and guide you around the city. I hope you're not spending your money imprudently and not lying to me that you were unharmed by the earthquake. I foolishly picture you in a dispensary writing your letters, my fountain pen gift in your good un-bandaged hand.

Looking forward to November rains. Lāhainā has been living up to its reputation for the last couple months. It'll be a lonely Christmas without you. I'll always have fond memories of us on Haleakalā playing in the snow. Oh, by the way, I never mentioned to anyone that something happened when we visited the crater. I was afraid of being called *lōlō*, but I know you'll believe that I'm not crazy when I say that I saw Lilinoe that day. I asked some *kupuna* about her. The elders told me that she is the snow goddess specifically tied to Haleakalā. She looked beautiful like a white winter butterfly, the wind whirling through her sheer *kapa*. I believe now that she was a good omen. She'll be there if and when you see snow. I pray to her and Jesus that you'll be safe.

I am busy working at the post office but now facing a dilemma. The King loved my *kapa* quilt and has ordered more. I work until five o'clock and am *maluhiluhi* at the end of the day. It's difficult to get the energy up for quilting because as you know it's a long process. However, The King's payments are almost equal to my salary at the post office. Queen Emma has made a generous offering for a cloth quilt, not to sleep under, too hot, but to cover the beds at Hale Ali`i. I approached The Missionary's Wife and she taught me the missionary way as how to make a patchwork quilt from all the pieces I gathered from anyone willing to donate (guilt, ha ha) for The Queen's quilt.

To cool off one hot Saturday, I moved my quilting under the *`ulu* tree in back. As I began to sew, the sun shining around the breadfruit leaves left a shadow on one of the white remnants. I thanked all the gods for the inspiration and outlined the *`ulu* leaf on paper. The Missionary's Wife told me later that it was called a stencil. I duplicated the stenciled leaves in cloth and sewed them all together. The Queen was ecstatic upon its delivery to Honolulu and suggested that I do the same thing with other indigenous leaves. She sent me some money to open a shop in Lāhainā that makes and sells the bed covers. I'll have to make a decision sooner or later whether I should quit the job at the post office and dedicate full time to quilting. Waiting for your next letter.

Me ke aloha,
Ho`oipo.

Before he fell asleep that night, exhausted by a late afternoon race between the forts with speed an essential requirement for the mission, he attempted a letter in return. He wrote around the incident of the previous night.

San Francisco, California
United States of America

Dear Ho`oipo,

So good to hear from you. I'm glad our letters are making it through, although it takes about a month to get here. Got a chance to see The Emperor again on our free night in The City. He treated us to a full `ōpū breakfast. Made a good friend. I call him The Irishman. We're both in the training program and will travel with me on our journey. He had too much to drink the other night and found himself being confronted by some challengers. Fortunately, I had the chance to pull him out a bad situation before it became worse.

Our days of training are coming to an end and we should be ready by January. I can at least tell you what I learned today. We will be taking a run down to Mazatlán, Mexico. It should relieve you to know that Mexico is like Hawai`i, neutral in the civil war. I'll be able to say to our children some day that their father traveled through two countries.

I'm happy to tell you that some money is on its way to both you and my parents, thanks to my good fortune and the teaching skills of the boarders at Lahainaluna. Perhaps you can use the extra dollars for your quilt shop.

Wishing that your love for me still holds.

Me ke aloha,
Mo`ikeha

The thought of Ho`oipo sewing under the shade of the *`ulu* tree, the sunlight flickering through its leaves, and her success at quilts secured him into a peaceful slumber. The fountain pen slipped from Mo`ikeha's hand as he completed the complementary close and his signature.

CHAPTER FIFTEEN
Mauve Crosses and Fool's Gold

Shortly before Christmas, The Commodore called all the trainees in for a more detailed meeting about their mission. "Good morning, gentlemen. You're survivors! Congratulations! You've completed some tough training. Some quit because they couldn't take the ordeal of cold, wind, darkness, and long periods without loved ones. Although most of you are not United States citizens, uninterested in committing completely to a stint in our military, or simply here for a generous monetary compensation, we've observed your personalities under stress, your leadership capability, your ability to work as the member of a team, your maritime skills, and your dedication to the mission. Those here have passed with flying colors.

I'm not surprised if you've heard some details about the mission through the rumor mill so let me set you straight. I'll take questions after. You will be joining up with Admiral Farragut and the other members of his fleet in the Gulf of Mexico to penetrate the Confederate blockade of the Mississippi River. General Benjamin Butler will be moving his troops into the area in the land offense.

Confederate cruisers have been patrolling around The Horn so movements of ships in that area would be spotted, reported, and perhaps even destroyed. Because we want this to be a surprise, we have commissioned American ship contractors to build us a number of vessels in Vera Cruz. You will pick up those ships when you get to your destination. So, come January, you'll be transported down to Mazatlán where you will take the overland route by stagecoach to Vera Cruz—about three plus weeks—and meet up with The Admiral on Ship Island in the Gulf of Mexico for more specific instructions.

I remind you that you signed a contract promising that any information I share with you is not to be discussed with anyone, including friends and family formally in correspondence or casually in conversation. Successful implementation of the Anaconda Plan may help end this tragic war quickly and save many lives with your cooperation."

Mo`ikeha took a deep breath and looked over to The Irishman with a look of "We're part of something big." If Ho`oipo knew that the mission was dangerous, she would certainly object. The Young Man was glad that he could later blame The Commodore for his pledge of secrecy.

Before anyone could ask the obvious question, The Commodore brought up the possibilities of risk. "You've been trained to get in and get out without being spotted, reducing the element of risk. But war follows no logical course. You've completed a successful training in firearms. If you must defend yourself, do so. You've also practiced watching each others' backs, now it's time to do it for real."

December 25 rolled around. A Mexican girlfriend of The Irishman invited him and Mo`ikeha to spend Christmas with her and her family down in San José. She was a startling beauty with raven black hair and skin as brown as Mo`ikeha's. Her father was the latest grower in a line of fruit farmers dating back to Old California. As was customary, the girl's entire family attended Midnight Mass at Santa Clara Mission, the church filled with the warm orange glow of a hundred candles, flaming red poinsettias, and balmy scented evergreen garlands that draped the pews. The Young Man had never attended a Catholic ceremony although he once peeked inside St. Anthony Church on Pū`ali Nani's sands down the hill from his `Īao home.

Earlier that evening, they witnessed the final *posada* of Advent. After being purposely rejected at two other houses, the members of the procession that included a girl and boy playing Mary and Joseph were finally accepted at The Mexican Girl's House. A clay figurine of the Baby Jesus was placed in the waiting empty crib. The Christmas Eve festivities proceeded with full gusto. The children tried to swat at the huge star *piñata* as the meal of *tamales*, *atole*, and *buñuelos* was laid out on the table. *Ponche*, the hot fruity drink spiked with cinnamon and brown sugar, was poured into cups, the sweeteners a necessity to keep everyone up and alert for the midnight mass. Of course, the men added a dash of liquor to enliven the birthday celebration.

In one way, celebrating with *la familia* was taxing to some degree for The Young Man. He observed the love of The Mexican Girl's family for each other and was filled with the most gnawing loneliness he had as yet felt since he had left Maui. The temporary depression dissipated at the party to celebrate Jesus' nativity. The clan took Mo`ikeha and The Irishman to heart, making them feel at home. They found out eventually that Mo`ikeha was not Mexican but Hawaiian, so, after a filling dinner of *bacalao*, roasted pig, and renditions of *villancicos* or carols, he was urged to sing a few Hawaiian songs.

Each of the children finally received *aguinaldo*, their small gift from the Infant Jesus along with a bag of cookies, dried fruit, and candy. The entire entourage then poured out of the house into the cold air to watch the children wave around the *luces de Belén*. The tiniest *keiki*, too young to play with fireworks, held on to Mo`ikeha just as his brother and sisters once had, as colored sparks lit up the skies of Christmas, 1861.

For New Years Eve, The Mexican Girl joined The Irishman, Mo`ikeha, The Emperor, and The Grand Chamberlain for the farewell dinner at The Poodle Dog on Washington Street. It was Mo`ikeha's treat, the funding from his success at poker. At fifteen cents a person, the menu included soup, fish, meat *en bloc*, veggies, a mixed salad, unlimited fruit, Mr. Krug's wine from Napa, and a huge draft of beer for an extra five cents.

The Emperor and his courtesans then sauntered down the streets to the Embarcadero to watch the fireworks show. After the last aerial punctuated the finale, the group re-huddled to fight the chilly night air and continue their commentary on the way of the world. The party broke up when The Irishman had to hail a buggy and accompany The Mexican Girl back to her relatives in the Mission. The remaining friends, on their way back to the Eureka, discovered a small coffee shop still open to sober up inebriated midnight revelers. There, over several cups of java, they continued their talk marathon.

On January 2, 1862, The *U.S.S. Wyoming* pulled along-side Mare Island. The men with a mission lugged their bags up the gangplank. The Emperor, the Grand Chamberlain, and The Irishman's Mexican girlfriend were there to wish them well, and perhaps make one last attempt to talk them out of what they suspected was a dangerous mission.

The Ship passed through the *Chrysopylae*, and veered south to Mazatlán.

There they would stay for a night and catch the overland stage to

Tepic some hundred and seventy miles south. The Commodore had provided the travelers with a list of necessities for the seven hundred mile plus journey to Vera Cruz from pants to pins, blankets to buttons. They would dress like common *gringos* to avoid questions. Each of four coaches in successive days would transport three adventurers to the port city in the gulf, one in each group of three able to speak Spanish. The Young Man and The Irishman would travel with, as Mo`ikeha called him, The *Hapa* Sailor, half British, half Mexican. His father, a maritime man from Liverpool docked in San Francisco, impregnated his mother who was a native of Santa Cruz, and hightailed back to England without word. Mo`ikeha recognized that The *Hapa* Sailor had risen above the indignation and tried to make things *pono* or right.

Several weeks later, the passengers on the *Wyoming* spotted Cerro Crestón, the five hundred foot hill and landmark of Mazatlán, the port that had boomed during the Gold Rush. Many a fortune hunter had traveled through it, up the Pacific Coast, and on to San Francisco. It was already late afternoon when the ship docked off Olas Altas Beach. The overland stage would leave early the next morning. The nautical trio raced to the Hotel Luen Sing in the Plaza Machado, checked in, dumped their bags, threw on anything resembling swimming trunks, and headed to the beach to test the famous warm waters. It lived up to its good name. The swim would be their last pleasure before taking on the bumpy dusty roads to Vera Cruz. After dinner, they hit the sack, the town lacking anything festive.

The Irishman, Mo`ikeha, and The *Hapa* Sailor looked like a couple of real life cowboys when they boarded the stage the next morning for Tepic. The journey would be accomplished in stages with stops between twelve and twenty miles at way stations depending on the terrain and weather.

Before boarding, The Stagecoach Driver and The Armed Guard gathered the passengers and in Spanish announced the no no's of traveling by coach. The *Hapa* Sailor mimed out the warnings to Mo`ikeha and The Irishman. "No liquor. No pipe or cigar smoking. No rough language." On the latter *kāpū*, Mo`ikeha pointed to and waved his finger at his Irish friend. The Stagecoach Driver continued. "No snoring. No firearms. Don't jump out of the coupe if there are runaway horses. And no striking fear in the passengers by talking about stagecoach robberies or uprisings."

Normally the stage could fit up to nine in the cabin with fifteen inches of seat. Luckily for this first part, there would only be six passengers. The long legs of the Irishman rubbed up against a pole-thin tax collector on his way to a bureaucratic job in Guadalajara. Mo`ikeha's knee caps joined with a woman taking her son to join her husband working in Tepic, the Capital of the State of Nayarit. The Boy sat quietly at his mother's side, poker-faced, probably never having ridden a stagecoach nor overwhelmed by unknown faces. He was dressed neatly as those from the middle class. At thirty cents a day, the stagecoach was not the means of transportation for the poor.

Mo`ikeha noted that the road out of Mazatlán was smooth but dusty, the trail well worn from taking gold miners to and from the fields. Twelve miles out they did the same thing they would do many times in the trip. The passengers got out, stretched, rubbed their bottoms, drank, smoked, and nibbled on jerky while *caballos* were unhitched, watered, and replaced by fresh horses.

After five days and nights traveling, the stage finally pulled into Tepic. It would be an overnight stop, the stage leaving at 5:00 a.m. while the weather was cool. After bouncing up and down for days, the passengers were relieved to abandon their cramped positions and actually lie down. Like Mo`ikeha, they had dreams in their sleep of floating to their destinations on soft white clouds.

The smell of fresh coffee and what the *señora* of the home station called *chilaquiles* woke the passengers before the Stagecoach Driver did. The Woman Passenger and Her Son had disappeared into Tepic. They were replaced by a burley Mexican blacksmith, his tools clanging as he threw it onto the back boot. He smelled of metal. "Did you notice The Grass Cross at the end of the street?" he asked his fellow travelers in Spanish. He pointed to the area. The *Hapa* Sailor translated the question and the shared knowledge of The Blacksmith. They looked up the main avenue towards the town's only landmark. "Tepic is in constant drought but the cross of grass stays green all year even when it reaches over a hundred in the summer. It is a miracle."

The *Hapa* Sailor added, "Death, and specifically the death of Jesus by crucifixion, is an obsession of the Mexican people. The Day of the Dead is one of their biggest celebrations. Skelton masks are seen everywhere. We see crosses in everything. Even the wild purple orchids that grow in the uplands take the form of a cross."

"Aren't all cultures obsessed with death?" asked Mo`ikeha. "Perhaps, unlike the Mexicans, the rest of us tend to conceal it." Before the chatter became more morose, The Stage Driver loudly summoned the passengers to board.

The next stage of the trip was to Guadalajara, some two hundred and fifty miles to the southeast. Two stops later, in the waning afternoon, thunderclouds had formed in the distance.

After a quick supper stop of greasy bacon and beans, not the best combination for an enclosed vehicle, the stage was off and running. As the dawn painted the desert skies with a pastel purple, the coach came to a sudden halt. A winter downpour had created a huge chasm in the trail. The Driver decided on an alternate bypass around a clump of towering cactuses. The option resulted in a situation inevitable for veteran stagecoach travelers. They were bogged down in the mud. Normally, the inconvenience would irritate passengers. Instead the snag came as somewhat of a relief from what Mo`ikeha called an *`ōkole* busting trip. All the travelers had learned, among other words, the Hawaiian word for one's behind. They all got out, happy that they had the brawn of The Blacksmith to assist them. They moved to the rear of the stage and leaned their shoulders up against the back of the coach while the driver whistled and yelled "*Yee hah*!" at the horses to pull the vehicle out of the muck. It wasn't as easy as they thought it would be. They all started to sink.

"*Arena movediza!*" yelled The Blacksmith. Mo`ikeha, The Irishman, and The Pole-Thin Tax Collector, now up to their knees in the goop, looked at The *Hapa* Sailor who was trying to writhe himself out of the mud. "Get out. It's quicksand!" He turned to yank his fellow travelers from the ooze. It was a struggle to tow out the sludgy commuters little by little, but they were all finally liberated.

The driver bellowed orders in Spanish. "Go get wood, sticks, rubbish, anything to cause the wheels to grab." The mud monsters spread out in search for branches, *manzanita*, tumbleweed, and flat stones. Mo`ikeha wandered off farther than the rest and came across some old fence posts from an abandoned corral. He spotted a small pond and stream in the distance. He expected congratulations as he pulled the poles toward the halted carriage. "*Loco*!" yelled The Driver, continuing his tirade in Spanish, "Don't wander off. There are rattlesnakes out there. Coyote. Wild dogs." Luckily, The Young Man's lack of Spanish kept him from the full impact of the reprimand. The rest were more grateful than the driver who continued with more commands. The *Hapa* Sailor told them that The Stagecoach Driver wanted all their belongings and baggage off the wagon so that it would be lighter. After everything had been tossed outside, the fence posts, debris, and *manzanita* branches were laid across the mud. After two tries, the stagecoach finally broke free from the captive quicksand.

The *Hapa* Sailor heard The Stagecoach Driver mumble about the mess the muddied men would make in his coupe as the travelers piled baggage back onto the coach. The interpreter relayed The Stagecoach Driver's concern to his fellow sailors. Mo`ikeha offered some advice. "Tell him there's a stream and pond where I found the posts."

"*Señor*, my friend says there is an *arroyo* in the distance. Perhaps we could clean ourselves, wash the mud from our clothes, and put on some fresh ones."

Considering the pride he took in his coach, The Driver gave an okay. "Only fifteen minutes," he added loudly as they raced to the *arroyo*. Twenty minutes later, the stagecoach with its washed passengers was headed on the road to Guadalajara, the coupe's top decorated with the fastened wet clothes flapping in the wind.

Within a week of multiple stops at way stations, the travelers looked forward to a night's stay in Guadalajara in Jalisco State. Mo`ikeha had been informed that the second largest city in Mexico had the title—The Pearl of the West—because of its beauty. The stage pulled into its station about noon. The Blacksmith and The Pole-Thin Tax Collector, finally at their destination, shouted *Vaya con Dios* to their fellow mud buddies. Across the street was The Francés, a hotel built during the colonial period, where the sailors would spend the night.

The three mariners checked in and tested their beds by bouncing up and down on them like children. The soft mattress and a soak in the hot water bathtub would be a relief for their aching bones. After a short afternoon nap and as evening began to turn violet and pink, the trio headed to a recommended restaurant along the Avenida Vallarta. The city was now aglow from the golden fires coming from the lit gas lanterns. Twilight strollers ambled down the promenade past banks, libraries, and schools. Mo`ikeha was absorbing what all the books called the romance of Old Mexico: a warm night, guitar music punctuating its mystique, a full moon rising above the Nevado de Colima. The naval men settled for a restaurant called Carne En Su Jugo. Besides the dish for which the *cantina* was named, the waiter suggested the *tortas ahogadas* and *birria* and the men agreed to try out dishes particular to the area. Each agreed to a beer with the meal.

While they waited, The Irishman's attention wandered off to three beautiful *señoritas* with midnight hair and red lips sipping drinks at a sidewalk table. Mo`ikeha grew concerned when his partner's eye began to wander for women. The Irishman got up and sauntered over to invite the ladies to the men's table. Mo`ikeha placed a ten-cent bet with the *Hapa* Sailor that these girls would decline an invitation to a stranger, much less a *gringo*. He paid up as they headed toward their table.

Mo`ikeha was uncomfortable with situations like this. Who'd match up with whom? What about his promises to Ho`oipo? What was the point of an overnight relationship? Whatever the circumstances, Mo`ikeha would still express his Hawaiian hospitality despite the language barrier. Luckily, the pretty maidens shared his feelings; they were charming, non-aggressive, eager to learn about San Francisco, and, when they discovered the brown young man was not Mexican but from the Sandwich Isles, they became more curious about his homeland.

"You have drunk tequila?" asked The First Señorita.

"Tequila? Isn't that a town not far from here?" asked The Irishman.

"We three and the drink are from there. My grandfather makes it from *agave*," said The Second Señorita.

"We come here to sell it to shops and *cantinas* for Father," added The Third Señorita, pulling out a bottle from her weaved bag.

"Very clever father using *tres bellezas*, three beauties, to sell," proposed the *Hapa* Sailor.

The Irishman called the waiter for glasses. He returned with tumblers that were filled with the prize tequila by the salesladies. The six clinked glasses. Toasts were given in three languages: "*Salud!*" "May you be in Heaven a full half hour before the Devil knows you're dead!" "`*Ōkole maluna*!" Everyone reacted joyfully to the drink as it slid down.

The Irishman was up for more fun, his mind filled with thoughts of sneaking the girls into the hotel. His fire was dampened when one of the *señoritas* mentioned that her uncle was the night clerk at The Francés. Mo`ikeha observed The Irishman's disappointment and whisper-mumbled to him that a stretched-out body and sleep were currently more important. The Irishman whisper-mumbled back, "And even better with a woman by my side."

The Beauties from Tequila walked the men to the hotel and wished them a pleasant journey, hoping they would return to Guadalajara someday. The Irishman climbed the steps to his hotel room displaying the face of a sad puppy. Mo`ikeha was aware that meeting them again would probably never happen. In his travels he was learning to seize the moment and appreciate the people who marched, if only for a short time, in the *posada* of his life. Early the next morning before the sun had not yet highlighted the distant Cordillera Neo Volcánica, the stagecoach left Guadalajara.

The Blacksmith and The Pole-Thin Tax Collector had been replaced by a bald lanky professor of history headed for a position at the Royal and Pontifical University and a quiet man with eye glasses whose only statement was that he was bound for the presidential capital now that Benito Juárez was in power again. The question of the reserve of The Quiet Man by the three sailors was answered at one of the way stations in a hushed tone. "Conservatives like him are targets of assassination. In Mexico, at this time with so many factions vying for its control, it's best for everyone, including you, to feign ignorance about politics and avoid a casket."

This would be their longest trek. Guadalajara to Mexico City spanned some three hundred and thirty miles, and they would slowly climb higher each day up to an altitude of over seven thousand feet.

The Professor, avoiding any political statements, volunteered to fill the men in on the history of Mexico City and its conquerors before its revolution: The Aztecs, The Spanish, The North Americans. Like a good student, Mo`ikeha listened like he listened to his teachers at Lahainaluna. This time it was school for real. He learned that Mexico City, once called Tenochtitlán, had been built on an island in Lake Texcoco that was quickly being drained as the city added more roads and buildings. The Professor said, "You'll recognize the city from afar with its skyline of cathedral towers dedicated to a litany of saints including Peter and Paul, Francis of Assisi, Teresa of Avila, and Philip Neri. The immensity of the city with close to half a million residents will be obvious when we cross over a hundred city blocks and its eighteen main streets that run north to south to get to city central."

The free lessons of Mexican history helped the days go by. Finally, one day about a hundred miles outside Mexico City, The Quiet Man broke his monastic silence with three questions in Spanish: "Where are you from?" "What do you do?" and "Where are you headed?"

The *Hapa* Sailor answered with the best lies he could come up with in response to the abrupt questions. "We are returning from California.

The mines have all dried up. We are going to Vera Cruz to do what we did before we got gold fever. We are going back to farm."

"What do you farm?" asked The Quiet Man.

All three in unison answered, "*Poi.*"

"*Poi?*" asked The Professor and The Quiet Man in harmony.

"It's a long story," responded The *Hapa* Sailor. At that moment, fortune was with them. The front wheel of the stagecoach busted loose and went flying past the wagon, the coupe leaning to the right.

"Whoaa!" yelled The Stagecoach Driver, followed by "Everybody out!" Familiar with the situation, the driver and shotgun rider set the wheel into place quickly and the ride into Mexico City continued on without incidents and without further questions.

Days later, the stagecoach pulled into the country's capital late at night. The exhausted sailors dragged their bags into the Hotel Gillow. They were in no mood for sightseeing. They washed the dust from their weary bodies and took their meal downstairs at the hotel *cantina.* Mo`ikeha insisted that after dinner he had to find a fitting souvenir from Mexico. After a short walk he found a small shop and picked up a gift for his mother back in Maui. The fatigued friends returned to Hotel Gillow and hit the sack.

At five a.m., the stagecoach departed. The Quiet Man and The Professor had been replaced by two homely sisters clutching their bags tightly to their bodies. They stared at the three men across from them. The trio heard the ladies mention to The Stagecoach Driver that this was their first trip on a stagecoach. They were going to Vera Cruz to work as clerks for a shipping company. To them, every little bump in the road was a mountain, every dip a canyon. Even the snorting of the horses alarmed them. A midmorning stop was finally made. The Two Homely Sisters offered the gentlemen some homemade fruit pastry. The Irishman winked at them after a bite and proclaimed, "*Bueno.*"

Soon the stagecoach was off and running. A few miles later it made its way through a narrow canyon of large boulders. Suddenly, a shot echoed across the ravine. "*Detener*!" yelled a masked bandit perched atop one of the huge boulders. The *señoritas* screamed. The Stagecoach Driver yelled, "Whoa!" stopping short of a tree that lay across the sandy red trail.

Another *bandito* jumped out from behind a rock at the front of the stage, a pistol in one hand, the reigns of two horses in the other. "*Tire su escopeta*!," he yelled in Spanish. With two guns now pointed at him, The Armed Guard sensibly heeded the robber's command and threw his shotgun off the stage. The Two Homely Sisters hugged each other in panic. Two more *banditos* appeared on their horses behind the wagon, dismounted, stuck their pistols in the window on both sides, and shouted commands to the passengers in the coupe. Mo`ikeha presumed it meant get out which The *Hapa* Sailor confirmed with a nod. The travelers stepped down, The Two Homely Sisters whimpering noticeably.

The Irishman looked beyond the bandanas that covered the thieves' noses and mouths and whispered under his breath, "They're just kids!"

"*Fuera los manos*!" demanded The Eldest *Bandito* who served as the ringleader. The command seemed obvious to Mo`ikeha. As he raised his hands, he confirmed The Irishman's observation. He figured them to be very young boys, the top dog no more than fourteen.

"We can take these babies," suggested The Irishman in *sotto voce*.

"One problem." Mo`ikeha murmured back. "These babies don't have rattlers. They have guns."

"*Gringo, calle la boca!*" yelled The Eldest Bandito. "Yankee, shut up," The *Hapa* Sailor translated.

Mo`ikeha noticed a fifth *bandito*, whom he guessed to be no older than twelve, lingering farther back from the stage, trying to pull up his kerchief mask that kept falling, his armed hand trembling dangerously. "Emilio, get your butt over here," the fourteen year old said to the other child in Spanish.

The Second Oldest *Bandito* complained in his native tongue, "I thought you said not to use names."

"Oh, since when you the boss?" retorted The Eldest *Bandito*, embarrassed by breaking his own rule.

"*Entregar sus pertenencias*!" yelled out another kid thief to the passengers, diverting the in-gang argument back to the situation at hand.

"They want our valuables," whispered The *Hapa* Sailor.

"No *tengo* valuables," protested The Irishman in bad Spanish, the prepubescent outlaws unaware that the cash the men carried had been tucked up into the leather flaps of the cabin interior in case a situation like this arose.

The Eldest *Bandito* commanded the two other accomplices to go through the sojourners' bags. They tossed the baggage out onto the trail and rifled through them, flinging their clothing onto the dirt.

They giggled as they tugged pantalettes from the ladies' bags, much to the embarrassment of the siblings, one *bandito* pulling the underwear over his head like a hat, asking in a high voice if he was cute. Finally, they discovered and confiscated twenty *pesos* from a small handbag. The Two Homely Sisters reached out and pled that the immature thugs not take it, insisting that it was all the women had in the world. The prepubescent purse-snatcher slapped their hands.

From The Irishman's bag, they took a pocket watch and fob his father had given him when he left Galway. The Irishman cringed at the thought of losing the memento of his homeland. Another keepsake, a silver cross, given to The *Hapa* Sailor at his mother's burial, was pulled from his satchel much to his dismay.

Finally, the desperados pulled the fountain pen from Mo`ikeha's clothes bag. "*Qué es esto*?" The Eldest *Bandito* asked, pulling it from the other thief's hand.

"*Pluma fuente*," volunteered The *Hapa* Sailor, and then, remembering Mo`ikeha's mention that the rare pen was from his girlfriend, added, "*de su prometida*!"

"*Pluma de amor*! Hah!" The leader mocked sadness and laughed boisterously, as he yanked off the cover. "*Cómico*!" He pulled the lever and squeezed at the same time. Purple ink sprayed his baby face. Everyone including his fellow robbers laughed. He pulled his kerchief mask off to wipe it.

"Your mask, Pablo!" shouted The Second Eldest *Bandito*. "You said not to take off your mask!"

"*Calle la boca, estúpido*!" the inept thief protested. "Emilio, bring the bag." The hand of the boy who obviously didn't want to be involved was trembling worse as he stepped forward. "Throw the valuables in it, boys…er… men." As Emilio tried to balance bag and gun, the pistol went off, shooting The Eldest *Bandito*'s horse. The Two Homely Sisters went catatonic. It was a near perfect shot to the poor horses' head; the animal dropped dead on the trail. The Eldest *Bandito* went into an uncontrollable rage, grabbing the littlest one by the collar and slamming him against the stage. "You've shot Moctezuma, my best *caballo*. Father will go *loco*."

He suddenly got back into the action at hand. He shouted to The Stagecoach Driver, "*Dónde está el oro*?"

"No gold. Only passengers," said The Armed Guard.

"Liar. Miguel, on top, at the back!" the boy boss ordered.

"I thought you said no names," reprimanded The Second Oldest *Bandito*. The ringleader gave him what Mo`ikeha called *stink eye*.

The now-identified Miguel climbed up on the coach and, unaware to him, stood on the concealed strong box that contained fifty thousand dollars worth of gold destined for Vera Cruz. He focused on the mailbag instead and dumped the letters and parcels onto the people below. He yelled, "*Feliz Navidad!*" as the missives fell down like snow onto the parched trail. "*Nada*," he yelled, jumping to the ground in one fell leap, spraining his foot when he landed.

The Eldest *Bandito* had had enough. "Let's go, clowns," he yelled, denying his own buffoonery. The gang leaped onto their horses. The now horseless leader jumped onto Emilio's pony; He swatted the child robber with his hat as they rode away and disappeared into the hills.

"Is everyone fine?" asked The Stagecoach Driver in Spanish. Everyone muttered okay, then dusted off and repacked his or her clothing. The Two Homely Sisters were still unable to utter a sound. They sat sullen all the way to the next way station. The men moaned at the theft of their keepsakes but were happy that all were unharmed. They were also content that their own money had been safe up in the leather flaps, though positive that experienced *banditos* would have discovered it. Each of the men offered the ladies a little cash to replace their money to calm their nerves.

The travelers spent more time that usual at the next way station discussing what happened, what they should have done, with hope that the rest of the ride to Vera Cruz would be peaceful.

After the second stop, the party's uneasiness had dissipated and the group was now laughing at the silliness of the bungling gang while expressing the sadness that the boys had taken to robbery. Suddenly, they heard a hooting and a hollering. They poked their heads out the stagecoach window. A gang of real men, not boys, was shouting, "Stop! Pull the wagon over!"

"Oh, no! Not again," was muttered throughout the cabin. The two women sat stiff as rawhide, their freshly powdered faces oozing new beads of sweat. The Armed Guard was prepared this time. He took aim but stopped. He saw no guns. He held off. They'd have to fire first.

"We have something for you. We are not robbing you," yelled the five riders as they approached. The stagecoach came to stop. The Armed Guard stood with his rifle pointed at the strangers. Was it a ploy? The men on the inside pulled their pistols out. The Two Homely

Sisters fainted on each other.

One of the five riders came forward with what looked like Emilio's bag. In Spanish he said, "We have come to apologize for the bad deed of our sons. We are the fathers of the idiot stage robbers. Here. I believe these are the stolen things: a watch, a cross, and a pen. Oh, and here are someone's twenty *pesos*."

"We'll give it to the ladies when they come to," said The Stagecoach Driver.

"*Gracias, Señor*. We again offer our regrets for the foolishness of our children. They have disgraced the good people of Mexico. Have a pleasant journey. We have a dead horse to bury and some switches to prepare for punishment." The five fathers rode back from where they came.

Mo`ikeha announced at the end of the week that they were nearing Vera Cruz. His fellow travelers questioned his prediction but he claimed he was right because, like back home, he could smell the *`ehu kai*, the scent of the ocean. Just as the sun dipped down *pūkoko* behind them, they spotted a sign—Vera Cruz five miles.

The stagecoach pulled into the Square of the Republic near the waterfront. "*Vaya con Dios*!" was exchanged by personnel and passengers alike. The men were excited and exhausted that they had completed their seven-hundred mile adventure. The Two Homely Sisters scurried off to a buggy, Mo`ikeha sure that the ladies' stagecoach riding days had come to an end. The three sailors dragged their baggage across the street to the Hotel du Commerce looking forward to a fresh bed and linens, a good soapy bath, and some renowned seafood from the local fishermen. The hotel clerk handed them a note that had been left at the hotel a few days ago by an unnamed gentleman. They decided that only after they had taken care of their hygiene and what Mo`ikeha called their *ōpū nunulu*—their growling stomachs—would they open the envelope from the anonymous man. Early the next morning they would find out what lay ahead.

CHAPTER SIXTEEN
Upon this Bank and Shoal of Time

The squawking of seagulls woke Mo`ikeha up. He looked out the window of the Hotel du Commerce onto the harbor below, already busy with ships coming and going. After the three captains had breakfast and read their orders, Mo`ikeha would head down to the custom house to see if a letter from Ho`oipo or his parents had arrived.

The Irishman burst into Mo`ikeha's hotel room blasting him with his pillow. "Hey, *poi* farmer. You up for breakfast? How I miss a stack of hotcakes."

"Well, if I wasn't up before, I am now, thanks to the hotel's Irish wake-up service."

After personal attention, the trio headed downstairs and asked the clerk if he knew a good Yankee restaurant. "The Golden Egg is what you're looking for. The owners, a couple of *señors* from Boston opened it after they didn't make it in California. It's over on Zaragoza Avenue. This is a cosmopolitan city so you'll find German, French, Spanish, American and, of course, Mexican restaurants and bars. There are lots of choices."

The Irishman had hotcakes that morning along with eggs over easy, bacon, and coffee at The Golden Egg. His colleagues joined him in the American breakfast feast. As they sipped the final drops of their second cup, The *Hapa* Sailor pulled the letter of orders from his coat. He read it for the others:

"Proceed south along the coast to Alvarado. There's a small boat harbor. Take up at The Papaloan Hotel. Contact the owner at Blackie's Shipyard. The Captain of Operation Yerba Buena will contact you and the other recruits that will be arriving shortly. When they are all here, we will proceed to rendezvous at Head of Passes on April 8. The Admiral will proceed from Ship Island and meet us there. Until then, enjoy yourself before you face The Confederates. Continue to maintain silence about the mission.

The Captain, USN.
p.s. Destroy all written correspondence.

The day would be spent bathing in the warm waters of the Gulf of Mexico at Boca del Rio—the long beach that ran along the coast of Vera Cruz. On the way back, the men stopped at the customhouse to pick up any forwarded correspondence. Everyone received a letter, Mo`ikeha two—one from Ho`oipo and one from his parents. They remained unopened until they reached the hotel where the sailors would savor every word. There in the comfort of a bed, Mo`ikeha read:

Wailuku, Maui
Kingdom of Hawai`i

Dear Son,

It's hard to believe it's been one year since you left home. Father fell down on his back the other day on a slippery rock in the stream. He's been in pain so a sip of *`ōkolehau* once in awhile helps relieve the soreness. Let's pray he gets better. Your brother has taken up the slack as soon as he gets home from school. The girls are growing and are very smart, getting straight A's in their mathematics and English classes. They say they want to be teachers when they grow up, but they're still so young. We'll wait and see. Sounds like your work is secret since you haven't mentioned anything about it except that you're learning how to sail all kinds of boats. We've been hearing horrible things about the war and hope you'll stay safe. Enclosed are drawings by your sisters of `Īao that they created while in bed with the measles.

Me ke aloha
Mother

Though they were not the paintings of daVinci, Mo`ikeha tucked away the drawings as prized treasures. He'd take them into battle. He then opened the letter from Ho`oipo.

Lāhainā, Maui

Dear Mo`ikeha,

Hope you are safe and have enjoyed your journey across Mexico. Went up to Hale Pa`i to read up about some of the cities you've probably traveled through to get from Mazatlán to Vera Cruz.

So did you meet any interesting *señoritas*? Just teasing. Can you believe that you've already been gone one year? I miss you and hope you'll be home soon. Pretty Boy, that's what you called your canoe competitor anyway, has been coming by more often. I told him I'm busy sewing a quilt for you that includes the places you've visited. I don't think he believes that you'll ever return. He wants to stir up doubt that you cannot avoid the ladies in other foreign ports. But I'm stronger than his advances. I finally opened the shop in Lāhainā and call it The Queen's *Kuiki*, since she gave me the seed money to make and sell the quilts. It's doing fair, considering that all businesses take a while to get established. I've let some of the other ladies skilled in *lauhala* sell their baskets and mats in the store. They give me a little percentage of what they make. I may start to sell *mu`umu`u*. The missionary wives call them Mother Hubbards after the nursery rhyme. It's like our old *holokū* except with no yoke and no train. The ministers' spouses are trying to combat the evils of the flesh by covering up our women. I'm torn by their thoughts that the flesh is evil. I often ask myself: Why did God make us of flesh if it is so evil? It's like a tool that can be used for good or for bad. Awaiting your next letter.

Aloha au `ia `oe,
Ho`oipo

Mo`ikeha felt bad that he would not write to her until after his mission had been accomplished. The next day the group was off to Alvarado where they stayed for a few days until all the men in the mission arrived from Mazatlán.

The Liaison to The Admiral met with the men at the home of the shipbuilder late one night for further instructions and the assignment of ships. Most of the men would be commanders of steam schooners and take on a full crew at Head of Passes on April 8. "There you will be filled in on more specific information. The final and rare assignment deemed by The Admiral before heading out is to allow you to christen your assigned ship with an appropriate name for sole identification. Do not identify it as U.S.S." They would depart in two days after the vessels were launched and munitions and provisions loaded.

The Liaison to the Admiral took Mo`ikeha aside for special instructions. "Your ship will be the only sail sloop. It will be the quiet ship sent in under the cover of night to sever the boom that straddles the Mississippi River and open a passage way to New Orleans." Mo`ikeha took a deep gulp, suddenly realizing that he would be in the thick of it. What would happen if they were discovered? The Confederation would pour all its fire and brimstone down on their heads.

Before he could even cast a doubt, The Irishman grabbed The Young Man around his shoulders and shook him firmly. "So good buddy, what you gonna call your schooner? I've decided to call my ship *Dagda's Harp*, the instrument that played the war songs of my ancestors that was followed by the cry, 'Forth to the fight.' You like?"

"I like, but I don't have a steam schooner. I'll captain a sailing sloop."

"Are you on a pleasure cruise? Everyone else is captain of a schooner," commented The Irishman.

He stated humbly, "I go in first to sever the blockade."

"Oh, I'm sorry. I never thought that you'd be doing the toughest job. Well, I know that we can all depend on the *poi* farmer. I'll be right behind you, brother, to defend your *`ōkole*." He paused for a moment then added, "Oh, by the way, what will you name your sloop?"

Mo`ikeha thought back to the seven waterfalls in his home in `Īao Valley. "I'll name it after the Seven Sisters of the Pleiades. "I'll christen it *Makali`i*. It means *Little Eyes* or the *Eyes of the Chief*. My new interpretation will be *The Little Eyes of The Admiral*."

Several days later, the ships left for the rendezvous at Head of Passes. The Admiral was the overall authority. Commander David Porter was in charge of the nineteen mortar schooners. The remainder of the fleet, eight steam sloops, fourteen gunboats, and seventeen war ships, would be divided into two sections, the first under Captain Theodorus Bailey, the second under Captain Henry Bell. And, of course, there was Mo`ikeha's sailing sloop, *Makali`i*.

Now at Head of Passes and with a full crew, Mo`ikeha was summoned by The First Division Captain on April 15 with orders to carry out a spying mission. The sloop set sail that night at 12:00 a.m.

Luckily, a stiff breeze favored the objective. The Admiral wanted to know the most current river situation around the two Confederate defenses: Fort Jackson and Fort St. Phillip. Undercover plants in the forts had confirmed several weeks earlier that there were about a thousand men split between the two bastions with about seventy guns at Jackson and fifty at St. Phillip. They also reported that the barrier that spanned the river between the two forts had been rebuilt after being damaged twice, first by a storm and then by an onslaught of massive driftwood.

Even though he was on a sloop and better able to navigate through shallows, Mo`ikeha was warned to keep on a lookout for jagged shoals or shifting sandbars, infamous along the Mississippi. He posted two men port and starboard on the bow to keep an eye out for natural or man-made obstacles. Poles were at their sides in case the river had to be probed. The sloop had been painted black and its sails were of dark canvas. The crew and captain kept their fingers crossed, hoping that they would not encounter a rebel ship patrolling the outer banks. They knew that they were at their destination when they spotted some lanterns hanging from the forts in the distance. No sentinels were spotted. The crew of the *Makali`i* was nervously elated that no one had discovered them, thus far. The murmur of crickets marked the night. Suddenly, Mo`ikeha heard a sound that he had never heard before. It was an irritating reverberation coming from a low clump of pines. He grabbed one of the local crew members. "What the hell is that?" he asked concerned that a rebel was hiding behind the grove.

The sailor laughed softly and whispered "Oh, that's a cicada, Captain." Mo`ikeha gave him a further look of confusion. "An insect, Captain, not a rebel, although as ugly as one. Sometimes they are in chorus but this guy's a loner, probably a refugee from New Orleans."

The ship sailed on in the stygian dark. He felt like Charon, the ferryman, the character from Milton's *Paradise Lost,* the epic poem he had endured at Lahainaluna School. Fortunately, the river was not the Styx but the Mississippi, their final destination was not Hades but New Orleans.

They approached the new boom stretched out across the river, the blockade made up of eleven hulks of discarded schooners chained together. Only the right end chain opposite Fort Jackson had to be dislodged. Once dismantled, the remainder of the useless ships would flow down the Mississippi and hug its left bank like a wounded river snake. Mo`ikeha grabbed a spyglass and looked past the boom into Plaquemine's Bend. There it was! The Mosquito Fleet! He counted ten wooden ships beyond the barrier and to his dismay—two Confederate ironclads, the *Louisiana* and the *Manassas*. They had seen enough.

Suddenly, he was spooked by a few shouts coming from the fort. Lanterns were moving about. It was time to go. He turned the *Makali`i* about and headed back toward Head of Passes.

The Admiral and his brother, The Mortar Commander, were elated at Mo`ikeha's clandestine effort. The latter suggested the shelling of the forts to soften them up before traveling through the *puka* in the boom.

The next day, April 16, The Mortar Commander's schooners moved into a closer position near the forts. At sunrise, the Union ships commenced firing shell after shell at the Confederate citadels on both banks of the river. The Mortar Commander called for a ceasefire to see if the Rebels would surrender, but after a brief pause with no reaction, return mortar recommenced from Jackson and St. Phillip. The Rebels were entrenched in the guts of the forts, prepared to put up a good fight. The Mortar Commander continued the barrage for several more days, inflicting the strongholds with another two thousand rounds of ordnance. The Southerners didn't budge. The Union fleet sat waiting for the call for a full attack.

When Mo`ikeha found out that he would lead with the *Makali`i*, followed by two steam schooners up to the abandoned ship blockade, the ultimate danger of it finally hit home. He gathered up personal items and rowed over to The Irishman on *Dagda's Harp*.

"*Hoaloha*, my friend," he said to The Irishman. "I just found out that we sail on the twenty-third. The *Makali`i*, the *Itasca*, and the *Pinola* will go in first and put a *puka*, a hole, in the boom. We'll be the first through but also the first to be fired upon." He handed The Irishman a small bag.

"What is this?" He looked in the bag, spotting among other things Mo`ikeha's personal keepsakes including Ho`oipo's gift—the fountain pen.

"Would you be so kind to pass it on to my family and *ku`uipo* if I should..." He paused and took a deep breath "...die in battle?"

"You're not going to die. But I thought the same thing. Here. Here's the pocket watch and fob. I don't have family anymore but I would appreciate it if you gave it to my Mexican girlfriend in San José if..."

A laughter of inconvenience emerged from Mo`ikeha's gut. "I thought you were going to visit Maui after the war but... sure."

"Good luck, my *poi* farmer!"

"*E mālama i kou kino, kanaka `Ailiki,*" he called to his friend, urging The Irishman to take care of himself. He climbed into the dinghy and rowed away.

From a distance, The Irishman called out, "See you upriver!" The words echoed across the shoals and sandbars of the shifting Mississippi where it was seized by a strong sea breeze and hurtled high into the heavens until it became a haunting whisper.

Ironically, Mo`ikeha had the most restful night in a long time, dreaming of `Īao Stream barely trickling on a summer day, cotton clouds gliding overhead, beads of water racing off Ho`oipo's brown skin after a plunge into the bracing stream, the loves of his life gathered round him.

He was awakened by the sound of men walking the deck. The cook had prepared a most hearty breakfast. "Like a prisoner's final meal," quipped The Second Mate, his gallows humor unappreciated. The day was spent with Mo`ikeha and his crew covering the crucial parts of the ship and volatile magazines with protective material including iron plates and chains. Guns were cleaned and loaded, final plans settled, all in preparation for the initial confrontation to control the Mississippi that General-in-Chief Winfield Scott called Operation Anaconda. Finally, the sun set on New Orleans like it would never set again.

On the twenty second of April, The *Makali`i* led the way up the moonless Mississippi along with the *Itasca* and *Pinola* as protection. The two ships stopped at a wide bend in the Mississippi where they would remain unseen by guards at the forts until Mo`ikeha's sloop returned from the boom with news of an open passage.

His point men would have to hack at the pole the size of a railroad tie that held the chain on the right bank and that would be noisy. As soon as the chopping was heard and the chains loosened, they anticipated gunfire, so they had to move out quickly back to the protection of the *Itasca* and *Pinola.*

The sloop slithered silently alongside the boom. The assigned men jumped out, axes in hand, and started slashing at the wood like crazed killers. They expected a "Halt! Who goes there?" but under the cover of darkness they had not been spotted, so far. The pole finally toppled, the chain dropping onto the second hulk. Unfortunately, the current was at low ebb and Mo`ikeha observed that the drifting hulks would take awhile to meander downstream and create a full gap.

The *Makali`i* headed back to the bend in the river to the *Itasca* and *Pinola*. The good news that the passage way was now open was passed on to The Admiral. The Mortar Commander insisted on another day of shelling. He felt that he was close to making the running of the blockade safer.

The Admiral was tired of waiting as well. "We must run the gauntlet," he announced in a strategy meeting after the somewhat ineffective onslaught of missiles. Finally, on the early evening of April 23, all the captains began lining up their ships like ducks in a row. They would break through at 2 a.m.

Finally, the call came. "Proceed to attack! Proceed to attack!" The *Makali`i*, *Itasca*, and *Pinola* looked downriver and saw the massive Union fleet coming their way.

As they approached the blockade, Mo`ikeha and the captains of the two ships noticed that the boom had drifted. The ship hulks had piled up and now blocked half of the river. Bells began clanging. The Union ships had been spotted! The forts came alive. Pounding feet and shouts of "Get up!" and "Under attack!" reverberated across the sandbanks all the way down to the bend in the river. It was too late and too dangerous for Mo`ikeha to clear the river completely. Luckily, there was enough of a gap for the ships to steer through, though one by one.

At the same time, the Union gunboats proceeded to shell the two forts to give cover for the ships breaking through past the barricade. Seventeen warships in single file squeezed through Mo`ikeha's *puka* including, among others, the *U.S.S. Cayuga*, *Kineo*, *Pensacola*, *Brooklyn*, *Mississippi*, *Varuna*, The Irishman's *Dagda Harp*, the flagship *Hartford*, and the schooners captained by the men Mo`ikeha had trained with in San Francisco.

All hell broke loose: mortars exploded, gunfire flashed from the forts and along the solid shoreline, rafts of debris were set on fire and pushed in the direction of the Union ships. Chaos reigned. What the Union Navy feared most were the ironclads. The one hundred and twenty-eight foot *Manassas* headed up stream to get into a better position but the *Louisiana* sat there like a swamp frog filled with buckshot. The Union Navy did not realize that the boilers of the *Louisiana* had been inoperable for some time while awaiting parts to make her battle worthy. She did attempt to fire guns from her ports but they were poorly built and hard to fire from. The commander of the impotent Confederate iron-plated monster, faced with futility, cut loose its moorings and set the ironclad adrift to make the Union sailors believe that she was functional. Instead, the C.S.S. *Louisiana* floated limply across the river until she ran aground. The human innards under heavy fire fled the river for land. Most of them never made it.

More gunfire erupted from the forts but the Union ships replied with a pounding barrage of mortars. Mo`ikeha, through all the smoke and din, moved the *Makali`i* upriver to see if the remainder of the Confederate Mosquito Fleet was coming to the rescue. The small, darkened sloop saw the ironclad *Manassas* returning with three rebel ships storming downriver towards Plaquemine's Bend. Mo`ikeha veered the ship windward into a dense clump of shrubs about twelve feet tall. His angels were with him. The *Manassas* and the three rebel gunboats passed the camouflaged vessel, their eyes focused on the inferno that lay ahead of them.

The rebel gunboats fired at their first target, the ten-gun Union sloop, *Varuna*. Their aim was accurate. The powder magazine was hit. A huge explosion rocked the shoals. Flaming debris, splinters, and shrapnel showered the ship next to it. Both vessels collided into each other and began to sink. A shiver ran down Mo`ikeha's spine when he saw both ships turn on their sides. The vessel alongside the *Varuna* was *Dagda's Harp*. With his spyglass, he scanned the waters around the ships for survivors but saw none. They were all floating face down in The Big Muddy.

Memories rushed in. He instinctively patted his coat pocket where The Irishman's father's pocket watch and fob had been secured. He whispered a little prayer to all his gods, Christian and Hawaiian, to receive his dear Irish friend and provide a place for him in heaven.

The sinking of the two schooners brought out the fury of revenge. All the captains, the men who had trained with Mo`ikeha, turned their efforts to the three gunboats. A barrage of mortar and gunfire showered down on the Rebels. The Confederate ships could not survive the onslaught of retaliation, so they turned to escape upriver. But Mo`ikeha was one step ahead of them. Two of the rafts of pitch pine, hay, and debris to be eventually set ablaze by the enemy had been left unattended upriver. He ordered his men to loosen the floatable masses and set them on fire. They got out the long poles and pushed the floating conflagrations into the path of the retreating ships. When the

Confederate captains saw the towering flames drifting toward them and felt the relentless bombardment from their rear, they ran their gunboats aground, yelling at all the Grays to abandon ship and head for the swamp.

Meanwhile, the bulky ironclad, *Manassas,* attempted to puncture the U.S.S. *Pensacola* with her large ram but it was to no avail. It turned its attention to the U.S.S. *Brooklyn* and U.S.S. *Mississippi,* causing some insignificant damage to both. The *Mississipp*i retreated temporarily, then returned with full vengeance. A mortar from it penetrated a weak section in the Confederate floating cigar and thick smoke billowed out of the *C.S.S. Manassas.* Its crew leaped into the misery of the Mississippi and swam away from the burning craft. The Confederate Goliath had been crippled. It floated downstream, ran aground, and exploded.

The Admiral, himself, had his hands full. Maneuvering to avoid the fiery rafts, he managed to run the U.S.S. *Hartford* aground into one of the sandbars. A flaming barge crashed into the Union command ship and set it on fire. Mo`ikeha, now free of vessels firing upon the *Makali`i,* headed to help. He ordered his men to grab buckets and to squelch the fire similar to his attempt to save the bowling alley back in Lāhainā. Working together, both crews put out the fire and, after several tries, the *Hartford* backed itself out of the soft mud.

And now there was silence on the water and in the forts. The levees around the forts had been breached and water poured into them. The Admiral let the Rebels remain in their squalid conditions until they were ready to surrender without more bloodshed.

Mo`ikeha surveyed the carnage. Bodies floated with and without burns, corpses mingled with the weeds on the muddy banks. The toll to the Confederate forces was devastating. Mo`ikeha had looked into the Eyes of the Beast.

Meanwhile, The Admiral called all his captains together to assess the damage, to take care of the one hundred and forty-seven injured, and to remember those who lost their lives for liberty. Mo`ikeha held the pocket watch tightly in his hand as *Scott Tattoo* echoed across the shoals, remembering the *kolohe* one, his rascal friend shanghaied from the Cobweb Palace, his traveling companion across Old Mexico, and that vivacious Celtic countenance in the glow of Christmas candles at Santa Clara Mission.

Thirty-seven Union bodies were dragged up along the banks of the Mississippi that night, their personal belongings on them placed on their bodies for burial at sunrise. Mo`ikeha re-claimed the fountain pen and his Mother's gift that lay on the chest of The Irishman. Now thirteen of the seventeen ships that had slipped past Mo`ikeha's *puka* in the boom would continue upriver to New Orleans, Baton Rouge, Natchez, and Mo`ikeha's final contracted mission—Vicksburg.

CHAPTER SEVENTEEN
All God's Chillun Got Wings

Mo`ikeha looked at the Mississippi River as similar to one of those new telegraph lines that had been strung up across the nation. News seemed to travel enigmatically upstream and downstream. Word came down the Big Muddy that upon hearing of the fall of Forts Jackson and St. Phillip, Confederate General Lovell withdrew his three thousand troops from New Orleans and sent them to join forces at Vicksburg. The Admiral and his Union ships sailed some seventy miles north of the forts and anchored just outside the Crescent City.

The citizens of New Orleans showed their outrage at the thought of surrender. And lacking strategic insight, its leaders had sent most of their able-bodied men to Tennessee to do battle for the Confederacy. New Orleans was now easy prey. Who were left behind were the elderly, women, children, and those too disabled to join their fellow brothers in the Western Theater. Mo`ikeha could see that a huge mob had gathered at the piers to defy the invaders, firing the few guns they had, brandishing pitchforks and machetes, setting fire to hundreds of bails of cotton that were then pushed out into the Mississippi. From his sloop, the Maui sailor heard the curses of the native sons and daughters of the Delta echo along the waterfront.

Mo`ikeha's feelings were torn. How would Hawaiians react if someone tried to take over their islands? But, at the same time, if the populace of Louisiana hadn't voted to secede and hadn't tried to maintain slavery, then blood would not have been shed and the war would have ended quickly. Finally, he thought of The Irishman. Weren't their sons the ones that had killed his good friend to perpetuate their misdirected ideals? Weren't they the ones that had chosen death, injury, and slavery over life, good health, and freedom?

With his spyglass, Mo`ikeha watched as two gutsy marines strode the gauntlet from the dock to city hall, the irate crowds hurling every imaginable epithet at the emissaries carrying the papers of surrender. Mo`ikeha saw both General Lovell and Mayor Monroe refuse the conditions. The two messengers were whisked off quickly lest the crowd tar and feather them.

The minds of the Mississippians changed days later when General Benjamin Butler arrived with his fifteen-thousand Union troops and surrounded the city. The concession of defeat traveled up the Mississippi and soon the troops at both Baton Rouge and Natchez pulled back up to Vicksburg. The Admiral continued to move the bulk of his flotilla upriver toward the Mississippi State stronghold. President Lincoln, advised of the capitulations by Confederate commanders, announced that Louisiana and the river were now open for the mail. Mo`ikeha took advantage of it and sent a short letter off to his parents along with the salary he had made for the first half of his assignment, his confidence high as a result of the recent victories.

The fleet of Yankee ships stopped to re-organize just north of Natchez, some seventy-three miles below Vicksburg.

It was a sultry night on the Mississippi River, the more intense humidity of summer a couple of months away. Mo`ikeha could hear the bullfrogs along the weedy banks of the river, a somewhat consoling song that he had heard coming from the taro *lo`i* in `Īao Valley after the sun went down. He heard a bump against his ship. "Permission to come aboard, sir."

"Permission granted," replied Mo`ikeha.

"Captain, The Admiral wishes to see you now if you are available."

"Please tell The Admiral that I'll be there shortly."

After he made himself presentable, Mo`ikeha rowed to and boarded the flagship. "Ah, Captain, thank you for coming," said The Admiral. "First, let me tell you how impressed I was at your performance in battle. You did several risky things and the United States is more than thankful. Your contract ends at Vicksburg, actually before Vicksburg. We want you to go on one final reconnaissance mission up the river, taking note of naval and land concentrations and how far down the river from Vicksburg the initial sentinels are posted. When you return, you are free to sail back down to New Orleans and around The Horn back to San Francisco." Mo`ikeha was excited to finally be released from the madness of war. "We will disguise your sloop as a Confederate merchant ship, change and age your sails, and give it a pro-Southern name. It should take a day or two and then we'll send you and your crew upriver. If there aren't any questions, that will be all."

"Yes, sir," responded Mo`ikeha. He saluted the celebrated admiral and departed.

When Mo`ikeha saw the *Makali`i* two days later, he almost didn't recognize her. She had been re-christened the *Pelican*, the bird that appeared on recent Louisiana flags. It was filled with a variety of merchandise including pots, pans, bolts of cloth, and articles retrieved from crippled Confederate ships. The Young Man from Maui and his crew were given appropriate civilian clothing to wear. That morning the faux crew of the *Pelican* set sail upriver. They would travel day and night and would not stop until they smelled the breath of Johnny Reb.

There weren't many signs along the way. Mo`ikeha had to depend on a rumpled old map. Upriver, their true colors went undetected. They even sold a couple of pots, pans, and thread to some white folk in a little shanty near the Big Blue Hole just outside of Natchez. Mo`ikeha made sure one of his Southern-raised men did the talking while he hid in the darkness of the hold. "Sure been slim pickins along the river here since the war begun," complained the eldest inhabitant. "They say that the Yanks will be a comin' this way; maybe they took Natchez already. Where you folks hailin' from?"

"We sell between Baton Rouge and New Orleans but, before the Yanks and that Farragut feller come into the City, we hightailed it out, considerin' they most likely steal our boat and the supplies," responded Mo`ikeha's Southern-raised crew member. "Well, we figured it best we's head up North to Vicksburg where we be safe with our own kind." The *Pelican* continued on, the captain and crew relieved that they had not been detected.

On the second day in late afternoon, the reconnaissance team was some thirty miles from Vicksburg, the winds whipping down the Mississippi at a brisk pace. The town of St. Joseph was nearby according to one of the few signposts along the winding Mississippi. As they neared Bruin Lake, they could hear the sounds of a vessel approaching. It was a rebel gunboat with a few sailors on-board. The crew of the *Pelican* became quite nervous. With the Confederate flag flapping, the *Mockingbird* pulled up against the *Pelican*.

"Where you folks headed?" yelled out The Captain of the *Mockingbird*.

"Escaping from Yankees downstream," shouted Mo`ikeha's crew member.

"You seen them comin'?"

"Nah. We hightailed before they come. You folks need anything to buy—tobacco, soap?"

The captain of the rebel gunboat jumped aboard the *Pelican*. "You not sellin' guns to the Yankees, eh?"

"We got a couple of guns only fer protection," uttered Mo`ikeha's man.

The Captain of the *Mockingbird* started to stick his nose around the boat. All of a sudden, he spotted an oilcan. He picked it up and examined it closely, reading the markings out loud, "C.S.S. *Louisiana*." Mo`ikeha took a hard swallow. They would next ask how the *Pelican* had acquired the can from the ironclad.

"*Hele aku*!" Mo`ikeha yelled out the Hawaiian signal to get the hell out of there. The Hawaiian rushed up from the hold and gave a full body blow to The Captain of the *Mockingbird*. He went head over heels into the muddy river. Before the Rebel captain could swim to his boat, grape from the *Pelican* pelted him. He got hit and sank to the bottom of the Mississippi. Mo`ikeha was so proud of his men as they fired away at the *Mockingbird*, incapacitating the remainder of its crew. Mo`ikeha turned his sloop downstream.

No sooner had they made the bend in the river, did they hear gunshots. It was a second gunboat heading towards them, its crew members gun crazy. A combination of minie' balls and bullets flew overhead, zinging the mast and sails. "Full speed ahead," yelled Mo`ikeha, grateful that the wind was at his back. Just then, as they turned another sharp bend in the river, Mo`ikeha was hit in the shoulder. The shot was enough for him to lose balance. He fell overboard into the cold water. He doggie paddled as best he could with his good arm and shouted at his men, "Don't stop. Keep going. Tell The Admiral they're as low as Lake Bruin. I'll wait here 'til you return!" The first officer faced a dilemma—retreat to deadly fire or turn back to retrieve Mo`ikeha. The decision was instant. If the *Pelican* returned for their captain, more crew members would be shot or caught. The *Pelican* reluctantly left its Maui captain behind. On his part, with all he could muster, Mo`ikeha swam underwater to the soggy bank. There in the river's reedy edge he hid. He peered through the duckweed and watched the rebel gunboat sail past.

"We'll get him later on the way back if he ain't drowned," yelled out the gunboat captain.

Blood oozed from Mo`ikeha's arm and mixed with the river. As a result of all the sudden excitement, the strenuous activity, and the stinging wound, he collapsed unconscious. The sound of crickets faded in and out. He noticed that it was now on the verge of twilight, the stars looking down on his poor pathetic self. He passed out again.

A stench woke him. He was being dragged and could only look back to where he had come from. He turned his head around as far as he could until pain shot through his arm and memory of its cause. He was looking at a mule's rear end upside down. "Scuse me. Bessie went and farted. When she does, it can raise the dead." The movement came to a stop. A black man got off the mule and walked around. A hound dog with a sad face also stared at Mo`ikeha.

"I was fetchin' biscuitroot and wild asparagus, grows thick here, when I hear the gunfire. Came over and found you among the reeds. Pulled you out of the river."

"Where… am I?" asked Mo`ikeha, weakly.

"You's in Tensas Parish, Louisiana, just above St. Joseph. We off to Big Pond where I got me a shanty to take care of you a bit. You got a mean woun' there. Was the white man takin' you back to the plantation and you run? Which one you work on?" asked the black man. "Oh shucks. Too many questions fo' an injured man along the trail here. You jes res'. Questions and answers will come in due time. Oh, by the way," he added, "this here's Gabriel, my old hound dog."

Mo`ikeha lay his head back down on the travois and fell asleep to the rhythmic clops of old Bessie and the panting of Gabriel as the journey to Big Pond continued.

Time passed. "We's here, mister… mister…By the way, what's yo name?"

Mo`ikeha tried to shake his grogginess to answer the man's question. "Mo`ikeha," he finally answered, looking up at a quaint shack at the end of a lake surrounded by moss-covered cypress trees.

"Sure is a funny name. Maybe your father an Indian, maybe your mama she's a negro lady? What plantation you come from? You runaway like me?"

"Oh, I'm not from any plantation. I'm a Hawaiian."

"Hawaiian? What's a Hawaiian?"

"I'm from the Sandwich Islands out in the Pacific Ocean."

"Well, I'll be. I ain't never meet a Hawaiian before. You folks eat each other?"

Mo`ikeha laughed. "No, no, no. We practice *aloha*—you know—love."

"My mammy tell me that all the time, before she died. 'Son, it's all about love.' Maybe she a Hawaiian. Here let me help you inside. My shanty taint much. I founded it when I ran away from the massa." The black man propped Mo`ikeha up under his good shoulder and lugged him inside. He lit a lantern after he lay him down in his bed. "I hope you don't mind if I wash you down seein' you kent do it yourself. You muddier than a pig in a sty."

The runaway slave started a small fire in the pot-bellied stove and soon the huge kettle of water was boiling. The man who had pulled him from the river washed Mo`ikeha from head to foot. "Just like Jesus washed the feet of his disciples," commented the Hawaiian as he was scrubbed clean.

"Oh, you knows about Jesus way out there in the Samwich Islans?"

"The missionaries brought The Word, although I still pray to the gods of my ancestors," replied the Hawaiian. "I doesn't hurt to have all of them pulling for you."

"Now this part bound to hurt the most. I got to clean this wound." The runaway slave examined the injury closely. "You went and got yourself a lucky wound. That minie' ball went right through clean. I goin' wash it all out good. Don't want it to get poisoned. Here, bite on this here rag while I scoop all that puss out." Mo`ikeha bit hard but felt better as his guardian angel applied some medicine and stuffed the wound on both ends with cloth. "This here black willow bark paste will heal you in no time. I promised the Lord no alcohol so I kent give you that fo' yoa pain, so here." He poured a cup of hot water and stirred what he called fumewort into it. "Drink. This will do the job, The Lord's natural way." Finally, he got a big red kerchief and made a sling for his arm. The black man took his only blanket and draped it across Mo`ikeha. "Now you jes relax there, while I cook us up a mess to eat."

Mo`ikeha's eyes got heavy now that he again felt secure. Time passed quickly after he tumbled into dreamland. He was awakened by the dinner call. "Hate to wake you, Mō`ī , but you need some fixins in yo stomach. Sorry, I didn't expec' to have people come a visitin' otherwise I would've spent the day goin' after a big bass, but I'm sure you gonna like this here crappie and some hoecakes. Here, let me prop you up." He handed him a worn plate and a mangled fork and poured him coffee in a cup that had seen its days.

"That crappie name don't sound appealing. What is it?"

"The white man call it perch. You heard of it?"

"We don't have too many fresh water lakes but I heard about it at school."

"You gone to school? And you a black man too. I wish idda gone but I work pickin' cotton since I was eleven. I got tired of bendin'. Nothing seemed to please the massa, so I got whupped with his cane. There's so much a man could take so one day I run. I didn't care. My family all died under the massa. I had nuttin to lose so I run. I decide to plant down here where nobody come cept some fishermens. Maybe if the North win, I finally be left alone. I jes waitin'."

"By the way, we've been chattering like two birds, and I haven't even asked you your name."

"Oh, I Henry," responded the black man.

"And what's your last name?"

"Oh, I don't have one. I take on the massa's name. I Mr. Henry's Henry."

"Well, Mr. Henry's Henry, I have a new name for you if you don't mind." The runaway slave shook his head in agreement.

"You are my guardian angel. You saved me from death and I'm most grateful. Can I call you The Angel?"

"I never considered myself an angel but you kin. That's why I give my old hound dog the name Gabriel. He's a runaway too. The chains that held him dug deep scars in his neck. He jes come up to the shanty out of nowhere one day and kept me upright during those first lonely nights. He my angel."

"Well, my Angel, you're not only a good doctor but an excellent cook. The crappie and corn meal cake was sure *`ono*...er...tasty."

"Now, you get some shut eye. It'll take some time for that hurt to heal and you mighty welcome to stay until it's mended. Besides, it's sure nice to have some company for a turn, much less a Hawaiian from the Samich Islans." The Angel put aside the dishes, washed his face, and curled with a shabby cloth on the homemade rug around the pot-bellied stove where he snored himself to sleep.

Mo`ikeha fell asleep too, dreaming of angels sitting on the giant basalt boulders in 'Īao Stream, their wings whiffling in harmony to the soft series of splashes from miniature waterfalls in the riverbed.

Days passed with Mo`ikeha in bed, The Angel re-dressing his wound, feeding him, and answering questions about life on the Mississippi. The Hawaiian assured him that The Admiral was coming upriver and with Vicksburg whipped he'd soon be free.

"Time to go outside and take a look at my backyard," announced The Angel one morning. "Maybe we even do some fishin' tomorrow." Mo`ikeha found the strength to walk out the door on his own. It was nice to take in fresh air and sunshine. He was feeling a hundred times better but filled with apprehension about what he was going to do when he was pretty much healed. Where would he go? How would he get there?

The Angel interrupted his anxiety. "Freedom is sure a beautiful thing. Makes you want to git up each morning. Doesn't it, Mō`ī ?" Mo`ikeha was amused. It was the same regal short-cut name The Irishman had given him.

Suddenly, Gabriel announced strangers with his doleful howl. Dogs were heard barking in the distance, followed by gunshots. "Dogs! Guns!" exclaimed Mo`ikeha, concerned that the two runaways had been discovered.

"No sense frettin'. They's hunters up round the lake on the other side after otters or muskrats fo' pelts. Time to get in anyhow."

Mo`ikeha wrote a letter to Ho`oipo that night. He didn't know if it would ever get to her but The Angel said he'd send it somehow. It read:

St. Joseph, Louisiana
On the Mississippi River

Dear Ho`oipo,

I hope you are well and the same can be said for my family. It's best that you relay this letter on to them and prepare them for it. My contract is completed so I'll be seeing you soon. There is one little problem. I've had to take sick leave. I was hurt in the shoulder but I'm one hundred per cent healed. I am in a most adequate medical facility. My nurse has taken good care of me. And don't get jealous. My nurse is a male. I call him The Angel. I can see only a small scar where I got hurt. I'm so healthy that we're going bass fishing tomorrow. Soon I'll be heading downriver to catch a boat home. I hope that the business is doing well. When I get back to Maui I can help you with the needs of the shop.

Homeward bound,
Mo`ikeha

The next morning with the sky still purple, Mo`ikeha was awoken by The Angel. "Best time to git em is when they's half asleep. You ready to get that big bad bass?" The Hawaiian mumbled a drowsy yeah. Today would herald another first—he would finally rid himself of his sling. The two men and Gabriel walked down the path to the lake and when they walked back later that afternoon, each proudly carried a big bad bass.

"This is quite a *pā`ina*," Mo`ikeha proclaimed that night as they finished grace.

"A pie na?" questioned The Angel.

"Yeah, a feast. Look here, bass over coals, hush puppies, collard greens and peas from back of the shanty, along with hot steaming coffee. You are as good a cook as the ones in the highfalutin hotels in San Francisco."

"Go on, now," The Angel motioned with his hands. The two men dug into the food with little talk, their smacking lips a testament to the gourmet meal. As the supper ended, Mo`ikeha asked again about the possibility of a letter getting down to New Orleans. "Well, there's a skinner that lives downriver a bit. We trades with each other what we's got. He a white man who run away from what he call another massa—the big city. He like to be alone and with nature. He says war is fo' crazy people and ain't takin no side. He got a canoe and go down to Natchez to sell pelts. Maybe when he go down, he take your letter. I take it to his reglar place tomorrow." That night after they tidied up, Mo`ikeha sang The Angel a *mele kahiko*, an old Hawaiian song about place, about `Īao Valley. The Angel replied with his rendition of *All God's Chillun Got Wings*.

The next day after breakfast, The Angel bid a good day to Mō`ī, loaded up Bessie with an early batch of summer squash and some smoked meats to pay for the delivery of the letter, and headed out along with Gabriel to The Skinner's place.

Hours passed going and returning. The Skinner was pleased with the gifts and said he was on his way to Natchez anyway. The Angel sensed discomfort all the way home. As he approached the shanty, The Angel felt very uneasy. It was too quiet. He slowly opened the door. Shotguns were pushed into his face.

“Henry,” the man behind the guns said. “Mr. Henry misses his hardest workin’ slave. Some hunters say they saw two negroes up hea. It was you and this other runaway. We kept a askin’ him, but he says he ain’t no slave.” The other gunmen laughed.

“Well,” said The Angel trying to get Mo`ikeha out of trouble, “he ain’t. He’s a sailor man from the Samwich Islans.”

“Oh, a sailor. Which side you fightin’ for, boy?” the man said to Mo`ikeha.

Another gunman spoke out. “Maybe he that Union sailor that was shot and fall into the river that they thought was drowned.”

The third gunman released his prejudice. “Can you believe that? Now those Yankee dogs got cotton pickers fighting for them.”

The lead gunman bragged, “Well, gentlemen, it looks like we got two black birds with one stone. The runaway goes back to Mr. Henry and the sailor from the Samwich Islans goes to the stockade in Vicksburg. Move em down to the river.”

Mo`ikeha and The Angel looked at each other intensely as they were shoved to the water’s edge. “*Mahalo,* my friend. *Imua*!” Mo`ikeha yelled out as the skiff with his Angel glided downstream until he blended into the low-lying clouds.

“You talking war codes, black boy?” yelled a gunman. He slapped Mo`ikeha on the back of the head. “And no talkin’ until we git to Vicksburg.”

CHAPTER EIGHTEEN
Ke Alahao: The Iron Road

Mo`ikeha noticed the bluffs above Vicksburg as the gunboat filed past a city preparing for battle. The Maui sailor assessed that The Admiral would have a hard time attacking the city; the Union Navy would be bombarded from the looming cliffs. The strong irons that held him in bondage were rubbing against and chafing his wrists. He was led from the pier through the streets like a slave, taunted and spat upon like a dog. Now he knew what it was like to be something other than white in America.

He was thrown into the local lockup with ten other men. He surmised they were sympathetic to the North. It was near dinnertime and a supper of bread and bacon was slopped into a dirty dented pan along with some red water. Reality finally struck Mo`ikeha that he was indeed a prisoner of war.

Sleep is an alternative to misery so most of the prisoners dozed off after they had swallowed their meals. Mo`ikeha's keen ear picked up a conversation outside the cells as he began to drowse. "Good news, constable, after everyone gets his biscuit, the wagons should be here to transport the jailbirds to the train station, say about eight a.m. I'm sure you're happy getting rid of these Yankee bleedin' hearts so you can stock your cells with your local criminals."

"Much obliged, captain. Where they off to?"

"The war come so sudden. We were caught without POW camps. I just gonna send these Lincoln lovers out to Richmond, let General Lee handle it. We gonna be too busy defending this town much less worry about providin' for prisoners. Night, constable. See you in the morning."

"I'm going to Virginia," Mo`ikeha said to himself, "by train!" He had never been on a train before, unless he counted the mud car he rode on in San Francisco with The Emperor. He was excited at the thought though he wished the locomotive ride were under more cheerful circumstances. He felt the same way about traveling across the United States—well, to be accurate—across the Confederate States. It was beyond his wildest imagination that he would end up on the East Coast. He knew there would be miserable times ahead, but the war couldn't last forever. He plotted to remain strong in all adversity. Thanks to The Angel, Mo`ikeha was physically fit to endure the long train ride to Richmond and his imprisonment.

At the train station the next morning, the men were piled into an old cattle car still smelling from the occupation of the former inhabitants. A large container of water with a ladle was placed in the cattle crate and the shredded remains of a blanket were tossed to each prisoner. A burley civilian guard was posted between the preceding car and the prison-on-wheels. In the train station, Mo`ikeha had noticed *The Vicksburg-Jackson Railway* emblem as they boarded. The latter would be their next stop.

"Anybody know where we headed?" asked one of the men out loud.

"Yeah, to a POW camp," responded another. The rest of the men laughed.

Mo`ikeha volunteered the overheard conversation from the night before. "We're going to Richmond."

"Virginia? How do you know, mister? You a spy among us?" asked a fellow captive.

The man next to Mo`ikeha defended him. "I don't think they gonna make a runaway slave a spy?"

"Oh, I'm not a runaway slave," said Mo`ikeha. He played his trump card. "I'm a Hawaiian."

"The Sandwich Isles?" asked a more knowledgeable captive. "You a long way from home, boy! Whatcha doin' in this here neck of the woods?"

"I came with Admiral Farragut. He's right behind me coming up the Mississippi River to Vicksburg. I'm just the raindrop before the storm."

"Word is it that General Grant is moving west along the tracks. Poor Vicksburg is going to be the center of the perfect storm," a concerned internee added.

"It doesn't hold good for us to be riding on a Confederate train heading towards the General. We're going to be in the crossfire," exclaimed Mo`ikeha.

"You better pray to your Hawaiian gods to protect us, witch doctor," said a quiet grizzly prisoner as he attempted to form a bed from the straw strewn across the car's floor. Everyone followed suite; the hypnotic clickety-clack of the steel wheels on the track lulled them to sleep.

The train pulled into the Jackson station shortly after noon. The searing heat and humidity of an Indian summer had lingered in September and more intensely in the enclosed cattle car. Mo`ikeha heard cicadas as he and his fellow captives were forced off one train onto another. The Adjacent Prisoner whispered, "I heard the engineer mention Grenada, so I guess you still might be right. We headin' east."

After the men were tossed onto an equally squalid car, after they were doled out hardtack and some withered apples, and after the new guard was posted, a blast of whistle and a clanging bell silenced the cicadas temporarily. They commenced their chorus as the Grenada-bound train, now some distance down the track, blended into a mirage created by the climbing temperature.

On the way to Grenada, The Adjacent Prisoner explained his predicament, one very similar to most of the captives on the train. They were not only against the civil war, but against war, period. They weren't for the North or for the South. They were for peace. And now they were going to suffer for their pacifism. Mo`ikeha continued to conclude that this whole war thing was a messy affair.

The sun was starting to sink low in the horizon as the prisoners' locomotive pulled into Grenada. In the twilight, the sweaty prisoners again changed trains. "Why are we always changing trains?" asked Mo`ikeha to The Adjacent Prisoner.

"Different gauges means different trains to change," he answered. "In fact, trains and tracks may decide this war. The Confederate tracks are a hodge-podge and change to different sizes in different counties. Ah, well, might as well get a snooze, got about a hundred miles to go. Should be there before the sun come up." The car was jolted by the train departure and in the night the train chugged on toward Grand Junction, Tennessee.

The prisoners didn't change trains at Grand Junction but the car door was slid open to let in some fresh air to combat the smells of the unwashed. Supplies were taken on. The new guard swatted mosquitoes with a dated newspaper he had tucked under his arm. Another short thirty-six miles and they'd be in Corinth. The whistle blew, bells pealed, and the new guard tossed the newspaper inside the car and shut and locked the door.

"Anybody read here?" asked the grabber of the paper. No one responded.

"I do," stated Mo`ikeha.

"Well, I'll be," teased one of the prisoners. "This native of the Sandwich Isles can read. I didn't know they had grass hut schools."

Mo`ikeha gave him *stink eye* then proceeded to read the headline. "Memphis temporarily falls to Yanks. Citizens fight bravely." The men hooted and clapped. "Memphis may be under Yankee hands but once the Blue Bellies are stopped at Vicksburg, the Mississippi River will be again under Southern control". Mo`ikeha read on that citizens living along the *Mississippi Central* should be vigilant for Yankees trying to destroy the rail lines and report them to authorities. Mo`ikeha read the propaganda published by the Southern newspaper. The men snickered at the outright lies, their eyelids drooping as the Maui sailor hummed on.

Suddenly, everything became too quiet. The train came to a screeching halt. The guard peered down towards the engine. "What's up?" he yelled to the assistant conductor.

Cupping his eyes and peering down the line, the assistant conductor replied, "Looks like the tracks are blocked," he replied. As he said that, shots rang out from muskets. Grape peppered the cars like lead rain. Even the prisoners' boxcar was under fire. Mo`ikeha dropped to the ground like the others. Now face-to-face with the filthy floor, he hoped that he wouldn't be killed by Yankees, the very ones for whom he had endangered his life. Then, the train started rolling quickly. Obviously, the engineer was preparing to run for it. As the locomotive gained a top speed, it plowed into the trees and lumber that blocked the track. Debris flew into the air, raining down on the successive cars. Now, the rear of the train, where Mo`ikeha and the men lay prostrate on the floor, came under heavier fire from snipers. One of the detainees screamed. A bullet hit him across his cheek and ear. Another prisoner crawled to the stricken man, pulled out his bandana, and applied compression to his wound. It was a good twenty miles down the track and out of the range of snipers when the driver of the train stopped for an assessment of the damage.

The Conductor strode along the length of the train, surveying the damage to each car. When he reached the boxcar of the shackled travelers, he cursed them. "See what your damn Yankee friends did. They went and killed the engineer and the fireman."

"Who's driving the train, conductor?" called out the guard.

"I am till we get to the next stop. One of the other workers will stoke the boiler till then."

When The Conductor found out that one of the prisoners had been shot, he returned with clean water and bandages. "Take care of your own kind," he grunted. "One of you can play physician to the injured traitor." He tossed the gauze into the car.

The substitute operator pulled the targeted train into Corinth at daybreak. The bodies of the dead engineer and fireman were removed from it. The guard yelled at the prisoners to get out and stretch, warning them that he'd pick off any escapees if they decided to run. Soon the curiosity seekers of Corinth were crowded alongside the dead men eager to learn of the valor of these Southern fighters. They also gawked at the prisoners of war. A new engineer and fireman were summoned while a new company of young boys in gray uniforms boarded onto an open car, their destination—Chattanooga—via the train's next stop at Decatur, Tennessee.

At the Decatur station, the band of prisoners was boarded onto a new line—the *Memphis and Charleston Railway*—bound for Chattanooga. A fresh guard escorted two new men not only chained at the hands but at the feet. "Here, join your fellow Judases," he said as he pushed them into the car. The prison-bound riders were content that this car was cleaner.

Outside, more gray coats filed past and onto another open car. "Lookout Mountain and Missionary Ridge is gonna see some real fightin' in no time," commented one of the captives who had once lived in Chattanooga. Mo`ikeha believed that the rumor was becoming reality. General Grant was coming and a major battle was looming.

"What you fellers do," asked one of the original prisoners, "that you shackled up more then us?"

"They think we part of Andrews' raiders that stole *The General,* the locomotive from Big Shanty," said one of the two new prisoners.

"Well, were you?" asked another.

The other new captive replied, "We was gonna be but the two of us over-slept. Never made it. Somebody went and snitched that they'd seen us meeting with Mr. Andrews and turned us in. We glad in one way that we wasn't there. Might have ended being hung in Chattanooga like some of the raiders. On the other hand, we missed all the action. Those boys did some mean damage along the *Western and Atlantic Line*."

Hours later, the train pulled into the Gateway to the South. The station was crowded with Confederate soldiers coming and going. Military bees were abuzz, some leaving their hives for Vicksburg. The two open cars of whisker-less boys who jumped off the train were most likely headed to halt the advances of Grant. The twelve prisoners again changed trains. Mo`ikeha had lost count of the number of transfers. *The East Tennessee and Virginia Railroad* now had the privilege of ushering them to their inevitable stockades.

It was getting close to dusk when the train pulled into Knoxville. The boxcar was opened again. In the quiet of the night, the prisoners saw lanterns headed their way. "Here's a loser from Chickamauga," said the new guard who'd take the prisoners the rest of the way past Lynchburg and into Richmond. Like the previous captives, the man was shackled hand and foot. The new arrival had a difficult time climbing into the car so Mo`ikeha extended his hand and pulled him up. The starved prisoners were handed some loaves of hard bread and stale mutton. They downed it as if dining on a gourmet meal at the Astor House in New York City. Within minutes, the train left the station.

"Thanks for the boost, sir," said the new prisoner. "Let me introduce myself. Colonel Thomas Rose, 77th Pennsylvania Infantry." Mo`ikeha tried to make out his face from the splinter of moonlight that squeezed its way into the boxcar.

"Captain Mo`ikeha, Admiral Farragut's flotilla."

Through that same moonlight, The POW Colonel noticed a non-white face. "A black man. I thought you folks were restricted from fighting. Although I must say The President is going to have to turn to y'all if we keep getting whupped like we did at Chickamauga."

"Oh, I'm afraid I'm more brown than black. I'm a Hawaiian from `Īao Valley, Maui. I was hired by The Commodore to aid The Admiral in taking New Orleans."

"Word come late but I heard you whupped em good."

"We did, but they put a minie' through my shoulder. A black man helped me recover but soldiers came to take us away, him back to his master, and me to Vicksburg. I've been on the train for days."

The POW Colonel added, "Then, because you're an officer like me, we're headed for the same place."

"Richmond?" asked the Mauian.

"Libby Prison to be exact, a hellhole for officers. Your fellow prisoners on this train and enlisted men will be held until they squeal like pigs, some sent to Belle Isle, the others let go. No more rooms in the stockades. I hear at Andersonville, another hell hole, they got em outdoors in the heat of the summer, in the cold of winter." The POW Colonel whispered, "But if you're like me, they ain't going to hold us for long. I'll try everything to be a free bird. There are no rules in war."

Their journey on steel wheels had come to an end. They had reached the Capital of the Confederate States under the high command of General Robert E. Lee. Mo`ikeha bid a fond *aloha* and good luck to the rest of his fellow traveling captives as he and The POW Colonel were led away down Cary Street to their prison on the James River.

CHAPTER NINETEEN
Escape from Rat Hell

Although the prison was several blocks away, Mo`ikeha, for once, was excited to walk the distance on his own two feet, having grown tired of riding the rails for so long. The guard that met them at the train followed the two prison officers a few steps behind. "Now, remember if we're separated," The POW Colonel whispered, "we'll keep in contact. There is a way to get out of there and we'll find it. I just don't want to sit around and die."

"I'll be happy to be on your team, Colonel," replied Mo`ikeha.

They arrived at Libby Prison on what was called Tobacco Row, a number of warehouses that stored one of the South's cash crops. Mo`ikeha noticed, besides the armed guards around the building, that the establishment sign was still posted over the door—Libby and Son, Chandlers. It brought back a time several years ago when he worked in the chandlery in Lāhainā. But this ship supply building would not bring good memories. As their papers were exchanged, the official transfer made, and the prisoners unshackled, both Mo`ikeha and The POW Colonel scanned the scene, making mental pictures of what they saw.

It was a conglomeration of three buildings with three floors each. Mo`ikeha noticed two signs down the hall that indicated that, besides the guards living quarters where he was standing, the kitchen was at the middle and the hospital down at the other end. "Can't be," said the receiving guard.

"Huh?" said Mo`ikeha distracted from his evaluation of the structure.

"Says here you're a ship captain," said The Receiving Guard. "Can't be. They don't allow no slaves to captain no boats. Perhaps you belong down in the slave cellar. You kin have it all to yerself. No boys there now."

"Oh, this man's a captain," argued Mo`ikeha's companion. "He sailed for Farragut. He got captured outside of Vicksburg. They paid him to sail for them. They wouldn't have brung him this far if he wasn't important. They'd have killed a slave on the way." Although it seemed harsh, Mo`ikeha understood that The POW Colonel was preventing the Hawaiian from ending up in a dungeon by himself and being mistreated like a black man.

"Hmmm, a negro captain. Now I know for sure that Lincoln's gone batty. Well, anyway. We got no room, almost a thousand men here. So you's going to have to bunk in the kitchen next door with some of those other late comers from Chickamauga. And don't blame us for it. They says they building more like this so we kin sen' some from this overcrowdin'."

The POW Colonel beamed at Mo`ikeha. The Chickamauga men would be helpful in finding a way out. "You'all gonna help prepare and serve the meals since you're beddin' down on the kitchen floor," ordered The Receiving Guard. "When cookie come in, you help em. Oh, and by the way, no snitchin' of food and no standin' by the window. You gonna end up being bucked and gagged. There's some soup on the stove for late-comers. Here's yer blankets, one to sleep on, the other for coverin'. Most of the Yankees are asleep so hush."

The two newly arrived prisoners downed the cold soup, happy to put anything in their stomachs. And although the floor was hard, it was fortunately still warm from the evening meal. They fell asleep on the last available space near a small, unused, outdated kitchen with a crumbling fireplace that hadn't been lit in ages. A bigger newer hearth had been installed in the newer larger kitchen. The clickety-clack of steel wheels, a remnant of their long days on trains, rocked Mo`ikeha and The POW Colonel to sleep.

The downside to sleeping on the warm kitchen floor was that Mo`ikeha and The POW Colonel had to rise early so that the kitchen was free for making breakfast. A banging pan woke the kitchen dwellers. Adding to the chorus were the notes of moans and groans vocalized by the risers as stiff as the boards they slept on. The kitchen squatters' responsibility was to feed their fellow men. This morning, like most mornings, the hungry prisoners on the second and third floors were served first, the skimpy meal usually cornbread and coffee.

Now, as they distributed breakfast, Mo`ikeha and The POW

Colonel could take a look at the two upper floors. There were four rooms on the second and another four on the third. Each room, about one hundred by fifty feet, held about two hundred and fifty Union officers of all ranks. The recent arrivals were in shock at the packed sea of humanity. The POW Colonel leaned over and whispered, "There ain't enough room in here to swing a cat." Bathing troughs surrounded the sides of the room, the ceilings were low, and the windows were barred but open to the elements.

Mo`ikeha leaned over to hand a tin of cornbread and a cup of coffee to a prisoner. "You must be new here. We hope your people be free soon," said a famished captive soldier. "But I don't know about us. Most come in with pneumonia and sleep by the window. They only git worse soon."

Another prisoner added, "You glad you wasn't here in summer—it was stifling. Hotter than a billy goat in a pepper patch. The smell from sweat—whew!—makes you want to heave."

The POW Colonel rendezvoused with Mo`ikeha on his fifth trip upstairs. "I heard the cellar's got three walled sections. There's a storage room on the west end, a carpentry shop at the middle where local woodworkers occasionally toil for the prison, and an abandoned kitchen on the east end with the moniker—Rat Hell. No need to explain why it's called that." Mo`ikeha knew what was on the mind of his train-traveling friend.

The sun came out the next day. The prisoners took their lunch outside in the fenced area so that the barracks could be cleaned and deloused. The POW Colonel took Mo`ikeha aside and told him that he had to take a look at the rooms down in the cellar that night. He wanted Mo`ikeha to help lower him down the abandoned fireplace flue so that he could take stock of the situation. He shared with the Mauian that he had been getting up after everyone was asleep and with a butter knife had removed the mortar from the bricks and admitted that he was emaciated enough to fit down the passage.

The gods were with them that night. A late fall storm had been brewing since the late afternoon. The noise of rain, rolling thunder, and lightning flashes commenced shortly after midnight—the perfect cover for the scouting expedition. The POW Colonel would drop down from the first floor into the carpentry room in the cellar.

A third man from the 77th Pennsylvania watched guard at the kitchen door for any movement down the hall. With a small candle tucked in his trousers, The POW Colonel was lowered with a rope comprised of confiscated rags knotted thick. Mo`ikeha pretended he had a large *ulua* on the line and like the prized fish he was not going to let this one go. The POW Colonel dangled and descended onto the basement floor.

As he tried to adjust to the dark, he was shocked to find a dark figure standing there. "Oh, crap," he uttered softly. He thought it was a trap. The Confederates had been waiting for him.

A pelting rain outside muffled the questions of the man in the shadows: "Who are you? What are you doing here?" Through the slivers of lightning that squeezed its way into the dark dungeon, The POW Colonel was a little relieved to notice that the specter wore a shabby blue Union jacket.

"Well, I'd like to ask you the same thing. But since you haven't immediately killed me or dragged me out by the collar to be bucked and gagged, I'll presume we're doing the same thing: trying to figure out how to break loose from The Bastille," answered the man in the blue jacket. "Major A.G. Hamilton, Captain 12th Kentucky Cavalry." A bolt of lightning crackled and boomed, highlighting The POW Major's slightly visible salute.

"Colonel Thomas Rose, 77th Pennsylvania. I'm puzzled how you got here. It wasn't down my entrance."

"Down the fireplace flue, eh? I considered that for the great escape, but for the inspection I simply snuck downstairs near the end of the workday. When the carpenter had his back to me, I slipped in and slowly slid under this thick straw. I will reverse the process tomorrow morning."

The POW Colonel scraped around at his feet. He bent over to discover that the straw that covered the dirt floor was over a foot high. He concluded that a hole covered with straw would be a good hiding place for excavated dirt.

"The best room to dig out of is the adjoining one, the abandoned kitchen. Unfortunately, it's called Rat Hell," said The POW Major.

"I already heard about it. But perhaps it's the best cover if you can stand rats. I can't. I hope that we find some men with true grit."

Upstairs, Mo`ikeha heard footsteps and slamming doors. Someone was coming. He yanked at the cloth rope, a signal for The POW Colonel to return. "We'll meet again," whispered The POW Colonel to The POW Major. The Union lookout at the hallway door heard the guards talking about prisoners who would be arriving in the morning. A losing debate ensued about where they were going to be put. The POW Colonel slipped his way out of the fireplace and onto his floor bed before the evening sentry poked his head in the door. The cacophony of snores assured him all was well. After his footsteps diminished down the hall, Mo`ikeha helped The POW Colonel refit the fireplace bricks and smother the removed mortar with soot.

While breakfast was being distributed the next morning, some sixteen new prisoners arrived, all in bad condition, suffering from pneumonia, diarrhea, dysentery, and wounds, some minor, some quite serious. Trails of blood led to the hospital. The patients with minor ailments were shown their sleeping spaces on the floor. The remaining men moaned in pain while awaiting treatment by the one and only doctor. Prisoners were enforced to clean up the blood. Dirty mops slopped up the vomit and feces from men that couldn't hold it. The smell of death permeated all floors. By morning, six of the seventeen seriously ill men had not survived the night. The bodies of the deceased with blankets covering their faces were taken out and placed on the weed and dirt yard, their final resting place to be decided. Mo`ikeha was hopeful that the Confederacy was humane enough to send the bodies back to their grieving relatives and friends.

Seeing walking skeletons enraged The POW Major and Colonel even more. They would discuss further plans of escape at the reading of *The Libby Chronicle*—a newspaper written by the chaplain to bring a little levity and fond remembrances of the prisoners' lives before the war. While the minister read "An Ode to Lice" and "Life in Pennsylvania", especially dedicated to the captives from Gettysburg, The POW Colonel and Major plotted. Escape night had to be no later than February 9 when the moon would start waxing. They would work on getting a maximum of fifty freedom lovers to join them. They both concluded that tunneling was the safest solution. The POW Major would serve as the logistics man up top, The POW Colonel, the tunneler down under.

The POW Major believed that the easiest way was to burrow an underground passage out of the carpenter shop wall into an abandoned sewer line. The large pipe was big enough to squeeze a man and would serve as an already existing exit to the outside.

The first dig to the sewer pipe was several nights later. The lack of proper tools made the excavation difficult. The POW Colonel had stolen some chisels from the carpenter shop. An old wooden spittoon served as a scoop. Handmade hoes, spoons, and lifted kitchen utensils were not the best implements for excavation but there was little choice.

"Duck soup!" said The POW Colonel when the men broke through to the sewer line. But the excitement of a possible escape was short-lived. Polluted, smelly water began to gush into the tunnel. The men clawed their way out. The sewer line was not at all empty but filled with foul contaminated liquid. "Plug it up, quickly" whispered The POW Colonel. The men filled the open end of the sewer line and the tunnel entrance with dirt as fast as they could. "Plan Two!" he proclaimed softly. The Union colonel showed no signs of defeat. Mo`ikeha admired his optimism despite the setback. The POW Major was of the same mind when he was informed of the obstacle. They were determined to try something else. A second tunnel was started but the digging crew ran into a mass of buried logs almost petrified. "Plan Three!" Undeterred, The POW Major worked the third possibility.

It was getting close to Christmas. The days got colder. Mo`ikeha was losing weight like every other prisoner. He had finally acquired some paper and a pencil. He had traded them for his pen. It was worthless with no ink. He would write a letter to Ho`oipo and his parents and hope that they would receive it. He found out that a pro-Union socialite who lived a short distance from the prison was a reliable postman. She was quite chummy with the guards who missed the affection of their wives and girlfriends back home. Some of the sentries ridiculed her and dubbed her "The Prison Hooker". She often appeared at the Libby doors with food and extra clothing for the Union boys in need. Of course, the guards selfishly had first pick of the gifts, the remainder thrown to the captives. The POW Major said that she mailed un-scrutinized letters that were tossed into her breadbasket that had a false bottom. He also mentioned that she would help them divert attention on the night of the escape. Mo`ikeha wrote:

James River, Virginia

Dear Mother, Father, Sisters, Brother and my sweet Ho`oipo,

I just wanted to tell you that I am safe and well and have traveled all the way across the United States by all means of transportation: ship, stagecoach, and trains and am now residing near Washington,

D.C. Who knows? Any day soon I may run into President Lincoln, himself. My stay should be completed by Valentine's Day—a day on which I'll remember you, Ho`oipo. As soon as I have some free time, I'll be taking a ship from the East Coast and hope to be back home to celebrate Christ's Resurrection at Easter. I hope you got the money I sent you on my way up the Mississippi River. I've met some really great people along the way both black and white. It's too bad the war doesn't allow everyone to travel freely. Perhaps some day when the United States is at peace, we can visit all the places I've traveled. I hope all of you are well. I miss you, Mother. I probably won't be able to recognize my brother and sisters when I return. I hope Father is better after his fall and all is well in `Īao Valley. Ho`oipo, snowflakes have begun falling as I writing this letter. Lilinoe, the Snow goddess, is watching over me as you predicted. The pure crystal gift from Heaven is an appropriate omen that my departure from here will be successful. Miss *kālua* pig and *poi*.

Me ke aloha,
Mo`ikeha

Mo`ikeha was careful to phrase his letter without outright truth least they worry about him. After all, he was a short distance from Washington, D.C., he did hope to soon be free, and he did intend to catch a ship back home. He would drop the letter in The Socialite's breadbasket the next day. His stomach rumbled from the murky soup he had for lunch made from spoiled discarded vegetables from a local farmer, but his days of rotten meals were limited. A new dig would start the next night out of the sidewall of Rat Hell.

In the meantime, plans were made to retrieve as many parts of Confederate uniforms as possible. Though the gray was standard, a number of southern companies wore a variation of other colors. Also gathered were basic civilian dress and work clothes. The Socialite provided this service by supplying many of the now one hundred internees with the proper attire for blending into the streets of Richmond once they had escaped.

The new plan was simple. Three relief teams of five men would climb down the chimney flue on a special ladder made out of old blankets into the abandoned kitchen in the basement otherwise known at Rat Hell. They would dig vertically into the dirt floor and then horizontally about some fifty feet under a vacant lot and resurface in an abandoned tobacco shed inside nearby Kerr's Warehouse.

The earth removed from the tunnel would be deposited into a large hole dug in the dirt floor, the soil from that hole spread out over the length and width of the room. Straw was scattered over the dirt surface in case a prison guard should poke his nose in the room. The straw was also a cover for one man who would stay buried under it until the next shift was in place and an update given. These shifts were made unknowingly by the prison guards who shouted out the hours at the change of their duty.

Christmas and New Year's came and went like other days except that a piece of unidentified meat and hush puppies were served at the evening meal. Memories of the holidays in Hawai`i with the family and Ho`oipo and in San Francisco with the Emperor and The Irishman caused Mo`ikeha to grow melancholic, but he felt that someday soon they'd again be celebrated with joy.

With everything in place, digging finally began around the third week of January. The POW Colonel had some dedicated men. The dig was anything but a cakewalk. It was dark, fragments of candles the only light. It was cold like most basements but even colder in minus thirty-degree temperatures. The near frozen ground made it harder to dig with improvised tools. In the initial days of the tunnel excavation, the stifling noxious air caused dizziness so bellows from canvas bags were devised.

Finally, there were the rats. Mo`ikeha couldn't stand rats. Several times he had to abandon his post on the first floor kitchen chimney and substitute for one of the members of the team and descend into Rat Hell. He dreaded their squealing that was enough to drive a man insane. But the taste of freedom superseded the furry creatures. The bold rats ran across bodies excavating the tunnel. They reminded themselves that reaching the tobacco shed was the goal and not being disturbed by the brazen vermin. Never before did that old Hawaiian saying, *Kūlia i ka nu`u*, mean so much to Mo`ikeha. He and the prisoners were indeed striving for the summit.

The digging was going along well. There were occasional close calls. Sentries passed dangerously near to the east wall of Rat Hell. The night watch strolled ignorantly over the tunnel being dug just below their feet. Occasionally a tool would strike rock and cause a clang. The Confederate guards would halt at the noise. The diggers held their breaths and went silent under the presumption that the sound may have alerted the sentries. The guards routinely presumed it was the noise of some pretty hefty rats scurrying through the bowels of Rat Hell.

February 9, the escape deadline, was quickly approaching. The POW Colonel believed that the tunnel had spanned the fifty feet, but he wasn't sure. That night Mo`ikeha was sent into the tunnel to dig a small hole vertically to the surface. Mo`ikeha carried with him the remnants of an old shoe. He was told to push it through the small *puka*. Sitting over the breach, the shoe would look like another piece of rubbish in the empty lot. The next morning The POW Colonel looked out the window to spot the position of the shoe. It was only a few feet from the fence that separated the prison from the tobacco shed. The tunnel would break through to the shed that night.

Word was passed on stealthily by Mo`ikeha and several other officers that February 9 was a go. The number of escapees was now at one hundred and nine. They would walk out of the tobacco shed and into the streets of Richmond in groups of three. They were informed to get out of the Confederate Capital as quickly as possible and either head out to the peninsula or to follow Polaris, The North Star, and head toward Washington and back behind the safety of Union lines.

Nervousness filled the one hundred and nine on escape night. One colonel would make sure that there was no discovery of the breakout for at least one hour so that the bulk of the escapees could get out of Central Richmond. The Socialite would come to the prison asking the guards to find her runaway dog last seen on the banks of the James River. She'd tie Leonidas W. Polk along the shore and later "discover" him. The search party would help give the prisoners the time needed to get out of Richmond proper. The absconders strapped their clean civilian or military clothes on their backs inside their shirts.

"Go," whispered The POW Major. The POW Colonel climbed down first. He went through the tunnel and hefted himself up into the tobacco shed. Mo`ikeha came next. His arms and those of The POW Colonel would pull up one hundred and seven escapees. The POW Colonel routinely peeked out the shed door. As soon as the guard turned the corner and was no longer in view, three men would be released. At about 3:00 a.m. the last man, The POW Major, came through the tunnel. The three men wished each other luck. The rope ladder was hauled up and stripped back to rags and the fireplace bricks were replaced.

Mo`ikeha and The POW Colonel put on their civilian clothes. The Maui sailor spotted something on the ground that had fallen from one of the escapee's pockets. It was Ho`oipo's gift. He snatched the fountain pen, looked out the shed door and, as the guard turned the corner, he and The POW Colonel bolted down the street. The two traveled for a mile through backstreets and alleys. Mo`ikeha and The POW Colonel came across a clothesline with less shabby attire, snatched the new duds, and changed into them in the middle of a magnolia grove down by a stream.

Almost an hour had passed since the escape. Both Mo`ikeha and The POW Colonel were giddy with the thought of freedom. But it was all short-lived. The sound of boot steps and shouts were heard in the dark. "Prison break! Prison break!" echoed through the streets. As they turned the corner, a group of soldiers in gray ran toward them. "Stop!" they yelled. The POW Colonel and Mo`ikeha turned and ran in the opposite direction.

"There are bogs," The POW Colonel yelled, panting, as they ran side-by-side, "a mile down to your right. You'll be safer there." The emaciated battle-weary Colonel could not keep ahead of the healthy youthful Confederate soldiers or astride with the younger Mo`ikeha. He fell back.

"Run, Colonel, run!" pleaded Mo`ikeha. The POW Colonel waved him on, stopped, bent over to catch his breath, his hands on his knees. Two soldiers grabbed The POW Colonel and led him away back to Libby. "All that, to be captured," thought the saddened Mauian as his desperation directed him to the swamps. The depression caused by the capture was replaced with a fond respect for the man that had saved his life and the life of many others. As Mo`ikeha sloshed down into the bog, he became convinced that this would not be the last escape of The POW Colonel. He would continue to escape until he was really free.

The North Star was shining brightly. Freedom was thataway.

CHAPTER TWENTY
Follow the Drinking Gourd

His initial goal was the Potomac. Once he was there, he would feel better. But he wouldn't stop. His best intention was to make it to the Boston area, perhaps New Bedford, a shipbuilding town, where there would be more immediate opportunities in getting a vessel to the Islands.

He had been soaked traversing the swamps and streams to avoid detection. He had to get some dry clothes to avoid illness and find a faster means to get to Washington. He asked God for forgiveness as he ran again through several backyards searching for clotheslines for garments of his size. He declared "Eureka!" loudly in his mind. The gold was a perfect fitting pair of britches, a heavy-duty shirt, and jacket. As the neighborhood dogs sounded the alarm of an intruder, Mo`ikeha headed for the open road. After an hour he came upon a route with a well-packed surface, obviously a used thoroughfare.

He was nervous. What if a platoon of Confederates came his way? He planned to dive into ditches or behind shrubbery that ran the length of the side of the road. Traveling at night with but a sliver of a moon was to his advantage.

The rest of Virginia must have been asleep or off fighting the war. He encountered not a single soul for a good time when suddenly a wagon pulled out of a side road and caught him red-handed. Since it didn't look military, he continued to walk on. He just hoped it wasn't a white man with Confederate leanings. The moon had already sunk into the Eastern Sky but even with the *mahina* down, he believed the wagon driver was a black man.

"Going my way?" said a feminine voice. It was a black woman, perhaps in her twenties.

"I'm going to Washington," said Mo`ikeha.

"Me too," said the woman dressed like a man. "On your way to Heaven like me?"

"Heaven?"

"Say, you must be a greenhorn to the Underground Railroad. The Pearly Gates is code for Canada."

"Well, not all the way to Canada, just to Massachusetts to get home. By the way, aren't you afraid that they'll arrest you and send you back?" asked Mo`ikeha.

"They could do the same to you. You got a plan for the white man?"

"A plan?"

"Yeah, like me. See all them vegetables in back of the wagon? I just tell 'em that the massa from the plantation want me to take the produce to the boys fightin' for General Lee and I give em a fake name of the massa, and says, 'I's better git back for my massa lay the whip on me.' Hop on. You be my husban' if anyone ask—that is if you don't mind."

"Oh, I don't mind. As long as I get to Washington."

"And if that don't work, maybe this will." She showed him a pistol that she had tucked under her shirt. "By the way, where you gonna stay in Washington?" asked the young lady wagon driver.

"Oh, I'm just going through. Gotta get a ship out of one of the Boston area shipyards," replied Mo`ikeha.

"You got money to go travlin' on ships?"

"I don't have a penny. I'll work for my passage back home."

"Well, hop on. I'll be your conductor on the Freedom Train. I must say you the best looking baggage I ever took on," said the woman. As the couple traveled the road to the Capital, they exchanged their names and their backgrounds. He told her of the famous Polynesian sailor that he was named after. He revoked her old name imposed by the master and re-christened her *`Ānela*, Hawaiian for another angel who had come to his aid. He spotted a ring on her finger.

"I see a small band there. Is that your wedding ring?" asked Mo`ikeha.

The memory of life with her husband stilled her for a second. "Well, kinda. We's poor but we did jump the broom."

"Jump the broom?"

"A broom is laid across the entrance floor and the man and woman jump over it. Once over, they married. The one that leaps highest controls the house. We agreed to jump the same height so we be equal.

Well, anyway, my man found this ring later when he was cleaning up after a fire in the main house. It was in bad shape. The massa told him to throw it but my man filed it down and cleaned it. Looks like gold but not sure. But it don't matter. As they say, 'It's the thought that counts.'"

She continued about her former life. Her husband had died of malaria. She worked with him in cotton fields outside Atlanta all her life, but the plants had all dried up. There were food shortages because, along with the embargo, the planters had refused to grow edible crops to starve the North. The plantation owners thought that the South would win the war and that the European nations would break the embargo and come to their aid. She heard recent rumors that General Sherman was coming to Atlanta. His neckties, train tracks twisted around poles, showed he meant business. She wanted to be on the safe side when he came. She was going to stay a bit with her cousin, The Station Master, in the Union Capital. "I'm sure my cousin will put you up for a good night's sleep. It's a long way to Massachusetts."

She, like many others, was initially fooled by Mo`ikeha's color then fascinated by The Young Man's background and travels. She was amazed that someone so young had come so far to fight for freedom for black folks like her. "Here's another plan. If we get separated or the moon is cloud-covered or down," she advised him, "the dead trees will show you the way."

"What to you mean?"

"Moss forms on the north side of a lifeless tree. It's another good guide like the Drinking Gourd." She explained to Mo`ikeha the slave-version of the Big Dipper.

Soon other wagons came onto the main road, they too taking their produce to market, or were they perhaps like his female driver heading for freedom? By evening, they had reached the outskirts of Washington.

"I'm a bit lost. This paper with the directions to the Station Master's house has seen its day. Can your read this?" asked *`Ānela.*

"Looks like Uptown. Boundary Street," said Mo`ikeha squinting as he read.

"I'll ask someone." The streets were empty. She pointed to the name over the large building with columns—" Look. The Treasury Department. That's where they make all the money. For sure, we must be in the Capital."

Mo`ikeha smelled smoke. Then he saw flames licking out the windows of the brick structure next to the Treasury Building. Like that night on the Mississippi when The Admiral's ship caught on fire, Mo`ikeha's instincts went into full alarm. "Wait here," he said to *`Ānela*.

As he raced to the entrance of the building, he could hear the neighing of horses. It was a stable that was on fire. He raced around the corner and found a bucket and a small well with a pump. He pushed down hard a number of times and filled the container as fast as he could. When he returned to the entrance, more people had gathered to help. Mo`ikeha pushed open one of the stable doors but he couldn't get close to the stalls with the panicked horses. The flames nearly singed him. He flung the water in the bucket into one of the stalls as far as he could. He sprinted back to the pump several times, hoping to at least save one of the horses. But his bucket of water was like a raindrop in Hell. The owner, a tall lanky man, finally appeared at the scene. He called out the horses' names hoping they would bolt from the blaze, but only terrified whinnies came from the inferno. Then there was silence.

The man slumped down on the street corner, staring out into the dark night, a red glow at his back, a glaze of defeat in his eyes. In the distance, the clanging bell of a fire wagon made its way to the conflagration.

An exhausted Mo`ikeha leaned against the wagon wheel, trying to regain his breath as the engine doused the remnants of the tragedy. He splashed some water from the bucket onto his heated face. He was concerned about the horses' owner. A man whom Mo`ikeha presumed was the stable master put his arm around his saddened boss, the futility obvious. He eventually pointed to Mo`ikeha, then made his way to him.

"The President would like to thank you for your dauntless effort. He watched you from the window of the East Room as he prepared to race down himself." Mo`ikeha and *`Ānela* gasped.

"The President?"

"Yes, of the United States." Neither Mo`ikeha or *`Ānela* had ever seen a picture of The President. The Leader of the United States despondent on a curb was not exactly the image they had ever expected to see. Mo`ikeha walked over to The President.

"What's your name, son?" asked The President.

"Mo`ikeha," he responded, " I served as a ship's captain with Admiral Farragut down in New Orleans. I'm on my way home."

"Terrific job, you fellas did. I wish all the fronts were as well handled as Farragut and Grant on the Mississippi. This bloody war would have ended sooner. So what state you hailing from?"

"Oh, not a state, sir, the Kingdom of Hawai`i."

"Hawai`i? You're a long way from home, son. Sadly, I just received a communiqué announcing the death of Kamehameha IV and sent a letter of sympathy to Queen Emma and Kamehameha V a few days ago. Alexander Liholiho lost his son like I lost Willie. What makes me particularly sad is that my favorite horse in there was Willie's—it brought back many memories of my sweet boy." The President reached into his pocket and pulled out some silver coins. "It's not much, son, but I hope it will help get you home."

The President walked over to *`Ānela* in the waiting wagon and reached out to her with two hands. "You have a caring husband. Good night." He turned to leave.

"*Mahalo*...er...thank you," Mo`ikeha called out. The President turned, put his hand on his heart, wrapped his shawl tighter around his stooped body, and slogged up the stairs into the executive mansion.

Still stunned about their chance meeting with The President, the couple continued their journey. *`Ānela* had gotten directions to Uptown from some passers-by during the chaos. They were there within the half hour.

"Got only one bed in back. Hope you and your husband find it comfortable, " said the hospitable Station Master of the Underground Railroad. *`Ānela* and Mo`ikeha looked at each other with a look of 'beggars can't be choosy'. The two travelers bathed with real soap and hot water from the stove. *`Ānela* shed her man clothes and washed the dirt of the road from her face; a beautiful countenance and body were revealed to Mo`ikeha. He couldn't help see, when she turned her back to him, the lashes across her spine that had been inflicted by the master. He was angered by what an insensitive ogre he must have been.

"Hope you enjoy these greens, ham hocks, and muffins. The church give it to me for the baggage comin' through the station. So eat up." Dinner was served by The Stationmaster, a warm man who could play a mean banjo. After a couple of rousing tunes, the musician plunked a soft tune to ease the two travelers into the arms of Morpheus. During the night in the narrow bed, Mo`ikeha unintentionally placed his arm across the back of *`Ānela* and touched the scars of slavery. The angel that had brought him to safety felt his fingers skim her wounds but said nothing. They felt the hurt and heat of each other's bodies.

Mo`ikeha kicked his pants off the side of the bed as he turned. The clinking of the silver dollars in them woke the Maui sailor. It had been the most refreshing sleep he had experienced in a long time. He pulled the coins The President had given him out of his pocket. He had not looked at them the previous night, what with all the excitement. There were five of them and upon closer examination he noted that they were minted for The President's First Inauguration. He would try to save a few of them as souvenirs to give to his family and Ho`oipo. Someday he'd tell his children about when and why The President gave it to him. The remainder would pay for his train ticket and expenses.

"Good morning, my Hawaiian friend. Did you have a good night's sleep like I did?" asked *`Ānela*, already up. "Cousin's gone to work and left us some hotcake batter and some coffee. You up for some breakfast?"

"I sure am," replied Mo`ikeha. He yawned vigorously. "Oh, excuse me, mam, I didn't mean to be rude."

"Oh, tis natural. You got the yawn of runaway that been travelin' for miles. By the way, our hider, The Stationmaster, left me a little map on how to git to New Jersey Depot, not too far from here. The *Baltimore and Ohio Railroad*. No rush on your part, now that we safe here in the city. When you feel like you ready to go, I'll take you. You wash up, I'll mess with the flapjacks."

"Listen," said Mo`ikeha, having thought about it from the night before, "why don't you come with me. I have enough money for two tickets. They're not going to bother black folks with tickets. They'll think we're freemen."

"Well, I don't know…"

"*`A`ole pilikia*…er…No imposition. You gotta go through New York to get to Heaven. You helped me. It's the least I can do. Oh, by the way, what about your wagon and horse?"

"No problem. Borrowed it from a white man whose face was covered with a towel in a barbershop. We'll leave it here for the needs of other baggage who'll be moving along the Underground Railroad."

Several hours later, Mo`ikeha and *`Ānela* arrived at the real, not underground, train station. Three of the dollars from The President were used to purchase two one-way tickets including meals that would take him and his angel all the way to New York City.

"How are we going to survive after we get there?" asked his traveling companion as they boarded. "I got twenty-five cents for a flophouse for one night if need be."

"I dunno," said Mo`ikeha, "but as one of my Lahainaluna teachers used to say, 'God takes care of fools and little children', and I certainly qualify for at least one of the two." They found their seats and shared their dreams of freedom as they rolled by rail to Manhattan.

"Communipaw Station!" hollered the conductor. Mo`ikeha couldn't believe that they were already in New York. Their impressions of Baltimore and Philadelphia were from their train window. At the two stops, the couple stayed glued to their seats less they be snatched up by the onslaught of boarding commuters. After the train left the stop in Pennsylvania, Mo`ikeha had picked up a discarded copy of *The New York Times* and became absorbed in the newspaper. He was so hungry to read that he even read the want ads. He had finally caught up on the war that had kept him busily involved. *`Ānela* had taken a deserved sleep. Now at their destination, he awoke her from her peaceful slumber. He slid the paper under his left arm that held a small sack of necessities provided by The Stationmaster at the Washington, D.C. house. With his right hand, he clasped *`Ānela*'s arm. "Stay close to me, wife," he teased. She giggled like a newlywed halfway through a yawn.

New York travelers were directed to a ferry and for just a few cents each, the duo sailed across from New Jersey to Lower Manhattan. With only enough money for a cheap hotel, Mo`ikeha had given up on the idea to travel by train to New Bedford. There was no other choice. He was pretty sure that he could get a pay-for-work job on a ship in New York to get to Nantucket. He got directions at a newspaper stand as to the location of the harbormaster's office and the couple started walking. *`Ānela* had to stop every couple of blocks to catch her breath. "Are you okay?" he asked her.

"Those long days in the field, the distance I've traveled are catching up with me," she said. "But let's move on." They strolled about twelve blocks taking in the outbreaks of late spring here and there and reveled in the thought that they were actually in New York City.

Mo`ikeha climbed the steps into the harbormaster's office; *`Ānela* sat on the last step catching her breath. The workplace seemed as busy as the harbor itself—people coming and going like ships. He waited patiently. "Can I help you, sir?" asked the clerk.

"Yes. Do you have a ship headed to Hawai`i or California? I'd like to sign on as crew."

"No ships headed that way lately, too dangerous, what with raiders out there. The *Alabama*, the Confederate warship, just put a hole in a whaler headed back to New Bedford. She limped into port here. Say, wait a minute, that captain and his crew have been stalled here for a spell. Heard the captain say they're building a brand new ship in Massachusetts destined to sail to San Francisco when it's safe, maybe by this fall if this war don't drag on. Anyway, they're still recruiting some ship's company." He rummaged through the paper stack. "Here you go. A company in San Francisco is buying it, not as a whaler, but to haul sugar from Hawai`i for processing in California. Hmmm. Here it is… black gang, boiler room assistant, steward, swabbie, swabbie, swabbie…"

Mo`ikeha heard the magic word—steward. "Where can I sign up?"

"The Boston Pier office. Just continue down this street about a dozen blocks. Big red sign. Can't miss it."

"Thank you, sir," said the excited Mo`ikeha. "Oh," he stopped and returned, "I've got only a little cash. Do you know where I can find an inexpensive hotel in case we don't sail for a couple of days?"

"There's a lot of cheap hotels on Broadway," said the clerk.

"*Mahalo*," said Mo`ikeha. He exited the building with a bound as if he had been born again. *`Ānela* shared his joy and followed him down the street toward a position on the new ship.

He wished his life so far would have been as easy as getting a job as chief steward on the as-then-not-named ship to San Francisco. "We'll notify you, probably after Christmas when we'll be transporting the crew to New Bedford. You know where you'll be staying?" asked the clerk at the Boston Pier office.

Mo`ikeha became concerned about the uncertainty of a departure date. "Not yet, but I'll come by tomorrow with my address. By the way, why isn't the crew returning as soon as possible to New Bedford?"

"No jobs there right now. Small town, you know. The war has put a damper on commercial shipbuilding, too dangerous to be transporting goods and passengers with rebel raiders prowling the Atlantic and the Eastern Seaboard. But, I suggest you head down to the New York Shipyard. They're always looking for able-bodied experienced men, what with the war going on. Lots of your fellow crew members are working there—you can make a buck a day."

Instead of walking, Mo`ikeha spent ten cents to get a buggy to take him and *`Ānela* up to Broadway. He was concerned about her heavy breathing. Perhaps she was coming down with a cold. "There," he pointed, after walking a couple of blocks. "Let's try that one." The Alexander Hotel seemed a symbolic choice, the name of the man who had helped Mo`ikeha get into Lahainaluna. They registered with a cheery curly-haired lady, paid their twenty-five cents a day rent, and, as *`Ānela* settled in, the Maui captain headed for the New York Shipyard in search of employment.

By the end of the day, Mo`ikeha had picked up a job as a supply clerk at the shipyard. It was not the most exciting job but it was only for a short time and paid the same as the hard-working blue-collar shipbuilders. The job was also not so tasking as to wear him out by the end of the day. He would have time with *`Ānela* to take in the sites of New York City in the weekday summer evenings and on Sundays. He wrote a letter to Ho`oipo and his family that very night.

New York City, New York
United States of America

Aloha Ho`oipo, Mother, Father, Brother, and Sisters,

Wanted to get this to you as soon as possible. Here I am in New York City. Can you believe it? I'm writing this letter to you now because I'm intending to be here only for a short time. My present assignment is a job at the New York Shipyard. The pay is good. Since I'll be here briefly and mail takes a long time to get to the Islands, it would be best if you would send a letter to General Delivery at Mare Island in San Francisco. I should be there sometime in the spring on my way home. I'm in good health. People have been kind to me and assisted me in getting here. My final step to get home will be to take a ship to New Bedford, a town in Massachusetts near Boston. The ship to San Francisco will leave from there. I'll send you another letter as soon as I get to The Bay Area to give you a heads up as to when I'll be arriving home. Dying to get back to warm weather, ocean, and my beloved `Īao Valley. Brother should be finished with secondary school. I hope I can get home for his graduation, but, Brother, if I don't make it in time, be assured that we'll have a special celebration when I get back. The girls must be getting beautiful. I'll have to get rid of some of those good-for-nothing boys that must be chasing them. Mother,

Father, I miss you. Stay healthy. And, Ho`oipo, what can I say? I think of you every day.

Aloha nō
Mo`ikeha

His room at the Alexander off of Broadway was on the north side and the winds from that direction kept the apartment cool during the climbing temperatures of summer. It was comfortable and secure, their neighbors hard-working men trying to make it in Gotham. During his leisure time he and *`Ānela* toured many New York nooks and crannies, especially the neighborhoods like Brooklyn and the Bowery. When it got too hot, they strolled through the completed sections of the new Central Park. During the Indian summer, they ambled along the waterfront or under High Bridge. They went to gawk at the fashions and holiday displays in the big windows of The Marble Palace, a huge building that the inhabitants called a department store. With the extra change left over from rent, Mo`ikeha practiced what he had learned from The Emperor—to dine in the finest of restaurants even if a cup of coffee was the sole purchase.

*`Ānela*'s health started to wane. Her difficulty breathing gave way to coughing. She seemed to tire easy and fought several bouts of fever. She finally gave in one day to Mo`ikeha's insistence that he take her to the hospital to find the cause of her affliction. He took her to the poor man's section and, after a lengthy wait, a doctor saw her. Within twenty minutes, the doctor and patient emerged. Mo`ikeha approached him. "Are you her husband?" asked the physician.

Mo`ikeha for simplicity's sake nodded his head. The doctor was busy and blunt. "She has a heart condition, perhaps weakened by hard labor, perhaps inherited from her parents. Avoid strenuous walking and work and make sure she gets lots of rest." He hustled away.

Thanksgiving was just around the corner. Mo`ikeha and *`Ānela* shared their thoughts about how it would be difficult during the holidays without family or friends. They agreed that they would stay occupied that day. An opportunity arose. Three great actors, Edwin Booth, Junius Booth Jr., and John Wilkes Booth would be performing *Julius Caesar* at the Winter Garden Theater on November 25, a fundraiser for a statue of Shakespeare to be placed in Central Park.

With five dollars from his second week of pay, Mo`ikeha picked up a wonderful formal-looking coat as well as a pair of pants, a white long sleeved shirt, and a tie from a second hand store off Broadway. *`Ānela,* likewise, selected a fancy dress, coat, a big flowered hat, and lady shoes, types of clothes that she had never worn. They were now dressed to take in the *theatah.* They tried to fit in as they strolled into the theater foyer but felt stared at first, then invisible to the hobnobbing knickerbockers in their tuxedos and gowns. They were relieved, however, when the lights dimmed to dark. The audience, comprised of the white rich and the dark skinned poor, were then no longer distinguishable as such.

"It must be by his death: and for my part I know no personal cause to spurn at him, but for the general," said Brutus as he began his speech as to why Julius Caesar should be killed. Halfway during the delivery, Edwin Booth, who was playing Brutus, was uneasily distracted like the rest of the audience by the sounds of fire engines and clanging bells. The water wagons seemed to be getting closer. Mo`ikeha and *`Ānela* grew as tense as the rest of the audience as the smell of smoke seeped into the theater. The couple wondered if they should leave, but no one else was moving.

The actor's mantra, *The Show Must Go On,* was indeed applicable to the performances by the professional Booth brothers. They continued despite the din of vehicles swarming around the Winter Garden Theater. Finally, after a break between the third and fourth acts, the fire marshal entered the theater. "I beg your pardon, ladies and gentlemen, but there is no need to panic. There has been a small fire in the La Farge Hotel above us. I have seen to it myself that it has been extinguished. Again, I'm sorry for the inconvenience. Please enjoy the rest of the show." The sound of relief rippled across the aisles.

The audience's fretful attitude resurfaced as they heard more engines and bells up and down Broadway. By the end of the play, everyone had discovered that there had been a number of hotel fires in the immediate area. Mo`ikeha and *`Ānela* rushed back to their residence, pretty assured that only the hotels of the rich had been threatened and not their little hideaway.

The Sunday paper was plastered with the previous night's commotion. It was a plot by Confederates to burn down New York City. The method consisted of a combustive concoction of sulfur, naphtha, and quicklime that once exposed to air could start a major conflagration. The firebombs had been distributed by a number of

Confederate agents in a dozen established hotels. However, New York's Fire Department had received tips and either raced to quickly put out the fires or prevented them. Mo`ikeha shook his head. The war had even come to New York City.

In a city, even one as exciting as Manhattan, Christmas was equally hard. Mo`ikeha's mother had always told him that when you give *aloha* to people in need, you won't spend time worrying about your problems. So on Christmas Day, he bought a pocketful of penny candies and *`Ānela* baked some cinnamon bread. They went to the Seamen's Hospital and offered their simple treats to the wounded sailors, wishing them speedy recoveries. Mo`ikeha shared his experience on the Mississippi and his incarceration at Camp Libby and they, in turn, related their stories. A light snow dusted the city as they left the hospital and returned to their hotel room. Mo`ikeha noted that a most heavenly smile adorned the face of *`Ānela*.

During the night, she began to heave heavily. Mo`ikeha began to panic. *`Ānela* was in a cold sweat, a burning fever across her brow, her inhalations arduous. He tried to lift her, to get her out of bed, to dress her, to take her to the hospital, but her dead weight made it difficult. "Angel," he called.

With some effort, she slipped the little gold band from her finger. "Here, Mo`ikeha. No need for this earthly thing. Give it to your wife to be. How lucky she is." She looked up at him, smiled, touched his cheek, and whispered, "As for us, perhaps in another time, another place."

She took one difficult big breath and collapsed on the floor. As he bent over to listen to her heartbeat, he knew already what the reality was. Her loving heart was silenced. He bent over her body and kissed her tenderly. Tears dropped onto her breasts. Mo`ikeha reflected on how she was never going to get to Canada but that she would certainly be ushered into Heaven. This baggage had come to her final stop on the Underground Railroad.

On a cold winter's morning several days after Christmas, Mo`ikeha rented a small boat and bore *`Ānela*'s body in a pine box to the Potter's Cemetery on Hart Island, a mile off of The Bronx.

He borrowed a shovel, was shown the next available space, dug a hole, and lowered the simple casket into the cold earth. He stuck a small wooden marker into the dirt mound that read "*`Ānela*, Conductress—Made it to Heaven, December 25, 1864. Rest in Peace."

He then offered a prayer to his Hawaiian gods and Jesus to take her into their arms. On the ride back to Manhattan, Mo`ikeha's spirits were as gray as that overcast winter's day.

Word came after the burial, that the *Morning Star* would be taking the crew to the new ship in New Bedford at the end of the month, January 1865—some four years since he had left Maui. And on January 31, Mo`ikeha bid farewell to New York City.

CHAPTER TWENTY-ONE
West through the Williwaw Winds

The tattooed crew member had been staring at Mo`ikeha ever since they had left the Port of New York. Tattoos ran down the right side of his brown face, onto his shoulder, and presumably down the rest of his body. Anyone confronting him in a dark alley would flee in fear. Mo`ikeha suspected him to be Hawaiian. The man moved over to Mo`ikeha and sat down next to him. "E, you Hawaiian?" he asked.

"Yes. *Aloha*." He extended his hand. "Mo`ikeha from Maui."

"Kamau`a`ua, Moloka`i."

"I'm excited to meet a Hawaiian. I haven't seen one in a long time. How'd you get all the way out here?" asked Mo`ikeha.

"Working on the whaling ships. Ah, but whaling days almost *pau*. I dunno if you heard but some guy in Pennsylvania set up one drilling rig and hit oil. No need to go out on the ocean and risk your life. More easy for just poke the ground. The new ship we'll be sailing on out of New Bedford is for sugar. Because of the embargo of Southern ports and Hawaii's head start in the sugar game, the growing of *kō* will be where the jobs are. And you? How did you end up here?" asked The Tattooed Hawaiian.

Mo`ikeha started at the beginning, noting that he had worked four years ago on one of the first ships that brought sugar from Hawai`i. By the end of the tales of his sojourn and The Tattooed Hawaiian's whaling adventures, the *Morning Star* was docking in New Bedford. Aware of Mo`ikeha's limited cash from their conversation, The Moloka`i sailor invited his fellow Hawaiian to spend the days before departure at his place at the Seamen's Hotel. There they often broke into Hawaiian and talked about their homes, their families, and all the things they missed.

On Friday, the crew and townspeople gathered at the pier as the owner of the ship, his wife, the Mayor of New Bedford, and the captain officially christened the new vessel—*Kamehameha I.*

She was screw-propelled, four hundred tons, a hundred and eight feet long and twenty-nine feet wide. The swabbies were exceptionally excited to have a virgin ship to clean, the smell of oak, pine, metal, and paint still fresh. The owner's wife climbed up on a ladder, smashed a bottle of champagne against the bow, and elicited applause arose from the throng.

The Captain of the *Kamehameha I* made a special announcement. "We hoped that the war would have ended by now so that we could sail to San Francisco without harm. The bad news is that we're still not safe so the departure date has been put off until further notice. The good news is that the Confederates want to sit down and talk. I'm not a betting man, but I'll wager that we should be out of New Bedford as soon as Lee surrenders. Finally, you need not worry about a salary. I will put you to work preparing the ship for eventual departure while I hire the remaining crew." The Captain of the *Kamehameha I* mingled with his men, and then headed toward Mo`ikeha.

"I heard that you were a captain of a ship in Farragut's flotilla that took Forts Jackson and St. Phillip and that you were part of the great escape from Libby," mentioned The Captain of the *Kamehameha I.*

"I was," said Mo`ikeha humbly.

"Great work, son. Does moving down the ladder to Chief Steward on my ship seem degrading?"

"Not at all, Captain. Less *pilikia*, excuse me, trouble. Besides, the steward makes people happy, well most. And, of course, this is my last voyage. I'm tired of war. I'll be so happy to get back to the *lo`i*, the peace of the *kalo* patches...and get married."

"Well, luckily you have a cheery and excellent cook as a partner. Welcome aboard, Mō`ī . When we get to Hawai`i, I'll let you take her into Honolulu."

"I'd love that, Captain." The Tattooed Hawaiian brought Mo`ikeha and The Captain mugs of celebratory rum. They clicked their cups and simultaneously saluted their impending journey with "`*Ōkole Maluna*!" Their interpretation for The Captain—"Bottoms Up!"—dissolved into laughter and hearty swigs.

During the next two months, The Captain of the *Kamehameha I* kept his crew informed on the progress of the war. Cheers went up when General Sherman captured Columbia, when Charleston gave in, when Petersburg was conquered, and, finally, when Lee surrendered to Grant at Appomattox Courthouse. They would long last set sail on April 10, 1865.

On that morning, the throng from the ship christening in January gathered once more at dockside, this time to be on hand for the departure. The Hawaiian flag was raised. A sense of pride filled Mo`ikeha. He looked toward the sailor from Moloka`i and could see that he too was moved by his country's ensign.

Hours later they were heading far out into the Atlantic. There they had a chance of avoiding any rogue raiders, gunboats, or Confederate vessels running up and down the East Coast uninformed about the end of the war. They cruised southeast by east until they were almost a thousand miles off of the Carolinas. An undisturbed ship could make it to California in several months but with all this evasive zigzagging, it was going to be a much longer trip.

Spring, or *`Ānela*'s poetic synonym for it, "When the sun comes back and the first quail calls," had arrived out in the middle of the Atlantic like it had back on the continent. After the scullery and kitchen had been cleaned and everyone fed that night, Mo`ikeha climbed up to the deck to relax with the other men and his Moloka`i friend. "We'll be losing the moon soon, Maui Boy," said The Tattooed Hawaiian, gazing up at the heavens at the waning *mahina*.

"It's to our advantage to travel under the cloak of night. By the way, how many raiders were out there?" inquired Mo`ikeha.

"A lot," said The Tattooed Hawaiian, "but most of them were for specific missions. The *Florida* and The *Alabama* were the most notorious. Most of the time they burnt the ships they captured; the bonded ones were lucky."

"Bonded?"

"A promise to pay the worth of the ship after the war was over and The South had won. The captain of the pirates, that's what we called em, comes up with a figure for the cost of the vessel and its cargo. They were pretty hopeful, eh? The sad part is that most of the crews of captured whaling ships were forced to make a choice of being set adrift or joining the raiders."

"That wasn't much of a choice," responded Mo`ikeha.

"Sadly, many of the indentured crew members were Hawaiians like you and me. Our brothers were forced to work for a killing machine."

The clouds gradually evolved into large fingers that pointed West.

"Here," said The Tattooed Hawaiian, handing Mo`ikeha a gift. "I made this for your father, obviously a good man from the description by his son. It tells the story of your sojourn in miniature. Look. Here's Pu`u o Kamoa—the Needle, the *Makali`ī*, the train, The President, your two angels on the bowl, and my tattoo all along the stem. Mo`ikeha hugged the man from Moloka`i in gratitude for the beautifully crafted pipe. Their *wala`au* continued until the sun was slowly swallowed by the sea and the two men became talking shadows.

The Captain's claim of possessing the best cook was not exaggerated. The men showed their appreciation after each meal by rubbing their *`ōpū* and sucking on toothpicks. Mo`ikeha, as Chief Steward, was the beneficiary of all the good cheer and compliments. Before long the ship was running alongside Brazil. Within a month or more they would be nearing the tip of South America.

The spring to summer weather continued to do its part in a great sail to Tierra del Fuego and through the Straits of Magellan. The bone chilling Williwaw Winds were, by reputation, the major accomplice to the destructive rocky shorelines and towering waves that made the strait a graveyard of ships. Even icebergs sliced open vessels passing through. But this time, the passage was kind to the San Francisco-bound travelers. Mo`ikeha started to feel more secure as they rounded the Strait. The ships of the Pacific Squadron would be there to protect the *Kamehemeha I.* By the end of a dozen days, it was four hundred miles off the Chilean Cost heading north.

Then, one day in June, a ship flying American colors came into view. It was the *West Wind* of New London out of San Francisco returning back to her homeport on the East Coast. They pulled up close enough to do some gamming and to exchange mail. The First Officer of the *Kamehameha I* called out, " Have you heard? The war is over. The South has surrendered."

"We heard," shouted The First Officer of the *West Wind*. "When did you depart?"

"The tenth of April," bellowed The First Officer of the *Kamehameha I.*

"Unfortunately we have some bad news for you. President Lincoln was assassinated."

Mo`ikeha gasped like the rest of the crew. "How?" yelled The First Officer of the *Kamehameha I.*

"Shot while attending the theater. John Wilkes Booth, the

assassin."

"How could it be? The actor?" Mo`ikeha brooded. "How could he kill the man who had been so gentle and generous?" Mo`ikeha squeezed the two silver dollars from the President that he always kept in his pocket.

"Oh, and watch out for the *Shenandoah*," added The First Officer of the *West Wind*.

"What do you mean?" hollered the officer of the San Francisco-bound ship.

"She's a powerful Confederate raider launched late in the war. They came through the back door around Africa and Australia into the Pacific torching all commercial ships along the way, especially whalers taking oil back to New England for power and munitions. End of March they set three American ships and one Hawaiian ablaze at Ascension Island. They're continuing their wave of destruction, unconvinced the war's over. The captains of the captured and bonded ships reported that Captain Waddell of the *Shenandoah* wanted proof. Be on the look-out for em." They exchanged good luck to each other and sailed on.

The gods of the sea kept the *Kamehehameha I* safe all the way up the coasts of South America and Mexico. Mo`ikeha met The Tattooed Hawaiian on deck after dinner one night as they neared San Francisco. "We'll be in on July 3. There's going to be one hell of a Fourth of July celebration in The City, what with the war over. The Emperor is going to be extremely happy that the brother-killing-brother carnage has ceased."

"The Emperor?" asked The Tattooed Hawaiian.

"A most eccentric, yet lovable San Francisco character."

"You going to stay in San Francisco for the fall until the ship is fitted for transporting sugar?" asked the Moloka`i sailor.

"I can't wait. I'll try to get a job on the next ship back to the Islands. I need to take care of a little business here, then I'm heading home," responded his Maui friend.

The ship cruised through the Golden Gate and docked on the afternoon of the third. After taking care of business, Mo`ikeha bid his farewell to The Captain and crew and a special *aloha* to his tattooed brother from Moloka`i.

He grabbed his ditty bag, collected his pay, and headed to the office of the harbormaster to look for a position on the next ship out.

"July 25th the *Barracouta* sails to Honolulu," said the clerk behind the counter. "She's a British brig looking for crew. You interested in any of these jobs?" He pushed the list of crew positions toward Mo`ikeha.

The Maui sailor saw the words assistant steward on the list. "At what dock do I sign up?"

"Vallejo Pier. You familiar with it?"

"Quite," said Mo`ikeha, recalling the adventures of the shanghaied Irishman.

After signing up for the *Barracouta*, he took a buggy to the Emperor's Palace on Commercial Street. Nothing had changed about the Eureka Lodging, except that someone had cleaned the sidewalk in front, an assignment probably ordered by the Emperor.

"Back from the war?" asked the receptionist who remembered Mo`ikeha during his training.

"Yes, I'll need a room until I sail for Hawai`i on the 25. Still the same price?"

"Yes, hon."

"Is the Emperor in?"

"I believe he's having dinner at the Occidental Hotel on Montgomery Street, you know, between Sutter and Bush. He left about a half hour ago. You can probably catch up with him and his retinue: The Grand Chamberlain, Bummer, and Lazarus."

"Bummer and Lazarus?" Mo`ikeha wondered who the two new retainers were that had joined The Emperor's *cortege*'.

"Two homeless dogs, hon," said the receptionist. Mo`ikeha chuckled as he climbed the stairs, dropped off his ditty bag in his room, mopped down his hair, and headed to the Occidental.

He again laughed when he saw Bummer and Lazarus consuming their evening meal out of silver bowls in the restaurant foyer. When Mo`ikeha entered, The Royalty of Commercial Street were imbibing in a pre-dinner cocktail. The Emperor spotted Mo`ikeha. "Ah, look Grand Chamberlain, our Hawaiian prince has returned from the war. *Aloha, aloha, aloha*." The Emperor gave Mo`ikeha a big bear hug, The Grand Chamberlain a hearty handshake. "Is that whole war thing insane as I predicted?" Mo`ikeha nodded his head in agreement. "Hey, listen. You're just in time. We're about to have dinner. Here's a menu. Choose anything you want. They may even give you ice cream and cake like they give all veterans returning from the war." After Mo`ikeha surveyed the meal list and ordered, he shared his yarns about Mexico,

The Mississippi, Libby, and New York. At then at the end of the meal, at the end of the stories, and at the end of the ice cream and cake, the trio and their two best friends sauntered out into the brisk San Francisco evening.

"I'll be leaving for home in three weeks," said Mo`ikeha as the men walked back to the Eureka Lodge.

"Well, the Grand Chamberlain and I must give you some memorable experiences for a great send off. We may never see you again." There was some plausibility about The Emperor's words. When they reached the hotel, the flamboyant friend invited Mo`ikeha to join them the next day for the Fourth of July speeches at city hall where they would snicker at all the pompous promises. Then they'd head to the marina to enjoy fireworks just as they had done several years earlier.

A week passed and Mo`ikeha had one last thing to do before he left. One morning he caught the newly completed *San Francisco Train* to San José. About two hours later, he walked from the depot up the Alameda to the house with the big veranda where he and The Irishman had spent a peaceful Christmas Eve and Day.

He knocked on the screen door. The Mexican Girlfriend of The Irishman appeared. She was excited when she saw Mo`ikeha but then pulled back at the absence of The Irishman. "Can I come in?" he asked.

"Oh, of course, of course. *Bienvenido*, Mō`ī ."

"*Aloha* to you."

"Where is my *enamorado*?"

It was difficult to say the words, so Mo`ikeha let his eyes do the talking. A tear slid down his cheek. "He's dead, isn't he?" she asked.

Mo`ikeha nodded his head with great difficulty. "He told me to give this to you." He handed her the gold watch and fob. "It was his father's."

As she grieved, Mo`ikeha told her how brave he was, how together they had opened up the Mississippi, how their efforts had shortened the war, and how he missed his friend as well. She retreated to the bathroom for a short time where she wiped her tears and tried to remove the creases from her skirt. "Come with me to the backyard." She grabbed two bottles of homemade beer from the icebox and led Mo`ikeha out into the backyard. In the shade of prune trees and the warm inviting San José sun they shared their feelings of love for The Irishman.

Her farewell seemed final as Mo`ikeha boarded the three o'clock *San Francisco Train* from San José back to The City. As he watched the

World go by outside the train window, he mused on Shakespeare's lines from *As You Like It* that the class had read out loud at Lahainaluna: "The World's a stage, and all the men and women merely players: They have their exits and their entrances."

During the two weeks that followed, The Emperor and Grand Chamberlain, when they weren't fighting for the rights of Chinese in The City, took Mo`ikeha to sites from Oakland to Monterey especially Father Serra's missions along the way. But July 25th approached quickly and soon it was time to go.

The Emperor treated Mo`ikeha—The restaurant paid for it, of course—to a grand dinner at the Occidental Hotel featuring prime rib, ham, artichokes, salads, breads, and desserts. The Emperor presented a toast before the Maui sailor dived into his last prized meal for many days. "Now that you have tasted life, its sweet and sour flavors, let's drink to your future sojourns. May they be filled with peace and *aloha*. *`Ōkole Maluna*!" announced The Emperor, remembering the Hawaiian version of a toast used by his Maui friend.

The next morning, The Emperor and Grand Chamberlain greeted Mo`ikeha at the foot of the hotel steps. A cab to the Vallejo Wharf was waiting for them. The sun was already giving the Golden Gate its name. "A most grand day for sailing," said The Emperor.

"For you," said The Grand Chamberlain. He handed Mo`ikeha a little gift bag. "Some souvenirs, humble tokens to remember your time with us."

"Perhaps the Grand Chamberlain and I will travel to the Islands to visit you," added The Emperor.

"I wish you would. I'll show you all the beauty of my homeland and *`ai* some fresh *poi*." Mo`ikeha turned and walked up the gangplank, occasionally turning and waving. Within the hour, the *Barracouta* was sailing toward The Sandwich Isles.

That night, after dinner, with the sailors singing a few ditties and doing necessary mending, Mo`ikeha opened his package. It contained the April 9 special edition of the *Daily Alta California* with the banner headlines—'War Ends!' There was also a gold coin minted by The Emperor's nation with a depiction of his executive mansion, the Eureka Lodge, on one side, and, on the opposite, an engraving of Bummer and Lazarus, his dogs, circled by the title *Emperor of the United State and Protector of Mexico*. The third souvenir was a can of San Francisco fog, with a note from The Emperor. "War, gold, and fog—all fleeting. Memories and love in our hearts—forever. The Emperor."

Mo`ikeha had never worked on a British ship before. They were organized a bit more rigidly than American vessels. However, everyone on the barque was cheerful and professional. Shortly after they left port, The Captain of the *Barracouta* gathered the crew on deck. He told them that there were reports that the *Shenandoah* was still out prowling in the Pacific. He shared some statistics of her size and power: two hundred twenty-feet long, thirty-five feet wide, one thousand one hundred and sixty tons, a single propeller, eight hundred and fifty horse power, three masts, and fully rigged. The impressive numbers of the monster boggled Mo`ikeha.

Concerns about an attack dissipated with the unending chores by the crew. Mo`ikeha, himself, was fully occupied with the feeding of the sailors. British food had the international reputation of something not to be desired so Mo`ikeha's expectations were not high. None of the mariners complained, though, a good sign that mutiny was not immediately on their minds.

A week passed peacefully for the around the world trip via The Hawaiian Islands back to Liverpool. On August 2, a crew member spotted a ship tailing the *Barracouta* and reported it to the First Officer who in turn ran it to The Captain. "Full speed ahead," was the order. The rear ship was persistent and gaining. It was at this point that The Captain presumed the worst. It must be the *Shenandoah*. His feeling was confirmed when she unfurled her Confederate flag. Finally, as it swung alongside, the pursuing ship fired a shell over the bow of the *Barracouta*. Her captain felt it foolish to run any farther.

After she came to a halt, a dinghy was launched from the *Shenandoah*. "Please present your papers!" the sailing master from the Confederate ship demanded as he came aboard the *Barracouta*.

"What is this all about?" asked The Captain of the *Barracouta*.

"Under order of Robert E. Lee and The Confederate States of America…"

The Captain of the British ship halted the order mid-sentence. "Before you go wasting your breath, I'd like to announce that there are no more Confederate States of American. The North has won."

The Sailing Master of the *Shenandoah* laughed. "A few other ships have tried that one to get out of the situation. They had no proof."

Mo`ikeha raced to his cabin, grabbed one of The Emperor's

farewell gifts, and bolted back alongside The Captain.

"Proof? What kind of proof do you want? My whole crew can attest to it."

"Your whole crew could be liars."

"Here, Captain," said Mo`ikeha. He slipped him the special edition copy of *The Daily Alta California*.

The British Captain looked at the headline and smiled at Mo`ikeha. "Is this good enough?" He pushed the paper into the *Shenandoah*'s Sailing Master's face.

The Sailing Master's jaw sagged. He stared at the headlines, read the stories quietly, and re-checked the newspaper back and front to make sure it wasn't a forgery.

The Captain looked over to the *Shenandoah* at the crew gathered at the rails. "I see dark skinned men on-board your ship." Mo`ikeha looked over and believed he saw Hawaiians among them. "Obviously, they have been impressed into service," continued The Captain of the *Barracouta*. "Because the war is over and the South has surrendered, you will hand over to us any crew members threatened and forced to serve on your ship."

The Sailing Master said nothing more except "Carry on" faintly. Mo`ikeha snatched his souvenir from The Sailing Master before he went over the rail. When he re-boarded the *Shenandoah* and relayed the news from the *Barracouta*, the Confederate crew's reactions quickly evolved from disbelief to a din of confusion. The babble formed like a giant wave that eventually crashed on a shore, its spume sliding across the sand in silence.

Within the hour, the first of two dozen impressed crew members changed ships. The Captain of the *Barracouta* asked Mo`ikeha to assist the Hawaiians, most of whom they eventually found out had served on the whaler *Abigail* that was torched at Ascencion Island. The Confederate raider's manifest listed them as William Bill, John Boy, William Brown, James California, James French, Alec Givens, Joseph Kanaka, Joseph Long, John Mahoa, and Cyrus Sailor. The nicknames supplied by the Captain of the *Shenandoah* indicated the lack of respect for those who wanted to live and serve on-board rather than be put in chains in the belly of the ship or abandoned on some God-forsaken atoll.

The *Shenandoah*'s plans to wreak havoc on San Francisco were immediately scuttled. Mo`ikeha looked back several times at the

Confederate raider until it was a mere blot headed for asylum.

The journey home after the scary encounter with the *Shenandoah* was rather peaceful. Oh, there were the usual squalls that tossed the ship about but nothing of significance. The Pacific Ocean was again living up to its name. They gammed with a few commercial ships headed for the West Coast who were excited that the war was over and that the threat to their livelihood had been finally eliminated.

Seabirds were appearing more frequently, a sign that the Islands were near at hand. The day came that Mo`ikeha had been looking forward to for a long time—the sighting of Diamond Point guarding the gateway to Honolulu. The warm summer breeze wafted Mo`ikeha's face. He inhaled the *`ehu kai*; the scent of the sea invited him home.

How Honolulu had changed in only four years! From the ship he could see more sidewalks, more streetlamps, and more buildings. Ships to haul sugar bound for California had replaced many of the whalers.

The ship docked at dusk. After taking care of business, Mo`ikeha thanked The Captain of the *Barracouta*. He, in turn, thanked Mo`ikeha for the quick thinking by providing proof to the *Shenandoah*. The last ship of the day to Maui had already sailed. He bought a ticket for the following day and headed for a port side hotel. He would leave Honolulu for Maui early the next morning. Again, and hopefully for the last time in a long time, he would sleep on a lumpy mattress. The slapping of lines against the masts outside his window and the lapping of waves against the piers in Māmala Bay lulled him into a well-deserved sleep.

CHAPTER TWENTY-TWO
Ho`i Hou i Ka Iwi Kauamo`o

Mo`ikeha remembered an old saying, *Ho`i Hou i Ka Iwi Kuamo`o*, as he boarded the S.S. *Kīlauea* to Maui. It literally meant returning to the backbone, figuratively that he was coming home. The morning couldn't have been more gracious. The purple streaks of dawn had gloriously dissipated over the Wai`anae Range, replaced by rich blue skies that he hadn't peered at for a long time, the harbor as placid as a well-protected fishpond. He had sent a letter from San Francisco before he left but there was no guarantee that they would receive it before he returned. Anyway, it would be fun to surprise them all.

A short time later they were passing Moloka`i, where The Tattooed Hawaiian had been born, Lāna`i in the distance where he and his ten year old cousin had sailed a dinghy much to the surprise of local fishermen, and, farther in the distance, Kaho`olawe and Molokini, the latter where he vied with the boys for the favor of Ho`oipo. The bouncy broiling sea of the Moloka`i Channel was crossed and replaced by the smooth waters fronting Lāhainā.

"Why aren't those boys in school?" he thought when he saw a band of young *kanaka* cutting back and forth on their *koa* boards on the combers rushing in toward Lāhainā Harbor. He had forgotten for a minute that these were the final days of summer vacation when, like himself years ago, long days were spent in the surf, the final serious celebration before delving into geometry and Shakespeare. A benevolent sun highlighted his alma mater, Lahainaluna, up on the hill. He wiped a tear, not of sorrow, but of happiness that he was finally back home with his loved ones.

He grabbed his bag and made his way onto the transit. As they moved toward the shore, Mo`ikeha noticed that nothing much had changed except that more sugar cane fields had sprung up. He walked through town looking for Ho`oipo's quilt shop. A lady carrying breadfruit pointed to the store with her free pinky.

Mo`ikeha peeked in the window and admired what Ho`oipo had done to the former grog shop. He spotted her busy re-rolling material, her back to him. He took out the pen that she had given him, the pen that had traveled thousands of miles.

"I think you dropped this, Miss," he casually said.

She turned around to the voice and stuck her hand out to fetch the fallen object. She looked at the pen in her hand for a second, a small crease of perplexity formed across her forehead. Upon realization, she screamed. "Oh, my God! Mo`ikeha! Mo`ikeha!" She cried out his name several more times.

A passer-by dashed into the shop thinking the proprietor was in danger. "Shall I call the constable?"

"Oh, I'm sorry. No problem," said Ho`oipo. "My love has come home." The passer-by smiled at the happy announcement and left.

Ho`oipo kissed Mo`ikeha, holding his face and staring at him. The boyish looks had evolved into a man's countenance, his eyes now filled with the experience of the world, his chin and cheeks covered with the stubble of virility.

Mo`ikeha stared back equally at the beautiful young woman. Her imbued self-esteem and confidence was evident. Her days without him had forced her to be independent. "I haven't finished your quilt that I started over four years ago," she laughed. "Now, I can add the last granny square to the other symbols of your trip. There's so much to say. Where do we begin?"

"Let's start with breakfast. I'm hungry."

"Oh, I'm sorry. You poor boy...I mean man. You must be famished. Let's go to the little café by the coconut grove. They make great flapjacks. After eating, we must leave for `Olowalu to see my parents. You can take my wagon to Wailuku, or better yet, can I go with you, maybe stay?"

"Of course."

After breakfast, Ho`oipo flipped the *open* sign in the door window and jumped on her wagon. The couple headed out to `Olowalu. Memories of that valley flooded his mind. He swore he could hear the *kapa* beats that drew him to Ho`oipo.

"Father! Mother!" Ho`oipo yelled. "Mo`ikeha has come back from the war!"

Ho`oipo's parents raced out the front door. "Mo`ikeha, so good to see you again. Look at you, a man all grown up, and healthy. Come sit down, tell us all about it."

"Father, let's save that for another day. I need to get our world traveler to Wailuku, to `Īao Valley. Is it okay to take him home? I'll stay there a couple of days with him and his family." Ho`oipo turned to Mo`ikeha for approval. He smiled as he nodded his head. She added, "Perhaps you'd like to take a good bath and a shave after traveling so long."

"Oh, I've been days without one over the last four years. Luckily, there weren't any ladies on the mission. They would have thrown us overboard because of the stench and bristles, but since I'm back to civilization…"

"Here," said Ho`oipo's Mother. "A fresh towel and washcloth and a clean razor."

Ho`oipo packed up her clothing and personal items as Mo`ikeha bathed and shaved. The war was washed from his body. Soon they were on the road to Wailuku.

The view from the *pali* never looked more beautiful. He imagined himself diving off its precipice into the deep blue sea, the winter home of the humpback whales. Mo`ikeha felt that he had new eyes. Haleakalā stood there patiently, as if waiting for her native son to return.

They finally turned left past the two story Ka`ahumanu Church. Ho`oipo commented, "Reverend Alexander's been gathering money to build a New England style church. The congregation has outgrown its present home." The name Alexander brought back memories of him and *`Ānela* in New York. "What's the matter?" asked Ho`oipo, noticing that Mo`ikeha had grown somber.

"Oh, nothing," he mumbled.

"Mo`ikeha, the only knowledge I have of war is in books. I'm smart enough to know of its horrors. If you don't want to talk about it, I understand. You're starting anew. Let's talk about the good experiences you had and ignore the atrocities you might have experienced. Let's talk about the future. Of course, when you want to share the traumas you faced, I'll be here to listen." Mo`ikeha grabbed her hand. She had said what he wanted to hear.

The wagon rolled down the hill to his home. From a distance, he could see The Twins throwing *kamani* pods at each other, until one cried. He was amazed at how tall and beautiful the girls were.

"Mama, someone's coming with Ho`oipo," yelled one of The Twins spotting the wagon.

Mo`ikeha's mother came out to the porch, squinting to see who the visitor was. The Twins ran out to the entrance. "Maybe Ho`oipo has a new boyfriend," exclaimed the other of The Twins, recognizing her wagon.

"I don't think so. Ho`oipo has promised to love Brother until he came back," said her sister.

Mo`ikeha jumped off the wagon as soon as they reached the house. "What? You don't recognize your older brother?"

The Twins were shocked. They squealed with delight and ran to him, squeezing him in the middle. "Oh, Mo`ikeha, you look so handsome. We missed you." They hugged Ho`oipo then raced up to the porch with the good news.

"Mama, Mama! It's Mo`ikeha! He's home at last." The girls raced back to lead their brother to Mother.

"Come," said Ho`oipo. "Leave Mother with our returning sailor. Show me that new puppy you got." The girls grabbed her hands and led her to the doghouse.

Mo`ikeha stood at the base of the stairs transfixed on his dear mother. He climbed slowly, noting that she had a few more strands of white hair but was still as beautiful as before. The peace of the valley had kept her young. She hugged him, trying to hold back the tears of joy. Then she turned serious. She softly said, "Did they hurt you, Son?"

"They tried to, Mother, but I'm a tough kid from Hawai`i. I survived."

"When you left you were a mere boy. Look at you now, a handsome strapping man. We're so happy to have you home."

"Where's Father?" asked Mo`ikeha.

"Here I am," said The Father. He hobbled up to Mo`ikeha, supported by a cane.

Mo`ikeha noted his halting strut and gingerly hugged him. "Aloha, Father. I'm so happy to see you. I missed the days when we would *wala`au* in the *lo`i*. What happened? Why the cane?"

His mother intervened. "Remember when we wrote you and said that Father had taken a bad fall on the rocks in the stream? We had hopes that his fracture would get better but Father had severely injured his backbone."

"Oh, I'm sorry to hear that." He gave his father another hug.

Mo`ikeha's Father dismissed the pity. "Well, I'm not dead, you know. I just can't work the *lo`i* anymore. The taro patches are now for others to work. The owner of the dry goods store in Wailuku has given me a job as a clerk so I'm still bringing in some money."

"I presume Brother will take care of the *kalo* patches. By the way, where is he? He must be taller than The Needle."

"Good news," said his mother. "Brother did get his diploma from Lahainaluna. Sorry, you missed the graduation. We did get your regrets from New York City. Ho`oipo's contact with the monarchy helped get him a job as one of King Lot's Royal Guards. You should see him, so handsome in his uniform. He wants to eventually join the military. He was so enamored by the dedication and service of his older brother."

Mo`ikeha pondered what he had ironically done. He had inadvertently encouraged his brother to become a soldier or sailor. How Mo`ikeha wanted to tell him about the barbarity of war and its effects that resulted in the injury and death of his friends. But he halted his criticism. It was his brother's life. Mo`ikeha had made his own choices. Now it was his brother's time to make his—whether they were sensible or foolish. All he wished to tell him when he saw him was to stay safe and come back home alive.

"Perhaps you can get down to Honolulu to see him soon. If not, I think he should be home for Christmas," said The Father.

"It would be fun to have a beer with him."

"So Father, who is in charge of the *lo`i*, what with your injury and Brother's absence?" asked Mo`ikeha.

"The King has hired Mr. Silva from Waihe`e to take care of it. He is a hard worker and knows his *kalo*. He's from Madeira, another island, out in the Atlantic Ocean. He stole away on a ship taking on water at Funchal, married a Hawaiian woman when he got here, and has produced some *taro* that rivals the sweetest from Ke`anae."

"Well, now The King's grower has me. We need to maintain our *kuleana*. I'll do everything to maintain it, Father."

Agitation came from his mother. "Oh, my God. Sorry. Sorry. The sun is going down and no dinner," exclaimed his mother as she scurried off to the kitchen.

The Twins and Ho`oipo returned. "Is it okay if I spend a couple of days with you?" Ho`oipo asked The Father. The Twins gave their approval.

"Of course, Ho`oipo, anytime," pledged The Father. "You know that someday you'll officially be part of the family. Right?" He turned to Mo`ikeha for a response. The Son responded with a poker face that suggested that decisions like that would be talked about later.

Within two hours with the help of all, a most lavish welcome home banquet had been spread out: grilled *`ōpakapaka*, sweet potatoes, poi, long rice, and sweet buns brought over by The Neighbor's Wife after The Twins had raced over to her house to share the good news.

The two men sat in the parlor sipping brandy that The Father had saved for visitors. Before The Neighbor's Wife entered the kitchen to help with the dishes, Mo`ikeha asked her how her husband was doing. She immediately turned sullen and mumbled something about "… letting your father tell you."

"Did I offend her, Father?"

"The Neighbor was taken away, Son, by order of the King. The Neighbor contracted *ma`i Pākē*."

"Chinese Sickness? What is that?"

"Leprosy, Mo`ikeha. The disease was spreading so fast that the afflicted have been taken to Kalaupapa on Moloka`i. Sadly, the poor people are on their own. The only way to it is by ship or down the treacherous mountain trail by mule. A boat occasionally drops off supplies and transfers letters. The Neighbor has written that after months of confusion, the industrious have begun to build wooden shelters on their own and started growing crops. The lazy or depressed sit under canvases, moping during the rains and occasional cold. Many family members believe that the isolation was a drastic measure but the King has promised to send some dedicated people there to tend to their health and needs."

The noise of pots and plates being washed and wiped finally ended. The women dried their hands and joined the men. "I'm so sorry," said Mo`ikeha to The Neighbor's Wife. "I've seen disease and death in my travels. Sometimes life deals us a lousy hand. I'll help you in any way I can to make your husband's life better. Perhaps I can write a letter to the King and demand that he recruit some angels, you know, those heroes out there who are willing to dedicate their lives to the afflicted."

She reached out and hugged Mo`ikeha and whispered, "*Mahalo*. Good to have you back." She headed to the door. "Good night, everybody."

"Did you bring back anything for us?" asked one of The Twins.

"Daughter!" complained Mother. "I swear you're acting like some greedy white people I know. Jesus talks like a true Hawaiian when he says that we should not get caught up in material things."

"Oh, it's okay, Mother. I did bring back some souvenirs." Mo`ikeha grabbed his ditty bag. He pulled out the coins and handed one to each of The Twins. "Put these safely away. They were given to me by The President."

"President Abraham Lincoln!"

"One and the same. I'll tell you all about it tomorrow."

"Father, here is a final edition copy of *The Alta California* with the 'War Ends!' headline and a pipe specially carved just for you by a fellow mariner from Moloka`i."

"For Brother, a can of San Francisco fog and a coin from The Emperor...to be delivered."

"You met an emperor?"

"And his Grand Chamberlain." The Twins gave their brother the look of disbelief.

"For Mother, a gold cross and chain from Mexico City." She smiled. A tear formed.

"And part one for Ho`oipo, a picture of her boyfriend taken in the first photography studio in San Francisco." He handed her the photo.

"You look so handsome and so serious in this picture," Ho`oipo commented. The Twins gathered round to see and giggled. It was passed on to the parents. "And what about part two?" asked Ho`oipo.

"To be given tomorrow after we take a leisurely hike up the valley."

"As good a hint for everyone to get to sleep," said Mother. "It's been a long day for Brother. I'm sure he's ready to take in the peace and quiet of `Īao."

In the middle of the night, Mo`ikeha got up to use the *lua*. He was attracted by the red glow of his father's new pipe coming from the porch. "Is that you, Father?"

"Yes, Son. I hate to smoke with this wonderful work of art, but at least you and your adventures will always be remembered every night when I come out to the porch." Suddenly, a sound came from the *kukui* grove across from the *lo`i*. "Can you hear it, Son? It's the *pueo* calling. You remember, I told you when you were a boy that the owl comes on special occasions, like tonight upon your return. Good to have you back and safe, Son. Good night, Mo`ikeha." The light from the puff highlighted the smile of pride on his face.

"Good night, Father."

The next morning after breakfast Mo`ikeha invited Ho`oipo to walk up the valley. The sun was shining brightly on the *kukui* leaves, spinning, as he remembered them. They strolled past the dam, the stream with barely a trickle as it was each summer. But soon, come winter, rains would fill and flood the parched bed.

Ho`oipo stopped Mo`ikeha. "You said you were hurt in the shoulder. Let me see it." She unbuttoned his shirt, staring at a more impressive physique than the boy who left after graduation. She ran her fingers across the scar. "It looks like a bullet wound."

"I didn't want to worry you. But, I'm as good as new. It's now a thing of the past."

"With your wound you've now earned your family name—*Pūkoko*." She kissed his shoulder. She held onto his shirt as they continued their walk, arm in arm.

They reached The Needle, the stone representation of the merman that had fallen in love with the beautiful `Īao, daughter of Maui. "No better place," said Mo`ikeha.

"For what?" Ho`oipo questioned.

"You forgot what I said last night? Part two of gift giving." He pulled out the ring given him by *`Ānela*. He slipped it onto Ho`oipo's finger, a perfect fit. "Ho`oipo, in our sacred valley, under the sacred bones of the *ali`i* high on the cliffs, in our *kuleana*, I beg you to be my wife."

"No begging, Mo`ikeha. Yes!"

The valley echoed with several refrains of "I love you, Ho`oipo!" and "I love you, Mo`ikeha!" as the lovers headed back down the trail.

KAONA

LEHUA MAU LOA

Everlasting Lehua

Dedicated to Kino`ole and Larry Speiler,
in memory of Henry Ho`olulu Pitman
who served in the American Civil War

`Ōla`a is darkened by the smoke of the land
Even Pele mourns with the red *lehua* rain
The young one weaves his way through the dogwood maze unlike the peaceful paths through Pana`ewa
The rain forest named by the demigod
Who protected him in his homeland
But a distant battle will shape the *kapa* beaters
Into weapons and gunwales
He will fight; he comes from great warriors
Protectors of Pai`ea
The red star reflects the *koko*
Hilo is proud
Come sew the first buds of *lehua*
The first buds of mayflower
Come make a *lei* for his sacrifice.

E INU O KA PŪNĀWAI MAU LOA

*Drink from the Eternal Spring

Dedicated to Edna Ellis in memory of James Bush
who served in the American Civil War

How cruel Hawea
How cruel war
The twins tormented by jealousy
The *koa*—the indignities of the color of skin
Live on, oh children
Live on, *e koa*
The siblings and the warrior share survival.
Eat the edible flowers and fruits
Eat the leaves and tender shoots
Eat the grasshoppers and the wild fowl
Ola—for another day.
Swim through the tunnel from Kanawai
The water spirits make safe passage
Burst out from under the *hala*
Behold the *punahou*. We are safe.

When you see the Wa`ahila Rain
When you see the mountain mist
Embracing at the heights of Mānoa
Remember those who struggled, fought, and survived
And now drink from the eternal spring.

*based on the Legend of Ka Punahou—The Spring of the Twins.

KA LAUHIHI

The Plumbago

Dedicated to the Memory of Joquina Martins Texeira

Mauna Kahālāwai dominates
The last rays punctuate Maui's western peaks
Soon purple shadows will stain verdant valleys
Nature's pastel palette adds an imperial hue
The *lauhihi*
A feminine compliment to sea and sky
The powder blue of tranquility
O intertwined hedge, magnet to *pulelehua*
A rainbow parade of common white and monarchs flutter past
To balance in the softness of her peace
O foreign flower
Your home is here now
Drought, wind, and heat are defied
You remain tolerant
Drink of the water not of battle
Drink of the pure from Violet Lake
Spill, sacred *wai*
Come nourish, flourish in the rich soil of Wailuku.

KA UA HO`OPALA `ŌHI`A

The Rain Ripened Mountain Apple

Dedicated to the Memory of Ida Rodrigues Moniz

Cheery Red
In a forest of stoic green
The forest flyers feast
They peck at your shiny coat
Sipping your sweet ambrosia.

Your white blossoms
Will yield bounty
So many will drop
When the sun is at its height
For it is the month of *Hinaia`ele`ele*
No need to strain, to stretch
To enjoy your company.

Come rest on a carpet of scarlet blossoms
Your bark makes birthing facile
Inhale your sisters' scents: guava, eucalyptus
Pale is the ring of *hinaulu `ōhi`a,*
Pele's compeer.

Not as large as the others of your kind
But small and plump hearts of cerise
Descendent of myrtle
Savor of pear.

O patient fruit
Waiting for summer
When the hungry will relish
Your festival of red.

KA PA`A MALE PAINA

The Ironwood Tree Couple

Dedicated to the Memory of Chuck and Marlene Powell

Follow either Huluhulupue`o
or Mananole Streams
They both rush *wai momona* from Lua `Eke
To nourish the ironwood at Waihe`e
The *paina* absorbs all
The aromatic branches, a berth.
Rest in the arms of fallen pines,
Listen to the wind whistle
Sweet dreamy tunes of peace.
Sacred this land of whispering conifers
Between Kealaka`ihonua and Haleki`i Pihana
Though twisted from the *puku kalina*
Its roots remain deep
Beneath the driftwood-studded shore
Occasionally a miracle occurs
A Jessamine is seen clinging to the pines
A flower that blooms holds such perfumes
As kindness and sympathy.
Paina seeds have fallen along the beach
Soon a grove of green will soothe the new weary
Fresh rustles will again whir echoes
Of *Aloha* and Contentment.

KA LEI O NO`E

The Lei of Mist

Dedicated to Charlotte Hanako Onna

Joy follows tears
Like a rainbow follows showers
So come sweet rainbow
After the storm
Bring us hope
Like God's promise of love after a deluge

Your reflection is everywhere
In the rain that strikes the sheltering canopies of Honolulu
In the mists of the Ko`olau
In the fog of Nu`uanu
In the waterfall of Kaliuwa`a
In the moonbow over Waikīkī

O perch of Kāne
We praise your colors
The red, orange, and yellow
Of roses
Of orchids
Of the turning leaves before the cold of winter
The green of the twisting *kukui* in Mānoa
The blue of the rushing waves at Makapu`u
The indigo of twilight above Diamond Head
The violet of sunrise over Lanikai
O Rose of Rainbows
Yours is the beauty of *ka hala o puna*
Our multicolored *`aumakua*
Gives us hope
When tears fall like rain.

NOTES ON THOSE FROM HAWAI`I WHO SERVED IN THE AMERICAN CIVIL WAR

The number of men who lived in Hawai`i and who volunteered, enlisted, were drafted, or were impressed into service in the American Civil War stands at over one hundred. The list grows as more attics and basements are searched and electronic research utilized. The list includes many whites, quite a number of whom are buried in the Grand Army of the Republic section of O`ahu Cemetery.

Over two dozen white graduates from O`ahu College (now Punahou School) volunteered for service and two of those men (Joseph Forbes and Eli Ruggles) died as a result of the war. Many of these volunteers were the descendants of pro-Union New England missionary families.

The list does include a number of native-born Hawaiians. Despite Kamehameha IV's Declaration of Neutrality, some independent Hawaiians chose to fight for a number of reasons including belief in the cause, adventure, or a pension. However, the major reason is that the majority of these future Hawaiian soldiers and sailors were coincidentally studying or living Back East when the conflict erupted. They were caught up either voluntarily or involuntarily in the web of war.

Even information about those Hawaiians who served voluntarily is scanty. In some cases there are records of only surnames (e.g. Kaiwi, 28th Black Volunteers). What is also obvious in this example is that several Hawaiians were thrown into "copper colored" regiments after Black Americans were recruited later in the war.

Many times these Hawaiian servicemen were given general names indicating their ethnicity like Joseph Kanaka, who served on the U.S.S. *Hartford.* So it was on the C.S.S. *Shenandoah* where impressed Hawaiian sailors from the captured whaling ship, *Abigail,* were listed with generic aliases on the ship's manifest like John Boy and Cyrus Sailor.

Here are some short biographies of a few white and Hawaiian men who fought in the war and who contributed to Hawai`i and the United States.

Samuel Chapman Armstrong was born in Wailuku, Maui, Hawai`i in 1839, the sixth of ten children of Richard and Clarissa Armstrong, one of the first Christian missionary couples to serve the islands. Samuel later graduated from O`ahu College (Punahou) and then attended Williams College in Massachusetts, graduating in 1862. After the war broke out, young Samuel volunteered, recruited a company, and joined the 125th New York Infantry. As a Captain, he was captured along with 12,000 men who surrendered at Harper's Ferry. After he was paroled he returned to the front lines in Virginia in the 3rd Division of 11th Corps. He fought in the Battle of Gettysburg, defending Cemetery Ridge against Pickett's Charge. He was raised to the rank of Lt. Colonel and was assigned to the 9th Regiment of the U.S. Colored Troops in 1863 and eventually commanded the 8th Regiment of the USCT. He led that regiment in the Siege of Petersburg and pursued the Army of Northern Virginia during the Appomattox Campaign. He was later sent with the 8th to the Rio Grande in Texas. President Johnson awarded him the rank of Brigadier General. After the war he joined the Freedmen's Bureau that helped him establish Hampton Normal and Agriculture Institute, known as Hampton University, in Virginia in 1868. Booker T. Washington was one of its most famous students. Samuel Chapman Armstrong was paralyzed in 1892 and died at Hampton Institute a year later. Fort Armstrong at Honolulu Harbor was named after him as well as buildings at Punahou School and The Tuskegee Institute.

James Bush was born in Honolulu, Hawai`i. His father, George H. Bush, was from England and married La`u. His brother was a Honolulu newspaper publisher. He enlisted as an Ordinary Seaman at Portsmouth, New Hampshire in September of 1864. He served onboard the U.S.S. *Vandalia* and then on the U.S.S. *Beauregard* chasing blockade runners off the West Florida Coast. He developed chronic laryngitis and spinal injuries and was discharged in 1865 from Brooklyn Naval Hospital. He lived in New Bedford, San Francisco, and Tahiti before he returned to Hawai`i in 1877. He lived in Keālia, Kaua`i where he was married first to Liloi and then to Sarah Kaloaaole Hiku. They bore one child, James Wood Keomana. James Sr. was a pastor of the Morman church at Keālia, a road supervisor, a tax assessor/collector, a truant officer, and a maintenance man at Kapa`a Jail until his death at age 58 in 1906.

Joseph Dutton was born Ira Barnes Dutton in Stowe, Vermont in 1843 to Ezra and Abigail Dutton. He attended Old Academy and Milton Academy in Wisconsin and after the war broke out he enlisted with the 13th Wisconsin Infantry. After seeing the horrors of war, he turned to alcohol. A marriage failed. Friends encouraged him to covert to Catholicism. After being a protestant most of his life, his new religion transformed him. He spent twenty months at the Abbey of Our Lady of Gethsemani in Kentucky in 1886. There with the Trappist Monks he learned about Father Damien's call for help to care for the lepers of Kalaupapa. He committed himself to Moloka`i. After Father Damien's death he founded the Baldwin Home for Men and Boys and later became a member of the Secular Franciscan Order. He passed away at age seventy-three on March 26, 1931. He is buried on the grounds of St. Philomena Church in Kalaupapa.

Nathaniel Bright Emerson was born at Waialua, O`ahu on July 1, 1839. He was the son of Reverend John and Ursula Emerson, missionaries who came to Hawai`i. Nathaniel attended O`ahu College (Punahou) and then Williams College in Massachusetts. In 1862, he enlisted with the 1st Regiment of Massachusetts Volunteers and was involved in the Battles of Fredericksburg, Chancellorsville, Gettysburg, and The Wilderness Campaign. He was wounded three times. After the war, he attended Harvard Medical School and Columbia University of Physicians and Surgeons in New York City. He practiced at Bellevue, then on his own in New York. He was invited by the Hawaiian government to work at Kalaupapa. Later, he practiced in Honolulu. He married Dr. Sarah Pierce and they had one child, Arthur. He held many offices including Vaccinating Officer of O`ahu, President of the Board of Health, and Prison Physician among others. He wrote and translated a number of Hawaiian literary works including *Hawaiian Antiquities* by David Malo, *Hawaiian Mythology*, *Hawaiian Revolutions of 1893 and 1895*, *Long Voyages of the Ancient Hawaiians*, *Pele and Hi`iaka (2 Vol.)*, and *Unwritten Literature of Hawai`i: The Sacred Songs of the Hula (2 Vol.)*. He died at sea at the age of seventy-six in while traveling with his son in 1915.

**Henry Ho`olulu Pitman** was born in Hilo, Hawai`i in 1843. He was the son of Benjamin Pitman of Boston and Kino`ole-o-Liliha, the last Hawaiian high chiefess of the Hilo/Panaewa ahupua`a. Benjamin

Sr. had three children: Mary Ann Pitman, Henry, and Benjamin Pitman, Jr. They moved to O`ahu to their house called *Wai`ale`ale* that was located in downtown Honolulu. Kino`ole-o-Liliha died young at the age of 28. Benjamin Sr. was married a second time to Maria Walsworth. She also passed away at a young age. After the death of his business partner, Benjamin Sr. moved his children to Boston to attend school. While there, the war broke out and Henry volunteered for the 22nd Massachusetts Infantry, Company H. He was captured in battle and placed in POW Camp Libby in Richmond. He was part of a prisoner exchange and was sent to recuperate at Camp Parole, Annapolis, Maryland where he died on February 27, 1863. He was 20 years old.

GLOSSARY

HAWAIIAN TO ENGLISH

`ae — yes
ā hui hou (aku) — until we meet again
ahupua`a — land division from the mountain to the sea
`ai — food, to eat
`āina — land
Akua — God
akua lele — flying god in the form of a fireball
akule — fish
ali`i — chief
ali`i nui — grand chief
Aloha au `ia `oe — Aloha to you.
ama — outrigger float
`ama`u — fern
`Amelika — America
`ānela — angel
a `oe? — and you?
`a`ole — no, not, nothing
`a`ole pilikia — no trouble
`auku`u — black crowned night heron
`aumakua — family or personal god
E ho`a koakoa! — Assemble!
`ehu — red tinge in hair
`ehu kai — scent of the ocean
E iho! — Descend!
`ekahi,`elua, `ekolu — one, two, three
`elepaio — bird of omen, goddess of canoe builders
hala — tree, lauhala leaves for weaving
hala o puna — pandanus tree
hālau (wa`a) — canoe house
hale — house
Hale Ali`i — house of the chief (e.g. `Iolani Palace)
hale koa — weedy relative of mighty koa
haole — white man

hapa — half
hāpu`u — fern with hairy trunk
hau — snow
haupia — coconut sweet
Hele aku! — Go!
hema — left side
Hiki nō? — Can do? Can do.
Hinaia`ele`ele — season for ripened mountain apples
hinaulu `ōhi`a — light ring around trunk of mountain apple tree
hoaloha — friend
ho`i kuahiwi — come back to the mountain
Hōkūle`a — navigational zenith star above Hawai`i
holokū — loose, seamed dress with yoke and train
ho`oikaika — be strong
hūpō — ignorant, stupid
ihu wa`a — bow of a canoe
`ilima — native shrub usually with yellow flowers
imu — pit
imua — onward
ipu — gourd/drum
iwi — bone
ka alahao — iron road
kahawai — stream
kahuna — priest
kahuna kalai wa`a — canoe carver
kakahiaka — morning
(E) kala mai ia`u — sorry/forgive me
kālua — baked
kamani — large tree
kanaka — man
kanaka `Ailiki — Irishman
kanapī — centipede
Kāne — one of the four great Hawaiian gods
kapa (tapa) — cloth made from mulberry
kāpū — forbidden
kau kau — (Cantonese) food
keiki — child
ke ka`a hōkū — star wagon
kelamoku — sailor

kepaniwai — earthen dam
kī (ti) — utilitarian leaf plant
kiawe – hard wood tree
kō — sugar cane
koa — hard wood for canoes/warrior
koholā — whale
koko — blood
kolohe — mischievous
kou — large tree used for dishes/utensils/old name for Honolulu Harbor
kuiki — quilt
kūkae — excrement
kukui — candlenut tree
kuleana — responsibility
Kūlia i ka Nu`u! — Strive for the summit!
kūlolo — pudding made from taro and coconut
kupuna — elder
ku`uipo — sweetheart
laua`e — fern
lauhala — long leaves for weaving
lauhihi — plumbago flower
lehua — red blossom of the `ōhi`a tree
lei niho palaoa — whale tooth pendant
lili — jealous
lo`i — kalo/taro patch
lokelani — pink rose of Maui
lōlō — crazy
lolo kai wa`a ka hala — breaking of the brains
lomi salmon — lū`au dish includes tomatoes/onions
Lopaka — name of Kamehameha's cannon
lū`au — feast (since 1856)
mahalo — thank you
mahina — moon
ma hope aku — later
maka hiamoe — go to sleep
Makahiki — Hawaiian Olympics
Makali`i — The Pleiades
mākaukau — ready
makana — gift

makapiapia — viscous matter in eyes
make — die/dead
makuahine — mother
makuakāne — father
makule — old, aged
(E) mālama i kou kino — Take care of your body.
mālie — calm
malino — calm
mālolo — flying fish
māluhiluhi — tired
mamo — black Hawaiian honey creeper (extinct)
manō — shark
manu — bird
mau hope — later
mau loa — everlasting/forever
ma uka — toward the mountains
mele — song
milo — large shade tree/carved for bowls
mimi — urinate
moemoe — sleep
moe `uhane — dream
mō`ī (kāne/wahine) — king/chief
mo`olelo — story
mūhe`e — squid
muli — stern of a canoe
mu`umu`u — Mother Hubbard dress
nai`a — porpoise
Nalowale i Ka Makani — *Gone with the Wind*
nānā — look
nīele — curious
nīoi — tree
noe — mist
nunulu — snarl like a dog
`ohana — family
`ōhi`a — tree with red blossoms
`ōkole — rump
`ōkolehau — intoxicating drink
`ōkole maluna — bottoms up
ola — health/life

`ōlelo hou — repeat
oli — chant
`olu `olu — cool/refreshing
`ono — tasty
o`o — mature, ripe fruit
`ōpe`ape`a — bat
`ōpae — shrimp
`opihi — limpet
`ōpū — stomach
O wai kou inoa? — What's your name?
pa`a male — married couple
pā`ele — to paint black
Pai`ea — name of Kamehameha I
pā`ina — party/meal
paina — ironwood tree
Pākē — Chinese
palaoa pae — whale's tooth
pali — cliffs
paniolo — cowboy
pau — finished
Pehea `oe/`oukou — How are you/all?
Pele — goddess of the volcano
pihi — scar/badge
pilikia — trouble
pōhaku — rock
pōhaku pa`a — basalt
poi — meal from pounded kalo
pōmaika`i — good luck
pua`a — pig
pueo — owl
puka — hole
pūkoko — blood red
puku kalina — sweet potato vines/Poetic-stormy winds
pule — pray
pulelehua — butterfly
punahou — new spring/area and school in Honolulu
pu`u honua — place of refuge
tsa! — I don't believe you.
tutu kāne — grandfather

tutu wahine — grandmother
`uki`uki — berry with blue color
`uku — flea
`ūlei — native spreading shrub
uli — dark color/ deep blue of the sea
`ulu — breadfruit
`ulua — fish
wa`a — canoe
wahine — woman
wai au`au— bath water
wai — water
wai momona — sweet water
wala`au — talk story

SPANISH TO ENGLISH

agave — plant basic ingredient of tequila
agunaldo — gift
arena movediza — quicksand
arroyo — small river
atole — drink made with cornflower/sweets
bacalao — dried salt cod
bienvenido — welcome
birria — drink/beer/stew
bueno — good
buñuelos — fritters, doughnuts
caballo — horse
Calle la boca. — Shut your mouth.
cantina — restaurant
chilaquiles — tortilla in chili or green tomato sauce
cómico — funny
de su prometida — from his girlfriend
Detener! — Stop
Dónde está el oro? — Where's the gold?
enamorado — in love
Entregar sus pertenencias! — Hand over your belongings!

estúpido — stupid
Feliz Navidad — Merry Christmas
Fuera los manos! — Raise your hands!
gringo — white man
Qué es esto? — What is this?
la familia — the family
luces de Belen — Bethlehem lights/sparklers
manzanita — shrub with thick roots
peso — unit of Mexican currency
piñata — container of treats hit by person with stick
pluma fuente — fountain pen
ponche — liquored punch
posada — procession
salud — to health
tamal — corn based dough cooked in leaf wrap
Tire su escopeta! — Throw down your shotgun!
tortas ahogadas — sandwich drowned in hot sauces
tres bellezas — three beauties
villa — house
villancicos — Christmas carols

HAWAI`I SITES

MAUI

Alanui Ali`i — King's Highway, Lāhainā
`Au`au — Channel between Maui and Lāna`i
Haleakalā — 10,000-foot volcano
Haleki`i Pihana — Heiau/ridge at Wailuku/Waiehu
Hale Pa`i — First printing press building, Lāhainā
Hale Piula — Two-story dwelling of Kamehameha III
Hānā — East Maui Village
Honokōhau Falls — Highest waterfall of Mauna Kahālāwai
Honolua — West Maui bay/surf spot
Ho`okipa — Beach/surf spot near Pā`ia
Huluhulupue`o — Land district near Wailuku/Waiehu
`Īao — Central Maui valley and stream

Ka`ahumanu Church — Wailuku Christian church
Kahakuloa — West Maui Village
Kahului — Central Maui port and town
Kama`ole — South Maui beach/stables
Kaua`ula — West Maui Valley above Lāhainā
Kaupō — East Maui village
Kealakai Honua — Ridge in Waiehu
Ke`anae — East Maui village/known for taro
Kepaniwai — Area/dam in `Īao Valley
Kūka`emoku — `Īao Valley's Needle
Lāhainā — West Maui town/ former Hawai`i capital and whaling port
Lāhainā Roads — Ocean area for anchoring off Lāhainā
La Perouse — South Maui bay near Mākena
Launiupoko — West Maui shoreline beach
Lele — Ancient name of Lāhainā
Lua Eke — Crater in West Maui Mountains
Mā`alae`a — Bay, village, and boat harbor at Maui isthmus
Mākena — South Maui beach
Māliko — East Maui gulch/bay
Mananole Stream — Stream near Wailuku/Waiehu
Mauna Kahālāwai — Another name for the West Maui Mountains
Moku`ula — Lāhainā residence of monarchy
Nāpili — West Maui beach and village
Nā Wai `Ehā — The four streams of Central Maui
Olowalu — West Maui village and canyon
One Loa — Big Beach, Mākena
Pāi`a — East Maui village and bay
Pūali Nani — Wailuku sandy area
Puamana — West Maui shoreline
Pukalani — Village near Makawao
Pu`u`ula`ula — Red Hill, Haleakalā
Pu`u Kukui — Highest peak of the West Maui Mountains
Pu`u Ōla`i — Cinder cone at Mākena Beach
St. Anthony Church — Catholic Church in Wailuku
Ukemehame — West Maui canyon
`Ulupalakua — Upcountry ranch
Violet Lake — Lake at Mauna Kahālāwai summit
Wai`ehu — Central Maui village
Waihe`e — Village/stream near Wailuku

Waikapū — Central Maui village
Wailuku — Central Maui town/county seat
Waine`e Church — Lāhainā Christian church

LĀNA`I

Kaunolū — Southeast Lāna`i bay/former village
Keōmoku — Central Lāna`i village
Lōpā — East Lāna`i surfing area
Naha — East Lāna`i valley

O`AHU

Diamond Point — Former name of Diamond Head
Honolulu — State capital, city, and bay
Kaliuwa`a (Sacred Falls) — Stream/valley at Hau`ula
Ko`olau — Windward mountain range
Kou — Ancient area name for downtown Honolulu area
Lanikai — Beach/area near Kailua
Māmala Bay — Ancient name Honolulu Harbor
Mānoa — Land section/valley/stream in Honolulu
Makapu`u — Beach/point near Koko Head crater
Nu`uanu — Valley above Honolulu
Wa`ahila Rain — Mānoa Valley rain
Wai`anae Range — Mountain range
Waikīkī — Beach/area near Honolulu

MOLOKA`I

Kalohi Channel — Channel between Moloka`i and Lāna`i
Kalaupapa — Peninsular village for lepers

HAWAI`I ISLAND (BIG ISLAND/HAWAI`I NUI)

Hilo — Big Island village and county seat
Kona — Leeward village
Lake Waiau — Lake near summit of Mauna Kea
`Ōla`a — Land division near Hilo
Pana`ewa — Land division near Hilo

KAHO`OLAWE

MOLOKINI

SITES OTHER THAN HAWAIʻI

SAN FRANCISCO/BAY AREA

Alameda — street section of El Camino Real in Santa Clara
Benecia Arsenal — large military reservation at Suisun Bay
Bohemian Club — private gentlemen's club
Camp Sumner — military post for mustering civil war troops
Camp Reynolds — garrison at Angel Island to defend bay
Embarcadero — area around S.F. waterfront
Fort Alcatraz — island in bay that held secessionists/later prison
Fort Baker — army post at Marin Headlands and Sausalito
Fort Mason — army post at Marina District
Fort Point — masonry seacoast fortification south side of Golden Gate
Mare Island — peninsular naval installation near Vallejo
Marin — north S.F. county and town across the bay
Market St. — main artery that runs from hills to waterfront
Montgomery St. — S.F. street named after Commodore Montgomery
Napa — county north of S.F.
Point San Jose — battery fortification/backup to Fort Point
Portsmouth Square — park near waterfront
San Jose — city and mission south of S.F.
Santa Clara — city and mission south of S.F. near San Jose
Washington Square — North Beach park
Yerba Buena — old Mexican name for San Francisco

OTHER AREAS OF CALIFORNIA

Fort Tejon — fort that protected San Joaquin Valley
Hetch Hetchy — valley in Sierra Nevada Mountains
Sutter's Mill — area where gold was discovered
Yosemite — valley in Sierra Nevada in East Central California

ARIZONA

Fort Mojave — post on banks of Colorado River

MEXICO

Mazatlán — city in Mexican State of Sinaloa
Cerro Crestón — 500 ft. mountain in Sinaloa
Olas Altas — beach in Mazatlán

Plaza Machado — old Mazatlán city center

Tepic — capital of state of Nayarit
Nayarit — western Mexico state

Guadalajara — capital and largest city of State of Jalisco
Jalisco — state in Western Mexico
Avenida Vallarta — main thoroughfare through Guadalajara
Nevado de Colima — 12,500 foot volcano near Guadalajara
Cordillera Neo Volcánica — range that runs east-west across Central Mexico

Mexico City — capital located in valley and lake in southeast Mexico
Tenochtitlán — Aztec city-state located in middle of Lake Texcoco
Lake Texcoco — lake that Mexico City rests on.

Vera Cruz — eastern Mexican State/ borders Gulf of Mexico
Alvarado — town south of Vera Cruz
Boca del Rio — city and municipality in center of Vera Cruz
Square of the Republica — heart of Vera Cruz
Zaragoza — main street of Vera Cruz

LOUISIANA

Baton Rouge — capital of Louisiana along the Mississippi River
Big Blue Hole — lake in Concordia Parish adjacent to the Mississippi
Bruin Lake — oxbow lake in Tensas Parish, Louisiana
Crescent City — alias for New Orleans
Fort Jackson — 70 miles south of New Orleans on west side of Mississippi River
Fort St. Phillip — 70 miles south of New Orleans on east side of Mississippi River
Head of Passes — mouth at main stem of Mississippi River breaks into 3 branches
New Orleans — southernmost city of Louisiana
Plaquemines Bend — anchorage of Confederate's Mississippi fleet
St. Joseph — county seat of Tensas Parish along Mississippi River
Ship Island — island in the Gulf of Mexico off the coast of Louisiana
Tensas Parish — area northeastern Louisiana

MISSISSIPPI

Corinth — city and county seat of Alcorn
Grenada — city and county seat of Grenada
Jackson — capital and largest city in Mississippi
Natchez — city and only county seat of Adams along the Mississippi
Vicksburg — city Warren County located between Mississippi and Yazoo Rivers

TENNESSEE

Decatur — Meigs County seat
Chattanooga — Hamilton County seat at Lake Chickamauga on Tennessee River
Chickamauga — area of major battle of civil war
Grand Junction — city in Fayette and Hardeman Counties
Knoxville — city in Knox County
Lookout Ridge and Missionary Ridge — sites in Battle of Chickamauga
Lynchburg — south central city

GEORGIA

Andersonville Prison — Georgia Confederate prison
Big Shanty — station where train was stolen in Great Locomotive Chase

VIRGINIA

Belle Isle — prison for non-officers
Carey St. — street near Potomac in Richmond
James River — 348-mile river that runs through Virginia
Libby Prison — officers' prison in Richmond
Richmond — capital of the Confederacy in Virginia
Tobacco Row — name given to area near Libby Prison

PENNSYLVANIA

Gettysburg — borough of Adams County/ South central town/ major battle site

WASHINGTON, D.C.

Potomac — 405-mile river that flows into Chesapeake Bay

NEW YORK

Battery — 25-acre park at the southern tip of Manhattan
Bowery — street and neighborhood in southern Manhattan
Broadway — oldest north to west thoroughfare, runs 13 miles through Manhattan
Bronx — northernmost borough of NYC
Brooklyn — one of five boroughs of New York City
Central Park — urban park 800 + acres in Manhattan
Gotham — alias for New York City
Hart Island — small island south Long Island Sound/part of borough of Bronx
Manhattan — island on which New York City lies
Winter Garden Theater — early theater in N.Y.

MASSACHUSETTS

Boston — capital and largest city of Massachusetts
New Bedford — south coast whaling, fishing, and shipbuilding town

THE CAROLINAS (NORTH AND SOUTH)

BRAZIL

TIERRA DEL FUEGO

Straits of Magellan — passage south of South America/North of Tierra Del Fuego
Williway Winds — sudden blast of wind from mountainous coast to the sea

CHILE

MADEIRA ISLANDS

Funchal — capital of mid Atlantic island of Madeira

ASCENSION ISLAND

SOME BOOKS ON THE SUBJECT

A Bibliography

Absolom, Absolom — Faulkner
After Fifty Years — Pitman
The American Heritage Picture History of the Civil War
Andersonville — Kantor
Battle Cry of Freedom — McPherson
The Black Flower — Bahr
Blue and Grey at Sea: Naval Memoirs of the Civil War — Thomson
Centennial History of the Civil War (3 Volumes) — Catton
Chancellorsville 1863: The Souls of the Brave — Furguson
The Civil War (3 Volumes) — Foote
The Civil War: A Narrative — Foote
Civil War Stories — Bierce
Cold Mountain — Frazier
Confederates in the Attic: Dispatches from the Unfinished Civil War — Horwitz
Confederate Raider of the North Pacific — Morgan
C.S.S. Shenandoah: Memoirs of Lt. Commander Waddell — Wadell
The Destructive War: William Tecumseh Sherman, Stonewall Jackson, and the Americans — Royster
The Fiery Trial: Abraham Lincoln and American Slavery — Foner
Gettysburg — Sears
The Glorious Cause — Shaara
Gods and Generals — Shaara
Gone with the Wind — Mitchell
Grant and Sherman: The Friendship That Won the Civil War — Flood
Hawaiian Antiquities and Folklore — Fornander
Hawai`i Chronicles (3 Volumes) — Dye
The Hawaiian Kingdom (3 Volumes) — Kuykendall
The Judas Field — Bahr
The Killer Angels — Shaara
Landscape Turned Red — Sears
The Last Full Measure — Shaara
Lincoln's Men: How President Lincoln Became Father to an Army and a Nation — Davis

The Lost Fleet: A Yankee Whaler's Struggle Against the Confederacy — Songini
The March — Doctorow
Mary Chestnut's Diary
Merchant Prince of the Sandalwood Islands — Dye
Mission Life in Hawai`i — Alexander
North and South — Jakes
The Oldest Living Confederate Widow Tells All — Gurganus
The Ordeal of the Nation (8 Volumes) — Nevins
Pirates, Privateers, and Rebel Raiders of the Carolina Coast — Butler
Race and Reunion: The Civil War in American Memory — Blight
The Red Badge of Courage — Crane
The Republic of Suffering: Death in the American Civil War — Faust
Rise to Rebellion — Shaara
Samuel Armstrong — Talbot
Sea of Gray — The Around the World Odyssey of the Confederate Raider Shenandoah — Chaffin
Shade of Grey — Reader
Shiloh — Foote
Shoal of Time — Daws
A Stillness at Appomattox — Catton
Story of Lahaina — Ashdown
Stories of Old Lahaina — Ashdown
Team of Rivals: The Political Genius of Abraham Lincoln — Goodwin
The Union Quilters — Chiaverini
Uncle Tom's Cabin — Stowe
Unforgettable True Stories of the Kingdom — Bell
The U.S. and The Hawaiian Kingdom — Tate
The Unvanquished — Faulkner
Unwritten Literature of Hawai`i — Emerson
Whaling Days in Old Hawai`i — Mrantz
The Widow of the South — Hicks
The Year of Jubilo — Bahr

PRIMARY SOURCE OF HAWAIIANS IN THE AMERICAN CIVIL WAR

Professor Justin Vance of Hawai`i Pacific University is the primary source in Hawai`i for information about Hawaii's role in the American Civil War.

THE HAWAIIAN ISLANDS

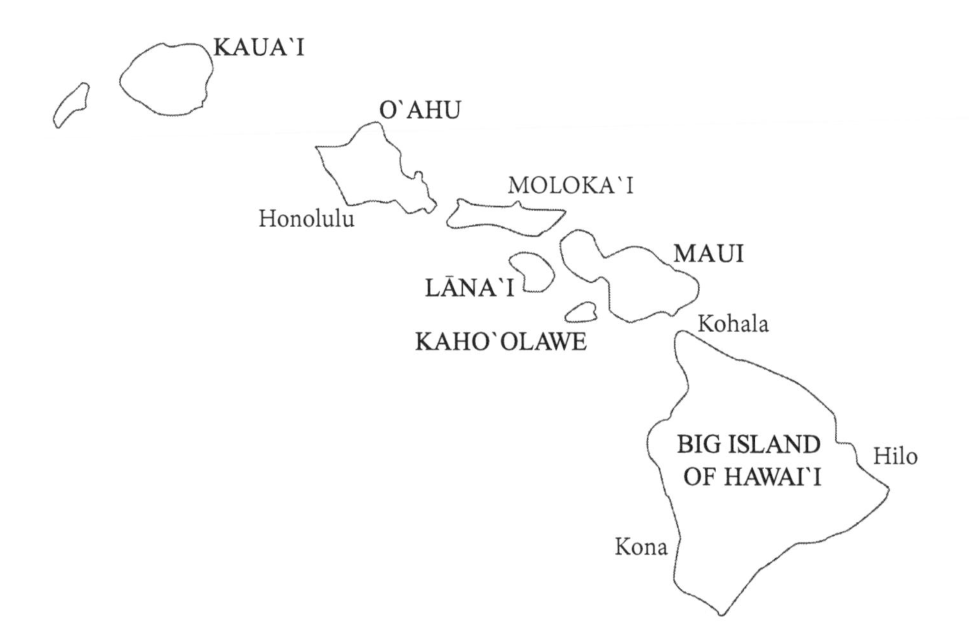

THE ISLAND OF MAUI

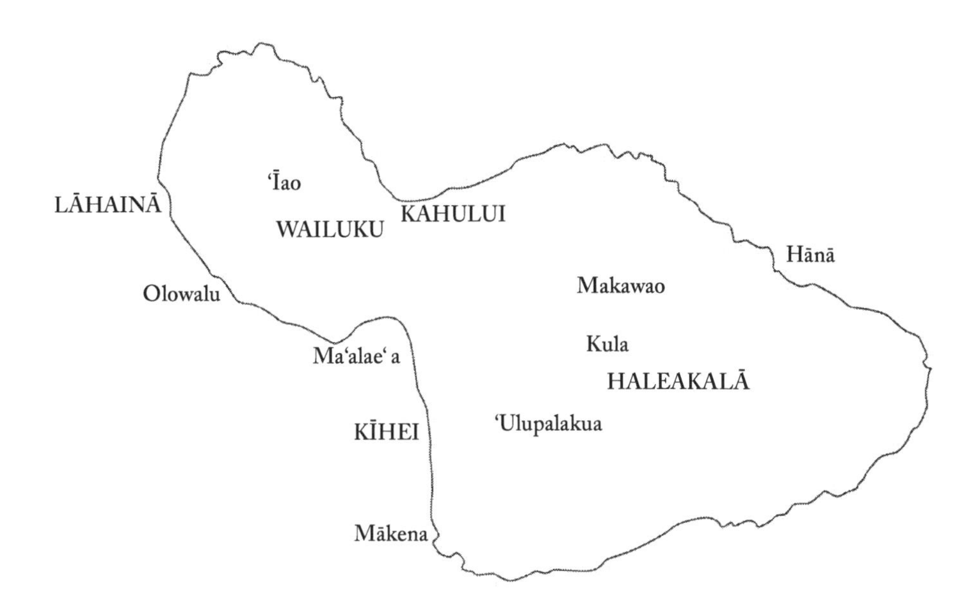

BY THE SAME AUTHOR

Born and raised on Maui, Wayne Moniz received a B.A. in English and Communications in 1968 from the University of Dayton, Ohio. In 1980, he was awarded an M.A. in Theater Arts - Film from UCLA. In 2005, he received the Cades Award for Literature, Hawaii's most prestigious writing prize. His short story collection of Valley Isle tales won him the Nā Palapala Po`okela 2010 Readers' Choice Book of the Year. Dubbed the "Dean of Maui Playwrights" by *The Maui News,* Wayne has written works that deal with the people, events, and issues of Hawai`i. They include:

PLAYS

***Still Born: Nā Mele o Kaho`olawe*** — the history and liberation of the island of Kaho`olawe - ©1990. Produced by Maui Community Theater [MCT], 1991. Published by Pūnāwai Press, 2000.

`Ili `Ili — a Hawaiian entertainer and the Spirit of Charles Lindbergh team up to save Hānā from a massive development - ©1994. Produced by MCT, 1991. Published by Pūnāwai Press, 2004.

Children of the Turning Tide — Hawaii's future monarchs as teens at the Royal School - ©1992. Produced by Baldwin Theater Guild [BTG], 1992. Published by Pūnāwai Press, 2000.

Under the Star of Gladness — three generations of a Portuguese Family and friends in Hawai`i - ©1997. Produced by MCT, 1993. Published by Pūnāwai Press, 2004.

People of the First Year — the first Japanese Christians on Maui - ©1994. Produced by `Īao Congregational Church, 1994.

Steamer Days: The View from Aloha Tower — a romantic romp through a 1938 Honolulu Boat Day with Duke Kahanamoku, Hilo Hattie, and Shirley Temple et al. - ©1997. Produced by BTG, 1996. Published by Pūnāwai Press, 2007.

Hawaiian Kine Christmas Carol — an 1889 Sprecklesville Mill kine version of the Dickens' classic - ©1997. Produced by MCT, 1997.

***Kamapua`a - The Exploits of the Pig God*** — ©1997, Produced by Hawai`i Leadership Conference for Nā Kumu `Ōlelo Hawai`i, Maui Community College, 1997.

***Pele and Hi`iaka: Sisters of Fire*** — the odyssey of the Pele Family and Hi`iaka's journey to escort Lohi`au from Kaua`i to Halema`uma`u - ©1997.

Tandy! — the libretto of an opera based on the rise and fall of Hānā born opera singer, Tandy MacKenzie - ©1997. Published by Pūnāwai Press, 2007.

Hibiscus Pomade — `60s musical when Hawaiian music met rock `n roll with Lucky, Aku, and the KPOI Boys - ©2002. Produced by BTG, 2004. Published by Pūnāwai Press, 2007.

Only the Morning Star Knows: In Search of Kamehameha — the search for the bones of Kamehameha leads King Kalākaua into the mind of Hawaii's greatest monarch - ©2003.

`Īao: Where We Walk Through Rainbows — the stories of the sacred valley from prehistory to modern times - ©2004.

SHORT STORIES

Under Maui Skies and Other Stories. © 2009. Koa Books.

Beyond the Reef: Stories of Maui and the World. ©2011. Pūnāwai Press.

Kepaniwai ©1969. Published in the University of Dayton Literary Journal, 1969. On display at the Hilo Tsunami Museum.

Aloha `Oe, E Ku`uipo. ©2006. Published in Maui Community College Literary Magazine, 2006.

Under Maui Skies. ©2007. Published in Hawai`i Weavers of Tales. National Writers Association - Honolulu Chapter, 2008.

POEMS, MUSIC, AND LYRICS

Wailuku, 1957. (Poem) ©2006. Published in Literary Breeze from Hawai`i. National Writers Association - Honolulu Chapter, 2006.

Maui Moon Blues (Music and Lyrics) ©1990. From his drama, *Still Born: Nā Mele o Kaho`olawe.*

Hibiscus Pomade. (Music and Lyrics) ©2002. From his musical comedy, *Hibiscus Pomade.*

The Makawao Fourth of July Parade. (Music and Lyrics) ©2003.

Ke One o Ka Pu`u Hale Nani. (Lyrics) Music by Pekelo Cosma ©2008.

22 Kaona (Hawaiian metaphorical poetry) Published in ***Under Maui Skies and Other Stories*** ©2009 and ***Beyond the Reef: Stories of Maui in the World*** ©2011

FILMS

The Chair Resistance. (Producer). West Valley Productions, ©1980.

Laugh Trax. Producer. (Segment Director). West Valley Productions, ©1981.

Standing in the Shadows. (Producer). West Valley Productions, ©1982.

Aloha `Oe, E Ku`uipo. (Screenplay), ©2008.

AUDIO BOOKS

Kula Keiki Ali`i by Rosemary Patterson. (Narrator). Maui Film Works. ©2013.

Under Maui Skies and Other Stories. (Narrator). Maui Film Works. ©2012.

ABOUT THE ARTIST

Joseph Aspell is an artist who lives in San Francisco. He has a BA in Literature, an MA in Art History, and an MA in Painting. His sculptures have been commissioned for churches and universities across the U.S. He recently completed two bronze statues of Father Chaminade. One is located on the Chaminade College Campus in Honolulu, the other at the University of Dayton, Ohio.

See his amazing work at: josephaspellstudio.com

- e pua'i wale mai ana -

Pūnāwai Press publishes dramas, screenplays, short stories, novels, poetry, non-fiction, and song lyrics about the people, events, and issues of Hawai`i.

To get more information, visit
waynemoniz.com
or write to:

Pūnāwai Press
1812 Nani Street
Wailuku, Maui, Hawai`i 96793

To purchase more copies of
Pūkoko: A Hawaiian in the American Civil War,
go online to Amazon.com
or the above-mentioned mailing address

For more about the book and author, Google:
Pūkoko: A Hawaiian in the American Civil War
and Wayne Moniz

To purchase the book of
Under Maui Skies and Other Stories,
go online to KoaBooks.com or Amazon.com

To purchase the book of
Beyond the Reef: Stories of Maui in the World,
go to Amazon.com or above-mentioned mailing address

AUDIO BOOKS

To purchase or download the audio book of *Under Maui Skies and Other Stories,* go to undermauiskiesaudiobook.com, audible.com, MondoTunes.com, and iTunes